Praise for Eleanor Bailey's **IDIOGLOSSIA**

"Eleanor Bailey's exuberant novel plays with the fate of characters struggling with the tension between inner and outer reality. Funny and sad and full of human sympathy." Jill Paton Walsh, author of *Knowledge of Angels*

"Highly original and beautifully written . . . [There are] flashes of a brilliant imagination and genuine psychological insights." *Sunday Telegraph*

"It's no wonder this deliciously inventive novel has taken the British literary world by storm. . . . *Idioglossia* is at once an intellectual puzzle and a sweeping epic focused on the intricately interwoven lives of four generations of women." *eye*

"Bailey's characters, who struggle to cope with life, love and loss, desperately latch on to any means of escape. Whether it is madness, mirrors, games or secret languages, Bailey skilfully threads these essential escape mechanisms into the narrative fabric. . . . An ambitious, sweeping family saga." *The Gazette* (Montreal)

"Bailey is an intelligent writer — eloquent about memory and women's stories. Her grip on poetic language is an assured one. . . . An ambitious first novel." *Independent on Sunday*

"A huge, sprawling work . . . *Idioglossia* is a novel determined to be generous. At its kind heart are Bailey's moments of uneasy love, found epiphany, unexpected love. Weighed against its darknesses, losses and severances, this generosity is *Idioglossia*'s achievement." *Scotland on Sunday*

"[Bailey's] unsentimental but sympathetic language penetrates the private world of the emotions in an impressive way. . . . [An] assured debut." *The Times*

W9-BPN-432

IDIOGLOSSIA

ELEANOR BAILEY

VINTAGE CANADA
A Division of Random House of Canada Limited

VINTAGE CANADA EDITION, 2001

Copyright © 2000 by Eleanor Bailey

Published in Canada by Vintage Canada, a division of Random House of
Canada Limited, in 2001. First published in hardcover in Canada by
Random House Canada, Toronto, in 2000.
Distributed by Random House of Canada Limited, Toronto.

Vintage Canada and colophon are registered trademarks of
Random House of Canada Limited.

National Library of Canada Cataloguing in Publication Data

Bailey, Eleanor
Idioglossia

ISBN 0-679-31125-4

I. Title.

PR6052.A3185I34 2001   823'.92   C2001-900860-0

www.randomhouse.ca

Printed and bound in the United States of America

2 4 6 8 9 7 5 3 1

For SMW

idioglossia (ˌɪdiəuˈɡlɛsɪə) *n.* 1. a secret language between a few people, a private language; 2. a lallation; the babble of babies or the murmur of lunatics.

In a study in the 1970s, volunteers were asked to choose between two geometrical figures. Men preferred a closed form. Women preferred an open form, with different parts unconnected. The psychologist concluded that a craving for definite structure and limits characterizes the male. The female, in turn, shrinks from rigid boundaries, the distinction of the inner and outer and sees the definite as a limitation.

On 24 March 1941 Virginia Woolf wrote in her diary about her sister Vanessa: 'I am imagining how it would be if we could infuse souls.' Four days later, she drowned herself in the river Ouse.

Contents

Grace

She dreamed she was a caterpillar in the bathroom. Over the day she turned into a butterfly on the window ledge while the sun moved across her body. Her hands became wings, green and opalescent. The veins dried up and faded until the wood was visible straight through them. Standing by the door was a man smiling. He said, 'They're never satisfied.' This seemed to make him angry. He walked towards her, his face narrowing, holding up his hand as if to strike her. He was shouting, his mouth contorting, his face red, but she couldn't make out the words. His shadow blocked out the sun; she could no longer see in the darkness but the heat was still intense. She lay pulsing weakly against him but he moved nearer and nearer until she couldn't see herself at all. There was nothing left of her. She could see the window ledge and she wasn't on it. When she woke thrashing, she was convinced it was reality; her arms were beating impotently in a sheet. It was wrapped around her, twisted like a cocoon.

Now she was awake, she felt calmer. She rose and stood staring out of the window. She held up her hand to the pane. It was cold. Her fingers grew damp. She traced a circle. Clockwise.

Yesterday had been a bad day. She had heard the angry man when she was awake too. He had told her that her mother was a witch. That she was a witch. He shouted until she had hidden her head under the pillow.

Through the window, next to her bed, was a large concrete yard divided by four white lines. Beyond that a bench and an

11

iron gate which led to the garden where, if she wanted, she could take a daily walk among the bushes, to the netting. Then, behind, the grey sky, nailed back by the black criss-cross. Grace was glad; the sky looked so grey and heavy, she was afraid if they didn't keep it away it would overwhelm them all.

There was a knock on the partition. Grace jumped but she didn't look round.

'Grace! Grace!' The voice was loud. 'Grace, you haven't been asleep again, have you?'

Not waiting for an answer, the woman – in her forties, hollow, with grey-flecked hair and the dull skin of a heavy smoker who now resembles the contents of an ashtray – marched across the bare floor to where Grace stood and turned her round to look her in the eyes.

'You have been asleep, haven't you? What do you find to sleep about then, I wonder? What makes you so tired? Sitting there all day, staring.'

Today, when Grace spoke, it was in a dull low voice. Evenly spaced words.

'Where am I going?'

The nurse breathed briskly. 'You've got a visitor.'

They walked along a low-ceilinged corridor. Every few yards a pair of white fire doors whistled over the polished floor and then settled back behind them. There were many twists and turns.

They arrived in the visitors' annexe. A large overheated room with clusters of chairs, and people arranged in groups of two and three. It was filled with the low hum of visiting voices and the shrill, uninhibited noises of the people they visited.

'Would you like a cup of coffee, Grace?' The nurse was pushing her towards the far corner.

'Grace doesn't drink coffee,' interrupted an older woman with the authority of a nurse, but she wore a dressing gown and a long white plait tapered down her back. 'She only drinks tea. I'll get her a cup.'

Still Grace stared ahead. The nurse gently prodded her to where a man sat waiting for her. At the noise of footsteps, he turned round and shielded his eyes against the light and looked up at her. Smiling tentatively, he stood up.

'Grace?' He held out his hand.

12

'Yes, that's right.' The nurse spoke for her and shunted Grace into a chair. When the man took her hand, she let him.

'Well, you've got an hour, darling,' snorted the nurse. 'Don't let her talk too much.' And she rustled away.

If the man was worried by Grace's silence and the eyes that focused somewhere across the room, he didn't show it, except perhaps by his smiling assurance.

He pulled Grace's hand gently towards him.

'Grace. My name is John. I'm a friend of Maggie, your daughter.'

She didn't speak, but he wondered if he imagined a sort of smile on her face. It was hard to tell. She must be seventy years old, he thought, but she looks . . . she looks no age. You couldn't put an age to her.

Her hair was white and soft as a mouse. Cropped around her head. Her cheeks were unlined but there were years gathered in her face. Like a statue, there was an age about it, but without any physical change. She lacked weathering. No dimensions, no emotional surgery.

At last her mouth opened and a slow sound came out. 'Maggie,' she said, 'that's a pretty name.'

1

The Boat

Even now, after more than thirty years, Maggie still felt the movement of the sea. Sometimes, in the morning, when she was almost awake, she could feel a shifting motion where her skin touched the sheets, the slight purring of the engine. And when she thought about it, she could see the dark green water through the porthole. Dazzling where the sun pierced the surface. She could still imagine the line of the horizon, flat against the sky. Infinite. It was the backdrop of her childhood.

When she thought back it was often to the morning of her eleventh birthday. She was dreaming of rain in thick drips. So thick and so fast that she was soon stuck to the waist in viscous liquid. Swallowed like quicksand. She woke up screaming, with a pain between her legs. She leaped from the bed and the sheets were soiled.

'Didn't your mother tell you this was going to happen?' said Sally Shezaar, irritated to be woken by Maggie knocking madly on the cabin door.

Maggie shook her head. Sally was not interested in the miracle of life reasserting itself on Maggie's bedlinen. 'Well, don't worry about it,' she said shortly, passing her a bundle of hooked white pads and a yellowing belt from a scruffy bedside cabinet. 'Here, use some of these. It'll stop in a few days.

'And put the sheets in bleach,' Sally shouted after her, her head already back on the pillow, 'or they'll have to be thrown away.'

Maggie had run shamefaced to her little room and curled on

the bed, afraid that her guts were falling out. She cried. She was dirty.

Her father made a point of forgetting her birthday. Her mother had forgotten everything. There was no celebration. So later, when the dragging feeling had stopped, Maggie congratulated herself and played a solitary game of quoits since there was no one else around.

The ship had moored in Morocco. Maggie knew this because all the passengers trooped back on board with red fezzes. Her world was endless water and day-trip souvenirs.

The ship was better empty. There were more corners and echoes. The kitchen's metallic reverberations, the sound of the waves. And she could run and run along the length of the ship without meeting anybody, listening to the rhythm of her feet against the metal floor and feeling her heat-swollen fingers against the rail. In the burning afternoon heat, the paint felt tacky. When the winds blew she stuck out her tongue and tasted salty lashings.

She lay on a deckchair looking at the sea through windows that she made of her hands. Since she thought she was alone, she was startled by the sudden approaching thump of someone else's feet.

After Sally, he was the only person who had spoken to her all day. He had a beard and an American accent. She found him interesting because instead of interrupting her thoughts like everyone else, he joined them.

She was thinking about quoits. Staring at the stacked rope curls. Sinuous fibres which, if she thought about it, made her teeth itch.

He picked up a quoit she had laid on the deck and threw it casually at the iron peg that stood some metres away. It flew gently through the air, was picked up at the last moment by a gust of wind and plopped satisfactorily over the spike.

She turned to face him for the first time, holding her hand over her eyes to shield them from the glare of the sun. He had a small dark face. Ageing. He smiled apologetically.

She said scornfully, 'What a fluke.'

He shrugged. 'I bet I can beat you,' he said.

'Go on then,' she said, lifting her body, her supine vertebrae, from the deckchair. In the heat she moved languidly like a woman, not a child.

Though he was a stranger the battle was intense. Neither spoke as they threw, walking silently to collect quoits at the end of games.

He did beat her, but only by a hair. In hours alone she had thrown and thrown interminably at the foot-high peg and now she was close to perfection. But he had dexterity. He explained by way of an excuse, 'I've had years of practice. I used to be a pitcher, see.'

She threw the defeat into the sultry sky with a wave of her hands. But she didn't know what he meant. Lemonade came in pitchers.

'It doesn't matter.'

All the time she was looking at his beard. It looked like an animal, furry and an unnatural deep brown, not at all the same colour as the thick crop on his head.

She sat back in her deckchair. He stared at the sea. After a while he said goodbye and walked slowly away. He had no bottom, she noticed. His trousers, although snappy, hung limply from his belt as if there were no body underneath. A bottomless man, she wondered, was that the same as a bottomless pit? She'd read about such things and they disturbed her; falling for ever in the darkness, what happened when you needed the toilet? When he had disappeared, she idly picked up a quoit.

Five minutes later she thought another man had come along.

'Hello,' he said, looking at her quizzically.

'It's you again,' she exclaimed in a scornful tone. 'You've just taken your beard off and stuck some funny eyebrows on.'

'I've n-n-never seen you before in my life,' the man stuttered. He put his hand on the painted blue metal of the ship's exterior. 'You must be mistaken.'

She looked at him slowly, the sun falling now, dazzling her. 'Are you trying to pervert me?'

'Trying to what?'

Her dark head went on one side. 'Pervert me. I've been told all about people like you. I'm not supposed to speak to perverts.'

'Are there a lot of them around here?'

She scratched her head. 'People go funny on this ship. Dad reckons it's the sea air but I think it's all those days of nothing but blue. You get really fed up after a while. People just sit all

16

day on deckchairs and look into the sea. Sooner or later it goes all prickly and there are strange shapes in the sea and they're deep-sea devils and if you keep staring they swim up and jump on board when no one's looking and gobble you up. They've eaten several people already but nobody nice, so it's all right. They almost got me once but I hid in the quoits cupboard until they went away.'

She let out a long sigh. 'Oh, it's so boring. There's nothing to do. I just get cross and sulk a lot. But the old people go funny, they're so bored.'

'How old are you?'

'Eleven.' She stuck out her chin. 'Nearly twelve.'

'Why don't you go funny?'

'Because I'm too young. Dad says you never go funny until you get older, when you can't think straight.'

He considered this, pulling up a deckchair next to her. Bumping it across the metal deck, its creamy canvas flapping in the breeze.

'And did it happen to him?'

She nodded matter-of-factly. As if such things were a normal part of adulthood.

'Dad was reading the newspaper and he went all pale. I said, "What's the matter?" and he said, "It's nothing," but after that he went to his room and didn't come out for a week. They had to put extra dancing on instead – I had to do an extra raffle and a song I really hate. Every day I went in and tried to get him to talk but he wouldn't. He was all grey and funny. He didn't eat any food. After a week he came out of his room. He went to the bar and drank beer for hours. Then he got better. Drunk as a skunk again but better.' She looked at him decisively. 'That's because he is old and old people go funny. The newspaper didn't do anything to me.'

She noticed that he looked at her with a fascination that she had seen in no one before.

'What was in the newspaper?'

'I dunno, I didn't read it.' She smiled with pride at the memory. 'I made it into a tree that holds water and everybody was really impressed.'

She wanted magic but he wanted frailty.

'Maybe if you'd read it, you would have gone "funny".'

17

She looked at him as if he were stupid. 'No, it's just a newspaper.'

'What does your father do?'

'He's a ventriloquist.'

The man nodded as if she were confirming his suspicions.

It was late. The sun had gone behind a cloud and the wind blew fresher. An elderly couple, sitting side by side staring out at the sea, shuffled to put on cardigans.

There was a silence while Maggie felt inside a pocket and brought out a small clockwork frog.

'That's Khrushchev.' To the man's questioning glance she said, 'I'm not a communist, you know.'

Winding him up, she placed him on the table and let go, at which he hop-hopped at a suicidal pace, racing across the lacquered table and over the edge. Throwing out his hand in a reflex action the man caught him, brought him nearer and screwed up his eyes to examine him.

'Hmm, greater blue-eyed bullfrog, I'd say.'

'I don't know what he is, but because he's really intelligent I think he must be a mongrel actually.'

'I see.' The man adjusted his eyebrows which were getting itchy.

'Of course, when he was younger he was less mottled and a paler green, so I don't know. I've asked for *I-spy Amphibians* for Christmas but I won't get it.'

'Oh dear.'

'We're only going to be in the Caribbean before then, you see, and they have nothing but useless books about love affairs and political scandals.'

The man was weary of frogs. 'Well, why don't you kiss him and maybe he'll turn into a handsome prince?'

'What would I want a prince for? I want a frog.'

'Well, then you wouldn't have to worry about your frog book, you could go and live in a castle.'

'It's not a frog book, it's an amphibian book and I don't want to live in a castle; my mother lives in a castle. They sent her to a castle because she was too mad to live in a house. She's a lunatic, you know. I think castles are horrible. And princes are horrible too. They just want to hold hands, and say, "Oh darling, I love you." They don't talk about interesting things.'

The frog was snatched from his hands. 'Come on, Khrushchev, stir your lazy stumps. There's work to be done.'

She turned to the man who was still staring at her with intense curiosity. 'Where do you keep your beard when you're not wearing it, or are your eyebrows the beard cut in half?'

He didn't answer but smiled and doffed an imaginary hat. 'I'll see you later.'

She went to the door. 'Are you the new entertainer then?'

'That's right.'

She came back and held out her hand. 'How do you do, I'm Maggie. I pull the raffle on Fridays and sing songs every other night.'

He put out his hand. 'Delighted.'

'What is your act?'

His face was enigmatic, as if it were used to keeping secrets. 'Wait and see.'

Annoyance flashed across her forehead, then the springy furrow bounced back; her skin was too young and too elastic for the anger to show for long.

'Secrets are rude.'

'Well, I'm rude then.'

'See you later, Mr Rude,' and she dashed away in case he booted her.

Her father was an empty man. She didn't understand him. It was as if there were nothing to understand. Neither her father nor her mother made any sense. Her mother stared dully ahead, but she was ill. Everyone nodded in hushed assent. That was the explanation. It was why she didn't smile or tell Maggie to do the dishes like mothers were supposed to. It was why sometimes she flew into rages that lasted for weeks. Maggie did not see her mother then, when she was violent, for Maggie was kept away. Once she had heard her mother scream that she was drowning. She heard her mother's screams through walls, then the sound of doors and voices. There was no water.

She did not understand but she knew it was something one should not talk about. Her friend Jenny used to come round on Saturdays to listen to *Children's Favourites* but she was not allowed to any more, after Maggie's mother fell ill.

Her father was meant to be normal. He lived in the world or, at least, *a* world. The cruise-ship existence was so cut off from everything else, surrounded by strange seas and stopping off at strange places, that it was hard to call it the real world. It wasn't the grey streets and red houses that signified normality.

He was ordinary but he had nothing to say. He spoke to her in short, perfunctory sentences. When he looked at her, it was with a confusion that seemed to question who she was. Perhaps because, as she grew older, she grew to look less and less like him.

As a small child everyone said she was her father's daughter but now she was changing slowly, inexorably, into her mother. The eyes more almond, the nose thinner, the hair darkening.

When she was old enough to think of such things, she realized she had no idea how her parents met. Neither the geographical details nor, literally, how it could have happened since neither of them had two words to rub together. Even before she was ill her mother was quiet. Maybe it was the mutual silence that attracted.

On the ship she had carved herself a routine. She liked to have a routine and no one else was going to create one for her. She went to see her father after tea, every day.

His tiny dressing room smelt of stale cigarettes and dusty velvet. A film of grey covered the furniture. She wiped her fingers across the chair, rubbing the colour back to life.

When she walked into the room her father was neck up in the cupboard, so she shouted, 'Hello, Dad.'

He emerged, blinking, frowning at the bright bulbs that surrounded the rather greasy mirror. He was, after all, a star.

'Can we play dominoes tomorrow, Dad?'

'We'll see.'

Her father frowned. His face was like a whisper, she could never quite catch it. He picked up Arthur Hodges. Maggie's eyes moved to the little shiny man.

'Hello, Arthur,' said Maggie.

Arthur smiled and opened his mouth, speaking in his chortling cockney accent. 'Blimey, wot's this then, a lady in my dressing room?'

Maggie laughed. 'I'm not a lady.'

'Well, what are you then?' Arthur took a closer look. 'Hmmm, you're not a cabbage, because your leaves ain't green.'

He pumped her arm. 'And you certainly ain't a refrigerator because your handle isn't made of metal.' He scratched his shiny chin. A light bulb popped on over his head. 'You must be a fish leaped out of the water.'

She shook her head and giggled. 'No. I'm an excuse.'

Arthur was confused. 'An excuse for a girl?'

'No,' she said, leaning on one leg, 'I'm "the bus was late".'

Arthur nodded and nodded. 'Ah – was late, eh? Was late.'

Once he started he couldn't stop. The whole of his waxen features bobbed back and forth. He stopped smiling and his eyelids fell down because her father had taken his hand away and dumped him on the bed.

'I'll tell you what you are,' he said thickly through cigarette smoke. 'You're a dummy. You and him. Can't shut the pair of you up. You're as bad as each other. Scram now, I've got to get ready.'

Her father could never get ready with someone in the room. This, Maggie decided, was because he was really two people. She was terrified that if she ever opened the lid of his dummy's box (which was forbidden) she would find her father's alter ego, glassy eyed, inside, staring out.

Arthur lay there during the day. He was all right, just an idiotic cockney joker who teased her in the riddles she loved, but attached to a hole in his back would be her father, dressed up for the show, his hundred-watt smile dazzling, lying inanimate. He must be there since she never saw him during the day.

She ran back to her cabin round almost the full deck, past a hundred little doors. It was time to put on the tutu that she sang in. No one explained why she had to wear a ballerina outfit to sing. She didn't dance, although she pointed her toes sometimes when she felt happy. Trussed up in pink, this wasn't often.

The ship that carried three thousand passengers had ten full-time cabaret artistes. A disgruntled group, none of whom could believe their dreams were reduced to this. On-board entertainment that was changed less often than the linen. The entertainment came all-inclusive, only the drinks were extra.

Mr Rude was to be Billy Bingo's replacement. Billy Bingo had jumped ship with a woman in Casablanca. Maggie was glad. Billy Bingo was angry like chopped onions. His outfit, the black-and-white checkered clown's trousers, the straw hat with the large daisy growing out of it, the pointy flat-footed red shoes, never disguised how dreadful he was either. He was a magician who could not perform magic.

Sally Shezaar, the late-night singer, told Maggie confidentially, looking across the silver sea one full moon as they stood on deck when everyone else had gone to bed, that Billy had been a child prodigy, better perhaps than Houdini. The apex, his triumph, was to cut people into four and hold up the dripping heads, the whites of their eyes swimming in red. When he put them back together, they walked trembling off the stage, a fire in their eyes. They had seen God, they said. And God was a formless wind littered with the souls of the dead. But just short of global fame (news travelled slowly back then) his bubble had burst. No one knew why. Some blamed an unrequited passion, some said he had begun to believe he was God and that this was his punishment. But, whatever it was, within two years he was struggling to pull rabbits from hats and eggs from ears on a cruise ship with Maggie and her father. And he never talked about his past.

'He was astonishing though, apparently,' said Sally huskily. Knowing the shabby, shrunken man he now was, this was hard to imagine.

Maggie knew that Sally, if no one else, had reason to miss Billy. It was a secret known to all that they had been lovers. She herself had heard Sally squealing and Billy snorting in time with the squeaks of the bedsprings. Sally must have taken pity on Billy, she reasoned, because he was so hollow, with his potato-coloured face, nose like a shrivelled mushroom and breath of sour apples; Maggie didn't believe that Sally would have done with Billy what people did, for any other reason. Sally was quite pretty, even if she did wear too much lipstick that she stickily kissed on to your cheek and you had to scrub it off.

On this, Mr Rude's début night, the dancing ladies were on first, with their bobtails and rabbit ears. Her father, the ventriloquist, was next, then Maggie singing 'How Much is That Doggy in the Window'. The ageing crowd always raised a sigh with this nostalgic number. It took them back to happy days. When they were young, when rock'n'roll was smart, before this cold new decade with its open-neck shirts. 1961 was the end; it could not possibly get worse.

Mr Rude was waiting backstage during Maggie's turn. He was wearing an elegant large suit and had slicked his hair back. She felt young and silly as the pink ballerina. 'I have to wear this,' she hissed at him when she walked off to a thin ripple of applause. Although why what he thought of her mattered she couldn't say. He laughed at her when she said that and she blushed pinker than the hateful tutu.

She in turn watched him. Mr Rude was very funny. He was a comic from Chicago and Maggie thought he was better than Danny Kaye. He never explained what had sunk him to the cruise circuit and nobody dared ask. For although he was unfalteringly cheerful and good-humoured he had a presence that was quite intimidating. And he never talked about himself, ever. No one knew what his real name was. From the first day he introduced himself as Mr Rude. Maggie didn't tell anyone that she had dreamed that up; he obviously had reasons for his secrets. Even though he stayed with them for five years little was known about him except that he liked his chilli hotter than the tropical sun.

Maggie had lived on this ship with her father, Harry, for over three years. Ever since, in 1957, her mother Grace had been judged mentally incapable of looking after a child. After that, Maggie and Harry were reluctant partners in their new life. Thrown together.

Her schooling continued patchily. Four hours a day with a minimum of supervision and books decades out of date. Her atlas did not know that the age of empire was sweeping a final bow. It was from the conversations of the wealthier passengers, talking in quiet distress, that she learned that Nigeria, Cyprus and Sierra Leone, in the real world, had won independence. Her map still had them painted proud in British pink. Maggie decided they chose that colour because it was the colour of British skin fried in the hot weather it tried to rule over.

The rest of the day she was ignored. She talked to herself since everyone else was too worried about their going-nowhere ambitions or their gonorrhoea or their tax bills to bother much with an eleven-year-old girl who was too old to be cute and too young to be interesting. She made herself laugh. Dropping bits of bread from the upper deck on to the heads of the people below and then whizzing out of sight when they felt their spattered crowns and peered upwards, wondering what this portent from the sky could mean. One old pair even lodged a complaint that they were being attacked by natives.

But now, since the arrival of Mr Rude, things had changed. After living so long in her own head she had someone to talk to. From the start he seemed to seek her out. Tracking her movements he noticed that she sat in cupboards, shutting herself away, seeking actual as well as social isolation. The ship had a wonderful choice of cupboards. A huge boiler room that hissed and chugged, iron machinery bigger than men, a linen closet with its gleaming smells and symmetrical piles of white folds, or a larder laden with fat cheeses wrapped in muslin and knobbly sacks of potatoes that she fell asleep on. She liked cupboards. They led to other worlds and not just Narnia. She asked her father for a fur coat to wear on her journeys. He looked disparaging. 'In this weather? Don't be stupid.'

Mr Rude laughed at her hiding. 'A definite case of cupboard love,' he said, creasing up. He asked her if she ever let anyone in the cupboards with her, only he said closets and had to explain what he meant.

'No one has ever asked,' she replied. 'Anyway, I don't need anyone else.'

'You're lucky,' he said sadly.

'I don't see why.'

His eyes glazed. 'People who don't need anyone else are never alone.'

She sniffed. She had never thought about this before. She changed the subject, as she often did when he talked about things too material. It meant nothing to her. And he was happy that she was not interested. He did not want to be either. She pulled him away from it all.

'Do you want a game of dominoes?'

'OK.'

Once they knew they could trust each other, Mr Rude taught Maggie to play poker. He loved to play, he said. Where he came from, gambling had been against the law. They had to play in hideaways. But that, of course, only made it more exciting. He took a sideways look at her to see if she

24

understood. He thought maybe she did. Children were always drawn to the forbidden. It was human nature untamed.

'But why was it made illegal?' she asked.

'Because it's a dangerous game,' said Mr Rude fervently. 'Once you're in you can't get out. I've seen men lose everything, their house, their family, because the game is more important.'

She nodded. She was older, in some ways, than her age.

They pretended to have money. Maggie kept diligent pencil notes of their fortunes. In little columns, which trailed through the pages of a pocket book. They had to be two people each to make up the numbers. Mr Rude played with a comedian he used to know called Bob Spitz and Maggie played with Danny Kaye.

They played late after the evening entertainment, in Mr Rude's cabin. Once she'd learned poker, she stopped playing dominoes. She loved the thrill of deception. And she was good at it. She had learned to cloak her feelings.

Then there were other games. Mr Rude played tricks on her. When she finally got to bed, there would be a note on her pillow, a riddle to find him, a sentence bent in the middle and twisted out of shape so that it pulled her head sideways.

Walk into my parlour, said the spider to the fly, I'm watching you, from a pool of blood, with my little eye.

Come through the wardrobe, to the land that's always winter and never Christmas.

Her body would be crying for sleep but her mind would be on fire, tormented by the puzzle. She had to work it out. He counted on that. When she found him that time, one chilling eye peeping through a gap in the industrial freezer in the larder, surrounded by frozen bloody carcasses, there was already a glacial film coating his eyelashes. She scolded him like a mother. Wagging her finger, she said, 'You shouldn't play games like that, you could have died if I hadn't found you.'

'What do I care?' he said, tying himself tighter in the blanket she had given him. 'Nothing is any more important than this. I only live for the games.' It was true. He was insatiable. He would forget to eat unless she told him. He milked her fantasies, which were rich and powerful, and she in turn had a foil.

25

All her life other people had tried to bring her down to earth. They had told her to stay in cold, dull reality. Only Grace, her mother, played with her. Her father, who worked in a fantasy world, would twitch with annoyance if she tried to play. 'For God's sake, Maggie,' he cried one time, 'don't you realize that I want a rest from all that bloody rubbish?'

Maggie wanted to run away. She didn't like the draught of her father's temper, her grandmother's rueing and wringing of hands, the way her life had changed. She had been forced into a new life. So she slunk into her head, to her familiar world. A world far from the sea. A murky reflection.

Mr Rude wanted to run away too. But he couldn't, he told her, because his brain was addled with thoughts of the world. 'That's why I need you, Maggie. You have access to other places.' She didn't understand since she was stuck on the ship as much as any of them were.

She was fifteen when it changed. She and Mr Rude had been friends for more than four years.

One late night after the show they were sitting like charmed snakes in identical laundry baskets, with only their heads visible from the top of the ovoid wicker tubs. They were sharing a hookah that Mr Rude had recently picked up when they stopped off in Alexandria. The tobacco had a heady aromatic flavour and it made them giggle.

Mr Rude was reading one of his favourite stories from the *Arabian Nights* and Maggie was watching him. A curious sensation that she had felt a lot recently but couldn't understand began to have definition. She found herself losing interest in the story and focusing instead on Mr Rude's lips. She had never looked at them properly before. She realized that although he was old, almost thirty, his lips were young and soft like a girl's. They were full and even and she wanted to touch them.

On her own at night, her friendship with Mr Rude was changing. When he wasn't there she kissed him. As she got undressed she put her lips on the slats of her wardrobe. And the wood did not feel unresponsive. She could feel his presence more strongly when she was on her own than when he was standing before her. In her head, he touched her with her fingers and lay between her legs under the thin sheet.

She knew that people never gave her what she wanted. She knew that Mr Rude would have adult reasons as to why their friendship should not change. He thought that she was a child and he was being a child by being with her. He did not notice that she had now joined the adult in him. So she had raised her game. And she was clever. If she confronted him he would have to reject her. So she would have to trick him as he had tricked her. She would be the spider and he would be the fly.

She was aware that she had newly swollen ammunition. Mentally too she was no longer an innocent. She had weapons, more lethal. She learned about women's sexuality from the dancing troupe flashing and flaunting on adult nights. She wasn't supposed to be there, but her father never locked her door and she could slip around the ship like a shadow. She knew every hiding place. She watched the show from behind the curtain, her eyes alive at the antics. More bizarre than the jangling breasts were the eyes of the men that opened so wide she could almost see in. Hypnotized by the twirling tassels that hung magically from the nipples of the women on stage.

What she knew about men's desires she had learned from pictures her father kept at the bottom of his cupboard under the shoes. She was not held back by the thoughts of girls of her own age because she didn't know any. Instead her formative years were full of the stories of loveless adults. There was an implacability about her that made desperate people want to tell her everything.

Mr Rude liked to drink and lately Maggie had started to drink with him. He balked at first but when she told him coldly that she could handle it and always did, he stopped being concerned. He taught her to like whisky by tipping a little sugar in. The spoon was so small and the canister big yet he never spilled a grain. He had very graceful fingers.

She had a plan. It felt wrong and exciting at the same time. She was shocked at the force within her that was making it happen. One night she left a note on his pillow.

Walk into my parlour, said the spider to the fly, water hides inside a glass and look straight through my eye.

At the end of the night, he came back to his cabin. Wiping tiredness out of his eyes, he smiled when, turning the cover of the bed, he saw the note. They hadn't played this game for a while.

He feared she had grown bored with such things. There would come a time, he was sure, when she outgrew him and he would be alone again. The note cheered him. It was not over yet. He looked for her, in a methodical manner, trying to make sense of the clue. But he didn't get anywhere. Frustrated, he turned back towards his bedroom. Maybe he would just rest a while and she would come and find him or jack it in. He needed a cigarette. He opened the door. He yawned. And there she was, in his bed.

'You didn't get it!' she shrieked in triumph. 'I'm not hiding. I'm where I always am, in your bedroom. I put myself where you would look straight through me, like water in a glass.'

He looked solemn.

'You may always be in my cabin, but you're not normally in my bed.'

She stared into his face. 'No.'

There was nothing to say. Her skin trembled and twitched. She looked at him across the room, his eyes tired with shadow growing across his face. She ached and burned.

He poured himself a drink and one for her automatically. Then he flinched. 'Don't you think we ought to go to sleep? We seem to be up later and later.' He screwed his eyes at the large wooden clock on the wall. 'It's half-past two.'

'Come to sleep then.'

He walked towards the bed. Confused by the surreal night. Well, what harm could it do to sleep there?

He climbed in. Afterwards he realized that he should have been shocked that she was naked. He should have leaped out. He should have firmly and kindly put her straight. But he didn't. She was so warm and soft and, frankly, determined that he found himself unable to do anything but respond. She was seething and pulled at him. Her skin was sweating. He didn't think about anything except the excitement coming out of her. In the darkness it felt perfectly natural. Her skin was taut to his fingers. She felt familiar. He found his eyes were moist. She was not a child at all. She was a spirit. A memory. He had slept with her before. With every woman he had dreamed of her. He had always known her.

Maggie's heart beat irregularly. Her body felt fragile. She felt her bones snap. The newness of it all. The reality could not be the dream. Exploration was a little frightening. Touching the body that she had only looked at and imagined. But in some ways it did not feel alien. For she had long watched how he moved. His fingers spreading a poker hand, with the grace of a woman opening a fan. His body had a slender delicacy, a femininity that was strangely familiar. He was old but he was also young. Everything was raw.

Dark blue daylight began to filter through the tiny porthole but the atmosphere was still early hours' madness, not morning rationality, and so it felt all right. She assured him in drowsy satisfaction that it was her scheme, her doing. She separated from him at last.

He lay, staring at the ceiling, his arms behind his head. When he breathed in he could smell his sin. But he felt uneasy joy. He turned and watched her as she drifted into sleep. Her young face. There was nothing written on it, no clue of the crime. It was as smooth as a billiard ball. He felt his own face. In contrast, the lines of sleeplessness, the scars of the years. As he rubbed his eyes he caught her scent on his fingers. He trembled.

This night had been a transition. She would be someone new tomorrow, today. He too felt different. He knew that it was his responsibility, that he should not have let it happen. But he could not feel regret. It could not now possibly be undone. It was too big.

He expected retribution. She would be traumatized, he would be vilified, dragged away in chains. In torpid half-sleep he heard her screaming, her delicate flesh splayed, contorted, tied up. He should pretend it had never happened. But it was too late. The fire was lit. It spread through him hopelessly. By now he could no more extinguish his lust than throw himself into the sea.

2

Cabbage and Chocolates

It was a long lunch. The old great-grandmother didn't go out often and when she did she liked to make the most of it. Despite her protestations that the food was inedible, too rich, too much. She was too old, her teeth were inadequate for the task, her stomach shrivelled to nothing. Despite this, she ate more than anyone. Steak, fries, a snivelling portion of peas ('Aah, you see! And you tell me, the old girl isn't getting enough vegetables!'). And they watched while she swallowed her pudding whole. They watched it shunting slowly down her neck.

As the restaurant emptied and the afternoon grew old, Maggie and her daughter Sarah sat around the table, their buttocks turning numb as the cheese that Great Edie toyed with while she talked. Time moved fast for her these days. An hour slowly falling from her lips seemed to her no time at all. Unfortunately it was not the same for her listeners.

'Of course, Levy couldn't keep his hands off me. He used to corner me when his wife wasn't looking. He tried to keep me behind closed doors. Of course I was available, wasn't I? That's how he saw it. Lumbered with two useless girls. Desperate, he was. Mind you, I wasn't short of offers. But, of course, I'd had me fingers bitten, hadn't I? Not that I was objecting to a bit of the other on a full moon. Why not? Do you think I was going to struggle on me own for nothing? No, I had me pick . . . What's the matter with you?'

For the first time in forty minutes she stopped talking. Great Edie had suddenly become aware of Maggie's face.

Maggie said, 'Burnt.'

Great Edie barely deigned to let an 'Eh?' slip from her nose.

Maggie smiled. 'You get your fingers burnt, not bitten.'

Great Edie curled her lip. 'You don't half talk a lot of rubbish. No wonder yer never got a man to marry yer.'

Maggie smirked. Her mouth tightened.

Sarah looked across the room to the waitresses kicking their heels, hanging from the tills, yawning, playing with the table-cloth, looking at their watches and smoking cigarettes. Time hung heavy. The second hand on the big wall-clock stuck.

Switching focus, pupils sucking back through the air, she looked again to her great-grandmother, bringing the lines on her cheeks back in sharp perspective. Great Edie couldn't see across the room. She lived in her own time.

Maggie swore the old woman felt heavier on the way back. Long shadows were already falling across the road as they struggled. The house seemed older, colder on their return.

The hallway was dark and narrow. Great Edie took minutes to shuffle along it back into her restricted universe, Sarah and Maggie held up behind. The walls closed in. Slowly, pre-cariously, they eased her back into her armchair where she would sit till the next time. Having talked all afternoon, she was finally exhausted. Finding a comfortable position for her hips – they waited for the clicks as the bones settled into alignment like plastic stacking – she let out a sigh and was asleep.

Still held by the spell of the house and the woman, Maggie and Sarah sat for some minutes in silence. They looked at each other, at the skeletal rising and falling, the bag of bones sinking into her seat. The threadbare armchair that was Great Edie's island of autonomy. She still controlled that. Otherwise her world was shrinking. Sometimes she could think no further than the stretch to her tea.

Maggie drew the curtain, signalled to Sarah that their duty was done and they tiptoed out of the room, prisoners escaping the sedated witch. Naturally the pressure of keeping quiet was impossible. Sarah's anxious left leg knocked over a bottle of gin which crashed to the ground. They both sniggered. The effort not to made it worse. With coy sideways glances, they ran out of the house.

Once out of the vacuum they exploded. Sparkling laughter

31

shattered into infinitesimal pieces. Swept into the air. Whisked away, glittering above them.

They looked at each other. Sarah at Maggie. Her mother, whoever she was. Whom she could still not entirely accept. Maggie at Sarah. Her daughter, whom she understood far more than she had ever wanted to. Mutual thinking. This was a rare moment.

'Do you want to get a drink?' asked Sarah.

'I'd better not.' Maggie said this anxiously, not wanting a refusal to be taken as rejection.

'Oh go on, why not?' Sarah touched her mother's arm. Casually, if that were possible. Maggie felt rigid.

She said, 'I'm going out.'

'Tonight?' Sarah stopped to give her mother a look of incomprehension. 'You never go out.'

Her mother smiled. 'Never is a bit final.'

'What are you doing?'

Maggie's smile may have hidden annoyance but she said laughingly, 'What are you, my mother?'

Sarah twitched. 'Well, sorry, I'm just interested, that's all. And the longer you don't tell me, the more interested I shall become.'

'Ah, the mistaken belief that withheld information is necessarily interesting.' Maggie became sententious when she was hiding something. Sarah wouldn't notice. Maggie continued, 'I'm sorry to disappoint you, but I'm going out with Annie. She's got a spare ticket for some play and asked me if I'd like to go.'

This could not have been delivered more flatly.

'Oh,' said Sarah. 'OK.' She looked at her mother rather oddly. 'What play?'

'How do I know? Some play. Something funny, I think. I didn't ask.'

'You didn't ask?' she said incredulously.

Her mother shook her head. 'I don't know anything about plays. What does it matter? It's just a play.'

'Well, who's in it?'

Maggie snapped. 'I don't know. I didn't ask. Goodness, Sarah.'

'OK, OK, I'm only interested. You should be pleased I care.' Sarah lifted her chin in defence.

Her mother spoke with a weary annoyance.

'Annie rang up. I was in a hurry, I was meeting you two and I was already late. She said, "I've got a spare ticket for a play, supposed to be really funny, do you want to come?" I said, "Yes, sounds good." And it wasn't going to cost me anything. It didn't occur to me to ask who was in it. I haven't heard of anybody. I don't go to plays.

'In fact the last play, now I think about it, the last play I went to, you were playing a duck. I enjoyed that. So maybe I'll enjoy this one too.'

'Well sor-ry, Mo-ther.' Sarah elongated the sounds. 'Sorry that I show any interest in your life whatsoever.'

They had reached the bus stop. From here Maggie could be home in half an hour. Sarah would walk further, to the overground station. The mood between them was light enough. Bickering signified connection.

But as she walked away from her mother, Sarah found herself groping for the edges of something amorphous. Difference. She could smell it. Even at this tired bus stop on a shabby South London street. She could hear it caught up with the litter cartwheeling in the wind. She screwed up her face in an effort to work out what it was. Her mother was strange. Still she could not define it.

Maggie had a routine when the day was over and she was at last alone. First she locked the door behind her – bolted and chained. Then she poured a glass of wine. She took her shoes off and replaced them in the perfect space that they had come from that morning. She slipped into her house shoes – plain black Japanese soft-soled slip-ons (she was too young for traditional slippers and too old for irony). Then she washed her hands and face. This ritual was an essential. She could not relax without it.

This evening she put on music. Early Fleetwood Mac singing the blues. She liked the melancholy but quietly of course. She sat in a chair in the sitting room. After suppressing it all day, she at last allowed herself to give in a little to her emotion. She took a sip of wine and carefully replaced the glass on the table (inner turbulence was no excuse for a stained carpet). She sat back and her eyes glazed a little as she thought. Her face grew hot, and for the first time in years, tears filled her eyes.

The shock of her reaction froze her for some minutes to the

chair. Her legs were pinned to the floor. Her clothes felt heavy on her body. I'm crying, she thought. I'm actually crying.

The sense of disbelief made her feel even more alone. She didn't move until the phone rang. Then she jumped. In her momentary fugue she forgot who the caller must be.

'Hello?'

'I'm ill. I'm sick. You need to come over.'

Maggie's face changed.

'No, Edie. You ate too much, you shouldn't eat that much in one sitting.'

'What? What?' The old woman's voice was almost a scream.

'Calm down, take a Rennie. They're in the drawer to the left of the sink. It won't take you five minutes.'

'You've got to come over!'

'No, Edie, you'll be fine. You just overstretched yourself. You starve all week and then you eat all that rich food, it's not surprising.' Maggie spoke slowly, comfortingly, like a mother.

'What food?'

'When we went out, earlier on,' she explained patiently. 'You, Sarah and me.'

'Out? I haven't moved all day. Come over! Come over here now, you wicked girl! It's wicked of you to leave me all alone for so long.'

'I'm going now, Great Edie.'

The shrilling softened. 'You coming over?'

'No, I've only just got back, and I'm meeting a friend this evening. We're going to a play.'

A pause, then inchoate screeching again. 'Then sod you.' Bang.

Maggie put the phone down too. She went back to her chair and drank more wine. She listened to the music. Blues notes that trembled through her spine, the voice a dark figure in the shadowy corner of the room.

She rubbed her face. Her fingers were damp. Her face felt aged. Flimsy like cloth, the years had passed. She felt a stab of shame that she should be crying. Over nothing. A letter. A letter she hadn't even opened. A letter that she was afraid to open. Afraid of what opening the letter would open in her. And she was right to worry, wasn't she, a stupid old woman, reduced to sobbing, to a child, at even the thought?

The letter. It was in her bedside drawer where she had placed it unopened on her return from the hospital two days ago. Delivered by hand. The nurse who passed it on to Maggie was not the nurse who had originally received it. She spoke to no one who had seen him. She'd just been told that a man called John or Rudi had wanted to get in touch with her and had left this letter.

When she was alone she had allowed herself to look at it. She felt the surface and raised it to her nose. White paper laced with the smell of the hospital day room where it had lain for nearly a week, in uncertain limbo between addresser and addressee. Anything else was her hopeless imagination.

The handwriting, however, was instantly recognizable. The copperplate curls gone wild with impatience and personality. It seemed perhaps a little fainter. Age.

The phone rang again. This time Maggie was expecting it.

More scraping on the E string. 'What friend are you seeing?'

'Annie.'

'Tell her you can't see her.'

'I'm not going to tell her that.'

'Tell her I'm ill.'

'Great Edie, you are not ill.'

'One day I'll be dead in my chair and you will know that it was because you neglected me and you will feel guilty for the rest of your life.'

Maggie sighed and rested her head in her hands. 'Why don't you watch some television?'

The scorn was palpable. 'Television! You think everything of this television. You'd watch television at my funeral. You'd get that Noel Tarrant, wouldn't you, to give away me money at the cemetery? Television, is it a dummy now to shut me up, is that it?'

'I'm sorry, Great Edie, I've got to go now. I think you should rest quietly and you'll feel better in the morning.'

'You know your problem, Maggie, my girl?'

Maggie was looking through the sitting-room door to the bedroom door, through which sat the bedside cabinet and the drawer and the letter.

'Tell me.'

'You're selfish. Completely selfish and you always have been. Just like your mother.'

35

Maggie shuffled. 'OK, that's enough now, Grandmother. Put the phone down and go to sleep.'

'And ungrateful. After all I've done for you, you leave me for dead. I hate you.'

'Yes, OK, I'll speak to you tomorrow.'

Maggie put the phone down and walked to the bedroom to pick up the letter. She did not miss stairs since moving to the flat; she liked a compact space. She carried the letter as if on a silver salver but paused, the mention of her mother prompting her to look into the second bedroom. Grace's room, kept for the periods that her mother spent out of hospital, when Maggie had to care for her alone. Maggie feared these times; the unpredictability of her mother's behaviour, the reliance on drugs she did not really understand, the terror that she would come back from work and find the flat smashed up, if the balance of her mother's mind shifted from dopey pliability to violent self-destruction. The majority of the time, when Grace was in hospital, the bare room lay unused, a constant chiding reminder. Maggie shivered at the feel of the letter in her hands. She put it on the glass coffee table in the sitting room.

Great Edie's tantrums often made her hungry. She went to the kitchen and opened the fridge. A tagliatelle and ham TV dinner was earmarked for Saturday night. The packet sat in a well-behaved pile of ready-to-heat meals. She opened the salad drawer at the bottom and sighed at the Little Gem lettuces and salad tomatoes that were waiting to accompany the meal. All planned.

Her eyes scanned the fridge. Hesitantly she took out an unopened box of Black Magic. A gift from one of her clients, she had meant to pass it on. With a sudden thrill of violence, she slammed the fridge door behind her so the whole white box shook. She nearly walked clean away but on a second thought she opened the door again and took out a dish of cooked dark green cabbage. Couldn't let it go to waste.

She had never eaten cabbage and chocolate for tea before and she found the combination strangely exhilarating. The good and the bad together. All the while she ate, she watched the envelope on the glass table in front of her. It didn't move but the letters may have wobbled slightly, in her direction.

'For Maggie Lockyer, daughter of Grace Lockyer. By hand.'

When she lost touch with a person, the memory reduced to one prevailing emotion. The impression was shaken through a sieve, the variety drained away and she was left with a solid whole. Her mind understood that person in a single way – hatred, love or boredom. So that, after they had gone, whenever she thought of them, she would feel that way. Eventually she thought that was all they had ever been. The living, breathing, panoramic person was gone. Only when there was a tangible reminder, some fresh evidence of their physical reality, did the rich ambivalence that she felt towards people return.

For more than thirty years Maggie had felt not hatred, not bitterness, but just despairing numbness when she thought about him; now she began to remember other things.

She finished the cabbage and was sick of the chocolates. She carefully folded the lid of the box back down and thought to return them to their place in the fridge – but for once she didn't, she just left them on the glass table. Profligacy.

The letter. She picked it up. Played with it between her fingers, stroking the surface across her mouth. Then put it down on the table again to give her distance. Space to think.

And the letter looked so small.

Opening it was one thing, bringing its own problems. But what if she didn't? What would that do to her? She was almost cross with him for the first time in thirty years. He had placed her in a terrible dilemma. And that made her laugh inside. Trust him to do that. For the first time since he left she remembered how he had made her laugh. She didn't really want to.

So say she didn't open the letter. What then? Could she return to where she was two days ago? Hardly. She was not that strong. She had shut him away for this long only because he was gone. Really gone, disappeared with no word, no information, no contact. That she dealt with. But now there was a change. He was back even in this small way. Even the folded piece of paper inside the envelope, which she held to the light, squinting. She could see it inside. It was him.

She had forgotten what it was to be tempted. She was tempted now. Tempted to open this letter and tempted to toss it away as an ultimate act of defiance.

She stood up and went to the kitchen to pour more wine.

On the way back, she hesitated and turned slowly into the bathroom, pulling the light cord.

Obviously some previous occupant had been a head or so taller than her and had fixed the bathroom cabinet accordingly. Maggie had never got around to changing it though she had lived there five years. It wasn't so bad. She could see most of her face if she stood on tiptoe. The whole of it, temporarily, if she jumped.

Sarah, of course, got cross that the only mirror in her mother's flat reflected the top of people's heads. But Maggie didn't feel the lack of it. She wasn't very interested in looking at herself.

Tonight she took a chair from the bedroom and wedged it against the bathroom wall.

While she wasn't a vain woman, there was a thought in her mind. Should she open the letter and, presuming that act led to meeting him again, how would she look to him now? (She did not wonder how he would look to her. He would always look the same.)

She clambered up. She could not ignore the thin layer of dust, after years of being zealously clean, but nor could she bear to fetch a duster so she compromised and wiped the mirror with her flannel. She felt regret almost at once, when she saw the lines of grey fuzz on her white flannel. She would have to put it in the wash now, early.

'You see,' she said, 'you're getting to me already.'

She looked at herself. Or through herself in a way she had not done for years. It was a shock. There was the face, the brown eyes with fine lines radiating outwards. She saw the strong nose; she saw her cheeks no longer taut, sagging slightly. She saw her mouth losing its fullness, pinched with anxiety. That was all as it should be. What made her gasp was something else.

Since she had received the letter, two days ago, something inside her had changed. Inexorably, beyond her control, the letter had taken her back. And all the while the letter was still there and she could still open it; while it lay just moments away from her scrutiny, she would continue to change.

In the mirror she was seeing her face with a new self or rather the melting return of her old self, her vulnerable self. So the face on the outside was no longer the face on the inside. It was like looking at someone she recognized but could not put a name to. She was terrified.

With adrenaline coursing through her body she staggered off the chair. Her head pulsed in flashes of black and white. She ran faster than she had run for years and fell on to the floor in the sitting room by the glass table, by the letter. Images were flooding her mind. Forgotten scenes of who she used to be and things she used to feel. Nothing solid, but tenebrous views through the trees. She was looking into a dark forest.

She knew what Sarah would say. Sarah would have opened the letter immediately. Sarah would say of course she should read it, meet John, perhaps she would enjoy herself for once; there was, at least, nothing to lose. But Sarah was young. An older woman did not have nothing to lose. Over the course of thirty years she had created a calm. Walking again into those feelings? At forty-nine? She was not at all sure. She had felt what the future after opening the letter might be and it was too hard.

She picked up the letter and determined to burn it, unopened.

The phone rang. She didn't answer it but thought instead of what play she could say she had been to. She took the chocolates and put them back in the fridge.

3

The Bed, the Sofa and the Bath

Sarah had been taking this twenty-minute train journey for less than a month and already it was beginning to terrify her. She had realized that what she saw when she sat in that carriage at six forty every evening was a perfect reflection of inside her head – the crowding, the confusion.

Every day she was trapped by a wall of flesh, bodies wrapped together. Pink on brown on olive on white. The smell of skin slow cooking, of hot carbon dioxide expelled. The heat on this August day was pressing. There was no space, no air to think. She tried to move but was pinned to her seat by a man standing right in front of her, his trouser zip an inch from her nose. So close she could eat him. This uncomfortable thought flashed in front of her eyes.

She wondered what people looked like naked. It was a habit, the way other women play with their hair. Except hair fiddling was a sign of insecurity while her habit was just a quirk. She didn't tell people, they would find it odd, but not telling them wasn't so easy either.

Her neighbour, a large man, took more than his half of the seat. She was squeezed, her thighs glued together. Selfish bastard. Didn't he know what it was like wearing a skirt in this weather? He was reading about salmon fishing. Making your own hook. Interesting. Really.

His hands, she noted, betrayed a life of solitude. That pale, pudgy, hairless look of the terminally single. She peered at his hands to confirm their ringlessness. And she was right of course, she was good at that kind of thing. Little details that other people didn't look at. She liked to watch. The crisps he was eating sent a fishy smell into the air. In a confined space, such behaviour was insufferable. Sarah looked away and tried to focus on a gasometer out of the window and imagine, as it fell, a cool breeze hitting her face. But there was no relief. For as soon as she escaped from the stifling carriage, when her spirit floated through the stale window, thoughts of the evening crept insidiously into her mind and she sank.

The evening that lay before her had become a hole in her life. She was dreading it. It was a hole she had dug for herself exactly seven days ago.

This time last week she was stuffed not on a train, which was at least suffocation with a purpose, but in a bar, with 'work-people'. A terrible mistake. She didn't like them and they did not like her. It was her fault. Her latest unconvincing incarnation as a wages clerk in a small computer company was proving painful for everyone. She hated working in an anthill – the hierarchy, the politics, the running around after things that did not matter – but she needed the money and they needed someone cheap.

The bar had been full, with people spilling on to the road outside, glad of the rain to cool down. Ant-slaves feverishly destroying themselves with alcohol and dull conversation. Sarah was moody and the bad atmosphere was boiling into a row. When the manager's crappy PA, of all people (the same girl for whom Sarah had picked up a chocolate brownie that very afternoon, the ungrateful bitch), said, 'Well, why don't you leave then if you hate it so much? No one will miss you,' Sarah finally fled, wishing only that she'd done so earlier and wondering why she hadn't. She pushed through the crowd, blinking into the storm, her face immediately wet, her limbs tied in tight knots for hours sprung free.

Walking through rain for some minutes, she had eventually stopped at another bar which called her with mournful music through its doors like a drunk. Ululating, come in, come in. No one else had heard. It was almost empty. At the far end was a scratched wooden square of floor where an old man in a suit was squeezing a young girl with blond hair as if he were the only thing holding her up.

Sarah sat on a stool by the bar and studied a display of beer nuts in front of her. Packets of Mr Nutz, in top hat and tails, danced before her, covered in dust.

Pfffff, she tried to blow it off from where she sat. From nowhere, there was a man sitting next to her. Dark, thin, late twenties, looking at her from behind small gold-rimmed glasses.

She turned her head round mechanically. He smiled. 'I wish it was raining in here.'

She asked him why, not because she wanted to know, but because he wanted her to ask.

He smiled again. 'Because since your shirt dried I can't see your nipples any more.'

There was a silence. She looked at his lips. He was so obviously respectable.

'It's not a shirt, it's a dress.'

'Well, I'm sorry.'

He picked up his glass pointlessly and swirled the contents. There was a small silence that he was quick to fill.

'So what are you doing here?'

'Drinking.'

He laughed.

'Well,' he said in an easy tone, 'I don't know what the hell I'm doing here. I was with a friend, but I lost her. Somewhere in the crowd, you know what Soho's like on a Friday evening. We were together and then I lost her. Can you believe it?'

'No, not really. She must have done it deliberately.' She spoke the truth when it was going to cause offence.

He laughed again. He had very even teeth. Unnaturally white.

'No, no, that's all right,' his elbow on the bar, being cool, 'you don't need to make me feel good about myself. But go on, what are you doing in here on your own?'

'Yeah,' she said, 'I know. Can you believe it, me, on my own, and with nipples like mine? Extraordinary, isn't it?' She looked at him witheringly. 'Really, I'm just drinking. Is that so unusual?'

'But you haven't got a drink.' And he leaped at the opportunity, thrusting his hand into his pocket in a dramatic gesture. 'What can I get you?'

They sat in silence for several moments, facing the bar, staring at bottles. She couldn't quite read the labels, they jumped when she blinked.

She felt him speak in her ear. 'I tell you what. We sit at that table over there and you try and read the labels of each bottle in turn. Anything you can't read, you have to have a shot of, OK?'

There was an inevitability about it.

'Oh, OK then.'

She lay on her back on her bed and stared at her body, so extraordinarily white. They weren't nipples, they were cherries on cupcakes.

She thanked God for alcohol. It stopped her giggling when she was meant to take things seriously. Like the words that were falling from his lips in a gushing patter.

'You have a wonderful body, I love a woman who is not ashamed of her body.'

She managed to turn her laugh into a throaty expression of gratitude. 'Mmm, thanks.'

His body was lean and pleasantly cool and she suspected that he had drunk rather less than she had.

It wasn't erotic or sordid, it was nothing. And nothing was fine, anaesthetizing. It didn't feel like her, and since she didn't like being her, this was good too, a welcome release. Maybe that was why she was doing it. Certainly, she was too drunk to feel anything – it was like watching someone else having sex on TV. She kept wanting to turn the sound down, with the delusion that Maggie might hear.

He couldn't contain his enthusiasm. Men never can. Cool as they liked beforehand but when it came to the actual doing, the ins and the outs, they couldn't stop their tails wagging.

'You drive me crazy,' he groaned, eyeballs rolling. Then it was over.

Sleep didn't come with a strange body in the bed, his elbows dug into her side. He weighed down the mattress so she was lying on a slope. When she came close to sleep her mind rolled downwards and she was immediately tense, totally awake.

She heard the rain stop. She adjusted her focus to the red blobs on her clock. It was a quarter to five and dawn was splintering through the blinds. She eased herself off the bed and padded into the sitting room. Curling on the sofa with a blanket over her, she pressed the video. Marlene Dietrich sat at a table, legs apart, playing a moll. Frank Sinatra tinkered on the piano. It was a film she had seen perhaps a hundred times. It was a comfort to have them three feet away and know exactly what they were going to say next. She liked that kind of world. A world of stylized certainty. Marlene, open lips, eyes glittering. Her unbroken spell. No one saw her in the morning.

Sarah stretched out her hand to touch the screen that vibrated in the darkness and she yawned.

'Can I get some coffee anywhere?' The request was tentative, the voice unfamiliar.

She woke with a start. The blanket was on the floor. Her skin looked whiter than ever in the light.

'Oh. Yeah. Sure.' Oh God. Her clothes were in the bedroom.

He grinned as his eyes followed the length of her body with slow satisfaction, remembering.

'Aren't you cold there?'

There was a sweatshirt lying across the chair, discarded three days ago after yoga. She grabbed at it, he made to take it from her but he was joking. Funny.

'Coffee's in the kitchen,' she murmured, rolling off and into the sweatshirt. Walking to the kitchen brought her stomach to her throat and a pricking swell of sweat.

He followed, chatting too much.

'I couldn't remember where I was when I woke up. Particularly when you weren't there. I mean, like you were my only clue. So I thought to myself, "Who do I know who goes to the opera?"'

Opera? What opera?

'Oh yeah,' she recalled, 'that poster in the bedroom.'

It had been on the wall when she moved in.

He was already saying something else.

'But I couldn't get it from that and I didn't recognize the view out of the window.'

'There isn't a view out of the window.'

'Hey,' he paused for comic effect, putting his hands through his ruffled hair, 'it's an interesting wall.'

The coffee tub ripped her nail as she pulled at it.

'If you like bricks.' The words were just audible as she sucked her finger. 'Shit.'

'Let me help you.'

His fingers brushing against hers – by accident, she hoped – made her shiver and she ducked to the kettle and hastily filled it with water.

'No, no, it's quite all right.'

Quiet finally, he watched her pouring the boiling water into the filter machine. She inhaled the coffee and watched the brown water dripping. If she kept her head down she could only hear his breathing, not see his face. They walked silently back to the sitting room.

She sat on the sofa hugging her knees, the sweatshirt pulled over and down to cover her rude bits. She rested her forehead on her knees. Her hair, straight, dark brown, shoulder length, fell like a curtain. She said, 'I hate people seeing me before I've seen myself.' She looked up around the room, her eyes narrow. 'Is it late?'

He looked at his watch. (Had he worn it throughout?) 'Ten twenty.'

'Ah.'

There was a pause.

'Look, I'll go.'

No doubt she should have said, 'No, don't rush off, stay for breakfast,' but she had done enough lying. So she just stared at him.

Her silence was communicative. He said, 'Just let me get this coffee down, then I'll be ready to face the world. You could do with some sleep after last night.'

She almost smiled. 'Are you saying I was drunk?'

'We both were.'

For a moment she thought there was a meeting of minds. That he was saying that the experience was the same for him. That they had chosen each other like an all-night garage – the first and nearest, not the one with the best pumps. A functional experience, forgotten instantly, until the next time she needed fuel.

Then he stammered, 'But hey, don't get me wrong, I didn't just come back because I was drunk.'

'No?' He missed the disappointment in her voice. Instead he was being reassuring.

'Of course not, you're a really sweet girl,' he looked up coyly, 'and you look great first thing in the morning, really. So tell me you'll meet me again next Friday and then I'll go.'

'Sure, OK.'

'Fantastic! Here's my number.' He pulled a card from his jacket. Silently she begged him to be a Japanese porn translator. But then he probably wouldn't have business cards. He was a development manager, whatever that was. He smiled in a way she was already tired of.

'My name's Richard.'

'So it is. I'm Sarah.'

And the week had passed. She shook her head in silent regret at the recollection, which despite the drunkenness was stubbornly vivid. All the escapes that her mind had dreamed up had failed to materialize. She was still alive. He was still alive. In an hour and a half's time he was expecting a repeat performance. She wished she understood herself. She had no idea how she had got into this situation, still less how she was going to get out of it. She was trapped on a train.

She remembered a career counsellor who had sighed stagnantly and dropped her CV back in her lap.

'I can't work miracles, you know,' he told her. 'I have never seen such a lack of continuity. Is there nothing you've stuck with?'

This was a bit upsetting since she had paid the man for his optimistic prognosis of her future but she couldn't deny his insight. He had been more right than he could possibly have known. She suddenly wished she were having dinner with him.

It's not my fault, she thought. I just have a problem with commitment. I am a victim of the modern age. I'm raging against nothing. I have nothing to complain about and that is precisely my complaint. I am beating against air. I have choices: real coffee, twenty-four-hour supermarkets, freedom and daytime television. And none of them does it for me. The joke is that I'm still totally fucked off.

Someone in the carriage was crunching an empty Coke can, an irregular rhythm. Sarah winced, shut her eyes and tried to breathe.

When she opened her eyes the salmon man opposite was entirely nude. His over-tight suit had melted away revealing the

46

limpid skin beneath. She couldn't look away. The anaemic chest hair, little beads of sweat, matting it into a fuzz. Sagging nipples, the line of hair an arrow pointing down over the blue-white convex stomach, towards the mass of thick pale curls below.

Sarah shook her head. She blinked. She stared at the fat woman opposite, immersed in a Maeve Binchy. But there was no relief, for the book rested on the woman's bare breasts. Nipples as big as apples sniffing the pages. And the zip man, swinging before her, had dropped his trousers and pants. His penis swayed like a pendulum as the train lurched through points.

She wondered if her own emptiness was what allowed her to see through other people. She had no doubt that what she was seeing was real. Maybe she was a non-person. Food went in and came out but something was missing in the middle, a part that enabled a person to join with the others in work, in play and in the mind. She felt dizzy. Much as she dreaded the end of it, the twenty-minute train journey felt interminable. She covered her mouth with her hand to stop herself gasping. She tore upwards to the window, feeling her skin flush, and threw her cheeks against the air like a drowning woman, her neck bent almost at right angles. Her face was stretched under cellophane, her features distorted. Air! Air! I'm going to be sick!

Whether she said this out loud she wasn't sure. There was an upsurge in sound as the train stopped at the station. A hiss of the doors and bodies falling on to the platform. The carriage emptied. The man with the swinging penis had gone. The fish fan closed his hook feature, put it under his arm and stepped over briefcases, closing and opening his puffy mouth.

Sarah looked round. She caught the eye of the fat woman, dressed again, in brown, who smiled.

She knows, she knows, thought Sarah. She knows what I see. Then she tossed her head and thought – well, I don't care. At least I haven't let myself get into that state. Serves her right. And she walked off the train.

It was seven o'clock. She was meeting Richard at eight thirty. A one-week reprieve had reduced to one hour. Seven days to cancel, to come up with some excuse and still she had failed to act. It was too late now. Once again.

She was numb with the thought. The noise of her shoes on the pavement felt like it came from someone else. She couldn't feel her key as it melted into the door. The flat smelt of bedclothes. The blinds were still closed from the morning when she had left in her customary hurry. The air was thick. Unwashed plates stank in the sink. For a moment she thought to wash up. But that would mean putting the plug in, her hands going through the slimy pile of dirty plates. She decided against it. She had suffered enough.

She ran a bath. That was dirty too.

She climbed in and lay steaming, sipping from a glass. Wine, so cold it no longer tasted cheap, the glass wet on the outside as well. Slippery between her fingers.

Since she was a child she had imagined her body as a desert. Her pale skin the undulating sands. Her button was a hollow that held on to the water when the flash flood came with the rocking of her hips.

Green oil poured from a thin-necked bottle, an algae film. She had turned the light off and the water was dark. A freshwater flannel swam beneath the surface, tickling the sides of her legs, the soles of her feet.

She had been in a long time, longer than she thought. She knew she was wasting time. Letting it slip through her fingers. The moments were dripping away. She dreamed of emptiness. It grew darker and the oil on the water had a silvery sheen.

At last she heard the click of the answerphone. She shivered and noticed for the first time that the water had grown cold.

A man's voice, shouting over a noisy background. 'Sarah, hi, it's Richard. It's eight forty-five and I expect you're on your way. Anyway, I'm going to give it a while. If you're not here by nine, or no, maybe by nine thirty, I won't wait. Anyway, I expect you'll be here any minute. Woman's right to be fashionably late, huh? Yeah, well, anyway . . .'

She heard no more because she slithered under the water. This time her whole face was covered. She saw watery stars. Wait for a whole hour? God.

She pictured him waiting for her. He would be wearing a stiffly ironed shirt. He would be standing where he could be seen, doing an anxious circuit every ten minutes in case she'd dashed in while he was blinking and hidden herself in a deliberately obscure spot. Like no one ever did.

She shivered uncontrollably and climbed into a towel and padded to her computer.

'You're horrible, Sarah.'

'People do this all the time.'

'You said you wouldn't do it again.'

'How dare he presume that I'd be there?'

'Because you told him you would be, Sarah, it wouldn't be an unreasonable assumption.'

'Oh God . . .'

Sarah paused on her keyboard, the words blinking at her. Then she wrote, 'I need to get away.'

The response was impatient. 'From what?'

'I don't know.'

'There's nothing to get away from. You have no responsibilities. You live only for yourself and you live like a pig. What's your problem?'

'You can talk.'

'I haven't left some innocent member of the public crying in a bar.'

'He'll be fine, he'll meet somebody else.'

'That's right, make yourself feel better. There are no excuses, you're a horrible person.'

There was a pause. Sarah stretched. Her neck was tight. She bent backwards over the chair, so far that she could see through the window behind her to the restaurant opposite where the chefs ran upside down. Bouncing on their hats. Always running, running, running while she sat still.

'I think', Alex was writing, 'that you enjoy it.'

'What?'

'You get some kind of pleasure out of the repulsion. I used to be like that about tomato juice. I hated it, but it was a perversely attractive hate. I drank it to torment myself. That's just like you. That's why you only go with men you can't bear – because you enjoy it.'

'Stop talking rubbish, I'm coming over.'

'You reckon? You abandon some poor bloke and then think you can come and amuse yourself with me.'

'Yep.'

'Oh, all right then.'

'See you.'

49

Sarah shut off the computer, threw on a dress and shoes and ran into the sticky night. Left, left again away from the main road on which she lived. The road was suddenly leafy, bigger. Breathless, she ran up the steps and rang the bell.

A tall man dressed in a pair of pyjama bottoms opened the door languidly, his thin frame haloed by the light.

'Come in then, date-breaker. You amoralist. Come in and see how little sympathy I have for you.'

She smiled for what felt like the first time that week. It had been so long, she was sure her lips creaked with lack of use.

'Hello, Alex.'

4

His Own Invention

Alex left the door for Sarah to close and slunk back inside. The hall was in darkness but Sarah followed the sound of his feet. Slamming the door, she clattered after him. Two floors up, thirty-six steps of wide bare wood. There was never a house with so many stairs. The oxygen was thin.

Her friend lived on the top two floors. The first contained the derelict kitchen, a room of his books, a dining or games room and the office. From here came the only light. Sarah walked in. Alex was back at the computer. It beamed an impish green across the room.

His workroom vibrated long hours of concentration. The mammoth computer, in the middle of the desk, dominated the room. Immediately Sarah flicked the switch, flooding bald electric light into the gleam. It revealed a pile of congealing takeaway cartons and empty beer bottles that must have fallen from Alex's hands the instant they were no longer required.

Sarah kicked them out of the way. Alex turned round to face her. A sallow complexion. A yellow luminosity from too long curled under electric light. Cadaverous cheekbones and short scruffy black hair.

'Hi,' he said again.

She always felt like she was interrupting.

'Been cooped up long?'

Hands folded under each armpit, Alex leaned forward to read a tiny clock on the screen. His lips moved as he counted.

'Eleven hours. I must be hungry.'

He stood up stiffly and slowly. Rigor mortis was setting in. Finally upright, how tall he was. She addressed a question to his neck.

'What you working on?'

He said it in the bass voice of a movie trailer. 'Revelation III: The Vengeance of Jael.'

'Ooh,' said Sarah who had no interest in computer games but liked Alex's preposterous story lines, 'and what does Jael do?'

The skin on his neck lifted a little. She craned upwards to see a small, satisfied smile curling across Alex's face.

'She drives tent pegs through the heads of the Canaanites and she's great at running away – you try and catch her and she stones you with her catapult. And she can hypnotize you. If you try and kill her from behind, she uses her ponytail as an evil pendulum and your man starts seeing the screen in slow motion.'

He spoke always in understatement. The low tones went with his unmoving face. Dark and wooden.

'Sounds good.'

'I'm quite pleased. Trouble is, strictly, she only appears in Judges. But I exhausted all the good bits of Revelation in the first two games.'

Sarah shrugged. 'Well, who's going to notice? I don't suppose many strict Bible fans buy your games anyhow.'

Alex nodded. 'There isn't a lot of overlap.'

'Let's have a look at her then.'

He bent down and manipulated the screen, his long fingers leaping round the keyboard in cabalistic fury.

'There.'

Sarah screwed her eyes up and laughed. 'She looks like an evil Girl Guide.'

He held his head sideways. 'Mmm, I see what you mean. It must be the tent pegs in my subconscious. It was meant to be biblical combat gear. Too blue, you reckon?'

Even though he was more intelligent, better educated, sharper witted, at least that was what she thought – he listened to her.

'Definitely. I don't think they even had blue then, did they?'

Alex pondered. 'They must have done, what about Mother Mary?'

She cocked a nostril in derision. 'What?'

'She always wore blue.'

An incredulous grunt.

'I'll make it orange,' Alex said hastily. 'They definitely had orange. I'm sure Moses wore orange in *The Ten Commandments*.'

'Like your research, pal.'

'Well, bloody hell,' drawled Alex, 'they don't pay me research fees.' He pushed the chair out of the way. A black leather, steel-framed 1970s office twirler that looked like it had been attacked with a knife. 'Do you want a beer?'

'Sure.'

In the corner of the room was a huge industrial fridge. It was Alex's only concession to modern interior design but one that gave him pleasure every time he opened the door and saw the brown bottles lined up in perfect symmetry. The order in his life.

Beers in hand, they went across the landing to the far larger, barer dining room. Rectangular, with ancient wallpaper which might once have been red. It was empty but for four red-leather dining chairs evenly spaced around a heavy oak table and an elaborate fireplace, with prick-eared, lolling-tongued gargoyles in the corners who looked as shocked to be there as the visitor was to see them.

On the table lay a mass of chess pieces, a board, dice and several sets of cards. Alex sat down, wincing as the chair leg grazed the floorboards with a grating squeak. He sat as he always did, relaxed but attentive. One long leg crossed over the other, his elbows slumped into the table. His hands propped up against his chin. Sarah sat next to him, tucking herself, as was her habit, into a ball. Arms crossed, holding on to opposite ankles. Her knees folded under her chin.

Alex switched on a small CD player. It let out a painful urban sound. An echoing dub bass overlaid with – what, scraped corrugated iron? Then came the singer; clanging, noxious, like someone throwing up in a dustbin.

Sarah looked at him questioningly.

Alex lowered his eyes. 'A friend of mine. I said I'd listen to it. Yeah, I know technically it's shit. But I think it's good shit. As opposed to bad shit. You wait until three in the morning, it'll sound really good then.'

'I didn't say a word!' She looked defensive. 'I think it's great shit. You know I hate anything with a tune. Who are they?'

'He's called Sour. It's just this guy I know.'

There were a lot of guys Alex just knew. He had always known people, despite his isolated life. His parents had known people. His parents had been part of a left-wing academic loose-skirted circle. While they were alive, the house was full of radicals – feminists, anarchists, thinkers, hippies – and the smell of burning grass. His childhood stank. Even his name was redolent of the time. He was named Alex, leader of men, lexicon, master of language, after the delinquent hero of *A Clockwork Orange*. It was his mother's Bible.

Both parents were now dead but Alex still knew people. He was reclusive by nature, but once you know people, you know people. He knew the sons and daughters of 'sixties radicals.

And nearly all, Sarah noted, became artists. Part-timers, tinkering with scrap metal and pornography and stereo equipment and lying about thinking about it. Drinking coffee, finding loft studios and building a rapport with their drug dealer. (They had drug dealers like other people have accountants.) Maybe because they could. Because they had big London houses to languish in. And parents desperate to sponsor culture in converted warehouses in Deptford.

Several times Alex had taken her to the exhibitions of 'this girl he knew', Leona. There was one called, no, *entitled* 'Unscrewing': a collection of NHS false limbs, mannequins' heads and plaster-cast imprints of Leona's own genitals screwed together into ill-fitting bodies. The genitals were always on top.

Helmet-haircut Leona escorted Sarah around her contortions. 'You see there,' she pointed, extending a skinny arm dressed in an exquisitely simple black Paul Smith sleeve. 'On the heads, that writing? It's lipstick. The material is the message as much as words. Modern thinking is all about texture. Lipstick, huh? Fake kisses? What a metaphor for the patina of celebrity.'

The sticky red words Sarah's upside-down head read were, 'Unscrew you, screw your head, unscrew me, the screw is dead.' She was glad the words weren't important. Because she didn't know what they meant.

But her favourite of Leona's exhibitions had been 'The End of Art'. Leona insisted all the 'people she knew' go to the private view. Sarah and Alex mingled with the gaggle of black-clothed, tractor-heeled guests sipping champagne. Waiting expectantly, using words like 'iconoclastic'. But then, the joke: there was no exhibition. Instead the warehouse was being demolished by the council to make way for a supermarket. Leona was filming the whole event.

It was meant to be a protest but Sarah missed the point. 'The power of that concrete ball to destroy everything!' she sighed. 'Fucking amazing.'

Now she was staring into space.

'So, go on then,' prompted Alex. 'This man you left hanging. What was wrong with this one?'

'Oh God,' sighed Sarah, looking at the ceiling. 'He was just so irritating.'

'Men you meet are always irritating.'

She raised her eyebrows and started picking at the beer label. 'So I'm unlucky. Either that or most men are irritating.'

'Or you're too fussy.'

She slanted her eyes. 'Hardly. I bloody sleep with them, don't I? That's more generous than a lot of women.'

'I didn't realize that it was for their benefit.'

'Well, it certainly isn't for mine.'

His mouth twitched. With what? Disapproval? He had a childish mouth. Full and smooth. To an extent it gave him away. It moved when his eyes were still.

'I see.'

She flicked a dead moth on to the floor. It spiralled lugubriously downwards.

Alex was gathering up the cards and counters and organizing them into heaps. The light hanging over the table flickered and buzzed. Sarah squinted and saw another moth sizzling. Little black body dazzled and then charred. Icarus.

Alex smiled hopefully and swiftly changed the subject. 'Shall we play?'

'OK, I know, enough. OK, let's play.'

Alex didn't like details. That is, not emotional ones. He had a passion for other details. That James Joyce was born on a cloudy day. That Elvis Presley liked watermelon-seed spitting competitions. He devoted weeks to proving to his own satisfaction that the square root of two was indeterminate. Those were the details that kept him alive. Shut up with books and computer was the best way, he said, to discover the world. But he wouldn't spend five minutes in psychosexual analysis. His face folded like paper.

People he knew talked about sex all the time. If they weren't talking about it they were expressing it in atonal music and art-house films, in unread poetry and high-concept multi-media performance art. Maybe this was why Alex never talked about anything. He would listen, for a while, then his face would retreat. Sarah knew what to look for. That folding twitch, the boredom maybe, or the discomfort. Suddenly he would look ancient and disapproving. At this moment one shut one's mouth.

The game they were playing was Alex's own invention. Before he designed computer games for a living, Alex had made board games. But they were always too complicated and too long. The market demanded a game that took an amusing hour after dinner. Alex's went on most of the night and invariably required tortuous decision-making and brain-blunting logic. Only when he moved into programming did he make any money. Complicated computer games sold. So long as they were brutally violent and highly offensive his punters didn't mind how clever they were. In fact, cleverness added to the appeal, giving the game a cult of endurance and a badge of machismo. But Alex himself had always preferred board games. A board felt more real to him. Computers made money, board games were a way of spending it. He built them only for himself. Intricate wooden patterns, hand-finished cards with a heavy wax coating. This game was called Alice-anti-Alice and it was Sarah's favourite. It was made of glass and painted wood. Three-dimensional, it looked from the other side of the room like a large doll's house. Close up it looked like a mathematical puzzle. With an Escher staircase leading nowhere. Everything that seemed solid fell apart. It was the third law of thermodynamics in action. Entropy in a night. It was a game version of *Through the Looking-glass*. One player played Alice, the other anti-Alice. Armed with a deliriously illogical landscape and a collection of obstreperous characters, anti-Alice aimed to prevent Alice, once through the mirror, ever getting back. To confuse into submission with time's arrow reversed, warped thinking and words that sounded ordinary at first but then didn't quite glue together. Players looked like they were trying to locate a fly between their ears.

The game rarely finished as Alex was always thinking of new details. New ways that the Queen could twist Alice's head. New complications that made it less a conventional board game and more a long argument into the night.

The only flaws in Sarah's mind were that when she played Alice she didn't really want to get back to the real world anyway, and that it always took for ever. Three in the morning and Sarah was still wandering the wrong way up the hill in the garden of live flowers and being tormented by a rose.

Alex stretched. He had an athletic body that needed to be running through forests catapulting wild beasts. So sitting down such a lot was uncomfortable.

She inhaled sharply. 'I bet that guy I screwed was a porn translator.'

Alex said tightly, 'I don't think porn needs translation.'

He spoke with such authority. Sarah looked at him. Dark shadow growing through on his face. His eyes, as ever, un-blinking.

'How would you know, you never watch porn?'

'One doesn't watch porn, one uses it.'

Sarah laughed at his evasion. When she laughed her face looked suddenly light.

They drank beer. Sarah tapped her fingers on the table. The silence had a late-night hum, darkness so heavy it throbbed.

'Oh God, Alex, I'm going to have to leave my job, it's driving me mad.'

'This is the job you started three weeks ago?'

'A month,' she said defensively.

'Right.'

'Things are coming to a head.'

'Already?'

'It doesn't feel like "already". It never felt like a new job. The personalities are the same, the work's the same. Every job feels like a continuation of the last one. Except that each time I feel a little more desperate and leave a little sooner. I don't understand how people put up with that shit all their lives.'

'So give up, do something else.'

She sighed. 'I can't, I need the money.'

'Come and do my cleaning.'

Sarah looked up at him to see if he meant it. His thin face was inscrutable.

She had thought about cleaning before. Her mother had always cleaned – in one form or another. As a child Sarah had hung around in other people's houses watching the magical process. The transformation of black-and-white floor tiles to a perfect gleam with a swipe of Maggie's steaming grey cloth. Sarah still thought of her mother when she walked through the smell of disinfectant. She shook her head.

'I couldn't. It would upset Great Edie. She hates my mother being a cleaner as it is. She's always going on about it. She says it's common. "If you make your money in the toilet, you live in the toilet" – or something like that.'

Alex raised his eyebrows. 'So why tell her? Keep quiet.'

'She'd know.'

'So lie.'

It was simple to him. He couldn't see how the whim of a half-blind, half-dead old woman could influence any decision. But then, Sarah thought, he didn't have a family.

'You can't lie to her,' she protested. 'She sees everything, she's bloody psychic.'

He was scornful. 'There's no such thing.'

She nodded, casting her eyes down to the floor. 'I know but she still is.'

He looked unimpressed.

Sarah went on in a higher-pitched voice. 'I'm telling you. She is. I was seventeen years old. I was in Spain on my own. Suddenly I get this letter. I recognize the handwriting at once. It's from my great-grandmother. She says, "I know what you're playing at, you dirty slut. Do you think I want another life ruined because another girl of mine can't keep her legs closed? Get rid of him at once." '

'But you're not another girl of hers.'

'I know, she's a bit possessive like that. But the point was I hadn't told anyone anything. She didn't even know what hotel I was staying in.'

'Your mother probably told her.'

Sarah shook her head energetically. 'She said she didn't. Why would she? And anyway, how would she know about what I was up to?'

Alex smiled. 'It wouldn't take a huge leap of imagination. That's what every other seventeen-year-old tourist alone in Spain for the first time is up to, I believe.'

'But the letter arrived the morning after I had been with this guy!'

'Well then! She must have written it before the whorish act had even entered your mind. That's not psychic, that's prophetic. Your great-grandmother is a prophet.'

Sarah looked at him, sighed and rested her face on the smooth, warm oak of the table. It was a release to unlock her back at last.

Alex began to tell her just how far such ridiculous superstition would not get her and was pleased that she didn't interrupt for once.

When he looked at her for an answer, Sarah was asleep across the table. It was four in the morning. He stroked her hair and went to get a blanket. After throwing it over her, he turned out the light.

She woke with her body still slumped over the table. The wood had flattened her cheek and dug into her ribs. She sat up painfully and squinted for a clock. There wasn't one. She trod warily through several rooms until she found a greasy dial in the kitchen, on the oven. Eleven.

She shouted aloud, 'Aaah! Great Edie!'

Scrawling 'A, thanks, bye, S' on a note propped up against the kettle, she ran out of the house, into her flat, splashed herself with water, thought of changing clothes and decided against it. There wasn't time. She bolted to the minicab office, looking anxiously in her purse and worrying about her debts.

The great-grandmother's house was nothing but corridors and stairs. What once were rooms were now overwhelmed by piles of belongings. As she had got older and weaker, Great Edie had lost control. It was like entering an untouched wilderness. Narrow paths that the old woman had beaten down, swiping her spindly arm like a machete, a route strewn with books, tins, photographs, empty spirit bottles thick with dust, and *Radio Times* and *Which?* guides piled head high holding open the sitting-room door.

Great Edie shuffled in holding a tray at a forty-five-degree angle with a slopping teapot, rattling cups and a plate of miserable-looking biscuits. She levered herself round to her chair and placed the tray on what might have been a coffee table under old newspapers.

Sarah was looking for a second chair.

'Underneath those blankets,' yapped the old woman.

Sarah picked up the dirty blankets with distaste and there was a simple wooden chair, while Edie lowered herself downwards and backwards into her armchair, her hip squeaking. Cup in hand, Great Edie opened her mouth and let the steam fall out.

'Aaah! Tea is simply the best thing for arthritis. That fool of a woman next door said give up cheese but she talks rubbish. Rubbish, all the time.'

Since Great Edie ate nothing but cheese and matzos it would certainly have been a sacrifice.

'All women my age eat cheese,' Edie was saying. 'The older you get, you don't want to eat something difficult. At my age it's all nibbling after a while.'

At ninety-five, the great-grandmother was whiskery. Beady-eyed and twitchy, in a house filled with dark rodent tunnels. For more than seventy years the great-grandmother had lived in this same house; all the time gathering and saving, never discarding. Now it seemed that the house fed off itself and the old woman in it merely scratched around on the surface like a rat. Sarah liked rats, liked their survival cunning. She felt less alone in a city where a rat was never more than two feet away.

Great Edie was sucking her tea. She enjoyed the sound of her false teeth clicking; at least, she enjoyed the effect it had on other people. Sarah shuddered.

'So, my girl,' said her great-grandmother, replacing the cup, crossing her withered knees that were almost lost under loose grey trousers. 'What do you want?'

Sarah smiled. 'I just came for a visit. You knew I was coming. Mum as well.'

The old woman twitched. 'What do you want?'

Sarah looked long into the tiny dark eyes, closed doors. She was hesitant. 'OK, I wanted you to do me a reading.'

Her great-grandmother played tantalizingly with the last drop of tea in her mouth. Click. Click. Click. Pause. Click.

'Why?'

'I don't know what I'm doing with my life. I thought you might be able to help.' She looked away and on to the mantelpiece full of ornaments. 'I've been feeling depressed.'

Edie's thin mouth became thinner and grimmer.

'Depression is a luxury of them with money,' she snapped. 'Nobody used to have time to have this depression. Now everybody has it. Nobody had this TV and video player. These parties and all the things you do.'

Sarah picked a snow-shaker from the mantelpiece. It must have been forty years old. Inside, two small girls were holding hands, wearing polka-dot bathing clothes under a parasol with 'Greetings from Blackpool'. She frowned and shook it while Great Edie's voice echoed.

'And you think my looking at the palm of your hand is going to make all the difference?'

'Please.'

Reluctantly, her great-grandmother took her hand. There was a smile in her eyes. Her walnut skin softened. 'Do you remember,' she said softly, 'when you were a child, how I used to take your tiny hands before lunch to check that you'd washed them?'

Sarah nodded, comforted. Edie stroked the hand slowly, looking at it carefully.

'Now, do you know what this palm is telling me?'

'No.' Sarah was breathless.

'It tells me,' Edie pronounced solemnly, 'that you're washing them a lot better these days.' At that, she shrieked with laughter; she only ever found her own jokes this funny. She let the hand drop. It fell dead against the chair.

Sarah slumped dejectedly.

'You great fool,' said Great Edie, 'of course I'm not going to read your palm. I haven't done none of that for years. It's a load of rubbish, you know it is. My God, and I get more sense out of that fool of your mother.'

'Please.' Sarah looked suddenly so small in her chair, her hands clasped together. Her face was drained, her eyes swelling. Suddenly, the old woman seemed tall, glowering, fierce. How could that be?

'I just feel like I've got to make some decisions.'

'Then make them.'

'I need a plan, I don't know which way to go.'

'Why does it matter? What happens, happens.'

Leaning back in her chair, Edie closed her eyes. Her bony face lost its animation, her floppy cheeks puffing like sails in a feeble breeze. It was a trick of hers; one had constantly to be attentive, to check that she was still alive. She began to speak. 'When I came to England on a boat with my husband to start a new life I had no idea what was going to happen. He believed, fool that he was, he would make his fortune here. Jack had plans. I had none. I thought, we will just see what will be. And look what happens.'

Impatient with the retelling, Sarah snapped, 'Sure, he dies.'

'Just two years later!' She raised her hands in scorn. 'So much for the fortune! So much for plans! Just enough time to leave me two young children to provide for and make me see what a complete fool he was. Children come much quicker than money. I told him. He didn't listen. He had so many dreams he fell asleep and he never wakes up. Me, no plans, here I am still.'

Yes, thought Sarah grimly, you are.

Great Edie spoke like the routes round the house. The only way out was straight, all the way through. Once on, there was no getting off.

'I didn't have no time for depression. That would have been a fine thing, with two young children. I had to make something of meself. The dead don't pay no bills.' (The more contemptuous Great Edie became, the more her grammar collapsed.) 'I'd rather have had Jack alive, empty liar like he was, than leaving me to work like a slave. But I am left alone. That's why I come up with something. I wasn't going to be a drudge, like your fool of a mother. I had more sense. I have a mind for money. That's when I discover my powers of intuition.'

Sarah's eyes widened. 'Was it as cynical as that?'

'Don't be such a fool, Sarah. Mysticism was big; it didn't take a clairvoyant to see that it could make good money.'

'But you predicted my birth, Mum always says so.'

Edie tossed her threadbare head dismissively. 'People get what they deserve in life.'

'But I don't know what I deserve!'

62

'Then you'll get a life of indecision. Isn't that right? There, now thank your old Edie for lifting the veil from yer eyes.'

From a tin with George V's coronation dimly visible through the rust, the old woman retrieved a gold and pink cigarette. It smelt of rotting wood. She lit it with a silver lighter, which her left hand – twisted so it really did look like the claws of a rat – retrieved from the rubble by her side. Inhaling was a struggle. Her eyes narrowed with effort, her face concertinaed into old folds.

They sat in silence. Sarah looked at the clock. At last Great Edie spoke again. 'Anyway, what about that friend of yours, what's his name?'

'Alex? What about him?'

'You want my advice?'

Sarah had begun to suspect that she didn't. 'Yes.'

'Stick with him.'

'But I'm not with him.'

'No?' Great Edie had been abandoned by her original eyebrows ten years ago but the pencil lines that replaced them now lifted in scorn.

'When a woman asks you to do the cleaning you are her slave. When a man wants you to do his cleaning, it's the bed next. That's the way men think.'

'See, I didn't mention the cleaning,' Sarah mumbled barely audibly.

If Great Edie heard she pretended not to.

Half an hour late Maggie arrived. 'You said you were coming at midday,' said Great Edie accusingly when Maggie had waded into the room.

'She remembers when she wants to, I see. Hello, love.' Maggie smiled at her daughter. Sarah smiled back. Sort of.

Great Edie was still angry.

'There won't be time for a bath now. I'll have to go like this.'

Maggie laughed. The weekly bath was always a battle. 'Oh no, there's plenty of time. In any case,' she added more threateningly, 'without the bath you're not going out. It's your treat for good behaviour.'

So Great Edie changed tack.

'I'm not going upstairs, my legs hurt too much. Dr Cohen said on Tuesday that I wasn't to go upstairs with my ulcers. You'll have to do it downstairs.'

She sat back in her chair, thinking this was checkmate. She winked conspiratorially at Sarah. Sarah winked back, pleased to be back in her great-grandmother's favour but still wondering how, after a week of nothing but sitting and sleeping, anyone could produce such a strong smell.

Maggie was thinking. She put a finger to her mouth, a hand on her hip.

'Hold on a minute.'

She left the room. Sarah stood up and peered after her. Great Edie sat in her chair, pulled her cardigan closer around her, hoping that this would make the bath more remote. For a few moments nothing, then a loud banging sound. Then Maggie's returning footsteps. There was a broad smile on her face.

'Gotcha!'

Great Edie sniffed.

'You know what I found, don't you?' Maggie was triumphant. She went to the chair and put her arm through the old woman's frail limb.

'Come on, Sarah, help me get her into the kitchen.'

Sarah was confused but obliging. The walk took some time with three of them and one fighting progress as hard as her feeble frame would allow.

'Ta-da!' said Maggie at last. 'Look what I found.'

It was a small tin bath.

'Where did that come from?' said Sarah. She had never seen a tin bath in her great-grandmother's house before.

'The back of the under-stairs cupboard.' Maggie looked slyly at Great Edie who was unexpectedly submissive in this defeat. 'That's the problem, isn't it, old girl, when nothing ever moves? That tin bath's sat there for the best part of thirty years, if I'm not mistaken. I bet you haven't touched it since.'

Great Edie sniffed. Maggie and Sarah started filling the bath with a bucket. The old woman looked forlornly out of the window. Frustrated that the hands that ruled a household no longer had the strength even to fill a bucket? Remembering some tin-bath tale that Sarah for some reason felt she couldn't ask about? Who knew.

The water was ready. Great Edie's clothes were gently

removed. The stains were tactfully not remarked upon. There had to be some dignity even in the family. Standing shivering on dirty linoleum that was not at all chilly, bare and scrawny like the skin on hot milk, Edie only turned to Maggie and said crossly, 'And mind you don't scrub me, I'm not one of your damn kitchens.'

They made a strange silhouette, later, the bath back in the cupboard, the three women struggling down the street for the weekly outing. Great Edie, wobbly, bent to the ground like she was following a trail of pebbles. Maggie, small but sturdier, propping up the old woman, and Sarah on the other side, so much taller than both of them, struggling to keep back her pace. Like some hopelessly ill-matched five-legged race. A cat, a shrew and an old, old rat.

5

On to You

Mr Rude wrote in pencil in a soft-backed 1966 diary. 'I am ashamed. I am more ashamed that my shame is not enough to stop me. That I am drawn to her, shuffling to her room like a married man seeking solace in a whore.'

He wrote in the mornings when he felt the regret. For by the afternoon his guilt seemed less certain and by the evening he was bewitched once more. The thick smoke of the clubroom threw a haze over everything. The tables wore gold brocade. In the evenings, wrong was harder to catch hold of, elusive.

The relationship, although he didn't think of it as that, had been going on for a year. They met most evenings; often there was a chase, a reincarnation of the games they played when Maggie was younger. He thought this was her understanding, that it was all a game. They lay in the clammy sheets on the single bed in the cabin so small that her discarded clothes swamped the floor. When he closed his eyes, he felt like a fly in a web; he clambered across her and she wrapped him. He went into a strange world of straight lines and soft sticky places. Things he didn't understand but craved. Her head was a vortex. To walk in was to forget everything. To lose the weight of the past thirty years.

He had expected her to grow bored, or his self-disgust to overwhelm him, but these things didn't happen. It wasn't even the sex that he craved, although that was extraordinary. It was the intensity of communication. That they never had a normal conversation. That he looked at her as one catches a familiar face on the street before seeing it full on and realizing that the person is in fact a stranger and that there are limited variations to the human face. With her he could live in a different world. What terrified him was that it wouldn't last. Some time, he knew, he would have to go back.

Maggie couldn't or wouldn't understand. To her it was still a game, a more thrilling one. If he said they shouldn't, she teased him. The best games were forbidden by the normal rules, her mother had taught her that. The best games are an escape. But he lived in dread of her father finding out. Even though the father was barely conscious most of the time, living alone, surrounded by the ocean and swimming in gin. Mr Rude had a vivid sense of what a normal father would do if he found out; that hung over him. He imposed a moral outrage on the unlikely figure of Harry Lockyer. That it would never happen was immaterial.

There was a knock at the door. He started from his thoughts of sin.

'Come in.'

'Hey, Rudi.'

He was called that by all now, since no one knew his first name. It suited him. Sounded East European. And he looked it, the raven hair with an almost oily sheen and the yellow skin.

'Hello, Adele.'

'Here.'

Adele, a thin young girl, one of the new dancers, dressed in a black-and-white can-can outfit, threw a pile of clothes at him.

'Mr Brown says you're to wear this tonight.'

Rudi stretched out one hand to catch the missile and grimaced.

'My God, Ali Baba again.'

The Masquerade Ball, as it was grandiloquently titled, took place at least once in every trip – twice in the three-month cruise. Everybody had to dress up. In great excitement, the passengers would ransack the ship for inspiration, stealing spare rope, cloth and metal and bribing staff for their uniforms. The afternoon before would be a hush of creation until hundreds of idle holidaymakers emerged from their cabins transformed, hurrying in search of the first cocktail.

It was the biggest of occasions. An excuse for opulence for people who still lived by the lessons of the war years. The make-do-and-mend generation taking pleasure in pleasure. In the size of it; the wide sky, the bountiful drink, the eternal sea.

The ballroom was festooned with ribbons and glitter that looked almost impressive after a couple of drinks. The ten-piece band roared jazzy numbers that called the faithful to Bacchanalian worship. In good weather the doors of the ballroom were opened and the music spiralled like smoke into the sky.

Maggie could hear the music and the sound of voices. It was eight o'clock in the evening. All the entertainers, ten of them, were required to jolly the party along until midnight. At sixteen, and now a salaried member of the troupe, Maggie was expected to join in.

Actually she didn't mind. Mingling in a party with hundreds of equally ridiculous-looking people was far less humiliating than singing on her own on stage. Besides, she could wear the Alice costume.

The costume wardrobe was looked after by the social director, Ed Brown. An insipid man with a chunky moustache always wet with spittle. On the night of the masquerade the potential of the costume wardrobe was stretched beyond endurance. Brown sighed with relief if he could get all his staff into something that fitted.

The extreme shapes were dealt with first. Her father always got the sorcerer's costume because that came with a matching miniature apprentice's outfit that fitted Arthur Hodges. Joe Moller, the barrel-shaped baritone, was a Dickensian character in a blue-and-gold-brocade Victorian jacket and three-cornered hat. There was endless argument over which Dickensian character it was since there was no original record.

Joe Moller was insistent that it was not Mr Bumble, seemingly on the basis that this was far too small a role for a man of his talents.

'Mr Micawber at the very least,' he asserted. 'I don't play cameos.'

'Too right,' drawled Sally Shezaar, 'you're strictly an extra.'

To her delight, no one but Maggie was small enough to fit into the Alice costume. But she knew better than to show her pleasure to Mr Brown.

Her costume was blue and white with a red headband. A long blond wig covered her own short dark curls. White tights wrapped her legs. She wore black buckle shoes. Best of all was the flamingo she carried under her arm for playing croquet.

Mr Rude, being of very average male size in those shorter days, five foot eight, lean limbed, was less certain of a good disguise. He ended up in whatever was left over. The sheriff if he was lucky, the Red Indian if he wasn't.

More often it was the Red Indian, because Mr Brown didn't like him. He had him down as a troublemaker. Mr Brown didn't trust a man who was never where he was supposed to be. Brown didn't know what Rudi got up to in his spare time. Not like the others who were irritatingly in evidence, loafing around the bar, lying on their elbows, smoking endless cigarettes. Not him. Rude appeared at nine in the saloon, walking out of the shadows like the Third Man, did his two-hour stint on stage and then went. Evanescent. Gone.

And even when Rude was there in front of a person, thought Brown, he wasn't. His head was somewhere else. You could see right through those hollow eyes.

The ballroom was full when Maggie skipped in. She was feeling the effect of the costume already. It crept into her skin. She could almost enjoy the party, staring at the strange people who were there by choice. She held her hands behind her back and walked jauntily up to the serving table.

'A glass of punch please.'

'It's got alcohol in,' said the serving girl primly. 'You're too young.'

'Oh don't be boring, June. If you'll give me some, I'll stand in front of you while you have a swig yourself.'

The offer was accepted.

The fat sound of Glenn Miller filled the room. Maggie stepped lightly, involuntarily keeping time. She went up to Sally Shezaar who was dressed as Ophelia with wet hair and flowers strewn all over her dress.

'Maggie, dear! Here you are, and dressed as Alice . . . again.'

'Ssh, Sally,' admonished Maggie, 'no one will know.'

Sally turned back to the man she was speaking to and smiled ingratiatingly. 'This is Maggie, the youngest member of our happy band.'

The man, dressed rather awkwardly in what was meant to be a kaftan but was quite patently an outsized towel with a pair of black trousers underneath, batted his eyelids.

'Ah!' he said through a cloud of cigar smoke and a voice full of fruit. 'Jolly good.'

Sally bent towards him confidentially as if she had something interesting to say. 'Maggie sings little songs in a tutu.'

Maggie pulled a face. She hoped that this would distance her from Sally, from all of it, but of course the man was not looking.

Sally spoke more loudly. 'Can you believe that this gentleman – Mr . . . – this gentleman has not been to the cabaret entertainment? Not once in three weeks. Isn't that unbelievable?'

Maggie did not find it unbelievable at all.

'I told him,' continued Sally – 'didn't I tell you?' she turned to the man – 'that if people don't come of their own accord, in the end we go and get them, drag them feet first from their rooms.'

The man laughed in slow unamused guffaws. 'Haw! Haw! Haw!'

'It's very nice to meet you,' said Maggie, shaking his hand and curtseying slightly, she didn't know why.

As she was walking away, Sally ran up behind and tapped her on the shoulder. 'He's a diplomat!' she whispered loudly. 'If I'm not down for breakfast, you can have my cabin.'

Adele came slyly up behind Rudi, who stood alone, frowning.

'What's wrong, Rudi? Fancy-dress night is fun. Don't you like fun?'

He frowned. 'Not this kind of fun.'

'What kind of fun do you like?' This was what she did for a living, walking the tables, sitting on laps and laughing with pleasure. Adele was blond all over. Even her skin had a golden quality, like a light was shining from behind. He hadn't answered her so she tried again. 'How long have you been here?'

He sighed. 'Oh, about five years.'

'On this same ship all that time?'

'More or less. Not the whole year of course, there's the three months off.'

'Where d'you go then?' Her voice was sucked into her punch glass.

'Somewhere else.'

Adele giggled in her little nose.

Maggie had joined her father. He was standing by the buffet, swallowing salmon. She could see his face distorted, upside down on the curve of the silver dish.

'Hello, Dad.'

He looked at her. His eyes were startled. He didn't say anything. Maggie felt angry. He was such a pathetic figure, drowned in that robe, the puppet next to him with the stupid grin on its stupid face. She wanted to shake him; shake him until he died.

It was past eleven. Mr Rude was bored. He had made conversation with at least a dozen overstuffed women. They had marvelled at his Chicago vowels, his sense of humour. They had congratulated him on his wonderful show. He had thanked them and felt bitter that anyone could enjoy his exhausted repertoire. Why couldn't they have shown more support when he was really trying? When he was full of hope? When it mattered?

Drink in hand, he wandered out on to the deck and looked out over the sea. The moon was covered in wild storm clouds, lighting the choppy water in the merest silver. He leaned over and watched the water churning a hundred feet below. He began to unwind and feel himself pulled downwards. Sometimes, the temptation was just to fall into the blue.

There was a tap on his shoulder. He turned round.

'Oh Sally, hi.'

Sally Shezaar beamed at him slowly. It began wistful and then it spread across her mouth, forcing her lips open.

He imagined she thought it winning.

'Got a cigarette, Rudi?'

'Sure.'

He reached into his pocket. She twirled round until she was resting on the rail next to him.

'Ahh! Fresh air, huh? Whoa, that's when you know how much you've been drinking. Bam' – she pretended to slap her face – 'like a punch in the mouth.'

He didn't say anything. She looked at him, first holding her head back and then under closer scrutiny, her eyes narrowing and widening, searching him.

'Where you coming from, Rudi?'

'Waddya mean?'

She controlled a hiccup. 'You know what I mean, all this mystery. You got something to hide, or do you just like everyone to think that you have?'

'I just like everyone to think that I have.'

She smirked. 'Some people think you're a communist.'

He looked aggrieved.

She pestered. 'Was it a woman?'

'Was what a woman?'

'The reason that you ran away here?'

He turned back to the sea. 'How do you know I ran away?'

'Well, you didn't come here by choice.' She scoffed, 'For Christ's sake, you're half decent. You're funny.'

'Chicago didn't think so.'

She shrugged. 'Well, Americans – waddya expect? Americans got no sense of humour.'

'But I'm American.'

'Don't tell me you're an all-American boy.'

'I'm not going to.'

Sally moved closer and nudged him. He looked away over the sea. Inside, the band was playing a Fats Domino number. The pace was quickening. He could hear the shuffling feet.

'So where you from then?' She wasn't going to let up.

'My parents were Polish.'

'There you are, you see.'

'What?'

'They didn't understand you.'

'Maybe I wasn't very good.'

Sally let out a loud cry. 'Of course you are. You're very talented. Anyone can see that.'

He looked at his watch. 'Do you want something, Sally?'

'Whoa, they gave you the right name, Mr Rude, or should that be Mr Rudowski?'

He laughed, in spite of it all, at the hopelessness of this humour, or maybe the hopelessness of whatever it was she was trying to achieve. Somehow Sally reminded him of the whole damn boat. The annual repainting could not disguise how it was falling apart. That golden age was over. The glamour was gone. Soon the cruise holiday would be a cheap alternative.

Sally smiled conspiratorially. Even in the semi-darkness he

could see where her make-up was wearing thin and the ageing skin surfacing. She touched his fingers.

'You don't have to be miserable all on your own,' she whispered. 'You can be miserable with me. I do it with such style.'

He took his fingers back and looked at her in horror.

She recoiled.

'What's that face for?' Her voice was cracking after too many cigarettes. 'Am I so disgusting?'

He looked at her impassively. She slammed the rail with her hand.

'What? Am I too old for you, is that it?'

He spoke now, trying to keep her quiet. 'No, of course not. I – I just don't think it'd be right in such a confined area. Other people wouldn't—'

'Don't give me that. I know that look. Men are all the same. Want something firmer to get your teeth into, I bet. Unless you're one of them – are you one of them?'

He winced. 'No. Calm down, Sally. I'm just not interested in anything right now, that's all.'

'I'm not asking for marriage, Rudi, just a little consolation. Something to make the time go.' She spread her fingers on his chest, stroking the skin in circles.

He looked at the sky in despair. 'I can't believe we're having this conversation.'

'What?' She looked at him in disbelief. 'This is a shock to you? You think this is something out of the ordinary? Look around you. Look in that ballroom! Look at all those trussed old fishwives spreading their legs on the dance floor with other women's husbands. And their rich husbands waving their cigars around, drooling like dogs. They don't mind the thought of me soothing their brows while their wives amuse themselves, I can tell you. I've got a dozen willing partners lined up in there.' She moved so close to him that he felt her sweet breath on his face. 'So what's your problem?'

Rudi shuffled uncomfortably. 'Maybe you ought to get some rest.'

She pulled herself up on the rail and bent one knee provocatively. 'There's not a man here who looked after himself all on his own for three months and I don't believe you do either. You been here years and still we don't hear anything. But I know men. The quieter it is, the more there's going on. You're into something. That's what keeps you so quiet. But watch out, mister, 'cause I'm on to you.'

He looked at her, his lips tight, a vein pulsing in his forehead. He said nothing.

'You're good,' she said, pointing a finger between his eyes. 'But you're not that good.'

It was his conscience talking.

Gathering together her dignity and her handbag, she limped off, her hips waving a wistful farewell as she swung back inside.

In the ballroom, the crowd was thinning. The lights were dimmed. The buffet was a wreckage. Trays of sloppy egg mornay and separating artichoke mousse. Empty bottles lined the tables. Ashtrays overflowed. People stumbled across the room, their disguises slipping.

Maggie was trying to extricate a long stub from an ashtray without getting her fingers dirty. She went in search of a non-judgemental light. She saw by her watch that it was past midnight. With a new urgency she strode towards the door. Past Sally Shezaar who was leaning against the fake Corinthian column, her shawl dragging the floor, her eyes half closed. Dark patches under her eyes that could have been mascara or unhappiness. She was talking to a man Maggie didn't know, a passenger. Whispering unnecessarily. He was looking anxiously through his wallet. When she saw Maggie she looked up and half smiled.

'Going somewhere, love?'

'Bed.' Maggie felt the floor sway.

'I bet you are,' she hissed, though the effect was marred by her sloppy lips and the words came out in more of a drizzle.

Somehow Sally, the dark reflector, prompted excuses.

'To sleep.'

'Right.' Impossibly, Sally lowered her eyes still further.

Maggie, who had paused, walked determinedly on, though there seemed to be a delay between her brain's command and her body's compliance.

'Night,' murmured Sally so low that for a moment Maggie thought she heard 'slut'.

Maggie ran along the deck. The ballroom was high in the ship. At the stairs Maggie turned and ran down and down. She didn't stop until the lowest level. She ran a winding path along the lowest deck past endless closed doors. At the very end she stopped and knocked. There was no reply. She opened the door and went into the darkness. The door closed behind her. She felt her way to the back of the tiny room lined with wooden shelves stacked with linen, her fingers her only sense. Then another pair of fingers felt her.

She let out a muffled shriek.

'Hey! You startled me, why didn't you answer the door?'

'You could have been anybody.'

He struck a match to light his cigarette and she could dimly see his face.

'Rudi' – she was reproachful – 'that was scary.'

Still alienated by Sally Shezaar, he said impatiently, 'I thought you liked cupboards.'

She switched the light on. The brightness was glaring. Her eyes adjusted first. The starched linen, rows of perfect piles of glistening cotton sheets and tablecloths. She began to feel very grubby. He was now sitting in a shelf, his legs tucked inside. He looked at her with watery eyes. She laughed.

'Hello, Ali.'

He raised his eyes. 'This dumb outfit, I look ridiculous.'

'So do I.'

'No,' he said. 'You look completely natural. That costume was made for you.'

'Even the wig?'

He nodded. 'You look great with long hair.'

She shrugged. 'I don't like long hair. Is that shelf comfortable?'

He patted the cloth he sat on. 'Come and find out.'

She bent her head and hoisted herself in. 'It's like being in a bunk bed,' she shrieked. She lay back. 'It's nice here,' she sighed, 'but it's a shame we've got nothing to drink.'

'That's what you think.'

Rudi fumbled behind his back and produced half a bottle of wine. She looked at him with the incredulous delight of the half-drunk who has discovered the means to getting even drunker.

'Lifted it from the dining room. That's one advantage of wearing this stupid cape.'

'But you're meant to be Ali Baba, not one of the forty thieves.'

'Alice?' He pulled her chin round to look at him.

'Yes?'

'Shut up and drink.'

'OK.'

She drank from the bottle. The speed of the flow took her by surprise and it spilled over the corners of her mouth and down the white front of her pinafore. She looked up at him and laughed.

They sat in silence under the disapproving eye of the light bulb.

Maggie said, 'Why did you want to meet here? We've never met here before.'

He sighed. 'Sally is suspicious.' This made him feel young.

'Of what?'

'Of this, of' – he said the word with difficulty – 'us.'

'Is she?'

He chewed his lip.

'Well, she doesn't know for sure. But she's on to me, she's looking to cause trouble.'

Maggie laid her head on his shoulder. When she closed her eyes, Sally's drunken face and dark swollen eyes were staring at her, so she opened them again.

'Why?'

'I don't know. Women can be difficult.' He moved her head up to look at her. 'Don't ever be a woman. Don't change.'

She laughed at him. 'But you're a man!'

'No, I'm not!' His voice was as urgent as a child. 'Well, not really, not here. How else could we be this . . . well, you know.'

She didn't really know what he meant but she nodded acquiescently, her eyes widening in concern since he sounded suddenly desperate.

She kissed him. He didn't push her away but neither did he respond.

When she moved away he slowly spoke. 'I have always worried, you know, about this. That the better it got, the nearer it came to burning itself out. I wanted to suspend it, suspend us.

But, of course, it's not possible.' His staring eyes refocused on her. 'What do you think?'

She thought that suspension was not always a good thing. Her mother was suspended, trapped in her own reflection. Sometimes change was life.

But she just smiled. 'About what?'

He smiled now. That she could not understand was his reassurance; they were still suspended for the moment. 'Looking-glass World, Alice. What do you think about Looking-glass World?'

'Ooh,' said Maggie energetically, glad that they were playing a game at last. 'I think it will be even more wonderful in the dark. Then we can play with the glow-worms.'

'What?' he said more lightly.

She leaped across the tiny room and switched off the light, hopping back on to the shelf before she had time to lose her sense of direction in the blackness. Feeling him with her fingers, she took the packet of cigarettes and the lighter from the pocket of his ludicrous pantaloons. The lighter flame flickered as she lit two cigarettes and put one in his mouth. Then she turned and sat back between his legs, her head on his chest.

They both stared.

'See!' she said, pulling her cigarette through the darkness, just the orange tip visible. 'A glow-worm!'

He clutched her arm and moved his own cigarette in circles. While he stared at it the orange seemed to leave a trail, a fountain of light.

He touched her hair. It felt rough and matted.

'Magic,' he said.

'Glow-worms,' she insisted and pulled the whole wig off. 'I don't like long hair.'

He moved his cigarette to hers so that the tips collided. They were incandescent for an instant and then, as he pressed harder, extinguished.

Grace

She was running through a field of tall reeds. They swayed in the wind but still came up over her head. She looked through them. The lines of dry reeds scratched her eyes.

The sound was loud. She couldn't see anything else. She couldn't hear her sister running. But when the wind blew and bowed the reeds into submission, when they parted for a moment to give her a view, she could see a flash of legs. She could see the bright red of her sister's dress, running away. The exaggerated movement, the circular patter of her feet.

'Ruth!'

Grace screamed but her voice was carried away to the birds flying over her head. 'Ruth! Wait. Wach Vlinder! I've caught you!'

She drew closer. She could feel it. She could taste it. She could taste her panting sister. She could feel her twitching round a corner. She knew her sister well enough.

The field was a mass of parallel lines. Like a piece of music. She saw it in her mind as she ran up and down chasing her slippery sister. Because it sounded like music. The rustling. The wind that had blown up as the afternoon progressed. There would be a storm.

She could feel the electricity. The hot wind on her skin. The back of her neck, damp with sweat. The thick air that was hard to breathe in. The sky yellow. The clouds looming. A spot of water on her forehead that made her hold her hand before her and wonder, is it raining, is it raining? If it did rain now she would not get home in time. She would be caught. She would be soaked through, the thin material of her slip dress translucent. Her hair dripping down her back.

She crouched on the warm ground. The earth was crumbly and moist. She rubbed it with her finger and looked through the reed stems for Ruth. Everything was quiet. The excitement, the fear, the waiting.

Patience was her virtue. Ruth could never wait. She was alive. But Grace was eternal. She could crouch, crouch down and stare at the earth for ever. If she waited long enough Ruth would betray herself. A beetle lay squirming on its back. She took a piece of straw and tried to flip it back.

'Aaah!'

Suddenly her sister fell upon her, knocking her to the ground.

'I found you! I won! I've got you!' Ruth pinned Grace's arms down and sat on her stomach. Grace struggled, rubbing dust into her hair.

'Pfff! Pfff! Pfff! Get off me! I can't breathe.'

Ruth sat next to her on the ground and said triumphantly, 'I won.'

Grace's face screwed up. 'No, you didn't, I was chasing you. You've just surrendered.'

Ruth looked at her crossly. 'No, you had to find me before I found you.'

'That wasn't the game. What kind of game is that?'

Suddenly it began to rain.

'Come on! Het regent, Vlinder!'

They were running and running. And they were laughing. Running through the rain was such a bad thing to do. Her hair was ruined. The curls that her mother had so carefully created, with rags and rollers, bounced irresistibly free.

The sisters laughed. They stopped still, choking with watery anarchy. Though Ruth was the younger and only nine, she was the more precocious. She was the first to revel in her wet skin.

'Look at me!' she yelled, tugging reticent Grace by the arm. 'I'm soaked through. The rain is so warm. Net, net.'

Grace was, as ever, more cautious. 'Shouldn't we find shelter somewhere? What if we get struck by lightning?'

'I hope we do,' said Ruth, rubbing the drips of rain on her

face so she was uniformly wet. 'I hope we get electrocuted together. We should hold hands so that if it travels it will go from you into me and we will always be joined together.'

Grace frowned. 'Don't be stupid, we'd die.'

'So?' Ruth had her arms held out and was twirling round in circles, dancing on the grass, churning up the soil. 'So?' she repeated. This was her answer to everything. 'Who cares?' Her voice lapped her, spinning with the rain.

Despite her misgivings, Grace relented. She held her palms out and felt the pattering of the storm.

'Mmm, smell,' she said. The deep lush scents. Heavy rain. 'Listen. It's so loud. Stop wailing, Ruth.'

Ruth, who had been releasing a cry to the wind, stopped and listened too. She took her sister's hand and said earnestly, 'I would only dance in the rain with you, Vlindi.'

Grace felt her sister's pulse racing.

'No one else would let you.'

It was more than a mile back to Aunt Rene's. They ran all the way. In gasps, stopping to catch their breath.

When at last they came to the lane and the back alley between the fences that led to Uncle Len's garden, they were drowned and muddied.

'You first.'

'No, you first.'

'You're the youngest.'

'Yes,' said Ruth, 'so you should go first.' With this logic, she pushed Grace roughly through the gate and kept pushing her as they both went into the house.

The door was open. They rubbed their shoes on the mat. The kitchen was steaming with the smell of mutton that had been bubbling for hours in the Rayburn. Cabbage was boiling to a pulp on the hotplate. Aunt Rene was chopping carrots on the old wooden table-top that Uncle Len had attached to the wall with a hinge on either side. She turned round to the gust of fresh air.

'Oh my goodness!' she said, eyeing the mud-spattered petticoats. 'Your mother is going to be furious. Those undies were clean on.'

The girls looked crestfallen. Quickly their aunt scraped away the carrot shavings and popped the vegetables into the pan.

She wiped the surface clean and lifted it to the wall. Tucked underneath the table-top was a white iron bath.

'There's plenty of hot water,' said Rene with relief in her voice. It was clattering against the metal tub. Aunt Rene had her knees bent and her sleeves rolled up, her pale skin scalding red as she sluiced the water around. Aunt Rene was so much jollier than Mother.

'Ruth, what have you got in your mouth?' Aunt Rene was mock stern.

There was a bulge in Ruth's cheek. Her attempt at innocence was spoilt by the guilty grin that spread across her face and opened it. A shiny piece of white potato.

Aunt Rene smiled. 'You are incorrigible. Now get your clothes off, the pair of you. Let's hope I can scrub the mud off your clothes before your mother comes down.'

But it was too late.

'Grace? Do you want this cup of tea?'

The nurse was looking at her and tapping her on the shoulder. 'You haven't touched it.'

Grace continued staring out of the window. It was still raining. With one finger she followed a drip on the windowpane from the moment it hit, pursuing its meandering journey all the way down the glass.

The nurse folded her arms and wedged her comfortable buttocks into the windowsill.

'What are you thinking about, eh?'

Grace didn't move but she said, 'We shared a bath that day.'

'Did you?'

'Mother was so cross. Aunt Rene had to scrub our clothes, they'd only been washed the day before. Mother was so cross.'

The nurse lit a cigarette.

'Mother was so cross.'

'Well,' said the nurse, patting Grace on the arm, 'mothers often are, aren't they?' She reached across the chair. 'Here, d'you mind if I have that tea if you don't want it?'

Grace didn't answer.

6

Pompety-pom

Sarah was back from Alex's, where she'd hidden since visiting Great Edie, breathing heavily as she stepped up the stairs. Yale key in the lock. Thin door opening into the fetid flat. Darkness inside, blinds pulled down against the sun. She crunched across the hallway into the living room. And sighed. The small black box blinked at her maliciously. There were three answerphone messages from Richard.

She listened to them as her skin froze.

His gathering anger almost sent her running back to Alex's again, but knowing that she had to be up for work . . . Work, oh God. Blackness overwhelmed her. It fell around her and was swelling up within. She slept fitfully, in and out of consciousness. She woke with her head spinning and her eyes raw. Like an automaton she prepared herself. Her face in the mirror. Her dark hair shapeless, the fuzzy silhouette. Her eyes were rimmed with red and the lids were heavy. Her skin was grey. Her urine came out slowly, reluctant too.

She left the house. Walked to the station. Stood on the platform surrounded by others. They looked so tranquil, so unreluctant. She couldn't understand it. Her body was screaming with every step.

At this dread moment in every week she always tried to distract her mind by thinking of a story she once read of an old turner, Pietro, who works a lathe in a huge and humourless factory. Sweating his guts out for a pittance. A ten-hour shift spent walking between two noisy machines. Yet even in this grim circumstance there is some release, he remains hopeful.

One part she could chant. 'For there is no prison that doesn't have its chinks. So even in a system that aims to exploit every last fraction of your time, you discover that with proper organization, the moment will come when the marvellous holiday of a few seconds opens up before you and you can even take three steps back and forward, or scratch your stomach, or hum something; "Pompety-pom . . ." '

Sarah walked into the office, repeating, 'Pompety-pom – pompety-pom,' the words becoming feebler as she went. Her head felt fuzzy and her stomach turned slightly. The clock on her computer said 9.04. Four minutes down on Monday. Ages and ages and ages to go.

She could not play the charade much longer. The effort, the back-stabbing, the greasing, the pretence, the boredom were all endured, as she saw it, only in order to work harder and spend more money on dry cleaning.

'Munning.' Ian, the head of finance, marched past, his word distorted with nasal briskness. A puff of lemon-scented chemicals followed him. He gleamed. Every morning he scrubbed in the shower, exfoliating his body as a motivational strategy.

'Morning,' mumbled Sarah gloomily.

He paused. 'Hey, missy, what side of the bed did you get out of today then?'

Ian spoke in perpetual clichés.

'My bed is against a wall,' she sneered.

'Very droll, very droll.' And with a clipped smile he disappeared into his office.

Sarah got up wearily and slunk to the coffee room. A squalid little box with a sink, a filter coffee maker, a kettle and dozens of mugs, some thick with mould. Sarah sniffed out a clean one. Scrawled in red it said, 'The world's greatest Dad'. This is a marvellous holiday of a few seconds, she thought. Pompety-pom.

The Pietro the turner passage appeared in an Italo Calvino collection called *Numbers in the Dark*. Like everything she read, it had come from Alex. He had stuffed it in her open mouth a couple of years previously to stop her moaning.

'Read the one about the hen,' he said. 'You'll find it good for workplace oppression.' Although how he knew was a mystery. He had no workplace.

She liked the story of Pietro and his chained existence. It comforted her a little, but mainly she thought that working on a machine would be preferable to what she had to endure. At least machines didn't say, 'I kid you not,' as they raised their eyebrows in smug sarcasm. At least Pietro was allowed to think in peace.

She craved a world where all she had to do was push buttons. Where she wasn't required to interact. A mechanistic world was sympathetic in that way.

She didn't read at all before she met Alex. She had thought that books were part of the reason she was miserable. Along with work, cleaning, her mother and playing hockey in the rain.

Alex had an entire room of books on the very top floor of his house. And not because he had to. Three walls were pinned by shelves floor to ceiling. Each shelf had books stuffed horizontally on top of the original vertical line. And now the shelves had overflowed, the books were climbing like ivy from the floor. Dark knotted lines creeping over the walls. As if he had been trapped inside his room for twenty years. By choice.

There was no order to the books. Nor could you make any assumptions from them about the character of the owner – except that he had eclectic tastes. Proust lay next to Andy McNab; Arthur C. Clarke next to the Gawain poet.

Alex said he kept only those books that served an emotional or practical purpose in his life. When the need arose, he would turn to the appropriate book for insight and consolation.

Unlike Sarah, he grew up with learning. And eclecticism. His parents had thousands of books. The house was an island, a colonial outpost of Allen Ginsberg in South East London. Surrounded by estate agents and solicitors, the books happily reminded his parents of what social rebels they were. In the hot weather his mother, Hilary, liked to read Chomsky on the patio and take off her bikini top when the man next door was mowing the lawn. She knew there was a hole in the fence. She had seen an eyeball through it once when she walked jauntily across the grass to inhale the honeysuckle.

Alex relied on books; unlike people, they did not suffer from mood change.

'People,' said Alex. 'You can't rely on them for anything. But books, they stand by their story.'

Sarah refused to believe that anyone had read so many books. So she liked to pick out a title at random and test him. So far he had always beaten her. *The Encyclopaedia of World Religions* he quoted verbatim.

'Page 223, "At the beginning the Universal Soul assumed the shape of man. This was Purusha. He did not feel delight. Therefore nobody when alone feels delight. He was desirous of a second." '

'But you aren't,' she said, not bothering to congratulate him on his accuracy, 'you aren't desirous of a second.'

He didn't answer.

Underneath this tome, the foot-wide paean to man's attempt to make sense of himself, crushed and lifeless was a thin, black hardback.

'*Covenant with Death*, John Harris,' she read aloud. 'What's that about then?'

Alex smiled. 'I read that when I want to remain stoic in adversity,' he said. 'When I am falling into the abyss. It's the story of a load of blokes from Sheffield called up in the First World War. Most of them die going over the top in the Somme. Screams of the wounded, people blown apart, buckets of blood sloshing in the trenches, dodging the sniper fire, yet they all stayed cheerful. "We have made a covenant with death and with Hell we are at agreement." I go back to it when I am indulging in woe – it gets things into perspective. It reminds you that no matter what shit you're in, everything can always be worse.'

'Pompety-pom.'

It was a slight disappointment to see that the coffee had already been made. That that two-minute holiday was already booked. Still, she poured the coffee as slowly as she could.

'Hiya, Sarah, good weekend?' It was Janet, the technical support. Sarah turned round.

'Not bad.'

Janet smiled. She was a plump, well-meaning redhead who wore too many floral prints and so would never get promoted.

'Anything wild?'

An image of herself sprawling on Alex's bed, white limbs wriggling, an octopussy, counting the tiles on the ceiling.

'Hardly, how about you?'

Janet giggled, as she did whenever attention was focused on her.

'Well, we finished the second bedroom.'

'You devil.'

Janet looked at her watch. 'Aah! Look at the time. If we're not careful we'll miss the nine-thirty meeting.'

'And that would never do,' said Sarah in a dangerous tone.

She sloped back to her desk, inhaling the sweet addiction of the photocopy room on the way. It did not help her headache. She sat massaging her temples and a trail of 'munnings' echoed around the room.

On Friday she had stared balefully into space while a pile of employee expense forms slowly decayed. The weekend was a cruel glimpse of possibility, like a prison window looking out over the beach. And now it was Monday again. She had hardly survived a month yet and already she was close to crisis point. For an explosion was building up. Rising inside her. A form of madness, if madness meant feeling not how others felt. Which it must do, she thought, it was the only explanation. Surely a dispassionate observer would conclude that corporate life was collective insanity? When her grandmother tortured herself, they changed her drugs.

Ten people sat in the meeting room in varying states of disinclination. The low hum came to an end when finance director Ian strode into the room.

'Munning!' he said faster than ever.

They all stood up and sat down again.

He let out a short breath and needlessly straightened his papers against the table.

'Al-righty,' he began. 'Mark, perhaps you can update us on the P35 complaint?'

Mark, immediately to his left, slumped down into his seat to hide his lanky height, fiddled with a greasy curl and rubbed his upper lip.

He has calves as long as my whole leg, thought Sarah, running a casual eye over the bony frame that made his shirt and trousers look hopelessly big, as though he was hoping to grow into them.

Her mind was just tortuously applying the long and scraggy look to his genital region when Mark sat up in his chair and her thoughts returned to the room.

There was a silence. He sniffed.

'Yeah, I called the Revenue about fifteen times but they still haven't got back to me, the bastards.'

'Well, that's fine,' said Ian. 'If you've called fifteen times, they'll have a record of the calls. We'll use it in our defence.' He looked at Mark witheringly.

'OK, maybe it wasn't fifteen times.'

'How many times did you call them?'

'It's work in progress,' said Mark sadly.

'Right,' said Ian, looking fiercely round the room and clicking his knuckles. 'Let that be a learning point for us all. There is no hiding your inadequacies. If you balls up, I know. And I kid you not, if you do balls up the only hope you have is to come clean before the fan gets hit by the proverbial. Your crisis is not my problem. Got it?'

There was a low murmur.

'Right. We'll come back to you, Mr Sutcliffe. Sarah. What have you got to report?'

Sarah, who by this time was counting the number of times she could sing 'Pompety-pom' in a minute, staring at the revolving hand on her watch face, heard her name and looked up smiling. The circle of people inside were out of focus as she stared far away, through the glass barrier of the meeting room to the open-plan office beyond. The lines of computers, the bent heads of ants. Her smile froze in the air and the rest of her face fell downwards as she realized that it was, inexplicably, her turn.

'Aren't we going the other way round?'

Ian tutted. 'What the hell do you mean?'

'Don't we always go clockwise?'

'What difference does it make?'

The words came from beyond her in a confused patter.

'It's-really-unlucky-to-go-anti-clockwise.'

She looked downwards. There was a stifled snigger.

Ian was puffing. 'Very droll. Very droll. I hope your comedy isn't a substitute for your progress report. Now give me the update.'

She looked up at him. For the first time she really looked into his face; the blue eyes that operated only in the world of ledgers and balances. Shallow eyes; she squinted to see better and was suddenly convinced they gleamed with evil. The blue seemed splintered with shards of black. Someone else was blinking back at her.

She turned to look at Brian, the finance manager, her immediate boss, pasty, stubby fingers, spilling out of his trousers. He looked back helplessly, as if he feared for her. She looked at the others. Sat there, in a meeting, chained to their salaries.

She was trembling. 'OK,' she said, 'I'm ready.'

'Well, thank you, madam,' said Ian incredulously. 'Only I'd appreciate a little hurry. You're not jumping out of an aeroplane, you know.'

The silence somehow became uncomfortable.

'For God's sake, girl!'

Sarah tried to enjoy the seconds it took her to get out her papers. The moment it took her to open her mouth. Pompety-pom. Pompety-pom. She felt conflict, a burning pressure within. She could sit in finance meetings no longer. Then, after this torment, a calm came over her. In a sudden moment of clarity, she knew what she must do.

She spat at Ian, 'I'm not going to tell you anything.'

He stared at her.

'I'm not going to be a prostitute to this crap! I won't do it. So stop giving me your P35 and your CT200s crap, stop lying that that's what you want.'

Suddenly she had grabbed Ian's chin between her hands. 'And fuck me like you've fucked everybody else!'

She pulled off her shirt, yanked off her bra and stood before him, an Amazon in the offices of Cellflo.

There was a gasp. Sarah stood with her hands on her hips and surveyed the scene. She felt powerful. Mark, for the first time since she had met him, laughed. Brian looked away but not before sneaking a red-faced glimpse.

Ian stood up.

'She's obviously drunk. Jill, take her away, get her some coffee.' He winced in frustration. 'Oh, for God's sake put your clothes on.'

Jill, a colourless blonde, took her sharply by the elbow and whispered, 'Stop making a fool of yourself, you silly girl.' She pulled Sarah's shirt around her and tugged her out of the room. The door banged open and Sarah could hear the audibly relieved voice of Ian saying, 'Well, you know, guys, I think there's a learning point here.'

Sarah sat by her computer sipping the coffee. Downcast like a child, glad it was over yet still feeling the shame. 'Do you think I've got the sack?'

Jill looked at once disparaging and incredulous. She didn't answer but raised her eyes and folded her arms more severely.

'Well, I don't mind,' sniffed Sarah. 'At least that means I won't have to work out a notice period.'

'Are you mad?' said Jill.

Sarah said, 'Probably,' but Jill wasn't listening.

'You've been here a month, what's the matter with you?'

'I don't know.'

'This is a nice enough company, there are nice perks, everyone treated you with respect. What more do you want?'

'Ian kept calling me missy . . .' She could not begin to explain, even to herself.

'Is that a reason to make an exhibition of yourself?' Jill grew more impatient as she was dragged into the conversation.

'Well, it's not a reason not to.'

'Oh, for God's sake.' Jill stood up. 'Well, frankly, we'll be glad to see the back of you. You've been a moody, uncooperative cow since your first day.' She walked off.

Sarah stared into her coffee. She could see her eyelashes winking on the surface. 'It's better out than in,' she said.

Nobody spoke to her for the rest of the morning. Since she hadn't been told otherwise she read a book called *Operating Functions – a corporate manifesto*. She scrutinized it for the hidden messages, evidence of the dark conspiracy.

And she found it. In the third chapter she fell on a chilling sentence. 'For synchronous parallelism, the processors used for a task are controlled by one central processor, so they are not independent of each other.'

A burning sensation ran through her skeleton. One central processor! Workers are eunuchs. The corporate world was a puppet strung on one hand. The morning train, the coffee room, Janet decorating her second bedroom, it was all a façade. If she walked behind them there would be nothing there, like the back of the mirror, a house of cards. Overused metaphors ran through her mind. She felt trapped. Watched. Traced.

Only last week, she had been sitting in a café. On the next table were three people. She had taken them for tourists. They were forever jumping up and down to take photos of their smiling selves, with arms around each other, gesticulating in faltering English. Yet at one moment, quite clearly, the taller man, his face hard to see behind those big glasses, had definitely turned his camera and taken a photo of her.

At lunchtime Ian called her alone into his office. A pitifully exalted box. His desk, bigger than everyone else's, was still fake wood. His importance was made clear by the corporate picture that hung on the wall. It was a landscape. A cluster of sheep by a stream against a hill. On the skyline a gate leading to another field. There were twelve clones in the cupboard outside. But no one else was allowed to put them up.

'I'm sorry that you're leaving us so soon,' he said cheerfully. 'When I recruited you, I thought that you showed promise.'

'No, you thought I was cheap.'

This was ignored.

'Such a short time with the company does not of course warrant any kind of leaving do.'

Sarah smirked.

'But' – Ian fiddled with his tie, his eyes focused on her now covered breasts –'I'm not one to harbour bad feelings. So I was going to take you out to lunch. Just' – he leered – 'to, you know, talk things through. It's useful for me, to know what I can learn from this.'

'You dirty old bastard,' she said and walked out feeling, for a moment, omnipotent. She felt strong in the lift, where her yellow reflection laughed with her. She strode through the revolving door in reception, wavering only slightly when the door picked up speed, smacked her on the arse and threw her on to the street. But the sense of her own strength could not surmount the coffee shop on the corner. She realized she could no longer afford their designer froth. No more skinny-latte-grande-vanilla. She would no longer rub fleeces with the fashionable sheep. It was over.

And much as she hated the corporate she did love the froth.

She wanted everything frothy. A pillow world with no sharp edges. Marshmallow cars. Roads of cotton wool. No crashes, only wobbles. No twisted metal and spiked heads. In a pillow world everyone would bounce. When she was in a plane looking out of the window at the clouds she was sure they were solid and fluffy. She wanted to jump out and fall through the elastic gossamer. Her hands and face smothered in softness. Her cheeks fat with iced candyfloss. She would be safe, wrapped in billowing whiteness. Just like her grandmother. She was happy in the clouds.

She looked again along the line of coffee hunters. Smartly dressed in shiny black, peering at the choices through little square glasses, tapping polished fingers on mobile phones. Frothy coffee was £1.50. She would have one last one. A goodbye to all that.

'Cappuccino to go, please.' She spoke brightly to the strapping dyed-blond Italian student who was confused by her unexpected appearance at two in the afternoon.

'You're going somewhere today, ha? You are not norm-ally in at this time.'

'No,' she smiled.

He was making her coffee. 'Well, lids and chocolate are over there.' He pointed to the corner of the gleaming counter. He always did. As if she didn't know where it was by now. Maybe it was the look of bewilderment on her face. He thought she was stupid. He didn't realize the look was ongoing disbelief that the coffee could cost so much and still she was expected to put the lid on herself.

These last moments of coffee pleasure, luxury between the lips. He smiled as he handed it to her. What a jolly man he was. Maybe because he was so young and his coffee-shop days merely a stepping stone. Today frothy coffee, tomorrow Fellini. I don't think so. Still, whatever got him through his life, she liked him. He was kind. Good looking too. She felt almost a frisson. Except, as the coffee left his hand and moved into hers, something horrible happened. As he was passing it over, he rubbed his nose with the other hand and a nostril hair fell silently into the cup.

It was an omen.

He didn't appear to notice and continued smiling. Unless it

was deliberate. She shook herself. Pull yourself together. Why would he want to do that? And even if he had, it was such a risky insult. There was no way of guaranteeing that the hair was ready to fall. And even if there were, it could easily have floated in the wrong direction.

But she could not complain either. She was not able to say, 'Excuse me, you have dropped a nostril hair in my coffee. I feel ill.' His English wasn't that good. She couldn't shout over the frenzied jazz music and whooshing coffee machines. She couldn't bend over the counter and try to explain to a puzzled manager. She could just imagine several of them, crowding anxiously round her, trying to understand. And failing. 'Nostril hair, what is this nostril hair, Fabio? What has happened here?'

So she maintained a tight-toothed smile, took her lid and walked out of the shop. Once she was sure she was out of view, she dropped it in the bin. It fell. Goodbye, sweet world. It was rather appropriate really.

Alex poured her a glass of vodka.

Sarah looked up at him. Her eyes were watery and her face grey and drained.

He sighed. 'Yes, yes, of course you can stay here.'

'I'll do the cleaning.'

He nodded. 'I know you will. The house from top to bottom. Rotating. As soon as you finish one end you start the other again. This house will be sorted for the first time since my mother died.'

'I shall make it my masterpiece.'

Alex looked at her.

'Well, you have to find something to occupy your mind. I don't mind you staying but you mustn't interrupt. I've got a lot of work to do.' She agreed respectfully. 'Now, since you have no notice period to work out, I presume you can take up your new position immediately.'

'The sooner the better.'

'We'll get your stuff.'

Two holdalls, a suitcase and an oversized rucksack covered it. Alex insisted on hiring a cab. The cabbie, realizing that this job involved a two-hundred-metre drive and ten minutes' lugging, mumbled something about being 'no frigging removal man' but was silenced by the fat note that Alex stuffed in his hand. When the job was done, Sarah was surprised by Alex pulling her back into the cab.

'Where are we going?'

'Supermarket – I don't expect an artist to work without a paintbrush.'

Halfway there she realized that the reason Alex looked so pale was because they were outside and she had probably never seen him in the open in daylight. He had fine lines around his eyes. He was looking older yet he was two years younger than she.

It was also surprising that he should know of the supermarket at all.

'Have you been here before?' she queried.

'Mmm. I once wanted some celery. Naik's doesn't sell it and he sent me down here.'

'What did you want with celery?'

'I can't remember.'

Alex chose as big and fat a trolley as the supermarket made. He began throwing in vegetables, rice, pasta, beans, fish and flavourings.

'What's all that for? You only eat takeaways.'

'If you're going to be housekeeper, you'll need food.'

'I can't cook!'

He was breezy. 'Then we'll buy some cookery books, they have everything.'

The household section was their greatest indulgence. Alex was gathering blue and green plastic bottles. Sarah took plastic gloves, scrapers, scourers, dusters, sprays, polishes, bowls and buckets.

She liked the brilliant colours.

'Which fragrance?' she asked him.

'What's the choice?'

She bent down to read. 'Pine, mountain mist or spring dawn.'

He stopped and wrinkled his brow in thought – he might have been listening to a symphony. With his scruffy hair and stooped posture, he looked peculiar. Like he ought to be on a lead. A young mother pulled her child away.

'Well, I don't know,' he said after some consideration. 'I'm drawn to pine.'

'Oh, me too,' said Sarah with fervour.

He continued, the didact. 'But pine scent never smells like real pine. It has a unique and unpleasant smell all its own. It should rather be called pine-scent scent.'

'Well, what about mountain mist?'

'Oh, I don't know. Here, give it to me, Sarah.'

She handed over the duck-egg blue bottle. He undid the lid.

'Now close your eyes, smell it and tell me what it says.'

She did so. The supermarket, its bright disco dazzle, disappeared. For the first time she was aware of its muzak. Piped flurries of 'Do you know the way to San José?' hummed by a chorus of underwater Burt Bacharachs. Great.

The fragrance hit her stomach first. It stormed back through her alimentary canal. A sour flavour in her mouth and, finally, the smell.

'Well?' he said breathlessly in her ear.

'God,' she said, 'I don't know.'

Her eyes were still closed. She could feel him next to her. It was strangely intimate.

'Mountains?' he queried.

It did not smell of mountains. It was hard to describe. She had to climb inside. Open her inner eyes. It was a dark smell. Cylindrical, orange, plastic. It stretched away as far as she could see. As she looked it began to revolve, faster and faster.

'Misty?' he asked.

She spoke. 'The way you said that, it sounded like my name. No, not misty at all. The smell is very clear, very strong. Like being inside a cement mixer.' She opened her eyes and made a face. 'Not mountain mist at all.'

They were testing spring dawn which Sarah found more to her liking. Alex was explaining the importance of the right fragrance when one was planning a change of environment and Sarah said, 'Colour too. They used to paint my grandmother's walls yellow. It was to liven the depressives up.'

A middle-aged woman jostled between the two of them.

'Drug addicts!' she snapped. 'Go get your fix somewhere else.'

Alex was often misunderstood. He seemed to provoke the more conservative citizen. Whatever he did somehow looked suspicious. He saw beauty in strange places. He would point out the classic shape of a Victorian drainpipe and get questioned by the police. Sarah appreciated it but didn't always understand. He did not explain himself.

'I'm so glad,' she said when they were back and the door was locked, when the bags were dragged upstairs and deposited in one small room. 'I feel safe now. I don't think I need ever leave this house again. I am going to stop exploring the world and start exploring this house. It will provide me with everything I need. I'll start on the hall tomorrow.'

7

Grey and Grey

Grace never knew she was living through a psychiatric revolution. That she was lucky. By the time she was diagnosed a schizophrenic the doctors had something to treat her with.

Psychotropic drugs were first developed in a Paris pharmaceutical house in 1953. Chlorpromazine was the first in general use. It meant that, for the first time, the ravages of psychotic illness could be tamed. In the wave of professional optimism that came with the breakthrough, the family was told that Grace might well recover. There was real hope that the next decades would see the end of mental illness.

And, when the wave blew through the sprawling Victorian hospitals, it did change things, for ever. Maggie never saw her mother fighting off her imaginary enemies, cowering in the corner in a thrashing fit. But while these more terrifying visions of bedlam vanished, it slowly became apparent that though the new drugs alleviated, they did not cure. Grace had never recovered.

She sat on her chair beside her bed that was one of ten in the small ward. Each patient was granted a little privacy with a plywood partition. Maggie held her mother's hand.

'Glassy-eyed today then.'

She had been watching her mother for all of her adult life. Grace had gone into hospital in 1957 when, after years of deterioration, the mania triggered by the sudden death of her younger sister was deemed permanent and her practical life came to an end. For thirty years she lived in the same building, a nineteenth-century palace. She was comfortable there.

But she was again an unwitting participant in progress, a guinea pig in the social experiment. In 1989, in line with new British mental health policy, the main part of the hospital closed. The great sprawling bulk was evacuated and smaller-scale care was now provided solely from the modern, low-rise block buildings that had been put up on-site in the early 1960s.

Grace, along with about half the resident population, was sent home. This of course meant staying with her daughter – at first in Sarah's old room and later in her own room in Maggie's flat. For the last decade she had lived a split existence. She was with Maggie during the 'good' times, when her mood swings were under control. But when her health deteriorated, as it did at least twice a year, when she became a threat to herself, she was returned to the arms of the hospital, normally for three months at a time.

Maggie was much happier when her mother was in hospital. For it was a cessation of responsibility. During the reprieve she could go into the kitchen in the morning without the fear of finding her mother slashed by a knife. She was still chilled by the memory of the smell of gas hitting her nostrils. It was shortly after Grace left the hospital for the first time. Daily she had expected disaster. But when Maggie walked into the kitchen, where Grace lay with her head in the oven, her fears were unrealized. Her mother was asleep. The gas was coming from one of the rings. Grace had turned the wrong knob. She lay breathing sweetly, her head resting on the iron oven floor. She didn't feel pain.

Even during her bad patches, some days were more lucid than others. Maggie suspected that to a large extent her mother could still control her behaviour. Sometimes she thought she saw a look of cognizance. Sarah agreed. She said Grace was positively normal. That she too felt like Grace most of the time but that such behaviour wasn't enough to get you locked up these days.

Today Grace was, again, looking out of the window. Maggie wondered about the endless fascination of the concrete slab. Sometimes she stared at it too, wondering what could be in it. If the blankness itself was the alchemy, a screen projection for what was left of Grace's brain. Maggie, with her head in the present – the bus journey, the contents of her fridge – saw a concrete slab. Grace, removed, saw a space of endless proportions.

The room was like a prison. This was Grace's choice. She tore off attempts to liven up the walls with photos. Other patients had clumsily stuck up family snaps with Blu-Tack (drawing pins are weapons of self-destruction). Her single bed dipped in the middle. A grey coverlet that Great Edie had bought years ago lay unforgivingly on top. It mingled well with the hospital walls. The nurses always asked if she wouldn't prefer a duvet. To bring a little comfort to the severity?

Maggie said no. Grace must be tightly tucked in. She needed to feel safe. She woke up screaming if the covers loosened during the night.

Vulnerable though she was, Grace had weathered the changes in mental health legislation and come through as disconnected as ever. She had held on to that. Weathered was right. She was in and out of hospital, in and out, in and out like the British sunshine. They couldn't get rid of her completely. For her tenacity, in a strange way, Maggie was proud of Grace.

As a child, Maggie walked along straight corridors to visit her mother. Highly polished floor, the smell of oil-burning radiators, her face flushing with the sudden exposure to sickly heat. Just how hospitals were meant to be. White walls yellowing. Air that felt thick and sweet with the medication coursing through the alimentary canals of long-stay patients. The gas of all that sugared coating.

Then Grace's life had permanence. She was in the same bed for years. Now it was a different bed every time she came in. And small, maze-like buildings that smelt of warmth and cigarettes, with corridors that twisted and turned. It took her time to settle.

The war on asylums was waged over Grace's head. It was declared at the annual conference of the National Association for Mental Health in March 1961. In front of two thousand delegates at Church House, Westminster, Minister for Health Enoch Powell vowed that in fifteen years' time half of the hospital beds in mental institutions would be redundant. Seventy-five thousand beds would go. He knew it would not be a silent struggle.

'There they stand,' he orated. 'Isolated, majestic, imperious
. . . the asylums which our forefathers built with such immense
solidity. Do not for a moment underestimate the power of
resistance to our assault.' He was, he promised, 'setting the
torch to the funeral pyre'.

Immense solidity. It burned slowly.

Grace was the perfect mother. She had never been angry with
her daughter. She accepted her completely. She had no expectations, no demands, no questions, no rules. She could not let her
down. Maggie considered herself fortunate. She believed that her
mother loved her. Not that she could ever say so. But Maggie
felt warmth. Great Edie, of course, dismissed that as nonsense.

'There's nothing in my girl's head any more. She's cold inside.
There's no pulse.'

That was Great Edie. She had declared her daughter dead.

Maggie imagined her mother as wise inside the silence. It was
equally delusional, doubtless. But she was sure there was something there. Grace dwelt in her own world, a world of snatches
and moments. Maggie looked in through a keyhole. She saw
splinters of light. Sometimes, if she looked into her mother, into
her round glassy eyes for hours, she began to see. Two girls
running. Always running. She could see both of them. Upside
down. Two tiny silhouettes, black, chasing. The image flickered,
a camera obscura, and then disappeared.

If Grace were allowed to stay in her own dreams, she seemed
content. If she were forced to join in with the real world, her
eyes clouded over and she was full of sadness. Or futile rage. She
flailed like a baby in mittens. Crying for hours, in a low tone or
a high screaming. It was all the same to her. Maggie knew that
she dreamed of her sister, Ruth, the younger by three years.

Maggie remembered Aunt Ruth in black and white. A woman
with a frozen laugh of delight. The picture stood on a mantelpiece at Great Edie's. It stood there still. She had looked at it as
a child, as a young woman with a child of her own. At the age
that Ruth was in the photo. Ruth never had children, but
Maggie wondered what her cousins would have been like.

She had only a memory of a memory. The young woman
snapped with a captured vibrancy. Maggie had no visual
memory of her aunt personally – she had died when Maggie was
three. Instead she remembered noises. The rustling of Aunt

Ruth's skirts against an apron. The feel of Aunt Ruth's stocking-clad knees against her own childish face. And she remembered the sound of her laughter. Aunt Ruth was always laughing. Wild laughter. Laughter that rang in the evenings up the stairs to where Maggie sat sleepless on the top step.

Maggie poured herself a cup of tea. She sat next to Grace, staring out of the window.

'I have a letter from him,' she said, finding the words inadequate when they left her lips. So short and insignificant. But her mother didn't mind. Words weren't necessary.

'After more than thirty years. What am I meant to say?'

Grace's pale unlined face was calm. She opened her mouth, as she often did, to sing.

> 'In the morning, when the sun is bright
> I'll hang out the washing in a line of white
> In the middle of the day when the sun is high
> I'll scrub the flagstones and leave them to dry.'

Maggie had grown used to talking in riddles. It was a language she spoke fluently. At least she was content for there to be no understanding. So much of what people said was pointless anyway, so someone who spoke undisguised nonsense was just as interesting. And if one listened, there were rhythms to Grace's nonsense. Lyrical cadences, emotional rhythm, sad syllables, joyful clips. She expressed herself in a more primitive fashion but maybe the result was profound. Grace was, Sarah pointed out (she would, thought Maggie), a post-modern conversationalist, an abstract human being. She was strange colours.

She never gave the right reaction, but she never gave the wrong one either. Not like me, thought Maggie grimly.

So she continued, unperturbed. 'Do you think I should open it, Mother? You see, I don't know how I feel. You know how I've been since. I changed. I changed the day he left and more since. I think I used to be more like you. Dreamy, I suppose. But I had to face up to things after that. I had to leave the cocoon. So I don't know. After thirty years, I've got used to things the way they are.

'My life is practical. I see you, I work. I look after your mother.' She smiled and took a sideways look at Grace's immobility – 'You know you still owe me for that one. I see Sarah. I listen to her problems. I worry about her. But she hasn't made a mess of it, at least' – she paused – 'not like I did. She's got more sense.

'Oh.' Maggie exhaled slowly and heavily and reached for her cigarettes. 'I don't know. I'm comfortable. Sarah can't believe it. But she's young. She doesn't know the meaning of contentment. The simple relief of an existence without anxiety. That just being free from the burden of constant fretting is enough for some people.'

Maggie stared again through the window. That yard of concrete. Ten metres by twelve perhaps? Solid at first but, as one stared, it deconstructed. Sparkling dots and larger patches of variegated greys.

'Grey and grey,' smiled Maggie softly, 'your favourite colours.'

There was a pause. Grace nodded.

'Sarah teases me of course – you know, you've seen her. Says I don't want to end up an old maid. But she's only joking. It would be the biggest shock of her life if I ever did meet anyone. She doesn't really think of me like that. I'm not a woman, I'm her mother. Not a very sweet one, but still her mother.

'And anyway' – her voice was more energetic and she raised her hands in the air to express herself more strongly – 'this is all pretence. He could want anything. I'm letting my mind run away with me. I'm halfway down the aisle and I haven't even opened the letter! He probably just wants his books back. I've still got several. Haven't read them.

'And you know me. My imagination. That's me. That's why I have to be sensible. Dignified. A woman of my age. I must get it in perspective. It was a big thing to me. I was sixteen. It was my first, my first . . .' she said the word with discomfort, 'experience.'

She did not add, and her last. Her mother did not correct her.

'He was thirty-two. An experienced man. I was a passing thing. A disgusting side of him. A perversion. A habit he wanted to kick. Embarrassing. He wasn't a bad man. That's why he felt so ashamed. Maybe that's why he left.'

Hmm. She turned to look at her mother who also stared outside. Strangely she felt calm in her presence. That her mother couldn't smile was sublimely ordinary. After the bereavement came acceptance. The tragedy had long escaped her.

Now she enjoyed Grace's patience. It was always a lesson, a meditation on how life could be. She had stared at this concrete yard endlessly, a myriad of grey dots. Maggie in turn was transformed in this room; she could stare with equal fascination at her mother's face. A hall of mirrors, where she stared for hours at her own reflection.

The fascination of a child or a madwoman. At some moments Maggie couldn't understand. Child behaviour, so celebrated, is sickness in adults. The stamping and wailing and sulking and dribbling is swallowed in a healthy maturity. But so is the fluidity of the mind. Where anything is possible. Where the world is a continual curiosity. Where the rattling coat hangers in her wardrobe really were the skeletons Great Edie had talked so darkly of. Real bones, dead bodies, terror under the covers.

That was where her mother lived. Her soft pink flesh. Sometimes when she kissed her goodbye, she tasted her skin. Soft and sweet.

Now Maggie took her mother's hand.

'So tell me, Mother, shall I open the letter? You tell me. You know how indecisive I am. Tell me, Mother.'

Grace continued to stare ahead. Even Maggie felt frustration. She dropped the hand back in the lap where it thudded dully against Grace's grey dress.

There was a knock on the partition wall.

The stolid voice of the nurse.

'Can I come in? Christ, it's dark in here.' She never waited for an answer. Her voice was split-level, cracked. 'Let me switch on the light.'

Maggie felt the click run through her. It was almost painful. She blinked to accommodate the shrill brightness that filled the space. It shrank instantly to a claustrophobic cube.

'How's Grace today?'

'Oh, fine,' said Maggie.

'Good.' The nurse turned to her after this perfunctory exchange. 'I hope you don't mind me interrupting but there's a man here to see you.'

*

102

Maggie felt like she was walking into death. Like every step was slow motion. There was an inevitability about it. She was trembling. Her head was floating. Her breathing was louder than thunder. Her mind was in total floundering confusion.

There was no doubt in her mind that it would be him. In the forty-two years that she had been in and out of this hospital no man had ever visited.

She stood behind the doorway and peered round. There he was. Sitting in the corner of the canteen. Clinging to two walls. Shrouded in a coat, a mac. It wasn't raining. He was smoking a cigarette. A cup of something in front of him. He was staring at her. Did he look the same, did he look old? She didn't know.

He looked shrivelled. Terrified, almost. She had expected something bigger. Her fear washed away and she felt more normal. At least she felt normal about being here, talking to an elderly man. As long as it didn't feel more significant. She walked across the room, conscious of every step. She almost forgot how.

'Hi.' False levity. She never said 'hi'. It was not one of her words. It implied an ease with life she did not feel. Her voice, she thought sadly, sounded rough and old.

He looked up.

'Maggie.'

She nodded. 'Mmm.'

How odd, she thought. How odd. There was a pause. He said inadequately, 'D'you want to get a drink?'

'Not particularly. Anyway there's nowhere to drink here.'

'We could get a cab.'

She started. 'I don't know what to say.'

'Well,' he smiled nervously. A quiver of winter sun. 'You could say, "OK".'

'OK,' she said, her throat compelling her.

He tried to smile again.

There is no need to speak during a journey. The noise of the engine, the presence – in the cab driver – of a stranger. The sense of the temporary, that one will speak when one arrives some-where else, these are all fine excuses.

So Maggie looked straight ahead. But in her periphery she

examined him. His knees, his trousers. He was wearing a suit, not new but respectable.

'You had this all planned then,' she said when the cab stopped at a suburban hotel, leafy, set aside from the road by a windy drive of bowing bushes.

'Is that bad?' he asked anxiously.

She laughed. Oddly displaced. One, an old man cringingly polite. Two, the object of the night-time thoughts of her entire adult life before her. She kept the mundane image in her mind. She did not want to analyse. That way she could stay in control.

They sat in a small dark lounge. A few pairs and groups talked indistinctly. Anaesthetic music was injected weakly into the room. He leaned back in his chair though his shoulders were still hunched. He rested his fingers together in a pyramid. The curls of his cigarette smoke licked across them.

'This is strange,' she said and laughed.

He looked relieved. 'You don't seem angry.'

'I'm not at the moment. It's a bit too odd to start manufacturing hysterics.'

'I can't imagine what it must have been like.'

She smiled wryly. 'I wouldn't try.'

He closed his eyes and nodded gently. 'Not yet, maybe you're right.'

Not yet? It was a question mark hanging in the heavy air.

He opened his eyes and drew nearer, staring at her in the semi-darkness.

'I'm so glad,' he said slowly, 'that I can't see you. I want to keep you in the dark. It would be too much of a shock otherwise. My mind takes a long time to adjust these days. I can't cope with shocks.'

Maggie slurped her drink.

'Shocks!' she spluttered. 'Let's remember who's doing the springing here.'

'Yeah, sure, sure.'

He was a paragon of contrition. Every line on his face. Bowed head, open hands, sorry frown. Nodding assent to her every comment.

'Let me guess,' she said brightly, making conversation with a stranger. 'You went back to America. You sound far more American than I remember.'

'That's right,' he said apologetically, ashen-faced. 'I went home. This is my first trip here.'

She regretted her words as soon as she thought them, they were too provocative yet they came out.

'Why did you come here?'

His voice was low, serious. 'I wanted to see you.'

'And how do I seem?' Her head tilted sideways. Her first petulance. Surely her first since . . . So long ago.

The acidity in her voice made his eyes water.

'It's still you, isn't it, Maggie?'

She ignored him.

He asked, 'Did you get my letter?'

Automatically she opened her bag and retrieved it. Still in the sealed envelope, white and unscuffed. He looked at it. It lay lifeless in her hands.

'You didn't open it?'

'No.'

There was a weighty pause.

'I'm glad, I think.'

'Are you?'

He looked thoughtful. Put a finger to his thinner lips.

'Well, I guess it must have meant something to you. It was a decision.'

'You are my daughter's father, how could I not think about it?'

He cast his eyes down again. 'Oh yeah.'

She looked stern, for the first time powerful. He feared her.

'Oh yes.'

More silence.

She said, 'Did you know you had a daughter?'

'I saw her visiting Grace.'

'That's spoilt my surprise then.' She said this almost monotonously, as if the conversation meant nothing. The truth was she had no template for this conversation; people she lost did not come back.

He spoke tentatively. 'She looks just like you.'

She stared into the middle distance, smiling warily.

'That's because you're doing the looking. So you can't see that actually she looks like you. Bloody annoying but there it is. I try to ignore it.'

It was a cruel joke. Each year, as Maggie could have forgotten, his face was delineated more strongly in her daughter. A genetic fault. A slowly maturing disease that made her daughter grow to look as she remembered him. But of course he didn't look like that any more.

'How did you know she was yours?'

'The age, I guess.'

She didn't want to think about it. Instead she looked at her watch.

She did not like this place. It was soulless. The gaudy fruit machine, the uncomfortable chairs, a few casually dressed people, a pair of teenagers snogging noisily in the middle of the room. 'I have to go.'

He jumped as though the words imploded in his head. His voice was hoarse. 'Go now?'

'You were right,' she said slowly. 'I need to look at you in the dark until my eyes adjust. Have you got a cab number?'

He grabbed her sleeve. A physical move, an impact of him on her. His fingers had moved her shirt. No one moved her clothing. She stared at him, open-eyed. He let go.

'I'll drop you off.'

She was stiff. 'Drop me at a station. I don't want you to know where I live.'

He put his hands in his pockets.

'OK, OK.' His voice was slow and deliberate. 'I could be a maniac by now. I could have been a maniac then, you might've been lucky.'

She darkened. 'I didn't say that.'

He bowed his head. He looked much older suddenly.

'You didn't need to. It takes a good degree of lunacy to be here at all. I know that. This is dangerous.'

She laughed. The moment snapped. Somehow it didn't feel dangerous. An old man. A middle-aged woman. Drinking whisky in a hotel. Her life was emotionally comfortable. The edges were soft. Everything was as always. There was no danger.

'Will I see you again?' He looked at her intently.

He was staring right into her. She felt her body rip. Like a hairline fracture in a wall that had been waiting to break. She held his gaze. That part of him was the same.

She sighed. 'I don't know what my husband would think.'

He looked serious. 'Do you want me to pretend I don't know you never married?'

'No. But I just wanted to know.'

He interrupted, 'I tracked you down.'

It was like walking into an old room, through cobwebs. She felt strange, displaced. Her head was light. 'I'm sure you did. I wouldn't expect any less. You were always thorough.' She bit her lip, annoyed that she had slipped unconsciously into a familiar tone. She wanted distance and space, solitude and her familiar quietness. She didn't want to be acting like a coquettish sixteen-year-old flattered by the attention. Like the last thirty-three years hadn't happened. Like her life was nothing without him.

'Oh God,' she said, 'I'm going now. This is ridiculous.'

'You'll meet me?' His tone was anxious and his eyes persuasive.

'What's to be lost?' she said.

That would have to be enough for the moment.

They stood up. The teenagers drew their lips apart and turned around like reflections. They all look the same, she thought, fat-cheeked insolence. They, in turn, looked pityingly at Maggie. As if, she thought, they were the only ones who had ever felt love.

8

Archaeology

Sarah woke up in darkness. Not knowing where she was or where the door was. Or where her head was pointing. Or if there was a window in the room. Or if there was a light, how she might turn it on. She didn't even know what she was lying on. Just that it didn't feel very comfortable.

Slow recollection followed. She was lying on a single bed in Alex's house. Her first night as a resident. The room was, she believed, on the top floor of the house, one floor above Alex's bedroom. But not directly above – probably. She couldn't be sure.

She stretched her arms out to feel for a wall. She found it on the left. She winched herself off the bed. It was an old-fashioned kind, two feet off the floor with a vast dusty gap underneath. Fumbling across the wall, she walked her hands sideways. I don't eat enough carrots, she thought. It was some moments before she hit a small flat box. The light. She switched it on.

The ceiling swirled before her. Her body surged like the ocean.

God, she remembered, last night.

She staggered through the door. Swathes of daylight hit her blinking eyes. Orientating herself she turned right, steadied her hand on the flat top of the spiralling square banister and lowered herself gently down. One step at a time. One step. Concentrate.

Alex was already in the kitchen. His short dark hair gathered in a little black tuft. His stubble poking wearily through his skin.

His eyes, black pinpoints surrounded by baggy skin. Blues music was playing. He was wearing a T-shirt with 'Fucker' written boldly across the front.

She sat gratefully at the table and rested her head in her hands.

'Ow.'

'Do you want coffee?' asked Alex without looking up. 'I've made some.'

'Thanks.'

'And here.' He stuffed something under her nose. 'Water. You might need some.'

'Thanks. What's that music?'

'John Lee Hooker. The man knows all about hangovers. Spent all day in bed with a bottle of bourbon but still made it out to play in the evening.'

She nodded, saying in time, ' "Boom boom boom boom" – yes, he does put it rather well.'

'Yes,' said Alex witheringly, 'but that's meant to be a gun.'

'Exactly, somebody let it off in my head.'

Alex sat down. The chair scraped uncomfortably across the floor.

He sighed. 'Last night is not to become a regular occurrence.'

'No, Alex.' She was humble.

'I'm happy for you to stay here. It will be useful for both of us. But we can't get smashed every night. I have work to do. I need a clear head to think. I can't have good ideas when my synapses are buggered.'

'I understand.'

He was talking, head bent down, not looking at her. 'I get lots of work because of my thought processes.' He raised his eyebrows. 'The people who commission me think the ideas are creative.'

'Aren't they then?'

He shook his head and, on realizing how painful it was, wagged his finger instead. 'People only want the mediocre. Sadly, the interesting things I have to do for myself. At least,' he sighed, bothered by how pompous this sounded, 'I like to think it's interesting.'

Sarah drank a little coffee. 'God, have you got any pills? My head is throbbing. What the hell did we have last night?'

Alex looked bored. 'We drank what we drank, what we took, we took. I'm not going to talk about it. Drugs are even duller in the talking about it afterwards.'

She pressed her lips together. And wondered why sometimes he sounded so hostile.

'Sorry.'

'No,' he sighed again, 'it's all right. It's not your fault. I just like to get on in the morning. Today I can't because I was arseholed last night and I feel shit now. It's not how I like to see myself. And yet I do it.'

'Well, you've got to give yourself a break some time.'

The kitchen was gutted. Ruins of his parents' 1970s decoration – pseudo farmhouse, mushroom tiling, every tenth floral, brown surfaces – were still in evidence but only just. The destruction was man-made. Some of the paper had been stripped. One kitchen unit was dismantled and propped against the wall. But the decorator had lost interest at a very early stage. And Alex had planted himself on top. The room reeked of the precarious lifestyle of the unattached male. Tins of male food – Irish stew, Vesta rice, papers sticky with Marmite and toast crumbs. A stainless steel juicer stood boldly in the middle of the table. It had yet to taste flesh.

The previous night had been Alex's idea after all, she thought crossly. Was it in an urge to get out of himself that he enjoyed being other people? It was a favourite ruse of his.

When the day had ended, after the shopping trip, they had sat together in the kitchen looking at one another with 'what now?' poised on their lips. Now they were living together. However haphazardly it had happened, however insignificant it was, somehow it changed them. If only temporarily, there was an injection of craziness.

Alex gleamed wickedly. 'Let's go out.'

That night a band managed by a guy Alex knew was playing a gig. They were a techno-thrash band. High-concept eco-anarchists. White dreadlocked scorchers who sang like disease. It was art. The newspapers said so.

Taken straight, the evening would be unbearable. For Alex was in no sense a joiner. He hated the fashionable, the faddish, the so-called cool. He hated to be associated. He stopped wearing his old school trainers when they became fashionable.

He hated that he was named after a cult. He said his parents were consumed by fashionable thinking. They preached alternatives and then lived a life like everyone else they knew. They were, as the *Clockwork Orange* 'bible' said, 'Eunuch Jelly'. He said this with venom.

But pretending was OK. Sarah loved to pretend. She would go along to anything. She loved to sit in different audiences and pretend to join in. Joining in with other people's passions was more fun because she knew it wasn't real. She liked dressing up, playing roles. Like it would be fun to be a Catholic with the incense and ashes. You didn't have to believe. This way she didn't need commitment to anything. And it didn't matter that she was thirty-two.

Maggie thought life was too serious and too short to have an identity. She didn't say so, but it was clear. Grace had an identity. Like a footprint it pushed in rather than standing out. Sarah had nothing. That was one thing she and Alex had in common. She had not thought that before.

So the previous night they were out with Karl – this guy Alex knew. He didn't make any money but his mother was Sonja Meier, the sociologist, and while *The War on Language* remained an undergraduate set text, this did not matter.

Sarah was not normally defined by her clothes. Her wardrobe was a homogeneous collection of grey and black. Her clothes masked her. She was used to noticing and not being noticed. It was interesting to live differently. Karl lent her something appropriate. Fuchsia strappy stilettos (four-inch heel and a size too big) and a triangular chain-mail dress that came down to her ankles. When she moved she sounded like 'Tubular Bells'. She covered her eyes and lips in lilac. The art-house crowd dressed like exhibits.

Maybe she should always dress this way. As they walked down the street people looked at her in fear and distaste. This felt right. It was almost as if she had her real face on. She was disturbed that normally she fitted in so well.

Alex's long legs somehow made him all the more authentic. Wrapped in metallic denim. Chains dragging behind like a soul in hell. Even though they matched, Sarah trotted to keep up. It was painful. Her toes kept rolling under and scraping along the pavement. But the blood dried.

When they got off the tube it was raining. Sarah's mascara was beginning to run.

They walked into what looked like a large underground garage. Tin walls, concrete flooring and even a vague smell of petrol. The gig was well under way. Sarah thought it sounded like sleet smacking against her ears. A throng of bodies heaved and sank in sweaty unison. Occluded by a fog of smoke, ice and steam, the rattle of metal clothing.

Karl came to greet Alex. He had quarter-inch ginger hair and a nose bauble that banged against his philtrum.

'Good turnout, eh?' he shouted.

'What?' mouthed Alex.

'I said,' Karl shouted louder, 'it's a good turnout.'

'Can't hear you, mate,' shouted Alex, lighting a cigarette. Which he did, when character required.

Karl smiled and with a wink handed Alex a small envelope. He was magically swallowed back into the mist.

Sarah didn't recall actually going to the toilet. She remembered being back on the floor. She remembered her body bending like hot glass. She was evasive and fascinating. She remembered the waves of sound against her ears and everybody reacting in unison. I have found my identity, she thought. These people have vision. I will become an anarchist, tomorrow. And so will Alex. Maybe there's somewhere here we can join.

And then the room seemed to turn into a hall of mirrors. It started from the ceiling. In a slow flow, like lava from the mouth of a volcano. It spilled around her so that she was sealed in an enormous sphere. And everyone else had gone. Except Alex, who was looming, his huge shadow stretched concave all the way from floor to ceiling. Whichever way she looked she saw him. Huge and inviting. And she saw herself. Fatter, thinner, older, younger. Then taller. With a neck that stretched and stretched and stretched.

That was last night. She didn't remember anything after that. Just that at four in the morning they were home and going to bed. And now it was morning and Alex was Alex again, not a monstrous yet alluring figure. And he was angry.

Sarah gathered herself up in the chair and spoke brightly.

'Why don't we discuss my employment?'

Alex looked pleased. 'You're not too ill?'

She smiled. 'Not at all. Just a little woolly. How sharp do I need to be to discuss cleaning?'

'Well, this isn't just a bit of dusting. It's an expert job. Very mathematical.'

His house was a living thing. His family had lived in the house since it was built a century ago. As far as he knew it had never been cleared out.

It was a tree. Each ring was another generation. He was just the latest on top. But his hold was precarious. He lived among the ruins of the others. The remains. The house had not changed since his parents had died. Except that it was slowly falling apart.

Perhaps he was the last. Unless he had children, and since he had shown no interest in women (or men) in all the time she had known him Sarah thought the chances rather remote. She didn't know what Alex thought. He didn't encourage questions. They joked but there was a line one did not cross.

He took a notebook from a drawer. The notebook was new. Half-covered in his erratic handwriting. She read upside down. It was a quote: 'The more head downward I am, the more I keep inventing things.'

'Here, I've drawn a plan.'

He turned the page. On a double spread was a two-dimensional map of one floor of the house.

Sarah gaped. This was forward planning. How long had the idea been in his head?

'OK,' he said. 'Each double page represents a floor of this house. I live in a few rooms on the top two storeys. I cleared those rooms when I first moved in, just piling stuff into boxes. They're all here somewhere. Then there are two lower storeys and most of those rooms I haven't been into since my parents died.'

Twelve years ago, thought Sarah. Alex rarely mentioned them. They were a phrase, 'since my parents died'. It was a dividing line: life then, life now. Never the same.

She knew they had both died of cancer, within a year. That they were both academics. Mathematics, logistics, phonetics with statistics, calculus with philosophy? She could never remember and she didn't understand anyway. She understood so little. He hadn't told her and she didn't ask. There was a picture in the main sitting room of the pair of them at some prize-giving, wearing gowns. Confident, lean, belligerent; fitting together like elegant bookends.

He didn't express sadness, or self-pity. He didn't say he missed them. He said he didn't like them. He expressed irritation that their early extinction made his life insurance more expensive. 'It would have been all right if they'd died in a crash.'

He was looking at her expectantly. He'd asked her a question when she hadn't been listening. Waiting for an answer. She took a wild stab.

'Er, no.'

'Really?' He seemed surprised.

She blustered. 'Well, you know, maybe.'

He sniggered, 'I think you'll find you do.'

'Yes, you're probably right.'

He hesitated. 'Well, I'll get you one anyway.'

'Oh, all right then.'

There was a short silence during which she felt embarrassed.

'Why have you never hired anyone professional to do this?'

'Don't you know what a professional would do to this house? They would scourge it. They'd raze it. I'd be left with a few thousand quid and a shell. I don't want demolition, I want archaeology. And I need someone I can trust.'

'But you've never shown any attachment to the things in this house before.'

'No,' he agreed. 'I've let it go. But I always wanted it preserved, I just didn't get around to it.'

Each map was drawn in dark grey pencil. Intricate, unnecessary detail, like an idiot savant. Except the view was from above. Everything was there, the fireplace, the cupboards, the windows. She stared at it in wonder.

He seemed to feel a need to explain. He said, 'I drew these up years ago but never got any further.'

'I would have thought it was just the kind of job you would enjoy.'

'Well, maybe. But I wouldn't be sufficiently detached to do it. Also I have a dust allergy.'

Sarah laughed.

'It's no joke,' Alex protested. 'I went into the first parlour a couple of years ago. I was looking for some music. A few

114

minutes in there and I was choking. Like I'd swallowed a vacuum cleaner. It was torture.'

Over the next few days she began to realize that it was not routine itself she hated. For her new life soon became equally rigid. Not because Alex had imposed it upon her. He wanted the work done, but as far as she could see there were no criteria to meet. No targets. No yardstick by which she was measured. Also, since he was absent, holed away, for hours every day, he had no way of knowing what she'd done.

And she was quite free to leave the house. She had a key. She needed it to buy the day's victuals. She could, if she wished, have stood with the old man and his can of beer outside Mr Naik's at ten o'clock in the morning. She could have talked his alcohol language, incomprehensibly, words with the consonants taken out. It wouldn't be difficult. Every day the old man tried to lure her in.

'Oo-aa-oo-aa.'

She realized not everyone joined in. That was part of the same conspiracy. That when she was walking to the train in the morning she was led to believe that everyone else was walking in the same direction. If she thought about it, she knew it wasn't true. She noticed many people did other things all day. Hanging around. Chatting to the shop assistant in Mr Naik's, as though they chatted there a lot. Buying their Tennent's at ten in the morning. The woman who served teas in the caff, earning money that was like eating celery – not enough calories to make it worth the chewing. A celery salary. She would enjoy it. It was perfectly normal not to function.

Often she hesitated and thought, why not? His vowels are as good as anyone else's. It might be rather pleasant to stand there all day. But instead she nodded politely and went back to her job.

She was forgetting what it was like to live in the real world. The train, the office, her cash flow, her washing machine. She couldn't forget her answerphone. She called in remotely and listened in dread to the messages. But even they dwindled. She had few friends and they were soon deterred by the barbed wire of her silence. Her mother called of course.

Only the previous day she had left a rather desperate-sounding message. 'Sarah? It's Mum. Are you there? Where are you? We haven't spoken for days. I need to speak to you, love, something rather important has happened. Call me back, can you? OK. Bye.'

Sarah smiled. Important to her mother meant Great Edie was having trouble sleeping or there was a sudden and dramatic change to the 159 bus route. Nothing happened to her. But she would ring her soon. She would.

Currently, she couldn't face telling her mother that she had left another job. Even though her mother, of all people, should understand the need to run away, her face would fold unhappily. She would put on her brave smile. And Sarah couldn't face that. It made her feel guilty. That, after all, her mother might hope for a little stability. And she never got it.

Each morning Sarah woke up naturally. Yet it was almost the same time every day. No more than a quarter of an hour either way. No later than eight, no earlier than seven thirty. She pulled on faded jogging bottoms and a sweatshirt. Scraped her hair back and brushed her teeth. Then she went down to the kitchen. She saw the coffee grains that Alex had left. She filled a pot of tea and took it on a tray two floors down. She did not eat. That was a treat saved for two hours' time.

She clunked downstairs, feeling the smooth wood banister cold under her fingers, the teacup rattling. Nine steps in each block, four blocks, thirty-six steps winding down and down. Into the darkness. She hummed as her feet echoed in the vast hole beneath her.

'Pompety-pom.'

While in her office it had been a slave song, now it was a tune of freedom, of self-determination – at least at first. Before she realized that she was not so much sorting out the house as being sucked into it. Into the skeletal lives.

After the hall, which just needed a complete clean to remove the clouds of cobwebs and dark brown smell, she started as requested in the front reception room. Since she had never seen beyond the closed doors in the first two storeys of the house, she had been apprehensive. The decorations, she estimated, were 1930s. Small yellow sprig in parallel vertical garlands for wallpaper that made the room feel like a cage. Several small tables, a red leather sofa. A writing bureau. Drawers filled with ageing

116

stationery. Best of all was a mountainous collection of postcards and letters going back years.

'Can I read them?' Sarah asked breathlessly.

'Of course, I want everything made note of.'

When it came to it, all the information was out of context. Interesting but ambiguous. Reading about another family was like overhearing a conversation in a café. A man tells his friend, 'It killed my wife': is he recommending poison or comedy?

She had hoped that the house would yield its secrets. Then she feared that there weren't any. That this was a blameless history. At the very least the significance was lost. She did not know the characters, the background; they were just names, and then faces conjured in her mind. For the moment she interested herself in the way that she was always interested in looking at faces or writing. It was information. The random nature of it meant that she could impose her own meaning. She could pretend its universal significance.

17 August 1916

Dear Aunt Ada

The Weather has improved since yesterday. Not hot enough yet for a bathe. We had tea outside yesterday though – Evelyn says to tell you, this was overly optimistic! We kept dry under the umbrella though. And at the very least, the air's fresh.

Love

William.

Sarah tossed her hands in the air, deliberately melodramatic since Alex had just come into the room. 'God, your family writes very dull postcards. I was hoping for adultery, passion, hatred. Instead I get the weather in Bognor.'

'Oh, I don't know,' said Alex, taking it from her and peering at the yellowing card. 'People were more subtle in those days. Bill was a grumpy old sod by the time I knew him. When is this dated?'

'1916.'

'Yes, well then he'd have been nine or ten. Surrounded by

women because all the men were away in the war effort. Probably really resentful at having to write postcards at all.'

He fiddled with the postcard like he was trying to fit a locker combination.

Then he let out a sigh of satisfaction. 'There, you see!'

'What?'

Alex looked pleased.

'Bill was cunning. Never what he seemed. This is pretty basic, but he was young. Look at it again.'

She stared, uncomprehending. The words slanted and fading, the picture a grainy grey shot of beach and promenade.

'What?'

'Take the first letter of every fourth word, starting from the beginning of the message. After "Ada".'

Sarah slowly read aloud. ' "I h-a-t-e y-o-u a-l-l".'

She laughed. 'No! That's too obscure.'

Alex's brow furrowed. 'Not at all. Bill loved codes. He taught me several. In the Second World War he was a code-breaker. He had to take some test in the Home Office where somebody timed him doing the *Times* crossword. He did it in three and a half minutes. Then he spent four years unravelling German commands stolen from the airwaves. Said it was the best time of his life.' He sighed. 'And he said it a lot. That was all he talked about towards the end.'

'Is that why they kept the postcard?'

'I doubt it. They just kept everything. Kept everything, understood nothing.'

'How funny.'

Alex put the postcard down.

'Now, Sarah, it's six o'clock.'

Sarah looked at him in surprise. This was a deviation from his normal line of conversation. She had never heard him make reference to time or place before.

'And?'

Alex suddenly looked almost shy. 'Three guys are coming over this evening. It's kind of a work thing but I'd like you to prepare food for us all.'

In all the time she'd known him he'd never entertained. He hated to eat in front of people. 'Alex, you know I can't cook!'

He shook his head.

'Don't worry. It's more assembly. Plates of cheese, biscuits, grapes, that kind of thing. There'll only be four of us.'

The friends arrived at ten in one cab. By this time, Sarah had diligently shopped for a sparkling array of food and drink. Spending someone else's money wasn't a problem. She had felt rather cheerful in the kitchen. Alex had opened a bottle of wine. He talked to her while she prepared the feast. But when the party arrived, the atmosphere felt different to her.

Alex introduced her to the three men. There was Hassim, a good-looking, long-fingered Asian who nodded politely. James, a small-eyed skinny weasel who twitched and scuffed. Though he could not look her in the eye, Sarah felt an instant horror of him. Then came Matthew, by far the most gregarious of the three, who fell through the doorway in a storm of ebullience, brandishing a bottle of Stolichnaya and a carton of raspberry and cranberry juice.

Alex introduced her as the housekeeper. Ironically? The three men seemed to accept this as perfectly normal but Sarah felt slighted. Knowing Alex, she reasoned, he said that to dampen any suspicion. For really, a single female, a stranger, living in the house? If they knew Alex at all well, they must have wondered.

'So, Alex,' shouted Matthew, who seemed to think they were all deaf, 'all set up for an all-nighter?'

'Absolutely.'

'Excellent.' Matthew smacked his lips. A theatrical gesture that would not have been missed from the upper circle. 'How about cracking open the Wodka then? I'm ter-ribly' – he drawled the word, enjoying the taste on his tongue – 'thirsty.'

Alex turned to Sarah and raised his eyebrows, indicating that she should do the job. Matthew looked her fixedly in the eyes. 'Easy on the juice. Just a tea-sing splash. Give her a rosy blush.'

While the guests were ushered into the upstairs sitting room, Sarah and Alex went into the kitchen.

'Am I playing maid all evening then?' Sarah kept the tone light though she was clearly annoyed.

Alex looked at her. He said very calmly, 'Not if you don't want to.'

'Right.' She was silent. No point in causing a scene after all. So she tried a brighter tack. 'What game are we playing?'

Alex, who had been smacking ice on to the table, stopped and looked at her. 'Oh sorry, Sarah, but you're not involved to-night.'

She felt a sudden coldness across her shoulder blades. 'What do you mean?'

'Just that. We are working on something. Sorry.' He didn't sound it. Remotely.

Sarah stuck her hand on her hip. 'Working on what?'

'Just a different game. They're helping me. It's very early stages, you'd find it boring. Anyway it'll take all night and you have to be up in the morning.' The last remark was evidently intended cheerfully but as he said it, Sarah clouded over. For the first time she felt like a servant.

She took a plate of cheese and the unfinished bottle of wine and walked to her bedroom. Sitting on the bed, staring glumly down to her feet, she could hear muted talking, like a smell of cooking wafting from the floor below. She felt excluded. Of course it was unreasonable, she knew that. Alex had his own life as much as anybody. She had attached herself to him. He had let her in but that didn't mean everything. Of course he could do his own thing sometimes.

Perhaps it was the game that bothered her. She thought that she was Alex's confidante. Suddenly, from nowhere, there were three men. Strange, elusive people who didn't fit together. Her mind threw in an image of how she had met Alex. Waking up; her unconscious body slow to rouse; looking into his thin face in bewilderment; a blur of shifting images. His concern, propping her up, giving her water. Were all his friendships formed as randomly?

Tired of her thoughts, she stood up. It was eleven o'clock but she was nowhere near sleep. The hum of the others made her more isolated than if she were in the house on her own. Pain ululated in her stomach. 'Where am I?' she murmured.

She tottered to the stairs and dragged down a few steps, round the corner to where she could see the closed door of the room the others were in. The door was outlined with the shining light from within. A bright yellow, powerful outline. Her light too, for the rest of the house was in darkness.

She could only hear the extrovert Matthew, the others were

indistinguishable. He spoke loudly and offensively, she thought. He sounded drunk.

'Where is it?' He was giggling.

There was a quiet answer.

'This is going to be fab-ulous, Alex. I love it. I love it.'

Sarah pulled her nightshirt, an oversized T-shirt of Alex's, over her chilled knees. She leaned against the banister and closed her eyes.

9

The Kiss

After four weeks Sarah was numb. She found herself unable to lift up the phone. Or she could lift up the phone but she let go in terror when her fingers started dialling the numbers.

After his friends had gone Alex had spent two days locked away. She was unaware of him coming out even to go to the toilet. He certainly didn't have any food. She knew better than to interrupt him. She turned instead to her own job and tried to lose herself in it.

It became increasingly easy. Her biggest fear, growing by the day, was the thought that one day it would come to an end. That one day she would have to make a decision about what to do next. Hiding away was the easy option. She couldn't live with Alex for ever. The longer she left it, the harder it would be to return.

She was amazed and fascinated by his family's capacity for hoarding, going back generations, as if they always suspected that one day someone would want to go through it. Not like her family which was more keen on throwing things away. Great Edie saved things because she was too lazy to get rid of them. Now life had overgrown her and she was forced to live in a jungle. Everyone else in her family kept nothing. She was sure that when she, Maggie and Grace were dead, they would leave barely a scorch mark. Alex's family had left a breathing scrapbook. It seemed deliberate. It kept them alive. Alex said he did not like to think of his family. Yet they were all downstairs. Enshrined.

There were so many letters. Hilary and Ted had kept avidly in touch with American intellectuals and the Beat scene. She found a pile of correspondence from Charles S. Perona, a San Franciscan poet. He talked a lot about writing and purpose. Sarah was interested that people then thought their ideas worth putting on paper. These were letters from a more optimistic generation which thought that what they did or said mattered.

Perona wrote:

18 April 1964

Had dinner with Ferlinghetti last week. He reminded me of the power of coincidence. That story of how he first got into Jacques Prévert? His fascination of the last 20 years. Do you remember? It bears retelling.

Ferlinghetti was in Paris on the day of liberation. The 25th? August '44. Ferlinghetti and some other junior officer took an abandoned jeep into the city. The jeep broke down and so they stopped at a café in Saint Brieuc for wine. While they were drinking Ferlinghetti noticed words scribbled on the paper table-cloth. A poem. The author was none other than Jacques Prévert. Of course, you know Ferlinghetti. He was a sucker for that anti-authority voice. And in the '30s too. He filched the tablecloth when they returned to the car and that very evening (so he says) began to translate *Paroles*. Well, you know the rest. It was published four years ago. By the way, he told me it's coming out in Britain soon. Penguin? He did say. Next year hopefully.

My point is that things get thrown at you. Just like it was chance that I bumped into Ferlinghetti again. And he told me. And I am telling you.

Ferlinghetti calls the job of the poet 'dissent from the official world of the upper middle class ideal and the white collar delusion and other systemized tribal insanities.' Let them eat poetry, eh? He's a cool cat.

I will be coming to London in May. Are you having a social?

Sarah put the letter down and rubbed her eyes in wonderment. She believed in coincidence. 'Systemized tribal insanities'? She knew all about them. Poetry she couldn't stick. No point. If it rhymed it was stupid. If it didn't rhyme, well, what was the difference between that and any other line of writing? Now wash your hands. That had a ring to it.

Every day her thoughts were carried on a wave of intangibles.

One day in the first-floor study, she found a box of hair.

No bigger than a shoebox and light though it was made of wood, the container lay in the bottom drawer of a chest, the key still in the lock. She opened it with growing excitement. Choosing to believe that it was important. Hair, three fragile locks, all tied up with silk and numbered, '56', '57' and '58'. She picked one up and unfurled it delicately between her fingers. She lifted it to her nose. It smelt musty.

When Alex finally emerged from his room he seemed different. She was alarmed at first. She had grown so used to the silence that footsteps on the ceiling, the creak of the stairs, were a shock. Then she remembered. Alex. And then she felt anger.

He came into the room. She was sitting on a red-carpet island surrounded by paper. He looked at her awkwardly.

'Hi.'

She didn't look up but mumbled a cursory 'Hello'.

He came and crouched in front of her. Looking a little rueful. And a little went a long way on such a cadaverous face.

'I've been busy.'

She didn't look up. 'So have I.'

He viewed the chaos. 'So I see. I hope you're keeping records of all this stuff.'

'Yes,' she snapped. 'I am. Of course I am. You told me to.'

He backed away. He looked at his watch. 'It's nearly seven. Why don't I make us something to eat and then we can have a beer and a game of Alice?'

Why should she be available on demand, like his damn computer, waiting to be switched on?

She said petulantly, 'I thought I did the cooking?'

'Have a night off.'

'I really wanted an early night.'

'Bullshit.'

She looked at him for the first time. Her face screwed up. 'I'm not just always available, you know.'

He rolled his eyes. 'Oh God.'

He was tired himself. He had been staring at a computer screen with increasing frustration. It wasn't working yet. He didn't know if it was going to. It could all be a total waste of time and he would have to spend the rest of his life making games for other people.

She knew when patience was running out. She smiled and lowered her eyes softly.

'Go on then. Make me something nice.'

Alex was a very good cook. He was, as in everything, precise and precision was useful in the kitchen. Everything he made looked exactly the same as it did in the book. Knowing she was bruised, he made an effort. He rolled fresh pasta while she had a bath.

While the dough settled in the fridge, Alex wandered down to the floors below his own living quarters. Sarah's work had made them more approachable somehow. He walked into the study where she had been today. Such dark walls, put up by earlier generations, years ago. He didn't know why his parents had kept it like that. It wasn't as if they studied in it. He looked round the room. His eyes fell on the open box of hair and were held there for a moment. He closed the door and returned to the kitchen.

Not even the waft of garlic and freshly chopped herbs could remove the childlike pout from Sarah's face when they at last sat down to eat.

'So who were those men round the other night?'

Alex looked steadfast. 'It's nothing remotely suspicious. I'm working on a special project. They're all involved with it.'

'Why won't you tell me about it?'

His tone was raised slightly and his face grew darker. 'It's nothing. It's not a huge secret. I'm just not supposed to go showing everybody. For one thing, it doesn't even work at the moment.'

'Everybody? Am I everybody now then?' She looked around her in mockery. 'God, if you told me, I'd just go blabbing, wouldn't I? All those important people I can tell. Maybe even the drunk outside Mr Naik's – we're pretty close now, you know.'

He didn't answer at once but cut his food. And took a sip of wine.

'Sarah, I am not under obligation to share everything with you. You are just staying here at the moment. We have to be allowed our separate lives. I don't demand every piece of information about you.'

She looked at him in astonishment. 'But you know everything about me.' She thought for a few seconds. 'Yes, everything. I have told you everything. What are you saying, that there is a load more of you I know nothing about?'

There was an air of impatient distraction about him now. 'Of course I don't know everything about you, don't be ridiculous.'

She broke into a simple smile, but her eyes were troubled. 'You do. Everything. There's nothing more to me.'

She knew she was heading downwards. At this stage there was still a choice. She could return to the air, or let herself be drawn into the dizzying vacuum of her own blackness. While it was not a pleasant fall, it was always tempting. But there was always the fear that she would never get out again. Like Grace. But Grace had an excuse, a trigger: she had succumbed to psychosis after the death of her sister. Sarah felt her own trigger was nothing. Nothing. That was the whole problem.

Alex had gathered up the plates. Breezily, like a mother, she thought. Her eyes felt hot. She could cry if she wanted to. She didn't. He turned on the hot tap and shot a green beam of washing-up liquid. Efficiency meant he must be nervous, or angry. It was a silent struggle between them for emotional control of the evening. Calm or hysteria. Like arm-wrestling. Just when she had nearly pulled him over, he dragged her back. But feelings are not like physics, she thought. The negative is always stronger.

'So are any of those friends of yours single then?'

He fired a look at her. Don't push it.

'I didn't see much of them, but one of them looked quite nice. What was his name? The Asian guy?'

He smirked. 'And you wonder why I don't want to introduce you to people?'

The words emerged slowly. 'You kept me out of it in case I embarrassed you.'

He looked away. They did not talk of such things. She was doing it deliberately. Acting like a nineteen-year-old. But it didn't feel like she had a choice. She often felt as if the last decade of her life had slipped by unnoticed one night. She just woke up in the morning ten years older.

But her behaviour felt deliberate to Alex. He could be deliberate too.

He said coldly, 'I see you found that box of hair. That belonged to my grandmother. My father's mother. She killed herself. She threw petrol over herself and set a match to it. My grandfather found out she was having an affair and was going to divorce her. She couldn't live with the thought of the scandal. She did it in the garden, this garden, when everyone else was out on an afternoon walk. My father said he came back and could smell the fire before they even came in the gate. They went through the house and the smell was horrible. Human flesh burns sweet and thick apparently. They ran out the back gagging but all that was left were a few scraps of clothing, some hair and bones.'

Sarah looked bored. 'That's not true.' She was pulling at a hangnail.

'Yes, it is.'

She would not be moved. 'No, it isn't.'

'How do you know?' he said defiantly.

'It's obvious,' she said. 'There would never have been any hair left. The hair would burn up first. Hair's dead and dry.' Dead and dry, she said it again in her head. She liked the way the words stopped so suddenly. There was no echo. 'Sarah' spun round maddeningly, endlessly.

So they played the game but this time there was a tension between them. They both felt it. Sarah didn't mind. It made her urge to win all the stronger. But Alex didn't like the confusion he felt.

They played almost in silence for two hours. The game was therapeutic. Despite themselves, they were drawn in, their previous thoughts in abeyance.

'The Red King,' shrieked Sarah, displaying her cards. This was a powerful position to be in. The combination hardly ever came up and the person who got it was for once almost certain to win. 'You are just my dream, Alex. You don't exist.'

Winning put her in a better mood. She smiled at Alex. It was eleven o'clock. Early, yet.

'Come and have a look at some of the other rooms I've been doing, you're way behind. I've done loads while you've been locked away, ignoring me.'

He bridled but didn't rise. And he felt very awake. After such an intense period of concentration as he had been in since Sunday, it was an artificial high. He would crash soon, but for now he was painfully alert.

'Let's go downstairs.'

The house seemed different at night. Old-fashioned lighting failed to penetrate its corners, the big house with such high ceilings and long rooms. Draughty, even now in summer, and always dark. Shadows in strange shapes that loomed and fell as you walked towards them. Alex had stuck to his own rooms for so long. At night, when he opened the front door in darkness, he would sprint up the three parental floors to reach safety. An imagination was not always a good thing. But then Sarah had known that for a long time.

Now that they were talking about the house she felt more comfortable. The edge inside her had blunted a little with the practical conversation. She gesticulated enthusiastically as she laid the plan in front of him.

'I'm on the first floor now. I was still downstairs before, wasn't I?'

He nodded, trying to remember. Putting his fingers through his messed-up hair. Rubbing his eyes. Trying to focus on this roomed reality, having been trapped inside the infinite dimensions of cyberspace for so long.

'I am just amazed at how much stuff there is. They have kept everything. I think I could write a day-by-day account of your family's life. I am dividing everything into categories and backing up all the information on the laptop. A lot of it I think you will want to throw away. It's just concert programmes, tickets, shopping receipts – somebody spent a lot of time in Carnaby Street.'

Alex smiled weakly. 'That'll be my mother. She liked clothes. My father couldn't stand it. He wore cardigans. She liked rainbow colours and beads in her hair.'

'So that's mainly rubbish, but I'm writing it down anyway – or do you want me to chuck out that kind of stuff?'

'No.' He was suddenly insistent, glowering intently. 'Save everything. I need to know everything.'

She looked at him peculiarly. He seemed strained.

'Oh, OK, OK, don't worry.'

They moved into the next room, which was the library. Six-foot-high shelves, rows and rows of, for once, neatly stored volumes. But the neatness was spoiled by the overflow. Chimney stacks of books on the floor. Sarah closed the door and sat on a tight brown-leather sofa. Shiny and ungiving, its skin stuck to her skin.

'This is amazing,' she drawled. 'I started in here today, as a break from all those files of academic writing. I'll go back to them later. But the library, God, I've never seen so many books together. Did they read them all?'

'I doubt it,' said Alex. 'They pretended to but sometimes weeks would go by when they didn't read anything at all.' He sighed and sat down on the sofa, rubbing his temples to ease the pressure. 'Besides, they inherited a lot of them. My family has been collecting for years. Some of these books won't have been looked at for decades.'

'There are some really crazy titles. So obscure. All that Greek mathematics! I'm cross-cataloguing them by subject, date and author.'

He was approving. 'That's excellent. Make sure you look in each one as well. Just in case there's something in them.'

Sarah sighed. There must have been several thousand books. 'What are you hoping I'll find?'

'Who knows?' he answered a little too neatly. 'I've left this house festering too long. My parents knew a lot of interesting people. The hippie thing. It might seem stupid now . . .' He broke off.

She was puzzled. 'Of course it doesn't. Nobody thinks that apart from you. Why do you despise them so much? If I were you, I'd love it. My family's done sod all.'

'Because' – he hesitated – 'they were all pretence. It was all image. Actually they were pretty stupid. They wrote fashionable things. It wasn't hard to be outrageous then. My father's semiotic interpretation of the common blasphemies caused a storm. They added a certain gloss to the crusty university image.' He laughed at the thought. 'My mother, at graduation ceremonies, with her see-through shirt under her academic robes, ha!'

The light, which was throwing a sickly lime hue, flickered for a moment and then died. They were sent into a buzzing darkness.

'Damn,' said Alex. 'Where are the spare bulbs?'

'Fuck knows,' she said with an abandonment in her voice.

He looked at her. At least, his head turned automatically to where her voice was, since he could see nothing. Strange how slow the mind is to adjust to a change in circumstances.

He went to feel his way through the books but she felt his movement and pulled him back to the sofa.

'No, let's stay here a while.'

'But I can't see anything!' His voice sounded strangled, with no mouth to it.

Sarah's voice was mellow, slow and entranced.

'I always loved power cuts. Because nothing was the same. In the 'seventies, I would be sitting in an ordinary bath, in a dull blue plastic tub, bored and probably cold. Then the lights would go out and suddenly it was terrifying. Eventually my mother would come stumbling in with a candle but before that, for the delicious minutes when I sat in petrified silence, anything was possible. The people I saw, the ships in the distance, the stormy waves. It was wonderful.'

'Well, why didn't you always have your bath in the dark then?' Already it was normal, sitting here, having this conversation. He no longer thought of leaving.

'Because it wasn't dark. The street lights shone through the frosted window. There was a constant orange glow.'

But it was perfectly dark in the library.

A silence of maybe a minute, then Sarah said, 'Is that why you won't talk about sex?'

She thought she felt him palpitate.

'Is what why?'

'Your parents.'

'I do talk about sex.'

She laughed. 'When?'

'Whenever I feel like it.'

'And you haven't in the last ten years?'

'Well, why do you want to talk about it all the time?'

'That's not an answer.'

This time he gave no answer at all. After more silence, she persisted. 'All the time I've known you, nothing.'

'You don't know that.'

'Well, tell me then.' She sounded frustrated. 'Share a little of your personal life with me.'

'No.'

'Why not, don't you trust me?' She sighed and hesitated, like she was thinking. 'You're my closest friend – probably my only friend. I could tell you anything, I think. I would feel safe doing it. Why can't you?'

She felt him stretch out his long limbs. They were sitting side by side, Sarah with her knees tucked.

'There's nothing to tell.'

'Don't you want to be with someone?'

'I don't think about it much.'

'Well, I want to be with someone. I think I want to meet someone really nice and settle down.' She meant it, yet it sounded hollow.

'Do you?' He sounded incredulous.

'Don't I? Isn't that what everybody wants?'

'I don't know. Not people I know.'

She thought for a while. It was surprising that Alex hadn't fled to the light outside. They were floating into danger. She hadn't expected him to come this far. Between them, he kept the relationship safe. He liked things to stay as they were. Even if they were bad. He hated the house but he stayed there, rather than face the challenge of change. In the same way Sarah went the emotionally turbulent route if she could. Normally he wouldn't let her. And his determination, in this, was stronger than hers.

'I mean,' she said, a casualness in her voice that was always ominous, 'why have we never had sex? You must be the only attractive man I've spent any amount of time with who I haven't slept with. You know me.'

Yes, he did. He didn't answer.

Now she had said it, the great, long unsaid; she was un-leashed.

'I mean, if we were in a film, wouldn't everybody think it the obvious answer? You're good looking, I'm available. So why haven't we?'

'You make it sound so appealing,' he said with a laced sarcasm.

'Don't you like me?' Her voice was belligerent, provocative.

He felt she was exposing herself. Not physically but it was just as disturbing. 'You know I like you.'

'How do I know? You've never told me.' Her voice was shriller, an improbable sound against the fusty smell of the books. The books tried to deaden noise. They disapproved.

He sounded perplexed. 'Well, I don't have to specify.'

'You don't even kiss me. Not even on the cheek. You hardly touch me. Why not?'

He paused. 'M-maybe I'm not a very physical person, I don't know.' He was floundering. He felt unable to stop it. He had thought himself immutable, but she had attacked blind. He had underestimated the power of weakness. Wasn't that just the mistake of her appalling great-grandmother, who had imagined that her strength could stamp out the frailty of the others? That hadn't worked. Strength always decays.

He drew his fingers along the sofa. Feeling the leather. To the nearest bookshelf, bumping along the concave spines, the pitted covers. Clinging to them.

She was talking.

'Why won't you kiss me?' She moved her hand in the darkness. She felt for his chin and turned it to face her. She could just make him out. The whites of his eyes, primarily, which were widening.

'I'll kiss you, if you want me to.'

Her hands were suddenly sweating. It was his first counterattack. There was nothing else for it.

'Go on then.'

It was very slow. He inched forward. She could feel his breath, not unpleasant, on her face. She expected him to peck her cheek, but he didn't. He clasped inexorably on to her lips. At first he was motionless, like he was making a print on a cold pane of glass. As if he were waiting to see what might happen. Then, surreptitiously, his lips began to move. He seemed to be tasting her, unsure whether he liked the flavour, or whether he had come across it before.

Sarah moved her lips too. They were the only part of her body that moved. The rest of her was frozen in shock. She thought her heart had stopped too. Her brain certainly had. Blank. It was so extraordinary she had no memory of anything ever having happened before. She wasn't sure, suddenly, who she was.

The kiss lasted for what seemed like hours. Alex was not going to pull away first. In the end, feeling she must get her breathing back to normal or she would suffocate, Sarah moved back to her part of the sofa. She sat meekly, her hands in her lap.

Alex spoke. His voice was not harsh but curious. 'Do you even understand what friendship is?'

'I'm sure I don't,' she said, like it was a revelation.

He stretched. 'I'm tired now. I think I'm going to bed.' He walked like a zombie, arms outstretched to navigate himself safely out of the room. He left the door ajar and turned on the landing light which brought a gauzy glow into the library. Sarah listened to his steps as they disappeared into silence. She rubbed her lips. They were cold. All of her was cold. She closed her eyes and felt for the bookshelf and picked the first book that came to her greedy fingers. Whatever it was, she would read it. It would contain the answer, the explanation for tonight. Coincidence. She was better off without choices. Since she didn't know herself.

She fell asleep some hours later, with the light still on. In her dream she was having sex. She didn't recognize him. But as it went on she was pushed further and further against the wall. She was motionless, faceless and dumb. But he was pushing so hard, so relentlessly, that the lips of her vagina split wide open, peeled outwards and pulled right up over her body until she was pulled right through. Until she was turned inside out and looking at her own raw purple-pink flesh from somewhere warm, deep inside.

10

The Storm

The feeling was entirely internal. It had no resonance outside. She felt she was in a vacuum. If she screamed, there would be no sound. So she could not shout. The joy had to be suppressed. It was a pressure, bubbles brewing inside her; she could feel them but there was nowhere for them to go.

No one had told Maggie that there were feelings like this. Great Edie shook her head grimly at the mention of men. Men were children. They created the mess that women cleaned up.

She had never known there could be pleasure too. To be in such a state of electrification that the slightest stroke on the smallest finger would send pulses through her entire body. This was unnatural, a product of the heat; in the long glowing evenings, in the motion of the boat, in the buzzing, the vibrating, the sticky sweetness of the liqueurs that she had developed a taste for, that her tongue lapped, leaving a glue around the rim of the glass. The sweet smell of tobacco, the darkness, the shadows, the wet sheets, her body, her mouth, the code between them, the broken messages. And the tension, the secrets, the running from noises. The wondering about the others, did they see her whole-body halo of ineffable power, her imperishable spirit? Her unquenchable thirst for the feelings, the essence, that ran through her like silver.

They lay in the darkness. She stroked his hand. It felt rough.

'What's your real name?'

He was silent. The darkness swallowed her words. She wondered how he would respond. But she wanted to know. It felt like a barrier between them. She had told him something of herself – he had asked endless questions. He was fascinated by her mother. He said he had so often feared falling over the edge himself, he was drawn to those who had the gall to do it. That comedy meant walking out as far as possible, looking over the edge, down to the raging waters and letting go and yet holding a balance. One had to be lucid enough to go back and make it funny. That's why so many comedians ended on the dust heap.

'Did you ever feel close to the edge?' he asked her. 'You must wonder, with your mother as she is. You must understand the impulses?'

'No.' She didn't. Perhaps she answered too sharply. He didn't believe her. But she had seen no precipice, she had felt no earth falling away.

She felt too solid. She had watched her mother crumble. Sometimes she blamed herself. That her strength, her independence, made things worse. She should have been with her mother when Ruth died. Been there completely. Or not been there at all.

She knew nothing about him. He might thrive on the separate existence of the boat but she was beginning to feel she needed something more. She repeated, 'What's your real name?'

He turned to her and smiled. An old smile, avuncular almost. Weathered like a reptile, a tortoise grey.

'Why d'you want to know?'

'Because it's such a basic piece of information. It is part of the jigsaw and it makes me feel uncomfortable that it's not there.'

She regretted that comparison. He was always teasing her about her innate need for order. She spun a web around him, but it was a web of perfect symmetry. She said it was a compulsion evoked by the disorder she grew up in. It was a protective line around her. She was brought up in chaos.

He continued to smile. He toyed with her hair.

'You have a name for me. Why bother with details?'

She felt almost angry and pushed his hand away.

'You say that. You use those words, but it's perfectly normal to want to know. There is no spell that will be broken by knowing your name.'

He felt he couldn't tell her. For him their relationship was a reprieve. A second chance. But it existed only in a charmed state.

He was terrified to do anything to break the charm. Once reality seeped in, a silent gas under the door, he would suffocate.

'Tell me who you are.' She wanted to stamp her foot. But she was lying down so she banged her fist hopelessly on the bed. The bed so old and soft that the noise was no more than a frustrated flop. Foetal limbs kicking noiselessly inside a womb.

Bad weather in July had chained them to the Port Royal, Kingston, Jamaica. The winds were catapulting chairs around the deck.

The storms of the last week had unsettled her. Normally Maggie enjoyed robust health but now everyone was ill. Some of the passengers had stopped off in hotels on land, so the ship was half-empty. The entertainment was lacklustre. The nightly shows were cut back and the troupe sat around playing hand after hand of poker, reading newspapers, listening to the radio when they could pick up a signal. Of all of them, only Sally Shezaar was lively.

She came running into the saloon whooping, her olive face creased in delight. 'Have you heard what now? Three days ago we beat Bulgaria three–nil. Today Brazil! What style! Eusebio is a hero, two goals, what a week!' she shouted, trying to rinse the inertia out of everyone else. Everyone else sank in their seats and looked assiduously in other directions. 'Oh Mamma Portugal,' Sally sighed, '1966 is your World Cup.'

Harry had not left his room for two days. This was normal in recent times. He had been drinking more than ever. Maggie was glad when he locked himself away. She needn't worry that he was going to fall out of or into anything or say something terrible. For the most dangerous time was before the stupor, when he would lurch round the boat chasing some abstract need.

He would reel around the others, ranting and offensive. It was the only time he talked. He became obsessed with trivia. He was determined, for instance, to find out the weight of Joe Moller, the rotund baritone. True, Joe was portly and irritatingly defensive about it. But still he didn't deserve such torment. In the bar, everyone was mildly squiffy.

'You fat bastard! You should be ashamed of yourself. If we sink in these winds, it'll be your fault. You fat bastard.'

Joe sat staring miserably into his beer.

Harry was also paying inappropriate attention to Sally Shezaar. At breakfast the next morning Sally was glowing. Maggie felt for her. That was desperation.

Her father emerged at lunchtime shouting obscenities and reeking of whisky. Maggie – with the help of Rudi – had battened him back in his cabin and sat with him until he fell unconscious. The door could not be locked from the outside. Unless he chose (as he often did) to lock himself in, there was no way of keeping him safe until his own storm had passed.

So Maggie was relieved that this time it was so bad he was already gone. In a few days' time, maybe when the ship was moving again, he would emerge. A little more hollow round the eyes, the chin a little greyer, the frame weaker. His skin somehow wetter, as if the perpetual soaking were Harry turning into drink rather than merely to it.

Even Rudi was sick.

'This weather!' he ranted. 'It's diseased!'

The wind raged feverishly. Maggie longed for a cool breeze but when she got up in the morning and pulled herself out on to the deck it was still the same noisome air. She tried to breathe but it was too humid. Like drinking hot bathwater. She lurched for the side that tilted as she ran and vomited noiselessly over the edge. No clean getaway: peevish winds pulled her vomit up and left a spattering across her cheek and hair. She groaned. Her body trembled, shook from inside. Everything felt dirty and sick.

On the third day stillness fell. The less sensitive thought this meant that the worst was over but Maggie knew that it was yet to come. The air was so heavy she felt her eyes pressing down on her skull. Her hair clung fearfully to her scalp. Energy drained out of her. The electricity in the air had consumed her; she was unable to think or speak anything but the most fatuous inanities.

The sky was gathering itself for something truly impressive. Purple giants bulged over the horizon.

She drank whisky to settle her stomach with Rudi in his cabin. He looked green. A muggy darkness was descending and she could hardly see him. All she could see was his mouth, set in a grim line, like he was holding something in.

'I wish this weather would change,' she said for the thirtieth time. 'I just want to be going somewhere, anywhere.'

'Why?' he said, his lips moving so slightly there was barely space for the words to escape. 'We're never going anywhere – just round in circles. We might as well be standing still.' It was true. They never got anywhere. The ship picked up and put down different people, new faces which always looked the same. The cruiser liner skated in arcs across the oceans but it never took them anywhere. The boat went as far as it was possible to go, didn't it? What else was there?

Maggie said, 'I just think if we moved I'd feel well again. If the storm breaks, if we get some air. I can't breathe in this fog.'

Rudi shrugged. Breathing seemed an overrated pastime. He had sunk to the level of inertia where he had lost the will to fight.

That night, though, the storm broke. It was not, by official measurement, a hurricane but Maggie swore it felt like one.

She had gone to bed alone, sick not only in herself but sick too of Rudi's doldrums. She did not have the energy to stir him to help her. She said goodnight offhandedly. She did not want to kiss him; her mouth still felt full of the taste of her own vomit. Endless rinsing could not wash it away. Hanging her head over the tiny sink, watching her spit swirl slowly down clinging to a hair, made her retch again and she had to force herself upright.

Rudi was too tired, it seemed, to care. He waved her away like a fly.

'I feel sick,' she said. 'I'm going to my own room.'

So Maggie lay sleepless, alone on her single bed. She turned the light off and lay in the semi-darkness, her sheets already creased and wet with sweat. She flipped from side to side in a restless anxiety. Huge figures loomed before her eyes. Faces of strangers, heads, trunks, sickly green sea, a sea of bodies. If she closed her eyes the nausea returned, churning, blending, folding her stomach. She could hear it.

She also heard laughter – probably Sally who seemed, of all of them, to thrive on unhealthy air. She was buoyed by patriotic excitement. Portugal, as the whole troupe had no choice but to find out, earlier that evening had marched triumphantly into the semi-finals with a five–three victory against North Korea. 'Only the English stand between us and the final,' said Sally through her many victory vodkas.

There had been electric storms all week so Maggie was unperturbed at first when lightning lit the small room. But this time, once it started, it did not stop. Relentless streaks of white light flashed through the room and, she imagined, her head. Thunder crashed against her ears. She clung to a blanket until confusion saw her toss it aside. Didn't wool conduct electricity? She knew it was stupid but stupid thoughts were all she was capable of. She wanted to run to Rudi.

Then she heard the rain, stinging at last, falling on the decks. So loud she trembled. Her clock had stopped. She had been too tired to wind it up. But now she assumed that somehow time had been struck by the storm. Human momentum broken by nature.

As the storm lashed on – for half an hour, an hour, two hours, more – her head, from feeling all week like a stone, now felt irrepressibly light. She feared it would detach from her neck and float away. When she blinked she saw a balloon that slipped through her fingers – her own terrified face imprinted upon it. The pain from her head was released but in its place, more terrifying, was a sense of unleashing. Gravity was no longer guaranteed. The fragile physics that held her to the earth, the strings, the puppetry, had been cut. And nothing would ever be the same again. She was loose, on her own and every stab of lightning that ripped through her bed cut her further away from the illusory normality she had deceived herself with.

She did not sleep. At least she did not believe that she did. But with her conscious thoughts bewitched into alchemy it was hard to tell. She had a fever but the fever was everywhere. Outside and in. There was no clambering back to health. Memories, thoughts of her mother, her face – that formless smile, like a baby, when what seems like a smile is only wind. Her father didn't even pretend. He only smiled through his dummy. Arthur was always smiling. She saw his maniacal grin, the wooden teeth, the upturned lips, black and shiny, that trapped her curious fingers in a soundless velvety grip. His words that sounded, in the heat, like necromancy. 'Come here, Maggie, help me tie him up.'

'No! No!' Did she let out a cry or was it the waves or the winds that moaned and whimpered in her ears? Was this what Rudi meant by the precipice? Was this what her mother felt? Trapped in a storm under the drumming rain. Her eyes ached with tiredness. Her body flinched with discomfort. The bed, how could she ever have slept in it? It burnt like a rope whichever way she twisted. There was no one to turn to and nowhere to go. Simultaneously she craved and dreaded sleep. Her waking nightmares were horror enough.

Dawn came slowly. The sky was still black, the clouds fuming in the sky. But the wind had blown itself out and the rain was reduced to a steady pouring. She felt calmer. Her mind was quiet at last. Exhausted, spent, like the port that became slowly visible through the haze, a mess of fallen trees and battered boats. When she looked out she could see people, some swathed in waterproofs, some already too wet to need protection, venturing forward to survey the damage.

There was a knock. She was surprised to hear her own voice.

'Yes?' She sounded older. Several years had passed in one night.

'Are you all right, Mags? Were you scared?'

'Of course I wasn't,' she said irritably. 'It was just a storm – I've seen them before, you know.' She was learning to look after herself. Suffer in silence and enjoy the self-reliance.

Rudi's frame came round the door, stumbling. 'Did you sleep?'

Obviously he hadn't. He looked terrible, his eyeballs receding into puffy surrounding skin.

'Yes, most of the time,' she said. 'I woke up with a couple of the bangs.'

Rudi looked unconvinced.

'I don't believe you slept a wink.'

'OK then.'

They looked at each other and smiled. It was reconciliation. A making-up of the argument they hadn't had. The electricity had passed. The demons had moved on. Maggie still felt unwell although a little better. Staggering out of her room, looking overboard down the vast white acreage of the ship's exterior, she saw the waves were no longer chasing up the sides. They were reduced again to benign clouds, bouncing off the metal. Afterwards, the next moment seemed both instant and for ever.

Maggie remembered coming back into the cabin. Sitting on the bed and looking at Rudi. At his eyes which were smiling again with warmth and understanding. Their eyes locked in a gaze. Then there was a loud and urgent knock at the door. The intruder did not wait for admittance.

The open door revealed the tragi-comic features of Sally Shezaar. Her fluid body poured into the room in a trembling wave.

'Harry's dead!'

Silence. Maggie did not know how she should feel. Her first thought was, how do I explain why he is here with me and why I am in my nightshirt? Then she didn't think. She ran to the sink and threw up.

Sally too was in night-clothes. That also demanded questions. But not now. Nobody spoke. Somebody had to say something. Rudi let out an exaggerated and belated 'What?!' And stood up dramatically, French farce style.

Sally's face was pure white. Shock, horror, repulsion and terror all written in porcelain. Maggie did not know how long Sally stood there before she spoke. Everything. Became. Slow. Sally's mouth, her misshapen teeth, opened hesitantly. The words fell out.

'I woke up and there he was – lying on the floor. I th-thought he was unconscious but when I shouted he didn't answer. So I kicked him and his body was cold . . . is cold.'

Her voice tapered off and she fell theatrically into Rudi's reluctant arms. He put them out at the very last minute before she would have fallen to the floor. She was sobbing violently, uncontrollably.

Rudi felt weary. He sat on the bed, taking the doubled Sally with him and pushing her away so she lay on the covers weeping black streams of yesterday's make-up. After all the noise of the last night, her sobbing was the only sound.

Maggie turned to both of them. 'Well, hadn't we better go and have a look, tell someone or something?'

She sounded calmer than she felt. The news was a shock but unreal. She found within her a voice of reason. Somebody had to. It did not feel part of her. It was a useful discovery. For want of anything or anyone else, she clung to it.

'Which room is he in, Sally – his or yours?'

Sally did not lift her face from the bed but raised a trembling arm and gesticulated in answer to the undignified question.

'Oh, it must be his,' said Maggie impatiently. 'He hasn't

moved for days. Come on, leave Sally. Let's go and take a look.'

Maggie walked briskly to her father's room, Rudi trotting obediently behind. The door was closed.

She opened it with some difficulty. The room was a mess. Empty bottles, heaps of clothes, both male and female, and the air laced with alcohol. Maggie thought she might throw up again.

'Jesus Christ, that's disgusting,' grimaced Rudi. 'I'm not going in there.'

'Suit yourself.'

It was the first time she realized that, when somebody had to do something, from now on it was always going to be her.

Maggie stepped over the bottles and sat on the bed. She saw by her feet a huddled body. She balked inwardly but stayed solid outside. Just her mouth set a little firmer on her face. She opened the curtains. A feeble light fell on her father. He lay on his front, one leg bent awkwardly sideways.

She took in the picture in one uncomfortable moment. She looked away in distaste but the vision never left her.

He wore a red dressing gown. It was hitched up above his hips where he had evidently writhed in his struggle. His ageing body hung in bluish bowls of flesh. His chin strained from the floor, apparently gasping for air. His eyes, thankfully, were closed. A drool of saliva, with flecks of brown, clung to his mouth and neck and then fell in a viscous pool on the floor. His bloodless buttocks were stained.

It was not how she would have chosen to remember her father. There were years in which to reflect on who her father was. But at that moment she felt a profound sense of melancholy. A void, the body slumped before her. A washed-up soul.

She was left with nothing but a gnawing sense of what hadn't happened. Her father had been more missing than her mother was. Where was he? Who was he? All the things she didn't know. How her parents had met. What had drawn them to each other. When she had been conceived. Her parents were such disparate beings, so isolated from each other and themselves. She could not begin to make sense of it. They were jigsaw pieces – ones that did not fit together but had somehow, in desperation, been wedged, forced together. But of course, the two wrong pieces had ruined everything. Not just these two, but the ruin spread in a rippling force across the whole picture. She had always thought in pieces. Jagged, muddled, her vision was broken.

She held her head in her hands. Now she knew she was older. After a few moments she looked up to the mirror in the cupboard and saw her own face, pale and strained. Her eyes travelled wearily in no particular direction and saw the lips and yellow bow tie of Arthur Hodges, grinning at her.

'Well, that's shut you up anyway,' she said grimly. She had wanted Arthur silenced for years. His idiotic humour and stupid smile. Her father's alter ego died with him. She felt relief and then for some reason she felt guilty.

11

Death

The moment of passing is not death, for then there is still movement. Death is afterwards; death is the aftermath.

Mr Brown, the social director, was anxious that everything should be dealt with as quickly as possible. There had already been enough disappointment among the passengers with the weather over the last week. A local doctor was smuggled on board. After a discreet examination, during which he regarded the cadaver with disapproving nostrils, he was content to write off the death as a heart attack. He wrote in a thick fountain pen with a confident zeal.

'Yes, yes, a heart attack. Wiped him out. Nothing anybody could have done.' The doctor leaned over the body. 'Very sad, especially for the girl.'

He was handsomely paid for his efficiency. For the questions he didn't ask. Maybe Harry had had a heart attack but there had been plenty to investigate. The dozen whisky bottles that lay around the cabin, rolling lugubriously when endless feet disturbed the floor. But by the time the doctor came these had already gone. Tidied away.

Maggie thought more about her father over the next few days than she had ever done. While he was alive, she had tried to ignore him; to shut him out. Now he was dead she found herself clutching for memories. Even though thinking about him made her feel sick again. Despite this, she needed to remember.

Now he was dead, the ankle-deep human being that he had been, the inadequate parent, was overwhelmed by the enormity of his role in her. He was half of her, like it or not. She sat on the deck looking at her own hand, her fingers – his fingers, the long tapering elegant fingers, they were his undoubtedly. Fingers like a magician. She stared at them. The lines, the crossed lines, the veins like vines that climbed up her palms. Through this new looking-glass was a darker world. Or maybe the brighter world. She had been living all this time in a looking-glass world. And now, as she looked out, she was facing the other side of the mirror for the first time. Her parents were two-sided too. Since her breakdown, her mother was all reflected shadows, veiled, and her father was all false brightness. All surface. The stark light that blinded when it was switched on. The entertainer. The dazzling smile with nothing behind it. Her mother in darkness.

She had previously thought that reality was how you chose to see it. And that her mother had chosen hers. That was how she rationalized it. Now she realized that reality could be thrust upon you.

Nobody talked. The management was anxious that the passengers should remain ignorant. There was a small ceremony. The body was cremated and the ashes scattered in Kingston. Harry had no other relatives that anybody knew of. His wife was legally judged incapable of making a decision. Maggie was still a minor in the eyes of the law. Contact with the authorities in England confirmed there was no family to answer to. His wife's mother apparently said she had thought it would come to this but had no opinion as to what should happen to him. All this Maggie was informed of by the officer in charge.

'You understand that we need to get this cleared up and out of the way. No point getting stuck in bureaucracy.'

The disposal of the body became the responsibility of the state. The state, thousands of miles away, wanted minimum fuss. And no flowers.

She was called for almost the first time before the Captain. There were matters to clear up.

Maggie walked across the ship to the Captain's office. Her feet moved rhythmically. She found herself counting. The ship was a quarter of a mile in length. It seemed a long walk. Maybe because she had used to run. She was always in corridors.

Her father had been dead for three days. Since then the time had flowed beneath her. She held up like an island, smacked by the waves. While outwardly unmoved, it was a slow erosion.

Rudi was small, quiet, hushed. He spoke in a low tone. She did not know why. He was awkward around her. In truth he was awed by her presence which seemed suddenly huge and exclusive. Her large unblinking eyes. He could not read them. For the first time he was scared of her. Scared by the same self-containment that had fascinated him before. The weight of her sanity. He knew her father was a weak man, a loser, an inadequate. He did not know how it must feel to lose such a person. Had she loved her father? Had she hated him? He had let these issues slip between their fingers. Their relationship was a phantasmagoria. It shone in the dark. It was not real.

So he backed off. And loathed himself for it, realizing that he was not up to the task. So she walked alone into the Captain's office. Maybe it was better that way. She walked into the room, out of childhood, into the cold world.

He was a tall, pale man, unconvincingly imperious, shielded by his huge desk.

'Maggie, sit down.' He paused. 'My dear.'

She smiled warily.

He looked at her sharply. No signs of grief. What a strange child she was. So unapproachable, so unlikeable. He gathered some papers together needlessly.

'A very difficult time, a very difficult time.' He shook his head, like a metronome. Rhythmic. She counted the swings. Blinking on each turn.

He knotted his fingers together and rested them against his mouth.

'Of course we have dealt with the immediate problem of disposing of . . . of getting rid of . . . of sorting out the practical details.'

Maggie stared at him, waiting for his point.

He paused. If only she would not look at him like that, her gaze so damned accusing. It wasn't his fault, for God's sake.

'The issue I have to account for is . . .' He paused again.

Maggie stared at his desk, polished wood with inlaid green baize. An inkstand, a letter holder bursting with officialdom. Keeping it practical. Suddenly he spoke sternly, though with visible effort.

'You are aware that your father owed us a considerable amount of money?'

Maggie shook her head dumbly.

He loosened his collar. He coughed unnecessarily. 'It was something we had overlooked for some time. Your father had, of course, put in many years of . . . service in our company. We knew that and we were lenient. We did not bring it all to such an end. But in latter years . . .' His voice broke off.

Maggie could bear the missing word no longer.

'You mean the drink.'

He was grateful to her.

'Yes, unfortunately so. We chose to see it as money owed rather than what it was – theft. It was better that way.'

She spoke deliberately. 'I'm sure you were right to do so. He had a problem that got out of hand. He was not a thief.'

'Quite.'

He looked uncomfortable. He could feel her eyes burning on him. She studied him carefully. The thin moustache, the wavering mouth, the insubstantial eyes. She closed her own eyes wearily. Everywhere she looked she saw cracks, fissures in flesh.

He coughed conclusively. 'So we have decided to say no more about it.'

She said nothing. Was she meant to be grateful?

He stood up. 'Well, well. There, there, my girl. It'll be fine. Stiff upper lip . . .' he cleared his throat – 'and all that.'

She left the room. This was her inheritance; the word was a heavy one. She was sixteen years old.

Since the tragedy, Sally had been a mess. She was neurotic at the best of times. Now with her lover dead and, worse, the next day Portugal beaten by England, she began to think she was cursed. She swung between gushing floral melodrama, a need to be forgiven, an overwhelming disgust and a haughty superiority about her own tragedy.

In the evening, after talking to the Captain, Maggie sat alone on her bed reading – a rambling historical romance she had plucked from the library (afterwards she could remember neither title nor author).

Sally came in, abject, her head hung meekly.

'Oh God, Maggie, you poor, poor darling.'

Maggie smiled stiffly. 'Hello, Sally.'

Sally looked into Maggie's eyes. The woman's pupils dilated in fervour.

'Darling, if you knew how I felt for you.'

Maggie looked at the floor. This outburst was not going to be helpful; she braced herself.

'I want to confide in you, Maggie.' Sally stumbled, 'I-I think it might be of help to both of us.'

Maggie tried to keep the scorn from her face. Sally put her hand on Maggie's arm. Her hand felt cold and clammy.

'I think you could do with a drink,' said Sally.

Maggie wanted nothing less.

Sally sat down uninvited on the small shabby stool by the mirror. She rested her elbow in emotional exhaustion, knocking over a brush. Maggie felt suddenly violated: the tawdry display, this cheap woman. Sally broke into her thoughts.

'I think you're old enough to know the truth, Maggie dear.'

Her heart sank. It was too much that she should bear the burden of other people's confessions.

'What do you want to say, Sally?'

Sally was only temporarily arrested by the new authority in Maggie's voice. It clashed with her chosen image of an innocent bereft. But she pushed these thoughts aside.

'Maggie, you need to know that your father and I were in love.'

There was a pause. Sally sighed dramatically. Maggie tried to smile encouragingly but it was difficult. Somehow there was an odour coming from Sally. A sour, unwashed, dried-up odour that made her heave again. She bolted up her stomach and commanded herself to get a hold.

Sally looked at her with wobbly eyes. Could there yet be more tears, mused Maggie, in those eyes that had been wrung to distraction?

'One day, Maggie, my child, you too will know what it is to love.'

Between each sentence there was an audible gulp. The voice became louder, more drawn out and extravagant.

'When it happens to you, don't be afraid. Of course,' she smiled to herself in happy recollection, 'you may not feel as I do, so deeply. I am a particularly passionate and feeling woman. I have experienced sorrow and pain. I have known loss, such loss, Maggie. When I am touched by love now, that new love must scratch the scars of the old wounds. To love again, I must reopen that pain. Love and pain, the two go together.'

Sally looked up from the spell she had cast upon herself. Maggie suspected she had forgotten to whom she was talking.

Sally laughed a curt laugh. 'Ha! Oh the pain, little Maggie, if only I could protect you from it.'

Maggie doubted very much that she could.

'I want you to know, Maggie, that your father and I loved one another very much. Ours was the deep, deep passion that comes to weary souls who have found at last a place to rest.'

Alarmingly, Sally, fortified by her drink, which had been refilled twice since the beginning of the soliloquy, now took hold of Maggie's chin and pulled her face closer to hers. Maggie felt a hot, alcoholic air hit her nostrils.

I'm not going to be sick, I'm not going to be sick, she muttered inwardly. Yet she could hardly bear to keep her eyes open. The wrinkles of Sally's face seemed lined with grime. Grey mucus, malodorous tears, the gritty mouth pinched with soggy lipstick.

'I think you ought to know that your father was not alone when he died. We had enjoyed a wonderful night.'

Sally was peering at Maggie as if from behind a pair of pince-nez.

'You know what love is, don't you, dear?' she asked severely.

'Er . . . I think I know what you mean,' spluttered Maggie.

Sally sniffed long and hard, an inverted sigh.

'Well, your father and I enjoyed the greatest of physical passions. We confided together in our loneliness.'

'I see.'

'I hope you do. If you understand, it will be of the greatest comfort to you.'

Maggie couldn't see how this news could comfort anyone but Sally. She didn't comment.

'One day, my pure sweet innocent child, I pray you will know love like I have experienced.' Sally examined Maggie minutely and sighed again. 'It may not be, it is not for all.'

Maggie looked around the room. The bare furniture, the few possessions scattered limply with no sense of their belonging to her. The bunk falling apart. The threadbare rug, crumpled against the pale blue walls, paint peeling. Her life seemed so thinly attached to anything. For the first time she felt a ball of emotion rise in her throat, clouding her eyes. It was not for her father, it was for herself.

Sally saw. 'Cry, cry, my poor darling, we must all cry together.'

This thought was intolerable. Sally had barely acknowledged her father until three weeks previously, when, as far as Maggie could work out, she had finally failed with every other male on board.

'Leave me, Sally, please. I don't want to be rude but I need to be alone for a while.'

This was a deliberate ploy to complement Sally's sense of the dramatic. It worked.

'I understand,' she swooned. 'I understand. We can talk more later. I'm here for you. Of all people, I understand.' With this she stood up shakily and limped from the room.

Maggie felt relief. She turned and laid her face on the bed. Her nose tickled by its flaking fibres, she was seeking the familiar smell but feeling unutterably alone. Not suddenly bereft, but as if she had always been alone and only now had she recognized her true isolation.

She had come here, to this ship, on this journey, because there had been no better alternative. The decision had been made in the early days of her mother's illness. Maggie had been seven years old. She could barely remember. That period was such a blur. There was a time before that when her life was like others', when she lived in a small house with two parents. She lay face down like a child to remember. There was, she recalled, little communication between her parents, but that too was normal. She had loved her mother. A quiet woman, reflective. A dreamer according to her grandmother. Great Edie preferred the more extrovert daughter, Ruth. Maggie had been a little frightened of Ruth, her aunt. Frightened of her noise. Of the cacophony of excitement that buzzed around her. There was something dangerous about Ruth, whereas her mother was so gentle. Such a flimsy spirit, so easily knocked down by everyone else. So quiet. Great Edie despised it. But Maggie loved her mother. She loved the security she felt when she sat in her arms. That, she remembered like a shadow on her skin. The softness of her mother. Her head held by those soft, cold hands. She remembered looking into her mother's eyes. Grace. It was a good name for her.

When Ruth died, it took four years for her mother's fragile self to snap. Great Edie cursed and swore. Her father, always uncommunicative, fled from Maggie's needs. Great Edie shouted. So loud, even Harry heard. Shouted that he had driven Grace mad and, as usual, she was being left to clear up the mess that men left behind. Inadequate, fool, dolt, schmuck, no-good. Her words beat him out of the house like dust before a besom stick.

She heard the discussions. Draughts of words, when doors opened and closed again. Maggie sat in the parlour of her grandmother's house playing with the carpet. She heard their reluctance, the mutual begrudging.

'I wash my hands of my daughter the day she married you. I told her it would end in disaster. I'm not responsible, Harry, for the mess you find yerself in. She's your problem, Harry. I've reared enough children. I've got a daughter dead and the other a useless fool to take care of. I don't want to bring up a grandchild as well. She's going to be like her mother. I can see it in those eyes. You look into them and they're somewhere else. I tell you I don't want nothing more to do with it.'

There was nothing for him in London but incriminating looks and heavy conversation. He had been a small-time entertainer in big houses and small town halls. It could not have been hard, thought Maggie, to find badly paid work afloat in the golden age of cruising. With luxury liners spanning the globe, thousands of passengers desperate to shake off the post-war austerity and be part of the good times. The cruise life seemed like rock and roll.

He had not wanted to take her with him, she knew that. And really, she understood. A seven-year-old child, the one reminder of the mess that was left behind. She forgave him for that. She was a memory of the woman he could not talk to even in the time of her clarity.

And as she grew older, tormenting her father with her chatter, her life, her neediness, he became less and less able to give her what she needed. She reminded him of all the things he hated.

The mind games, that damn family. The darkness that had drawn him to Grace, that had fascinated him and repelled him just as quickly. And worse, she looked like her mother, she knew. Alone in her cabin, Maggie held up a hand mirror and looked at her own almond eyes. She stared at herself so that she would feel close to her mother. But, since this was another reason her father feared her and loathed her, she hated her face too.

All these thoughts kept her clinging to the pillow, shaking with fear. With a fear of the nothing that lay ahead. Or rather, hardly nothing. She felt ill, but now she had begun to understand. And the tears came. Hot tears, not remembering the past, but fearing the future.

12

Tongue

Sarah was convinced that she was looking for something. Why else would Alex check so often through the day's findings? If he was so fascinated why didn't he just undertake the process himself?

After cataloguing the library and finishing the study – her system now ran to thirty pages of meticulous text divided into different files for each room – she had moved on to a series of rooms that seemed largely for storage. Places where possessions had been stuffed as if the rooms were never intended to be walked into. The second was full of games. Dated games. Piles of them. Sarah was consumed with a desire to play them all. To open these decades' neglected boxes of entertainment. It seemed so cruel. Alex told her not to be silly.

The kiss. No word of it had been spoken since. She wondered what Alex thought, whether he was wondering, like her. Whether he was as completely uninterested as he seemed to be. She knew better than to take appearance as an absolute. One thing he could never disguise was his ability to give nothing away.

After a fleeting discomfort that she felt meeting his eye the next morning – that was the moment when he might have said something.

She walked into the kitchen later than usual. She hoped he would have moved on to his office already. But maybe there was, after all, a confrontational need in him, for he was sitting at the table surrounded by toast crumbs. Rings of orange juice and coffee overlapped in patterns.

His head was hidden behind the newspaper. He never read newspapers. The economic section too.

'Good morning.' She tried to speak brightly, then thought it sounded false and tried unsuccessfully to normalize the tone halfway through. It came out like a spoof Swedish accent. She blushed.

'Hi.' He peered over the newspaper. He looked exactly the same. Only maybe his look was a little too unflinching.

She sat down too. 'What are you up to today?' What a stupid question. What did he do any day, every day?

He sighed. 'I am near deadline on Vengeance. I have to finish it by next Tuesday.'

'Oh, what day is it today?'

He smiled. 'I'm not sure. I've got a feeling it's Friday. That's why I'm in a hurry. It could be later than that.'

She screwed up her eyes to read his newspaper.

'It says Wednesday on here.'

He was nonchalant. 'It's an old one.'

'Monday 6 June 1994. So it is.' She looked back to him. 'Why are you reading that?'

'I found it on the floor.'

'I mean, why are you reading an old newspaper?' She spoke impatiently.

He sniffed. 'Why a new one?'

'Is that a genuine question or a life philosophy?'

'Both, maybe. Newspapers are the same old shit over and over, right? The paper is recycled. The stories are reusable. If anything, old newspapers are more interesting because you can see how wrong we were.'

Banter. How reassuring. Even though she would shortly be lowering herself back down the black hole. Even though she knew things were different. It was nice to pretend.

He interrupted her thoughts. 'Oh, by the way . . .'

She hesitated and turned her head back.

'Yes?'

'Those guys who were here the other night are coming round again this evening.'

'Oh.'

He heard upset in her voice and sighed. 'No, don't sound like that. What I was going to say was I'd like you to join us. It was wrong of me to exclude you the other day. It must have been very irritating.'

Irritating. What an Alex word. Her emotional depths translated in his language into a pothole in the road. Maybe. Unless. Underneath.

But she looked at him warmly. 'I did feel a bit left out.'

'Well, please join us tonight.'

When she was searching through the room that day she came across more hair. This time a whole box full of it, a small, cardboard box. It was a relief not to be opening yet another faded 1960s board game. The lid was a little stuck and pulled off with a growl. More and more locks, evidently from different heads. If his grandmother really had died in a fire, Sarah mused, she must have taken a lot of people with her.

This time the hair was placed in small plastic bags though some was just wrapped in greaseproof paper. There must have been well over a hundred locks. All different shades and textures, from fine doll blond to wiry black. Each lock was tied with a length of fine cotton. Attached to the cotton, a tiny label with more numbers. Sarah stared, rubbing lock after lock between her fingers.

The locks were alive, evoking the heads they had adorned. Though it was silent, this house was so full. It was impossible to make an impression on it. Her own self was choked. Which was odd, because she was not aware of having had a sense of self before. Yet now it was suffocated. When her earliest memories were of being closed behind doors, away from conversations, it was strange that this house should make her feel so on edge. And Alex was no more accepted. He stuck to his portion of the house.

She had to stop herself dropping the box. The hair seemed to be writhing. Her chest tightened. She breathed in wildly and tore her eyes away. She looked up across the dark room and was surprised to find that she was alone. She expected people. She got up and was drawn to the sketchy vision of the photos on the wall. University events. The 1970s. Midi-skirts, thick-framed glasses, man-made fibres, the self-conscious smiles of the people, young and clever. Their eyes following her. She reached the edge of the room and touched the closed curtain. It felt fragile in her fingers. When she pulled it back impulsively, dust showered into the air. The French windows behind were grey and dirty. An old handle with a vertical bolt. She was surprised that it moved easily. The wooden windows, twenty winters swollen, burst open on to steps down to the back garden. A forest of brambles. She had never been out here before. A patio of broken stone lay before her, weeds piercing the slabs. Rusty garden furniture, black iron latticed in diamonds, was still arranged in a sociable circle for cocktails. The only drinkers were an army of snails who lapped the rainwater that clung to the metalwork. She was imagining what the garden must have been. She turned slowly round 360 degrees. The right-hand fence, the long grass, nettles, trees, the left-hand fence, the patio, the window, the view through the curtains, almost black from here. And then she heard voices.

Shrieks, whoops, yelling, long-syllabled voices trying to step above one another and, underscoring, a low beat of music and, distinctly, the smell of marijuana. It was over in an instant.

Alex did not like drama, especially when he was working, so she saved the discovery. Then, when they met again in the early evening, she said, 'There's something I must show you. I found something so odd.'

'Really?' There was an instant enthusiasm. Like he knew what she was going to produce. Or at least he hoped he knew.

But when she brought out the box it was clear that this was not what he was hoping for. There was still something else. The palpable disappointment on his face was total. For a second. If she had not been waiting for his reaction, if she had not known to look out for such a nuance in him, she would have missed it.

'Oh – that,' he said flatly.

Sarah spoke in an incredulous voice. 'Alex, it's a box of hair!'

'Yeah.'

'Why?'

'Why what?'

He could be unbearable.

'Why is there a box of hair in your parents' house?'

'It's my house.'

'Yes, I know.' She tutted at his obfuscation. 'Your house then. I spend so much time looking through their stuff, I forget, I muddle words up. But the point is' – she jabbed with her finger as if to push the conversation physically back in the direction she wanted it – 'the point is, what the hell is a box of hair doing in there?'

He paused. Searching for an answer.

'I've no idea.'

'But you knew it was there?'

He looked her straight in the eye. A sure sign of deception.

'It's been in the family for years. No one knows how it got there. My mother thought it might be her great-aunt's; she was an eccentric old woman. Just the kind of thing she'd do apparently. Ask total strangers for a lock of hair to complete her collection.'

Sarah looked at him, unconvinced. One eyebrow up, quizzically, the mouth pursed, almost amused. An expression that was more usually pointing in her direction, stuck on Maggie's face.

'And the story about your inflammatory grandmother?'

He looked, unusually, coy.

'Yeah, I admit I made that one up.'

'Hmm.'

'Still,' he said, half-heartedly, 'good work.'

'Thanks . . .' She was reluctant to mention it since he was being uncooperative. 'And I heard voices.'

'Oh, how strange.' That was all he would say. What was it she was looking for? She played with the thoughts in her head. Juggling them round as they sat in silence. Resting before the evening preparations.

It was clear to her now that the house was merely a subsidiary job. Not a complete bluff – the work needed to be done. But it was not what she was here for.

Maybe it was something to do with the game. That, of course, she would discover tonight. She felt fresh air blow through her. Being kept from the secret had been gnawing away at her, cutting her up. It had been poisoning her thoughts, slowly. She could never stand not knowing. Like Maggie said, not knowing didn't make the unknown important, by virtue of its secrecy. But it enthralled her. The secrecy alone made it inflate in her mind until she thought she would burst.

Alex had seen that she needed to know. Maybe, better still, he had felt the need to tell her. He wanted to tell her. That thought warmed her. She felt loved, even if his oddball friends already knew.

They arrived, like last time, a little after ten. Matthew came first, in an extravagant pair of black leather trousers and a purple shirt tucked in tight so his generous stomach bubbled over the top. His voice boomed through the door. 'Alex, sweet. *Nous sommes arrivés.*'

Next came thin James, the weasel, in tired denim, bright eyes taking in the hallway. Then Hassim, long, elegant, wearing, for some reason, a suit, dark, sharply cut – so incongruous in the surroundings and with the overwhelmingly shabby clothes on everyone else.

'Hi.' Matthew spoke to Sarah automatically, as a presence in the hall. He bit his lip before doing the same to the hatstand. And he looked back at Sarah properly, as if to check that she was not, in fact, a piece of furniture.

Seeing this, she shuddered and mumbled, 'Hello again.'

Alex ushered them in. If the men were surprised that Sarah was joining them this time, they didn't show it. Sarah had more opportunity to take in the three of them. What a disparate group. As she handed Hassim a vodka, he looked like some Bollywood James Bond. She felt underdressed, as if she should be in some shimmering black plunge number, hair tied up in a knot to set off $60,000 diamond earrings.

When she gave a bottle of lager to James she felt transformed into rough. Or at least, a rough's bit of stuff. He looked like an undernourished fake perfume salesman pitching up on an orange crate on Oxford Street. For him she felt impossibly smart. Why dress up when she was about to be stood round a piss-stained lamp-post, tapping her foot?

Matthew was tall. But more outstanding was his girth. He must be twenty stone at least. Sarah wasn't sure how she should be dressed when she handed him a red Martini. Maybe an entertainer's assistant. A bunny outfit, with fluffy ears and laddered fishnets. She could see him running a lap-dancing club. She had worked in one for an afternoon and the manager there had the same oily forehead and lascivious breathing, the air grating over his fatty throat.

She and Alex drank red wine. That made her feel good. That they were similar while the others were different. As she poured for Alex, she felt inexplicably proud. His thin pale face looked intelligent, concentrating on the red liquid as it fell. The lines on his face pleased her.

They ordered a Chinese. Again this was, she conceded, promotion. She was less a serving wench, even though the guests sat around, legs stretched out over the floor, sinking into their seats, indicating that it was her job to open the door and dish it up. Alex sat upright but he still didn't move.

Had he told them that she was going to be introduced to the new game? That she came higher in his list of priorities? That, as his closest confidante, naturally she would have to know the secrets of the game? That they, whoever they were, wherever they came from, would have to defer to her ideas?

Had he told them – was he telling them, she wondered, as she collected the greasy bag from the delivery guy – that they two, in fact, had a more intimate knowledge of each other now? No, of course not. He had told her nothing in ten years; he was hardly going to talk now to these acquaintances. While she wanted them to know her status, she didn't want him to tell them. Maybe they would feel it, the atmosphere between them, the unspoken communication. That Alex was different in an indefinable way. She carried the bag into the kitchen and awkwardly picked out the tin trays. A trail of sauce dripped down her fingers which she licked. She tasted, in sequence, the sour, then the sweet.

Why, she wondered, did a few physical seconds with Alex feel more emotionally demanding than almost anything else? Not that it was a particularly pleasurable memory. No. It was just affecting.

They ate. Discussing a string of topics loosely connected. A concatenation. She was not participating but taking in the scene. She never performed well in groups. Perhaps because she saw it as a performance. She felt judged. Instead, she drank the conversation along with her wine and looked forward to the beginning of the game.

Alex never seemed to enjoy himself.

The evening wore on, soporific conversation continued. Alex brought out more wine. 'I can indulge tonight,' he said to her questioning glance. 'I'm not working tomorrow.'

She looked at her watch. Midnight already.

She caught Alex on her way back from the toilet. She hadn't liked to do it, to speak out of turn, but she could wait no longer.

He was filling the cheese board. Stacking biscuits precariously. Concentrating so closely he did not notice her presence. She touched him lightly on the arm.

He shrank back, startled, which made her wonder how unconcerned he really was about the library. He gathered himself up and smiled a slightly boozy smile. Not unwelcoming. She pushed forward.

'Alex, don't keep me hanging on any longer . . . when are we going to start the game?'

He looked at her blankly. 'What game?'

She became shriller, less dignified. 'The secret game, the game you play with these people.'

He stared at her. Perplexed, a lack of comprehension for a moment. Then, cognition and discordance.

'Oh.' He spoke hoarsely. 'Oh, we're not doing that tonight. No, they've just come round socially.'

She stared in turn at him. No game?

'No, Sarah.' he was speaking again, more abruptly. 'That other thing is strictly between the four of us. No one else can know yet, I told you that.'

'So I'm still not allowed?' Her voice was clipped.

He sighed and uncharacteristically ran his fingers through his black hair. He was not given to gesticulations. His face was immobile and his body taut, wooden. But now, under pressure, he squirmed.

'It's not a question of not allowed. I don't know why you're making such a big thing of something so insignificant. It's just another job. I've signed a privacy agreement. We all have.'

The excuse fell weightlessly to earth. A feather flying from his mouth. Sarah felt anger.

'So all the while you knew I was thinking that we were going to play the game, you knew that we were going to do nothing of the kind. You let them all know how stupid I was. Everyone was laughing.'

'Oh, don't be ridiculous,' he said, half shouting, half laughing. 'You've had too much to drink. Either have some more and calm down, or go to bed and sleep it off.'

'Go to bed?' she said slowly, aghast. 'You are telling me to go to bed? Oh, OK then. I'll go to bed if you want me to, Alex. I'll go to bed, you know me.'

She remembered children laughing, from a long time ago, cruel screams. She turned and walked out of the room. Slightly disturbed, Alex returned to the dining room. Matthew was swearing that he could fit the entire length of a candle up his backside. Alex felt the control of the evening slipping away from him.

The conversation was interrupted by loud bangs through the ceiling. The others looked startled. Alex spoke hastily. 'Sarah has some furniture to move back before she can get to bed. She wanted to do it before she got too tired. You know she's sorting the house out, don't you?'

But the justification was largely for himself and attention had already moved on.

It was gone one when Sarah returned. They had begun a poker game. James had rolled up and tickly sweet fumes filled the room.

Her eyes sparkled.

'Got everything sorted out?' Alex asked quickly.

She looked at him airily, coldly. She could shut out anybody if she wanted to. 'Of course.'

'Excellent.'

She walked jauntily to the table.

'Do you want me to deal you a hand?'

'Oh, don't worry, Alex, I'll just watch. I don't want to . . . interrupt proceedings or get in the way.'

She smiled beatifically.

'Oh, you wouldn't be interrupting,' he said icily, hating her sarcasm and wondering what he had done.

'That's awfully sweet of you. I'll just slip in quietly here.' She sat between Matthew and Hassim.

'Sure.'

If he could exclude her she could exclude him. She could make him feel what she felt. The outsider. She had that power. As they played, Sarah clapped and shrieked in exaggerated girlishness. Having thought her distant and uninterested, the men began to warm to her new mood. If they spoke she laughed with a delighted tinkle.

James did not receive the brunt of it, being opposite, but Hassim and Matthew were showered with praise.

'Another flush, Matthew! You have the luck of the devil. Or is it more sinister than that?'

By now her sentences were completed with a touch, a stroke on the arm. A coda to reinforce her phrase. At first they accepted her physical flatteries wordlessly.

Then Matthew began to make little asides. Little nods in her direction, acknowledging glances. She was surprised that of all of them, he should have taken the bait. She had assumed he was gay. But maybe he just had the largest appetite. When his new hand was dealt, she pulled it towards her. So that they two might share the secret. To get a good view she had to lean in towards him. With each round the angle increased. Five degrees, ten, twenty. By the forty-five-degree point she had to put her hand on his thigh to support herself.

'Matthew's got a wonderful hand,' she slurred. 'You should see what I can see.' She sounded childish and she did not care.

Alex took no outward notice. He did not see that, at the mention of Matthew's wonderful hand, Sarah pulled the obscured other hand on to her own lap. 'A wonderful hand,' she echoed. 'He'll beat you all, I bet.'

For the first time the unnatural loudness in Matthew vanished. In silence he turned to her, eyes widening as hers narrowed. He looked at her, all of her. Or all that was visible of her slumped form cut in half by the table.

She noticed perspiration breaking out on his upper lip.

He held his breath. She smiled. A dirty smile. All lips and promise.

Matthew yawned suddenly and broke the silence. 'Do you know what, lads?' he said.

The others looked up.

'I'm fucking knackered. I'm going to have to call it a night.'

Sarah smiled. 'Well, it's very late. I expect we're all tired, aren't we?'

She looked steadily at Alex. He said nothing but looked grim. He knew, she thought, painfully satisfied.

Alex could not sleep through the noise. He left his bedroom and drifted down to the room with the TV. He watched a film, any film, about a woman who lived alone in a country mansion with her Chinese manservant and had an identical twin who arrived in an old Rover, sweeping up the drive.

'And do you know the most amazing thing?' said Sarah, who had mercilessly woken Alex up on the sofa the next day. For a moment he forgot how he came to be there and welcomed her presence. Then he remembered. He didn't speak.

'The most interesting thing about having sex with Matthew is that it answered something I've often wondered. Which is what it's like to have sex with a fat person.'

Alex pushed his face into the cushion and tried to pull it round his ears. It wouldn't reach and anyway her voice, shrill, insistent, penetrating, was not going to leave him that easily.

'I mean,' she continued with false brightness, 'what it's really like. It's not as different as I thought. Maybe' – she put a finger on her chin quizzically – 'that's because he's a young fat person and the rolls of flesh are still relatively tight. Anyway, to be honest I didn't have the courage to go underneath. I was afraid of coming out with my breasts two sizes smaller, or twenty years older, all the life squeezed out. It had to be one or the other.'

She paused for breath to survey the damage. He still didn't look at her. He looked rather ill and stared ahead, gripping the cushion defensively to his chest. He didn't understand her motives. And he didn't care to. She seemed to seek out misery, making things worse, less comfortable, harder. He couldn't understand that.

'In fact I rather enjoyed it. You know what you said about tomato juice. You were right. Such an acrid flavour, but kind of savoury.

'Another thing though, scientifically speaking, strictly in the name of biology, I must report that there was one thing I noticed that distinguished fat sex from all the thin sex I've had over the years. Shall I tell you what it was? I bet you'd never guess, unless you've slept with a fat woman, that is. Have you, Alex?'

She zoomed close up to his eyes, knocking his nose. He winced. He could not escape. Not even in this bald room that he'd created for himself, TV and bare floors.

'Fat sex? Have you, Alex? Hmm, no answer. Well, I'll tell you. It's the tongue. You never would have thought it, would you?

But it is. The tongue itself gets really fat. Matthew's tongue was so fat I thought I was going to gag. Can you imagine? It was such a curiosity. The rest, the thighs, the bulbous belly, the rolling neck, that you don't notice if you close your eyes. I suppose our bodies are less sensitive. But the mouth, Alex, that was really something.'

She shook his catatonic shoulders. 'What do you think?'

Then he overwhelmed her, grabbed her arms and brought her shaking to a halt. His eyes were like stones.

'I think you're disgusting.' He trembled with violence. He threw her aside and stormed out of the room. A few minutes later she heard the front door slam. She was left to wonder what she had done.

13

Pine

She was worried about Sarah. She wondered why she hadn't called. She worried how she could tell her the news about her father. But Sarah was only part of her thoughts.

Maggie had seen John – or Rudi, as she found it impossible to call him anything else – twice since the first meeting. He was undeniably pleasant company. But she had not called him as he had requested. After all these years she wanted a little dignity.

He was waiting for her again when she next visited Grace. She went every Wednesday. Her client Rosa, an elderly Spanish Catholic, a wealthy widow, lived in her childhood and believed that the shops closed at lunchtime.

Today Grace was noisy.

'Sailor Jim, Sailor Jim
I couldn't get enough of him.'

Just that. Over and over. Sometimes sung, atonally. Sometimes not. Maggie was developing a headache. The woman at the next table thought she was the Virgin Mary.

'I've got thirty-five children, you know. Michael, the eldest, he's an arkycheque. John works on a lathe. Peter, he's me rock of course. Then there's Jesus, he was boiled in oil – only thirty-three . . . it's no age, is it? No age at all.'

The afternoon passed slowly. At last Maggie left the heat of the sealed room and escaped into the breeze with a sigh of relief. As she walked out she passed the main entrance of the old

Victorian building. And there he was, leaning against the Gothic porch, an intricate façade of peeling glory.

'You're here again,' she said.

He smiled. 'You've lost none of your observational skills then.'

She wouldn't play.

'I can't go for a drink tonight, I'm seeing a friend.' And it was true this time.

'I wasn't assuming you would. I was, you know, just staying in touch.' His eyebrows knotted together defensively. 'I don't want to lose touch again, Maggie, it's been a long time. A hell of a long time.'

He talked like an old American. A crusty Texan walking against the sun. She tutted at such foolishness, and then sniggered. She remembered herself and looked at him sharply.

'This is ridiculous. It's too ridiculous. I can't make sense of it. The whole thing. I don't know. I've lived a whole life since I knew you.'

'Me too,' he said.

'Well, doesn't that count for something?'

'What do you mean?' He really was puzzled. He stood up from the building. A teaspoon of stone crumbled away. He said, 'See, we're all getting old.' Then an interested afterthought: 'This is the building that she used to be in, right?'

Maggie looked up at it and patted the white stone. 'Yep, they took everything out in the late 'eighties and they built those new buildings.' She gesticulated at the squat cream bungalow complex from which she had come.

'Why don't they knock the old building down?'

She shrugged. 'I don't know. Ran out of money. Historical interest? I think at one time they were hoping to turn it into luxury flats but nobody liked the neighbours.' She shrugged again, then stopped and looked at him rather desperately. 'How can I talk to you now, meet you now without making everything else invalid?'

'We're old friends, what's wrong with that?'

She felt relief, then disappointment – did she? Surely it could not be so straightforward. This was the tragedy of her whole life. It could not be dismissed in a sentence. They began to walk across the neglected grass.

'Were you married?' she asked in a monotone.

'Yes,' he said, as if unsure of how to answer.

'What happened?'

He looked at her anxiously. 'My wife left me fifteen years ago.'

'So why come back now?'

'It took a long time to get up the courage.'

She repeated insistently. 'So why now?'

'I couldn't leave it any longer. I'm sixty-five. I'm going to be an old man soon.'

He looked up. His head before had been bowed. 'Also it was watching my father die. Last year. He was ninety-one. Finally went. Eighteen years after my mother. He'd been seriously ill for at least ten. I couldn't leave when I thought he was going to die. And we had so many false alarms. Every time we'd all rush over. My sister from England. My brother from New York. We'd all be there, hanging around the bed. He'd be sitting wrapped in his old blankets looking like a bum. Babbling on, in a string of incomprehensible mucus. But we all had to listen, he needed an audience. We'd tiptoe round the house, whispering. Then he'd get better.

'A few months later we'd go through the whole damn thing again. He couldn't get enough curtain calls. You know he used to be an entertainer too? Amateur stuff. Except when he retired and he took to the streets. Even then he didn't need the money but I guess people threw him coins because he looked so old. He used to tap dance even though by the end his feet could barely lift off the sidewalk.

'And as long as the audience kept coming back he wasn't going to let us down.' Rudi's pupils were dilating in hazy recollection.

Maggie thought wildly, father, brother, sister, what was this? This was all new. A family? A parent he was devoted to? He had never mentioned any of them before.

'At least once a year we'd all rush over,' he continued. 'You can imagine how frustrating it was for the others. At least I was in town. Then my sister couldn't make it one time. I called to tell her that the doctors said he could die at any moment.

' "Yeah, right," she says. "But they don't mean Dad. They

mean any of us. I ain't got time for philosophy. Tell him I'll come next month."

'So I told him and of course he died during the night. None of us were with him. We felt bad.'

Rudi sighed. She noticed that she was walking to his step. At his pace. Empathetic footsteps. It was automatic.

'His death was a turning point. It was like it crystallized everything. During my lousy marriage, I pushed you to the back of my mind. Now, with everything gone, it became urgent. Nightmares where you were being tortured while I just stood by and watched. Or I dreamed about who you were now. You had grown taller and you spoke to me with total indifference.'

He turned to her, his face framed by the walls of the old building. 'And that I knew your father had died just before I left, hurt even more. I had my father all those years. You were so young and I left you there.'

And suddenly he burst into tears. His head bent down, shamed in his hands. There was no hair at the top of his head.

Maggie didn't know what to do. So she sat on the bench which they had unaccountably now settled on and looked into the greenery, the hospital grounds, scruffy rhododendron bushes. Herbaceous borders dying back after the height of summer. How often, as a child and as an adult, she had sat in this verdure, watching the revolving seasons.

For a few moments he shook silently.

'There there,' she said, stiffly tapping him on the back.

His head rose slowly upwards. His eyes were red. He looked at her.

And they both laughed. A painful laugh but there was still humour inside it.

'Maggie, I'm sorry. Forgive me.' He wiped his eyes.

'What for?'

'I know I have no right to cry.'

'You go ahead. I'm sure we've all got reasons to cry.'

'I'm sorry for everything, though, I don't know . . . It sounds so phoney, inadequate.'

She smiled. And breathed in. Summer air, sweet florals, so peaceful suddenly.

'Well, it's certainly pointless. I don't know if I want apologies. Nothing you say will ever make you feel better.'

'No.'

Then surprise registered in his expression as it hit him that her sentence had not finished as he had anticipated.

'What can I say to make *you* feel better?'

She sat serene and played with her hands, rubbing the arm of the bench, picking at pale green moss like a scab.

'Oh, I felt better a long time ago.'

'Really?'

'Well.' She hesitated and looked coolly into his eyes. 'Not really, really. I recovered. I got over it. I suppose I forgave. I didn't forget. But I had to get on with it. I had a child.'

'A daughter to raise,' he echoed.

He looked in danger of crying again, she noticed. She spoke hastily. She had used this technique on herself.

'So do you have any children?' Then, if she hadn't been too old, she would have blushed. She wiped her thick fringe away from her face and felt that her forehead was moist. 'I mean, any other children.'

He swallowed, coughed, moved a little. 'Three.'

She thought about it but it didn't affect her.

His hurried voice continued apologetically, 'All girls.'

'Oh. So you're used to them then?'

'I'm sure they're very different from Sarah,' he said supportively. 'My other three are so very all-American.'

'Well,' she pondered, 'Sarah is certainly very British. Although she's very dark.'

This felt to Maggie like the kind of casual conversation one might have with the dentist, while he was screwing the drill together. Overtly light but both parties know there is pain ahead.

She looked at her watch.

'Oh, God, I've got to go. I really have. You can accompany me back if you don't believe me.'

He raised a confused eyebrow. 'Why shouldn't I believe you?'

She smiled. 'Well, I don't know. Sarah never believes me when I say I'm going out.'

He clicked with exasperation. 'Aren't they always like that? They grow up and they think they invented going out. I have to keep quiet in front of my kids so no one panics.'

'What are you up to that might cause panic?'

169

'Don't even think about it.' He smiled. ' "Old man occasionally still goes to movies" – it's not front-page news, is it?'

'You should stop calling yourself old,' she said, almost crossly. 'You might consider yourself old. I'm barely middle-aged.'

'I know,' he said encouragingly. 'Why d'you think I'm so interested?'

It was a curious mix of the sacred and the profane. They came across topics that were suddenly shocking and then slunk back into the almost funny and idle curiosity. Maggie was not sure which was worse. Or better. Surely there could be little harm in seeing him like this, while she felt in control?

She was almost proud of her performance. Not just outside but within. She felt calm. Seeing him, being tested now, was a confirmation of her success. After years of working on it, she was able to control her emotions to a large extent. After the initial shock, which had nearly killed her, she was now well defended.

They walked out of the grounds. To their right was a wilder garden, with towering trees, hiding the road.

'Is that where you played?' he said. 'The place you used to talk about?'

'Mmm.'

This time he had a car. 'I rented it,' he said to explain the lurid red sheen.

They were easier with each other. She felt that he was pushing her a little. In an attempt to, what, move things along? She shuddered at the thought. She didn't have an acceptable way of thinking about it, even to herself. There were no words these days.

'You can drop me at home,' she said, aware of the significance or the potential for drawing significance, though really none was there.

'Not afraid of me any more?' He spoke lightly.

But she felt a flash of anger. It came from nowhere, a bullet.

'Don't imply that I was some stupid girl for being wary before. That was just sensible. Don't insult me. I'm not a child any more, you know.'

'OK, OK.' He held his hands up, as if he, not she, faced the bullet. 'I'm sorry.'

'I know, you said that.'

Suddenly he saw the indifferent face of his nightmares. Flustered, he said, 'I didn't mean it, I was just kidding. I don't want to upset you. Christ, that's the last thing I want.'

She stared at him angrily. Looking into his old eyes. Warm and anxious. He struggled, but he held her immutable gaze.

After a few seconds' searching, she spoke: 'Well, OK then. But for God's sake—'

'Yes?' He was meek and breathless.

'Don't be so bloody afraid of upsetting me.' She shouted so loud, he jumped at the wheel.

He looked confused. 'Oh, OK then.'

They continued in silence while she directed him to her flat. A halting combination of truncated words and hand signals.

The car hummed through the suburban streets. Past houses, cluttered gardens. People, scruffy, shabby people, heads down, laden with bags. The air dusty, squally winds blowing dirt. She wound down the window and inhaled the familiar incense; petrol, dirt, sweet wrappers, stale batter, kebabs, rubbish over-flowing industrial bins.

He stopped. 'So this is where you live.' He craned his neck to look out of the window. His wrinkles stretched in the strain. He saw a tidy façade. A trim block of flats. Fastidious. Newly raked gravel to either side of a path.

She saw her opportunity.

'You haven't lost your observational skills either then?'

He looked appreciative. And yet it was as if seeing her rejuvenated him. He seemed younger now. She got out of the car.

Euphemistic coffee invitations from a hundred black-and-white films ran through her mind. Jack Lemmon, Cary Grant, Walter Matthau.

He wound down the window. 'Would it be too much to ask for your number?'

Although she actually wasn't, she felt angry again, as if that were the right way to be. She felt muddled. This constant shifting. Was this what she had felt like as an adolescent or was this more like the menopause? She turned briefly round, bending down slightly to his level.

'Yes, I'm afraid it would.'

'OK.' He tried not to sound too humble. He needn't have bothered. She wasn't listening.

She was wondering if what she said had sounded suggestive. It did to her. From nowhere her mouth opened and words, unplanned words, came out. And her hands were on her hips.

'Look. I don't know what you want. I won't say "and I don't care", because of course I do. But I'm not about to have my life pulled sideways by your mysteries.'

She took a deep breath.

'If we are going to spend any more time together, you are going to have to explain exactly where the hell you've been and why. I refuse to continue blindfolded. It may have been all right when I was a child—'

At that word again he winced visibly.

'—but it's not now. You could have left me alone. You chose to come back. So you face the consequences. Stop pussyfooting around. Do you understand?'

He nodded and straightened himself as if this outburst were a relief. But it was a bizarre conversation to be having in the street.

'Fair enough, I promise.'

She walked into the flat. Away, alone, tiredness assaulted her. She had not realized it before, but the whole experience was entirely exhausting. Utterly. She sat on the sofa and found her forehead hitting her knees. With a sigh she picked up the phone.

'Hello, Julia? Hello, yes, it's Maggie. What? Yes. I am. Exhausted. Can we have that dinner next week instead, do you think? Yes. That's right. Yes. Mmm. Mmm. Really? Mmm. Just as well then. Yes, much better. OK then. Yes. Yes. OK, Julia. Mmm. All right then. Same time next week? . . . Yes. No, actually can we make it Tuesday? I'm rather tired on Wednesdays. My mother. Yes, yes. Exactly. OK then. All right. Yes. OK. Yes. Thank you. And you. Bye.'

She put the phone down with relief. Julia. She didn't get much out of seeing her anyway, to be honest. You couldn't keep reminiscing about a shared six months years ago. She wanted to be alone and reminisce about a whole lifetime. Suddenly, after all this time, she almost wanted to torment herself.

In the morning there would be work and Great Edie. But now

it was early. She would have a bath. A long luxuriant bath. A womanly bath. Hours in length and even deeper. Perfumes, oils, wafting fumes. The mirror would steam over and she would relax. With these delicious thoughts, she fell asleep.

'I'm not well, since you ask. Though I don't know why you did since you don't care.'

This barrage peppered through the door preceding the craggy features of her grandmother.

'I'm not decent. Close yer eyes.'

'They're closed.'

'Liar,' she snapped, more good-humouredly. Pulling the door open. Maggie pushed. It was, as always, a struggle.

Eventually Maggie and her grandmother sat together at the kitchen table. A rectangular, folded, yellow laminated table flecked with strands of black. Maggie inhaled staunchly.

'So, Edie, how've you been?'

'I don't know what you're so interested for. I mind me own business, don't go poking into your business and you don't go poking into mine.'

'Have it your own way then, you normally do.'

Great Edie clacked her teeth irritably. Maggie put the kettle on.

'What d'you want me to do for you today? Hoovering, change the bed?'

'That casserole you made me was rotten.' Edie enunciated every syllable. And if that wasn't clear enough, she repeated, 'Rotten.'

Maggie was unfazed. 'Well, I liked the bit I had.' Great Edie raised her eyes to the ceiling in despair.

'Well, what do you know, eh? You've never liked food. You're a skinny bleedin' bugger, always have been. And yer dinner's skinny too.' She nodded her head to her chin belligerently.

She didn't hear Maggie mumble, 'That's because I don't roll it in lard like you used to.'

The kettle was beginning to sing – a screeching soprano. The kind of singing, thought Maggie, that Great Edie would do if she could.

'Tea?'

Her grandmother raised her chin suspiciously. 'Make sure you don't put too much milk in it.'

'Well, why don't you put the milk in yourself?' Maggie tilted the jug towards Edie provocatively. It was a small cream-coloured jug, with frilly edges. A remnant of the past.

Great Edie sniffed in disgust. 'You know I can't pour no more. I'm as good as crippled. I've worked my fingers to the bone looking after this family and what do I get?'

'Not much, eh?' said Maggie. 'Just me slaving for you twice a week.'

Great Edie took no notice. 'My own granddaughter begrudging me a cup of tea.' Her voice trailed off into her wispy white beard.

So Maggie poured the milk. And placed the cup and saucer (which her grandmother insisted on despite struggling more every year with her shaking fingers on the delicate handle) carefully in front of her nose. It was only here that Edie would see it, for she was tunnel-visioned now. She could see almost nothing that was not in a direct line in front of her eyes. Of course she denied it, spitting vituperatively at anyone who dared to suggest that she needed help.

'So,' drawled Maggie, shifting uncomfortably against the hard wooden chair. Three slats dug aggressively into her back.

She tried again.

'What shall I do for you today? I don't think you're quite up for a bath, are you?' She inhaled distastefully. 'Not that it would be a bad idea. But no point being overambitious, eh?'

When she looked at the old woman she was clearly nowhere near the kitchen and the cleaning. Her eyes were almost closed. Great Edie slowly turned her head to Maggie. Her eyes were full of hate.

'Have you forgotten what that man did to you?'

She'd got it. It had to happen. It always happened. Maggie opened her mouth to say 'What?' – an incredulous '*What?*' – but nothing came out. She shuddered. The inevitability. The claustrophobia of being watched. If she felt like a dog in a cage, her grandmother would say, yes, a bitch. Great Edie saw everything. She always had. If there had to be a clairvoyant in the family, why couldn't it be a benign one? Great Edie spoke again, dragging Maggie out of her stupor.

'Because if you have forgotten what that man did to you, you're a bigger fool than that mother of yours.' Great Edie folded her arms with a new energy that made her suddenly years younger. 'And if you have forgotten, I haven't. Don't forget who had to support you because of him. A stupid girl. A child with a baby. Don't forget who gave you money, when I had precious little enough of me own, since I was dumped in it by my rotten husband. Oooh, I sometimes wonder if I'm the only one with any sense.'

Her husband's death she always used as evidence of his and all his gender's supreme stupidity – and selfishness. It would never have happened to her.

Maggie looked at her helplessly. She said nothing. She could think of nothing to say.

'How many times you seen him?'

'Four.'

'Oh my God!' Edie raised her hands in the air in a wave of woe. Her face creasing more, if it were possible. Her expression, even in neutral, was reminiscent of a woman who had toiled for years in Siberia without a coat. Now it was positively tragic. 'What will become of us?' she cried. 'What will become of us? The family is in ruins!'

'It's not that bad.'

Her grandmother temporarily stopped her wailing to look at Maggie in astonishment.

'Not that bad, she says!'

Great Edie exchanged a look of disbelief with the kettle. The kettle nodded malicious agreement in whispering steam. Maggie looked at it too. It was at least as old as she was. How could a kettle make her feel so censured? Somehow it did. Everything in this house disliked her. Disapproved. As if the utensils had a memory, engraved in their steel, that they had worked overtime for her and the baby just when they were looking forward to retirement.

She shivered. She always felt cold in this kitchen. It was too old and unwieldy. Never clean. Cracks between the cupboards. Great Edie disapproved of fitted kitchens. Too easy, for one who enjoyed suffering almost as much as she liked to wish it upon other people.

Ancient, permanently grubby linoleum. Yellow cupboards that

clung perilously to the wall, rattling when the South London trains rolled into Herne Hill. Glass-fronted – small shelves, stacked with ever-dwindling piles of porcelain, smashed and never replaced. And the old-fashioned utensils. The grater the size of a head. Hard black. The potato scraper, the knives, the egg slice all forged in iron and steel. All designed to cause pain. And how they did. Then and now.

She looked at Great Edie. 'What the hell does it matter?'

Edie made a face. 'And her language! She speaks to her own grandmother with such words. Wash your mouth out when you speak to me like that.' She added quixotically, 'You dirty bugger.'

'But really, Edie, I know what he did to me – to you, to Sarah. But what's the point in harping on about it? It's not going to do any harm seeing him now.'

Her grandmother could barely express her derision.

'And what about Sarah, I'd like to know? Your only child. Have you even thought about her? I know you didn't then, but have you now?'

Great Edie loved the moral high ground. She was so shrunken it was the one place from which she could still look down on people. Maggie glowered.

'I've called her six, seven times. She hasn't called me back. I'm rather worried about her actually, she doesn't normally leave it this long.'

'And what are you going to tell her? Have you thought about that?'

'I've thought about it, and I think I'll just have to be honest. What she does is entirely up to her. I'm not going to have any expectations.'

Great Edie snorted. 'What a can of worms. You don't know what you're getting yerself into.'

Maggie smiled weakly. There was apprehension in her voice.

'I know that it could upset Sarah. That's why I'm going to tell her alone. Give her the opportunity to have nothing to do with him. She knows the history. She's very matter-of-fact about it.'

Great Edie shook her head in derision. 'Fifty years old and she still talks like a baby. Still she learns nothing.' She picked up her cup. In her hand it wobbled dangerously, even though she tried to steady it with the other. Maggie never poured more than half a cup. Still there were many spillages. Great Edie's chair was spotted with stains.

'You're worse than your mother, you are. At least she makes mistakes only once. You make them again and again.'

This struck Maggie as particularly unfair. Her mother was no longer in a position to make mistakes, even less repeat them, since she was still living in the original. Anything she did now was exonerated. Her damage was not her fault, thought Maggie bitterly; if anybody was to blame, it was her lax daughter.

Maggie, however, was still fighting. Could she not have a little intrigue in her life? Did she still have to protect the daughter she had already given up everything for?

Everything, nothing. It was not as if there had been a glittering path winding before her. But still there would have been more chances. She could have ventured further if she had not been chained to the washing cycle. If she had not been financially indebted to the most ungracious of benefactors.

'So what else have you seen then, Great Edie?' She sighed at the dilemma always within her, not wanting to go along with her grandmother but wanting to know. 'Since you saw him, you might as well let me know what's in store.'

Her grandmother shrugged as she always did when asked for valuable information. She was garrulous only with trivia.

'I see very little. '

Between gritted teeth Maggie said, 'Well, tell me what you do see then.'

A heavy sigh. 'Always you prod what should be left untouched. That is your downfall. You never listen.'

Maggie smiled encouragingly, her exasperation disguised behind her teeth. Slowly, despite her conscious antagonism, Great Edie was being consumed by instinct.

The crabby old woman looked almost serene. Possessed. Her mouth opened. The voice was hers, but lighter. Unfettered by prejudices. There was somebody else in her seat. Maggie knew it. She remembered. That different voice rang through the house in the days when Great Edie had paying clients. A voice of reason. Yet it made no sense since Edie claimed she was a fake.

Her grandmother now sat more upright, life returning, her spine held up by something more than her own weak muscles.

'I saw him, some time ago. In a boat. At first I thought it was the boat you met him on. But then I realized it was not a boat but a plane.'

'Why didn't you tell me?'

'Why should I tell you? I hoped he'd be going somewhere else. I see all kinds of images. I dream all kinds of dreams. How am I to know?'

There was a sour note returning. Maggie said quickly, anxious that the other Edie, the wise Edie, should not vanish so soon, 'And where was he going, what was he doing?'

'There were a lot of shadows. Maybe the past, yours, his, I don't know.'

'But when we meet, what happens?' Her curiosity made her sound suddenly like Sarah, impatient and resentful. Great Edie strained for information. Suddenly Maggie had to stop herself laughing. With the old woman's eyes bulging, it looked like constipation. She managed to keep quiet and her grandmother continued, more rhythmically, quieter. And her other voice rang out.

'There is a small child. She is in a huge garden. Several hundred acres. She is lost. She looks around her and it is only when she realizes that she is alone, that her mother has disappeared, that she feels fear, real fear. Fear has become her. She feels it in her mind, in her fingers.

'In her bladder her muscles relax. She cannot stop the trickle of urine. She walks through a tunnelled arbour and comes to a herb garden. It is laid in geometric patterns. Circles within circles. Stone paths crossing in the middle at a sundial.

'She can smell rosemary. Remembrance. The smell excites her fear. She is trembling. Her breathing is short. She runs through a line of sharply clipped hedges that tower over her head. She feels them closing in around her. The light disappears.

'She runs through the garden and into another. It is identical like a mirror.

'Further on there is a wilderness. Tall trees sway in the gathering wind. Giant lean pines. A dark ceiling. She wants to cry, but her voice has gone. She is searching for her mother, or anyone. But the only voice is the wind. The wind is meaningless although she strains to make sense of it. Then – the edge. She has come to the end of the wood.

'The garden is gone and she looks down to a river. A sloping muddy bank falls gracelessly downwards. The river flows quickly. Dragging reeds and fallen branches. She stares at it transfixed. Held by the motion. She knows instinctively that she will not like what she sees. She wants to look away. She wants to but she can't. A voice inside her is urging her back, before it's too late. But something holds her there. She sees. Tangled in the flotsam, bloated and bloodless, a body, a woman. She screams.'

Great Edie stopped speaking. And then Maggie screamed too. The scream roused her grandmother from her torpor. She looked venomous.

'What the bloody hell's that noise for?'

Maggie was struggling for air. Her eyes were wild. 'I had that dream! I had that dream! I had it many times. At least . . . at least,' she faltered, 'I feel like I did. Maybe it was just once. I had that exact dream when I was young. Four or maybe five, a year or two after Aunt Ruth died.'

'Well, maybe you should learn something from it. Dreams keep coming back unless they're answered.'

Maggie was still aroused, her heart beating wildly. 'What message? What message?'

'How should I know?' snapped Great Edie. 'What do you think I am, sodding psychic?'

14

Thick and Fast

Maggie thought about the garden. The dream she remembered so vividly was one that she had had more than once on the ship. Yet the dream was not about Rudi. It was a dream she had when she was still very much a young child. When everything seemed magnified. Not just physical objects – the vast decks, the over-sized deckchairs with their huge tongues flapping in the wind. The sink in the cabin was so uncomfortably out of reach that she scraped her elbows. But everything. Everything was elongated. A day could seem interminable. The sea was endless. When she cried she would never stop. When she was happy, she would never feel sad again.

The dream was an exaggeration. An exaggeration of reality. For they did go to a garden.

She had not thought about the dream for years. She found it sad because she loved gardens. She visited London gardens. Kew was her favourite, the Victorian glasshouses a mysterious jungle. The smell of the damp, the dark plants and the drips that fell from nowhere on to her cheeks. More than this she loved the wild parts. Pine scents, damp bark and the green-black needles, the soft brown carpet.

Her mother loved it too. Her father didn't come if he could avoid it. Maggie thought nothing of that. Parents were not people who did things together. They were separate beings. Her father worked and drank. Her mother floated and cared for her child. Looking back as an adult, Maggie could see that Grace must have been difficult. So ethereal. She was a child, already regressing. She thought nothing of spending an entire day pretending to be a squirrel. Maggie adored it, but it didn't get the washing done.

Hearing the dream was like finding a freshwater stream and bending down to drink draught after draught of clear, clean water when she had spent so long surrounded by the salt sea. Craving liquid, seeing liquid, but knowing that she could not drink.

She was walking back from Great Edie's, a curious figure hunched in thought.

The dream was a dream of loss. She had lost two things in her life, her mother and then Rudi. Was this to remind her that she must not expose herself again – or something else?

She shook her head unconsciously. A young woman swerved to avoid her, with a scornful look at this staring-eyed creature making strange head movements.

It might be what Great Edie thought but she knew otherwise. She had spent too long denying herself the luxury of intimacy. It was not her problem any more. It was Sarah's. If she could change anything about her life it would be that, Sarah's childhood.

Sarah was brought up by her shattered self. A defensive half-mother. She had not allowed herself to be consumed with maternal feelings. She had kept a distance. Sarah had suffered.

Maggie had been, if not cold, then cool. Great Edie encouraged it; she was not a warm person. Maggie had had warmth and it had slipped from her fingers. Grace, the warmest person, had given and then taken away. Rudi had offered something. Not warmth exactly, but connection. That connection was abruptly severed.

At sixteen, she was too young to reflect. She had done what she could. It had been self-preservation. At the time it was the only thing she could do not to be swallowed under the sea. But now when she looked at Sarah, difficult, distressed Sarah, when she saw her daughter floundering she felt like a poisoner.

The walking was helping. The regular steps, the peripatetic conversation. Instead of taking the most direct route, she frayed into wanderings. The tatty streets of South London. The tall houses set back from the main road. A vertical line of bells, the big family houses converted into one-bedroom flats. Disintegration.

The streets were smarter in the days when she walked through them with Sarah. Then, when she pushed the second-hand pram, she felt dowdy next to the trim greengrocer's and the immaculate bread shop with its hot dough smell that foamed on to the street. Now, even casual as she was, she felt overdressed. Her conspicuous handbag clutched over her shoulder.

Sarah had always been a strange child. As if she knew that she had brought shame upon the family. As if she knew that her conception was a disaster, that her life in theory and in practice was an embarrassment and a regret.

Poor Sarah, because she was clearly a sensitive child. Deeply anguished eyes. The most ordinary situations could terrify her. More inward even than Maggie. She could not bear to be asked her own name.

Sarah must have been four or five. A period when many children are insatiably friendly. Before self-consciousness. Mr Vincent, the fishmonger, a dear old man. As twinkly-eyed, fluffy-haired, straight-out-of-the-bath-pink an old man as one could hope to find. That's what Maggie thought, along with everyone else. Mr Vincent loved children. When he saw Sarah with Maggie he smiled broadly, so that his cheeks puckered in dimples. He held out a sweet, saying, 'And what's your name, little one?'

Sarah was at that point staring, moon faced, through the glass counter. Mesmerized by the lines of pink and silver corpses framed in ice. The jewel eyes staring out at her. She heard the voice of the old man and slowly turned round, a look of terror on her face. It was as if she had stepped off the pavement and realized in that split second that she was about to be hit by a car.

She let out a piercing, unearthly cry of pain. Not loud but penetrating.

The old man shrank back as if he had been whipped. There was a sudden silence in the shop. Everyone, the assortment of mothers and their well-behaved children, closed their mouths and stared. Mr Vincent served Maggie the haddock without another word.

This daughter, as Great Edie never failed to remind her, was a stain on her reputation, blood on the carpet. She was not safe in public. She was not normal.

Thinking back now, Maggie felt a wave of self-loathing, as she always did. If Sarah had had Grace for a mother she would have received understanding. She would have been swept up into the embracing private world of her mother. 'Silly fishmonger! Poor Sarah. Stuff the shopping, let's go and play in the woods.' But Maggie was incapable of that. Life was too hard.

She thought of her own child self. Wondered how she would have taken to the child Sarah. Would she have found her impossible, as she did as a mother and adult, or just interesting? She suspected the latter. As a child, Maggie was able to enjoy difference. She lived in Grace's world. As an adult she had shut that away. It was the survival process. Her old self was trapped inside. Still there but, of necessity, locked away.

When Maggie was a very young child, Grace had a mirror on her dressing table. A long mirror in the middle with two smaller mirrors attached on hinges to the left and right. Maggie often sat beside her mother on the stool as Grace brushed her long hair.

The way the mirrors stood, the left and right turning in, Maggie could see a thousand images of herself and her mother, streaming back into infinity. She stared, transfixed. Grace stopped brushing and put her arm round her daughter. She pointed into the mirror. 'There, Maggie, that's where you and I live. In reflection.' Maggie had no questions. 'If other people are strange with you, it's just because they can't go there. But we can. Look.'

Grace pulled the left and right mirrors in at a tighter angle so the two of them were almost completely enclosed.

Maggie squinted up the line of images. She could feel her mother's heartbeat against her face. She was warmed by the heat of her voice.

'Look, Maggie, look at the end.'

Maggie looked harder.

'Can't you see us?'

Then suddenly she could. Suddenly she saw that not all the images were identical. That in the distance she and her mother were moving independently.

'Wave at us, Maggie.'

And Maggie and Grace lifted their hands to wave at themselves.

The pair in the mirror stopped what they were doing and waved back. Then they smiled and walked sideways together out of view.

'Where are they going, Mummy?'

Grace smiled. 'It's not "they", Maggie, it's us. We're probably going for a walk somewhere. In the garden maybe.'

'With the talking flowers?'

'That's right.'

Her old self was trapped inside. Still there but locked away.

Maggie realized that she had stopped, literally lost in thought. She was standing on the pavement on a busy suburban street, staring at her partial reflection in a tiny puddle. People were giving her a clear berth. She had long acknowledged that the best way to protect oneself was to feign insanity. Madness was thought to be infectious. She had travelled in safety late at night through the grimmest unlit spots by taking her shoes off, shaking her head and making strange loud noises. But this lunacy was accidental.

The paralysed posture was giving her backache. And she realized, since it had not rained for a fortnight, that the puddle was urine.

She walked on.

Since he had made his unsought reappearance in her life, she had been plagued with thinking. Thoughts that she had not had for years. Uncomfortable memories. Uncomfortable because they were both difficult and enticing. Her easy life, the comfort she had wrapped around herself, like a thin silk sheet, ripped with little resistance.

And once the memories started, thick and fast they came at last. And more and more and more.

And more. Sarah was at school. Great Edie was somewhere in the house. Maggie was delirious with flu. She must have been twenty-one, twenty-two maybe.

She had been sleeping fitfully for an indefinite time. One hour or ten, it felt the same. Then she got up. Perhaps to go to the loo. But by the time she was on her feet, her soles pricking and painful on the floor, her head spinning and rushing, she had forgotten why.

She stood swaying, her vision blackening.

Then for no reason she was drawn to the box containing

Arthur Hodges, her father's dummy. She kept it in the bedroom because there was nowhere else. He lay shut in his box gathering dust. He was part of the room, unnoticed.

Except now. For it struck her for the first time that he was kept not in an ordinary box but in a child's coffin. Why had she not noticed before? A white, rectangular box pointed at one end. A tarnished brass plate on the top, the engraving worn away.

For the first time since he was packed away when she left the boat, she walked slowly towards the box, swaying feverishly, and opened it.

Her heart jumped. Arthur Hodges wasn't in there. She was. Her own child self. Ashen-faced, open-eyed, smiling out at her. Eleven years old. A perfect human being, self-contained.

She came to on the floor. The wooden boards felt cool to her face. Her temperature was down at last.

In the dusty London afternoon, Maggie smiled at the memory.

She remembered feeling better, clearer. She had struggled to her feet and checked the box. Arthur Hodges and his impenetrable grin were back.

She had looked in the mirror then. Apart from the flu-drained features what did she see? What was changed from the child in the coffin? It was that sense of self. The self-sufficiency. Ten years later and she considered herself merely a mother of dubious morality. A woman who could not give her daughter even what she herself had received.

She had been walking now for more than two hours. Haphazardly, from street to street. So preoccupied that she had no idea where she was going.

Yet the pedestrian journey, which she had barely an impression of, just the unfocused noise of traffic and blur of people, had brought her to her daughter's flat. How odd.

She rang the bell and waited. No answer. Sarah was not one to go out during the week. Maggie had heard nothing from her for nearly a month. It was probably the longest continuous period she had gone without hearing from her daughter since the first squawks had come out of her mouth. Sarah had let out screams before she was even fully delivered. Maggie heard her before she saw her. At the time she was struck with the idea that Sarah was as reluctant to be born as she was to bear her.

As she waited by the unanswered bell naturally she pictured her daughter lying inside, murdered in stinking neglect.

She shook herself. Damn Rudi. Since he came back she had felt her grip on her mind slipping. All kinds of shadows hanging over her again. But if the shadows had returned, must that not mean too that the sun had come out again?

'Oh shut up, for God's sake shut up!'

She shouted aloud, on her own in the street. The sound of her voice stung like a slap in the face. Brought her round. What was she doing? A middle-aged woman shouting in the street. It was ridiculous.

Decisions. Sensible decisions. Order, organization. She straightened her hair. Sarah had probably gone away for a few days. She would come round with a key tomorrow and prove it.

She was making a meal for herself. Which struck her this evening as pathetically solitary. Dinner for one surrounded in foil. What an overblown image of the vanished family. Crystal metaphor. In the frozen fat of her Beef Wellington, the six-pointed ice flakes, scentless and cold.

She opened the fridge to get a carton of salad. As her hand was reaching towards it, she stopped, frozen too. There was a note, in erratic copperplate curls.

> ' "The time has come," the Walrus said,
> "To talk of many things:
> Of shoes – and ships – and sealing wax –
> Of cabbages – and kings – " '
>
> So Maggie come and see me then
> Place of which oft you spoke
> Your childish 'lurgey-blurgey den'
> The well-remembered oak.

And though it was more than thirty years she knew instantly what it meant.

It was nine o'clock at night. Her feet were aching from the walk earlier. Still she pulled herself out of the house. She walked on to the main road and half walked, half ran, left for the few hundred yards to the orange revolving light of the minicab office.

The hospital building, looming white in the darkness, was in front of her. She turned away and walked calmly into the gardens along the full stretch of the lumbering hospital to the furthest corner, to the trees.

Rudi was not instantly visible. The trees clumped too thickly together. Beech, sweet chestnut, wild cherry. There was only one oak. Though it was dark and she had not walked through this man-made spinney for years, she did not hesitate.

She stopped in front of him.

'Fancy you remembering that. What the hell did I mean by lurgey-blurgey?'

She spoke casually. Her first sight of him was the glimmer of torchlight by which he was reading. He sat on the roots of the oak that pushed out of the earth in twisted fingers. He looked up.

'You said "lurgey-blurgey" meant a closet without doors. A superior closet that was not sullied by the need to have boring old clothes hanging in it.'

'Cupboard, you mean. Did I? How strange.'

'Yes,' he sighed fondly. 'You always did like cupboards. You said that the oak tree you sat by in the hospital gardens was a cupboard. That's why you sat in it.'

'Did I say that?' Her face crinkled in bewilderment. She pulled her fingers through her hair and looked around her, as if orientating herself.

Rudi was quietly encouraging. 'Sit down. Have a drink.' He handed her a whisky. It was already poured, in a thick square tumbler.

'Where'd you hide that?'

He smiled ruefully. 'In the cupboard, of course.'

'Hmm,' she said, adding more guardedly, 'and I'm certainly interested in how you got into my flat to leave a note in the fridge.'

'Oh, that.' He shrugged. 'You left the back door open yesterday when you took the trash out.'

She stared. 'You lay in wait?'

'Yes. Sorry.'

187

He looked at her with concern. She stood tense. As if the enormity of it all was holding her up.

Then her body slumped. She fell on to the grass, her head in her hands, exhausted. When she looked up at him, the torch was illuminating his face so that it looked ghoulishly skeletal. He was staring at her in anxiety. There were tears in her eyes.

'Oh God,' she said weakly, 'why did you come back?'

She sighed. She looked so frail. He held out his arms to her and she took refuge. Despite everything it was a comfort.

'I couldn't leave it, Maggie,' he said softly. 'I had to make a peace for myself.'

She trembled.

'I want to tell you about myself,' he said. 'I want you to understand. I spent so many years in isolation. Nobody knew who I was. Nobody knows who I am, still. My wife never knew. But I'm an old man, whatever you say. I don't want to keep anything from you any more. I should have told you years ago. I should have trusted you. I realize that now. But at the time I didn't know you. I was a coward. I thought you were just a child. I was wrong and so I screwed everything up. I don't want to do that any more.'

She was lying curled against him like a cat. He stroked her head. It was terrible, but she felt a flame of happiness warming inside her. She despised herself. The darkness, always they had met in the darkness.

'Go on then,' she said after a few minutes, sounding stronger now, more like herself. 'Give me a bloody cigarette.'

She could feel him smiling as he reached in his pocket.

They smoked together, rich inhalations, as if it weren't killing them.

She spoke first. 'So tell me, what happened?'

He smiled.

She poked him in the ribs. 'And I'm warning you, it better be good.'

15

The Long Story of a Mature Person

But this was not the place for a mature person to tell a long story. To Maggie these trees were a sanctuary and she did not want it defiled. She lay in the darkness comforted by Rudi, a stranger yet part of herself. There was a quiet perfection in the moment. In lying together. Hearing a gentle wind in the dark night.

And yet they were mature people. However romantic the moment, with maturity comes the knowledge that it is only a matter of time before the body stiffens.

'My bony ass,' he said, breaking into the silence. 'I gotta get some cushioning.'

Maggie felt a momentary pang for their mutual lost elasticity and then she checked herself. What good had padding ever been to her?

'Yes,' she said, tired now, 'we're too old for this kind of stuff.'

He bristled. 'Hey, don't say that. We're not too old for sitting on the ground in the dark. I'm not too old to leave dumb notes in your refrigerator. We're never too old.'

'Oh, OK then.' Maggie walked meekly beside him. She was still as unsure of him as he was of her. Whatever there was between them now, it was in constant shift. A kind of unsettling process. Sometimes one seemed more accepting, one more defensive, one more forward-looking, the other living years ago. Back and forth. Momentarily they hit a synchronicity and then again they were years apart.

They walked together out of the hospital grounds. He took

her home. Barely a word passed between them but the atmosphere was not silent. They agreed quietly to meet the following morning. Rudi would come round to Maggie's flat. She would make breakfast and they would deal with this unfinished business between them. And that was how it seemed. Business unfinished. She wanted to know and he, at last, wanted to tell her. That they could get no further without this transaction was self-evident but where 'further' was, neither knew. Sometimes consequences were best left to figure themselves out.

Rudi never slept through the night.

He thought, lying in the growing light, it will be dawn soon. Today is the day. When she will know. Is this a smart thing to be doing, he asked himself. Stirring up the past that was finally lying comfortable? Well, OK, he reasoned, not that comfortable, let's face it.

Was she as perfect as he remembered? Was she perfect then or was that time spinning a soft focus? Of course it was. She was an ordinary middle-aged woman. Well, he reasoned again, not that ordinary. He pulled up his knees and made a tent of the blanket.

Oh yes indeed. She is as haunting as always. She may not be perfect but the memory was. Was. Could was be turned into is?

The only reason why these questions did not worry him was because he felt there was nothing to lose. He had left the country that had become his home and it was hardly a sacrifice. He had never felt comfortable in America. His parents tried hard to disguise their identity – too hard. Seemed the harder they tried, the clearer it was they were different. That much he learned.

He half-listened to the unfamiliar sounds. The buzz of small engines that went by more frequently as the morning approached. He turned over. His body moved slowly. He was a fit man for his years but he was feeling the rust. Who could look back on their life and say: this is why? This is what I did and why I did it.

He rubbed his weary face with his hands. His mind, a mess of accounts. Explaining things he barely understood himself. Why he left the boat. Explanations sounded like excuses.

If there was one thing he feared it was confrontation. Yet here he was. He could have let the whole damn thing lie. Maybe he was too old to leave things behind.

He heard the first train crank past. Halting heavily, reluctant in the darkness. The fluorescent glare of his travel clock said it was five. Cool morning air hit his arms as he stretched them out from under the duvet. He felt the cold now. Used to be a one-man radiator. Even in the Chicago winter. Suzanne loved it. She would wrap herself around him at night. And in the morning the kids would crawl in, seeking out their Daddy heater. Melting round his legs like candy while the grey morning cut across the room. Suzanne would switch the light on. The girls would scamper away at their mother's instruction. Suzanne would rise, transforming, in her ascension, from woman to worker. Her shapely form barely masked by the ugly nylon nightdress, the synthetic material clinging to her skin.

He would watch her through half-closed eyes. The shimmering buttocks walking purposefully to the bathroom. She snatched her bathrobe – a horribly practical pink fleshly garment that had been bought from the Sears catalogue. It covered her body, evaporating sensuality. She pulled up the sleeves, put on her slippers, opened the door and clacked down the corridor. Clack clack clack. Leaving a vacuum in the bed, an indentation in the mattress, a lingering warmth that was all the more appealing because in his imagination it was not hers.

He listened then to the banging of pans, the rising and falling of childish conversation. Suzanne's maternal anger:

'No! Don't do that! OK, just one then . . . I said *one*, Lisa.' Then hiatus. Always a momentary lull before the explosion. 'No, *leave* it! You'll burn yourself.'

He pictured the struggle. Even if he didn't want to. Her back turned to the refrigerator, her glare averted for a moment. The crucial moment. A bang, of metal on stone, the pan on the freezing floor, an ominous hush, followed by the screams.

'Waa! Wa! Wa-aah!'

And the angry voice of Suzanne failing to conceal panic, shouting over the noise. 'You stupid girl! Didn't I say leave it? Didn't I?'

He heard the sting of the slap. It made him wince though he could not see it (he could not endure physical cruelty). The softer but more persistent sobbing and finally, after angry banging of pans and the resumed sizzling of breakfast, the reconciliation. 'Come on now, sweetie, come to Mommy. It's all right, it's all right.'

Lying here in London, in a cheap bed and breakfast, Rudi felt very far away. It was twenty years, three thousand miles and a divorce settlement later. He felt the distance. But no more, paradoxically, than he had at the time. Often the world went on around him while he just listened.

Later he took the train to Maggie's flat. It was such a straightforward journey, it is easy to assume that the decision was lightly taken on either side. It was not.

Rudi could not explain properly even to himself what he was doing at this time in this strange country where even the cars drove on the wrong side of the road. Where the rules were different. Where everything was different.

Where everything reminded him of a girl he once knew who liked Alice. A girl who said that she and her mother lived in the looking-glass. Then he didn't know what she meant.

He did now. He knew exactly what she meant. In fact he had begun to understand almost as soon as he left her behind on that crazy boat. As his life in Chicago unfolded. When the girl was gone and he lived with another woman, when he had children of his own.

By the laws of reflection it was only when he lived so close to a woman who didn't live in the mirror, who was completely existent in the real, in the unrefracted, it was only then that he finally understood. The difference between prose and poetry.

She opened the door. He held up his hand. Part in greeting, part in defence. He said as if to himself, 'You look so . . . young.'

She didn't understand. Her eyebrows lifted in query.

'I don't know why I said that . . .' he faltered. 'At least I can't explain.' He looked at her. He felt at this moment as if she were the only thread holding his life together. Without this woman, this ageing stranger before him, he had no past. Everything else was gone.

'Come on in then,' she said, pulling her cardigan around her. 'It's chilly standing here.'

It was chilly. There was an equinoctial air. Emotionally leaden. He had thought it was just him. But he realized, no, the season had turned. It was mid-September and the leaves were toasted brown. The air smelt of woodsmoke, though there was no fire.

She looked at him, wondering what he was going to say next. She could hear her own breathing. She thought that once she had known him. And that the way she knew him then, the manner of knowing – trust was too strong, the word was perhaps *unquestioning* – this was returning. Perhaps it didn't matter that as yet they had said so little. It was the fact that things were going to be said that was significant. This had begun to supersede the doubts. The doubts that had insidiously over-taken her memories; that their friendship was nothing to him, a casual dalliance to make the time pass on the sluggish ship.

Suddenly she had faith in him again. And with this hesitant revelation came a morbid conviction that he had always wanted her. As he stood in the doorway, with the glow of late summer surrounding him, it would almost not have mattered to her now if he had told her nothing. But here it was, she was going to know. On some level she felt even intrusive, as if she already knew what he was going to say. Intrusive for demanding information she had already understood.

On the glass table in the sitting room lay a carton of orange juice (concentrated), a jar of coffee (instant), a rack of toast (cooling, culled from a white loaf), a pot of butter (spreadable) and a jar of jam (without extra fruit). Maggie had no patience or money for the luxuries that Sarah's generation considered a necessity. Rudi blanched a little at the coffee. The slightly sweet smell, as the boiling water churned the granules into froth.

They sat side by side on the sofa with a foot-long gap between them. The plain, neat sofa. An impossibly pale cream. Surely she could not live and keep that clean.

Rudi held out some folded sheets of paper. His eyes darkened. He looked vulnerable.

The papers were aged slightly, curled at the corners. The printed writing on them was from an old computer. An early Amstrad perhaps. The laborious indentation of a now obsolete machine. There were about twenty sheets.

Maggie softly accepted the papers, if only to stop them

quivering in his grasp. She found herself saying, 'Are you sure you want me to read this?'

He smiled at her concern, at the turnaround. 'I owe it to you, you have a right to know.'

For some reason she said, 'There's no such thing as a right. Nobody has a right to anything.'

He looked at her, startled by her choice of words. He nodded. 'No, I guess not.'

'So,' she said with a forced normality in her voice, crossing her left leg over her right in a stiffly casual way, 'what is this?'

He opened his mouth to speak. It looked like an effort but when the words came out they were matter-of-fact. He had distanced himself.

'About ten years ago I took part in a documentary about Chicago's post-war immigrants. I hadn't talked in depth to anyone about my life before, certainly not my wife and my American friends, but actually I found it perfectly easy to give a factual account to a stranger. To talk into the black box of a camera was so unemotional that I found the process almost relaxing. Unburdening. Yet it was impossible even to imagine confiding in people I knew. Anyway,' he sighed, 'afterwards I asked for a transcript of the interview . . .'

Rudi's voice trailed off. He pointed at the papers with his nose, gesticulating dismissively with a jerk of his chin.

'And this is it.' Maggie filled in the words.

Rudi nodded. 'The edited transcript. Well, there are five of them but you don't need to read all of them, they're very long.'

'Oh.' She turned the papers around, gathering them neatly together and holding them on her lap. Almost as if chastised she said, 'OK, I'll read this then.'

Rudi nodded again and sat back on the sofa. While moments before his body had been taut, now he relaxed. The air sank from him. The movement sent ripples across to Maggie, still tense on the edge of her side of the sofa. Rudi closed his eyes. Maggie looked at him but there did not seem any possibility that he would be opening them again. So she turned her gaze to the papers and began to read.

*

Interview III

LS: So, you told us last time about the Jewish village – the shtetl – in eastern Poland you grew up in, your relationship with the Poles and your family life. Your father was a tailor.

JH: Yeah, that's right, he took over the business from my grandfather.

LS: So what happened to that after Piludski's death?

JH: Life was a lot more difficult. The right-wing Endecja party was in power and changed the laws. In the late 'thirties the Poles were allowed to set up in the Jewish business areas. The Endecja spread pamphlets about us. Saying we were morally corrupt, we were dirty, that we spread disease.

Before, I had gone to one of the schools that during the liberal period had started mixing Poles with Jews – unbelievable now. But with the propaganda, that soon backfired. Polish children who I had gotten along with, like good friends of mine, suddenly didn't want to talk to me any more. There was some violence. Jewish men would get beaten up, mostly by ignorant peasant thugs. Most ordinary Poles were not like that. Some of them even defended us. Sometimes the police still punished the perpetrators. But that happened less and less.

LS: What did you fear most?

JH: Uncertainty, without a doubt. Our lives in Poland had always depended on the tolerance of the law and the people. We were very vulnerable. We had no rights. The world closed in and there was no place else for us to go. That sense has never left me.

LS: Even though you're in a free country now?

JH: Even though I've been an American citizen for forty years now. It doesn't make me American. And America has treated me well. But that hasn't taken away the deep-rooted insecurity. I guess that's the point. An immigrant is always an outsider.

LS: So the Germans invaded Poland in September 1939 . . .

JH: That's right. The fear and paranoia that we experienced before the war were no preparation for what was to happen.

LS: And how did things change?

JH: A lot of different things happened. The only reliable thing was that each time the situation changed, it got worse. The Soviet occupation, for example, was bad news at the time, but with what happened subsequently, we looked back on it like the happy days.

We carried on a semblance of normal life. Details became so important. My mother would insist, for example, that we washed our hands and prayed before eating, even when we were moved to the ghetto and rats were running across the table. We never used to pray before. She was a total atheist. In 1941 they created a Jewish ghetto and from the surrounding areas we were herded together like cattle. There was a lot of disease, disgusting conditions, not enough food.

But even so, things could've been worse. People brought us food. Not enough but better than nothing. We were almost able to get on with our lives. Unbelievably my father still had orders for suits.

LS: But it didn't last.

JH: No, no, it didn't. It had happened already in other shtetls and in September 1942 it happened to us; they annihilated the ghetto. We heard a rumour the night before, and we had no doubt that it was for real. Complete panic broke out. A lot of people said Kaddish in their homes. Others burnt their possessions so at least the bastards wouldn't have anything afterwards. Others, like my family, fled for their lives.

LS: How old were you then?

JH: Eight years old.

LS: And how did you escape?

JH: Well, when I say my family I mean my parents, my sister and I. We escaped to the forest. The rest of the family didn't. My aunt, my mother's sister, never could face up to reality. The stupid woman said she couldn't risk taking her children into the forest. She couldn't cope with the obvious truth that hiding there was like hiding under the floorboards of a house. Sooner or later you're going to get discovered. There were no survivors among the people who hid in the ghetto.

My grandfather knew he was too old to survive in the forest. He knew he would hold the rest of us up if he tried. So he resigned himself to his fate. I don't know what he thought. Maybe he didn't think about it. I've often wondered.

The last time I saw him, it was one in the morning and my parents were making plans. My grandfather gave me a look I couldn't understand. I suppose it was fear or horror. He grabbed me, and Etta too. My sister was crying, she was four years older and understood more than I did.

Grandfather took me into the corner of our tiny house. He held me at arm's length for a minute as if he didn't want to lose sight of me. Then he put his hand into a box that he kept by his bed (made of packing cases, we didn't exactly have furniture any more). He brought out a glass jar that contained his collection of teeth. Every tooth he had ever lost. All the baby teeth and, by then, most of the adult ones too. I don't think he had anything else to give.

My grandmother wouldn't leave him. Even though she was a strong woman and she might have made it. She didn't want him to be alone, even for a few hours. We found out later, through the underground, that everybody was carried off in wagons the next morning. They went by train to Belzec and were all gassed a few days later.

LS: Where did you go?

JH: There was no great plan. We ran into the forests. There were several hundred of us at first. But this number got weeded out over the hours, days and weeks as the Nazis sniffed us out with those dogs.

My sister was killed when she went to take a pee. She went too far from where we were hiding – she always was too modest. There was a pair of Lithuanian soldiers recruited for the dirty work, walking through the undergrowth. We heard the shots. We couldn't see anything from where we were, sheltering in the back of a barn. Our first thought, I'm ashamed to say, was that in finding her they might discover us. They wouldn't have known for sure she was Jewish, they just killed her on the off chance. Twelve years old . . .

. . . They put so much effort into it. I could never understand why. It was like it was an obsession. They knew there were still some of us hiding in the undergrowth. And they didn't let up. What did it matter that a few weak, dirty families lived out the time in the woods? But there was no logic in it.

LS: So how did you stay hidden?

JH: Sheltering with compassionate – or crazy – Polish farmers who risked their own lives to protect us. I really learned that there are good and bad people in every race. I saw such humanity from people who had every reason to betray us – and I saw Jews who turned against us when the Germans invaded in return for privileges and protection for themselves and their families.

Some people hid in groups, making secret camps. But my father thought we were safer alone – and if we kept moving. My father grew cunning. He developed a knack for avoiding trouble. Not at all like the man he was before. He got a gun from a Polish communist sympathizer in exchange for my mother's wedding ring. We made our way, the three of us, towards Krakow. It was slow going. My mother was not that strong, we were totally reliant on good-natured peasants to give us food – and sometimes shelter. We spent many freezing nights just in the undergrowth. I thought about the rest of the family, particularly my sister. We had to leave her body, burying her was too slow and too risky. You can imagine what that did to my parents.

LS: What kept you all going?

JH: I think what got my father through was anger. He was so mad that his strength and morale kept me and my mother going. She would have given up, I think. I would never have survived on my own. My father was superhuman.

LS: How long did you spend in the forests?

JH: We were on the run for over a year before we finally made it to Krakow. We had heard that the big cities could be safer. The AK [note: the Armia Krajowa, the Polish resistance] could get you false ID if you were lucky. They even had a group to help Jews financially, the Zegota. We were lucky, or maybe it was just my father's brazen determination. We lived in hiding with papers that proclaimed us pure Aryan. We lived in the cellar of a butcher's. A barely lit, low-ceilinged, stone-floored room. It stank and we were permanently filthy. We had food poisoning all the time. Most of the meat was off, but it was eat that or starve. We had long stopped being fussy – there were pig carcasses dangling over my face in my dreams. But, really, after what we'd been through, I didn't care. We stayed there until the end of the war. Naturally we didn't want to remain in a country with so many memories. There was no future for us in Poland. But my father had a cousin in Chicago. And so in 1946 we emigrated to America.

End of Interview III

Maggie put the paper down. Though the page ended there, overleaf it moved on to the next interview which covered his arrival in Chicago. She put the papers together and looked at Rudi, who still had his eyes closed. He could be dead, she thought.

She shook him, rather hard. He opened his eyes and turned them to her, otherwise not moving.

She stared at him with tears in her eyes. 'Why didn't you tell me?' Her voice was beseeching.

He looked at her in surprise. 'Have you read it all already?'

She twitched in annoyance at this nugatory detail. 'No, just the one.'

'Well, you won't know the whole story then.'

'I don't care.' She raised her hands in despair. 'Why didn't you tell me this before?'

He opened his mouth and closed it again. 'I don't know what to say.'

The tears flowed more freely from her eyes, unblocked. 'I don't know you, I've never known you.' She was sobbing, not far from uncontrollably.

He bridged the gap between them and took her in his arms. 'Stop, stop, for Chrissake, stop.'

She breathed deeply, in an effort to control herself.

He said, pointing at the paper, 'This is not who I am.'

She didn't believe him.

'No, Maggie. I am the man *you* knew. That's who I want to

199

be. All this was a long time ago, a long time ago even when we met. Christ, it was almost twenty years later when I met you. You've got to remember that it might be new to you, but I lived with it nearly all my life. It's not me. It can't be me. I couldn't live if it was who I am. I had to get over it.'

'So why tell me now then, with no warning?'

He bowed his head. 'OK, it was too blunt. But waddya want? I'm not a psychiatrist. I wanted you to know everything. That was a pretty important part of my character formation or whatever bullshit the shrink says. I had to start at the beginning. Don't you see?'

'So you want me to say, "OK, that'll be why you're a bit secretive, fine, let's hear the rest of the story"?'

He looked small. 'I guess it doesn't shock me any more. I'm sorry.'

She turned her wet eyes away to the door, as if she thought suddenly of running away herself.

'No,' she sighed, 'don't be silly, it's fine. Why on earth shouldn't you have told me?' She was resuming her normal gravelly tone. 'It's terrible and shocking, of course it is. I don't know how to respond.'

'You don't have to,' he said with an open smile.

She turned back towards him and looked him unflinchingly in the eye. 'But another terrible thing . . .'

'Yes?'

'All the while I was reading that I was thinking, God, I have never had anything to complain about. And you know what?'

This being rhetorical, he waited patiently.

'I started to feel ashamed of myself.'

He laughed. And she thought, through her angry feelings at herself, that his face was very attractive still. And she despised herself all the more. For thinking something so shallow *and* for feeling angry at herself, at her age. For God's sake.

'What are you laughing at?'

'I don't know really. That you would be so stupid. All misery is relative, you know.'

She looked perplexed. 'What do you mean?'

'I mean OK, so some people might think I had more right to sympathy than you. But it's not a competition. You had a hell of a life. I lost most of my family. But, in different ways, you lost yours. You were all alone. I was never all alone.'

'It's hardly comparable. You were facing life or death.'

'Yeah, but at least it was finite life or death. Edie has been torturing you for years.'

She couldn't believe that he was being so flippant. 'If I said that, it would be appallingly insensitive.'

'Yeah,' he said, drawing out a cigarette, his first of the morning, with a relaxed pleasure, 'but you didn't, did you?'

She took one too. She had travelled across such a range of emotions in such a short time that she needed it. She looked at the clock that ticked loudly on the mantelpiece. It had struck against her heartbeat for years and yet this morning she had barely been aware of it. It was still only eleven o'clock. How exhilarated she was. She felt him looking at her. Penetrating her skin with his gaze.

She said slowly, 'And I have no patience for Sarah when she gets so desperate, because I think, what on earth does she have to worry about? And she knows that and I think that depresses her all the more.'

He nodded sagely. 'Suffering is all relative.'

She stood up and folded her arms uncomfortably. Her body was stiff with adrenaline. She stretched a little, keeping the cigarette close to her lips.

'Don't go away again.'

He smiled. 'I'm not going to.'

She wanted him to stay because she was becoming a child again.

16

The Cut-off

'Mrs Snoek, again there is no hot water.' His call was not angry, more beseeching. 'You did promise that I would be able to take a bath on Sunday nights.'

'I promised nothing of the kind,' snapped Mrs Snoek, who had reverted to her maiden name to create the exotic aura which was so good for business.

Maggie listened to her grandmother and wondered again why any paying lodger would put up with it.

Edie stood by the kitchen sink, peeling potatoes. The curling skin fell obediently into the bowl.

The sound of weary feet descending. The man entered the room. Forty-five, almost no hair, medium height with a slight paunch that was barely contained by the camel-hair dressing gown. A towel, far from clean, draped over one arm. White stick legs, too far apart.

'Mrs Snoek, I implore you. I can't go to work in the morning in this state. I'll lose my job.' He stepped gingerly across the kitchen. Maggie heard the soles of his feet peeling off the greasy floor.

Edie took no notice and carried on with the erratic scrape, scrape . . . scrape.

'Mrs Snoek, you did promise, did you not, when I took the room that a weekly bath would be included in the rent?'

'Well, you've 'ad one, 'aven't you?' Now she scraped her own bedraggled hair with the back of her hand.

This was the voice she often used to get her own way. A voice of long-suffered tragedy, as if she hoped the listener would think she had lost half her family to peasant violence and so give in.

George Crouch did not look impressed, merely grubby. So Edie tried another tack.

'Maggie, get yer fat arse out of that chair and make the man a bath.' She sighed dramatically and turned round at last to get a good look at her no-good granddaughter and demanding lodger. 'Well, do I 'ave to do everything round here? Do you think I've got time to go making baths for Mr Hoity-Toit, what with making dinner and having two clients this evening? D'you think I haven't got enough to do?'

Wordlessly, Maggie rose to her feet. She smiled cautiously at George Crouch.

She walked to the understairs cupboard. For some minutes her figure was half cut off. There was a banging, clattering sound. She emerged holding a tin bath by its handles. The weight rested on her protruding belly.

George Crouch came out of the kitchen. He coughed nervously.

'You shouldn't be doing that, love, not in your state.'

'Oh, that's all right, I'm quite able.'

'But still, when there's a man in the house.'

She looked at him coldly. 'Really, it's all right.'

For such a young thing, he thought, she was awfully old. Something about her. So constrained. Odd. Why, she could be no more than eighteen.

Filling the kettle so many times, walking to and fro, creating a draught, the on and off of the tap which never operated without a loud slurping sound. It all drove Edie to distraction.

'Gawd, Maggie, you don't half get in the way. You and that bloomin' bulge of yours. Cor, I never put on that much weight. How many babies you planning on havin'?' Edie drew breath. 'Gawd and if that kettle bloody whistles again in my ear! You want me deaf?'

The meal Edie was preparing was spreading. A diaspora. The corned beef tin sending its cloying smell into every corner. The plates, the cabbage, scattered leaves. The potato peelings blocking the sink. The savaged potato lumps recovering in the water. Maggie hustling in and out with the heavy kettle, her breath catching in the effort.

George Crouch sat in the front room next to the tin tub, his bare feet on a footstool, reading *The Times*. He rubbed them together. An unconscious pleasure, the toes stroking one another, seeking out rough patches and crumbs of collected sweat.

'Nearly there,' panted Maggie.

'Oh thanks, love.'

'No problem.'

He peered into the tub, at the dark water. 'Are you sure this is clean?'

'As a whistle,' said Maggie, with enforced cheeriness, hesitating at the door. 'I cleaned it myself last week. The water always looks dark – it's the effect of the metal.'

'Ah,' he said suspiciously. Not surprising if he didn't believe her, living in this house of dank and dirt.

She lugged in the last kettle, with the complaining voice of Edie still echoing behind her.

'Well, only seventeen kettles, not bad, eh?'

He didn't answer. He wasn't a man for irony.

'Do you mind if I have the bath after you?' she said.

But George was buried in his newspaper. Evidently he had not heard her.

He emerged, shining, half an hour later and seemed shocked when she said she would pop into the water before throwing it away.

'But it'll be too cold for you, love.'

'Oh it's all right, I'll only be a minute.'

A strange look was left on him. Squashed, like he'd been hit. She ran into the front room. The curtains pulled before dusk gave the room an exotic red tinge. She stripped quickly and stepped into the bath.

Goose pimples pricked on to her skin. The water felt sticky. The cheap soap (Edie felt little need of soap herself and therefore saw no reason why anyone else should enjoy luxury) was sloppy in her hands. George Crouch had left it swimming in a watery soup. Spiced with strands of his wiry hair.

Maggie shuddered and dunked the soap into the water. The bath. Always a necessary evil. Washing on the boat had been so difficult.

And here it was worse. The boiler had broken down some

years ago. No one could persuade Edie to get it fixed. She would not be reasoned with. She would not even discuss it. So there was no hot water. Instead endless whistling kettles and a tin bath that was coated with limescale flakes.

Maggie struggled to make a foam of her soap. It was a grim process. Twisting the cake round and round in her hands, yielding thin suds. Zealously coating herself though the smell was unpleasant. It made her stomach twist too.

The water was a grey opaque. She held her breath as she sank into it, wetting her hair that spread like moss through the water. She took the Amami shampoo and applied a meagre portion to her short crop.

Underneath the water she listened to the nothing. She remembered the advertisement and saw the pink lady saying, 'Friday night is Amami night.' Somehow washing her hair was never so luxurious.

But she liked the numbness, the cut-off. She was a cut-off herself. For the past five months, since she had come 'home' and realized how unwelcome she was.

She could not imagine having a deep bath where her legs could not reach the bottom. Where her knees were not crunched foetally up against her chin, where it was not impossible to be truly clean. This was how it should be. She was a dirty girl, who deserved to live in the dirt.

Edie certainly thought so. Since Maggie's return, an already difficult relationship had deteriorated considerably. Maggie was surprised that Edie had let her stay at all. She suspected it was only because, under her watchful eye and pay, she was less of a liability.

'We'll say your husband died. You married abroad. He died of something. Um, what? What?' She scoured the air with her hands for inspiration.

'Typhoid,' said Maggie dully.

'Yes, typhoid, that's it! Foreigners are always dying of typhoid in those nasty hot countries.'

It was odd that anything that wasn't England was 'nasty' when in fact Edie was a nasty foreigner herself.

'Why can't we tell them the truth?' Maggie asked out of resentment more than curiosity.

'Because, you stupid girl, that would be the end of you. Do

you think you could stay in this country after that?' Edie's face screwed up into malicious lines. 'Ooh, you can't even begin to guess what it's like, arriving in this country, with their snobbery and their suspicions. After all these years, now I've got a bit of respect. I'm not going to let some stupid careless girl pull it all apart.'

This was a vast exaggeration. If Edie lacked respect it was more likely because of the state of her home and the string of strange people who trailed in and out seeking supernatural advice. But there was no telling her. Maggie pulled her fingers through the water and watched the combing effect. Her eyes focused on the wetness that seemed to have changed in consistency. She pulled her fingers out of the water in surprise and examined them. A semi-transparent glue. Oh God. George Crouch. Ugh.

Like a flash she saw again his look of horror at the knowledge that she was following him into the water. Oh God. She leaped from the bath, snatched the towel and scrubbed herself roughly. Rubbed away at her loathing. Everything around her was so sordid.

She sat wearily on the stool and looked at the mantelpiece against the wall. In no hurry to return to the greasy kitchen, the annoyance of her grandmother or the egregious shame of the lodger. And the parlour was warm, thanks to a coal fire, and clear since it was barely used. At least there was space to think.

The mantelpiece displayed the family photos. Different eras, different settings and sizes thrown together in discord.

Half the people she couldn't put a name to. They were wedding photos mainly. In one Edie, much younger, next to the dreadful husband Jack, the one who died so selfishly after their arrival in England. Actually he looked quite sweet. A bemused expression, looking into the camera as if he did not know what it was.

This was in the early days of their married life. Edie looked upright, energetic. Her husband looked desperate to please. She didn't recognize the bridal couple. Presumably part of the unknown family in Holland. Edie hadn't bothered to stay in contact. For a while there were birthday cards from a Hanni and Petr, an Ulwe. Strange names that ran through Maggie's ears at one time and then faded away.

Another picture. Edie as a child. She looked entirely different but for her eyes. That iron determination was just the same. Maggie smiled. Edie was hand in hand with a small, darker girl. Some long-forgotten friend. Edie claimed she left the photo up there 'because it's the only picture of me I like'. The friend looked uncomfortable, almost sullen, but Edie was loving the attention, a glorious wide smile, glittering teeth, plump cheeks uplifted. It was certainly a different vision of her. There was – what was it? Maggie thought – there was a trust in her.

Maggie's eyes ran along the shelf. They were stopped by the biggest face of all. A golden frame, elaborately ridged. Inside lay the smiling face of her aunt Ruth. It looked disproportionately large because it was taken only from the neck up. The little figures in the other pictures would fit easily on to Aunt Ruth's nose.

Maggie suddenly felt the cold of sitting in the room in only a towel – or was she chilled by the eyes of her aunt? By the eyes that chased the viewer round the room. That captured smile. Frozen energy that exuded life. The other figures looked stiff and self-conscious by comparison. Except for Edie herself. She, like her dead daughter, looked born for the camera.

Further along still, right at the end, almost obscured by a snow-shaker of Blackpool – the casual observer might tend to assume it was placed there on purpose – at the very end, was a picture of Maggie herself.

She was standing under a pine tree in a public garden. She looked like she was going to cry. She looked seriously into the camera. Thinking, yet confused. A pair of dark eyes that were trying to work something out.

She remembered that afternoon. It was before her mother was ill. She remembered running through the pine trees, the summer before Aunt Ruth died. The thrill of the whirling wind, the buckling trees that swayed and moaned.

'I'm coming to get you!' shouted Aunt Ruth, her infectious laughter wending through the twisted space between them. Maggie ran. Panic-charged adrenaline running through her toddling legs.

She sprinted through the wood, crying with delight. Then halted for a moment and, panting, looked behind her. The wind too paused and there was no noise. She could no longer see the brilliant red of her aunt's dress. And she had lost sight of the little group. Her mother, her father and grandmother. For an instant she was filled with pure terror. She ran, her long hair falling loose, her sock elastic collapsing. She ran round and round in search of the edge of the trees. Then at last she saw the yellow field of wheat where they had picnicked. At the end the family. She ran and ran and collapsed sobbing into the arms of her mother.

Grace laughed quietly. 'Calm down, little one.'

Maggie lifted her red cheeks from the cool skirts of her mother and looked up into her sympathetic face.

'It's all right, Maggie. There's nothing to be afraid of, I'm here.'

Her mother stroked her head. With the weight of the fingers upon her, Maggie felt her scalp relax. Her mother always sounded calm. She looked into her daughter's face, searching it with an intelligence deeper than sight. Maggie saw those beautiful almond eyes and smiled again.

Aunt Ruth came striding out of the pine trees. All laughs.

'Ruth,' said Grace softly but admonishing, 'you frightened poor Maggie half to death.'

Ruth let out a long guffaw, 'Ha- ha- ha- ha!'

Maggie felt suddenly humiliated. Scared of her aunt and confused about her place in the world. She clung tighter to her mother. Grace responded with a reassuring squeeze, her arm around her daughter like a safety rope. With her there she would never fall.

Her aunt, before so exciting, seemed suddenly sinister. When she laughed so widely her mouth opened so far. Inside, at the back the teeth were black.

Maggie looked at what was left of the picnic. The rolls, the rug and the bottles of barley water. She looked out at the yellow field. What had looked beautiful now looked merely jaundiced. She trembled. Grace pulled her chin towards her so that she could look into her daughter's eyes. Maggie felt a glow inside, a burning love for her mother.

Edie laughed, loud like Ruth. 'That girl's a coward just like you, Grace. You should send her out in the woods more often. Teach her to fend for herself.'

'Oh Mum, don't be so cruel.'

Maggie curled up in her mother. Grace rocked gently, reassuring. The wind blew lightly. She could feel it through the hair at the top of her head that was the only part of her body not protected by her mother. Pushing down further, Maggie could see under her mother's arm her father, Harry. He was lying on the grass, staring at it intently. Maggie closed her eyes and crept in closer.

Aunt Ruth broke the spell.

'Come on, Maggie, let me take a photograph. Go and stand under those trees.'

Maggie sighed and dressed. Eventually she returned to the kitchen and her grandmother, and, promising to empty the bath later, sat down at the table. Edie acknowledged Maggie's return to the kitchen with a sniff.

In the meantime Edie had sat alone in the filth, enjoying the moments of solitude, a cup of tea in her hands and the customary hot-water bottle between her legs. It eased her fictional arthritis.

The arthritis had come to her in a flash of inspiration after Ruth's death. The point at which Edie stopped. Stopped cleaning, stopped eating, let things fall apart. The thin barrier that before had separated her from filth fell away. She let the house, and herself, go.

Thirteen years later Maggie was given the job of cleaning. It was a job to which Edie attached no importance. She did not care if it was not done. But Maggie had to do something. That it was her job felt most appropriate to Maggie. Only when she was down on her knees painfully grinding a cloth into the floor did she feel that she was getting what she deserved. Wicked girl. Bow down at the altar of dust.

When Aunt Ruth died, some woman, Maggie forgot who, probably a neighbour meaning to be kind, said, 'Let me get you a nice meal, Edie love. A nice roast, a nice warming pudding, nice and filling, to warm you up inside. You look half-starved.'

And Edie yelled, 'What do I want to be comfortable for? My daughter's dead. Do you think food will fill me up? My beautiful daughter, still barely more than a child. Oh, you stupid woman.'

The smile fell from the woman's face, smashing like a plate on the floor. Edie walked into her bedroom, slamming the door behind her. Harry, of all people, was left to voice a stammering apology. Maggie stood staring by the door, scraping one leg behind the other.

Edie survived on matzos and cheese. And strangely, that was when her whiskers started to grow. Almost invisible at first, thin grey strands on her chin. To begin with she plucked them out. Later she couldn't be bothered and her eyesight was fading and what she didn't see had never mattered to her.

Maggie struggled in vain against the dirty house, armed with the acrid scouring powder that stung her nose. Every time she removed one layer of dirt there seemed to be another underneath.

Cleaning was the backdrop of her swelling stomach. It became harder. As she grew bigger, she felt the baby kicking inside. No one told her how she should feel, so she felt perplexed. The baby seemed to like the carpet sweeper. It was soothed perhaps by the rolling motion. It made Maggie smile wryly. Lucky baby. Since the carpet sweeper was so ineffectual the baby got rolled a lot.

She called it baby to remind her. For she felt nothing maternal. No great acceptance of her fate. She felt very unnatural. Even her nightmares were better than this. This was beyond imagination. It had never happened to anyone before. She was an aberration. For a while she believed she was giving birth to a demon, she could feel its tail flicking inside her.

It was a curse thrown upon her. She had inhaled a pleasure and wallowed in sin. Now she was punished. It was easier to think in fairy-tale melodrama. She was a fallen maiden forced by the old witch to lick the hearth with her tongue, or close enough. Easier than thinking about the reality, for that reminded her of Rudi and she couldn't bear to think of him. That hurt more than anything her body could put her through.

As she grew bigger the curse grew too. The more people could see, the more shamed she was. It was not so bad with strangers. Edie made her wear a ring. She got it cheap from a contact in the East End.

But the people who knew her, the neighbours, the callers, the shopkeepers and the postman, they did not believe Edie's story, this child-bride granddaughter, with a dead husband who had never been mentioned before.

At last out of the thoughtful silence, which was almost too big to fit in the cramped kitchen, Edie spoke.

'Now, Maggie, you should go to your bedroom. I can't have clients seeing you. Not now there's no hiding it. Don't want people thinking this is some kind of knock-up shop.'

Maggie sat on the wooden chair with the slats that burned into her back. She had barely been out of the bath five minutes, but she was already glad to get away from her grandmother's hectoring and the chance that George Crouch might come back and she would have to look in his eyes and know.

Edie went to change into her professional costume. A ludicrous combination of brightly coloured sheets and table-cloths, gold hoop earrings, a black tasselled headscarf that normally covered a side table and still bore the indentation of the lamp which stood upon it, creating a strange illusion of a halo on her grandmother's head. She looked the part in a vastly overblown fashion. She deserved to be laughed out of her tent but the clients seemed to like their mysticism spread thickly.

Maggie went to her bedroom. Her room was cold. It had no heater. Even under the covers she seemed to shiver, whereas everywhere else she was so hot these days.

She tried to sleep but she wasn't tired. The light was feeble. A neglected electrical system meant the bulbs in the top of the house flickered and dimmed. It was uncomfortable to read. In any case she was too unsettled. Too distracted. And the books in the house were all her grandmother's nineteenth-century romances in soggy pink covers. Tall dark strangers and low-cut heroines who flitted through picaresque episodes with a grinding inevitability. She had no books of her own.

Downstairs she heard the doorbell. Edie greeting the client. Fake East European accent wafting up the stairs.

'Ah, Meesus Bowles, come een, come een.'

'I'm sorry I'm late, Mrs Snoek.'

'Do not worree, my child, of course I zaw the delay.'

'Really?'

'Yis, of course, I zee everything.'

'That's amazing. And you know, what you said about my husband was true. He *was* fed up because of having to visit my mother every weekend. You were right. How could you possibly know that?'

'I tell you, Meesus Bowles, I zee everything. I know you and your husband like I know myzelf.'

'Oh!' the charmed client let out a shriek of excitement.

It was quite a performance.

Maggie closed the door and lay back in her bed and stared at the ceiling, following the lines of imperfection. The unaccountable stains. As if someone had been tossing raw eggs.

From under the pillow, she drew out a scruffy envelope.

It was all she had. A short one-page note. She had found it in her drawer a few days after Rudi had disappeared from the boat. While she was sorting out her father, the confusion, wondering where the money was going to come from and how to appeal to her grandmother who didn't have a charitable side.

She wondered if she wouldn't rather have no letter. She could have filled a complete void with a selfless tragedy. He was dead. He had thrown himself overboard to save another or had been swept into the sea by a freak wave. Instead she had this lack of information. Of course, it would have been impossible for him to compose.

Why did she have to be the understanding one? She was young, bereft, he should have been excusing his behaviour. Instead, as usual, she thought self-pityingly, it was she who was making the excuses. He didn't want to hurt me. He didn't know about the baby. He loved me. But something happened. Something he couldn't tell me about. It was probably a protection.

26 July 1966 [as if she were going to forget]

Dearest Maggie,

I know this is difficult. Believe me, I would not have done it, but I had to. Try not to worry. You're young of course and so resilient. You will meet some other guy later, I promise. More respectable, closer to your age. I don't think Edie would like me much, do you?

I'm sorry not to say goodbye. I'm sorry to be mumbling these old clichés, but it is easier this way.

Ever yours

John (I'd told you I'd tell you what it was one day, didn't I?)

Often she had wanted to throw it away. When anger alleviated the hurt. But it was all she had. And later, when she was weeping in indulgent grief, she was glad.

She opened her eyes and watched the ceiling swirl. If she concentrated she could twist it around. And when it was twisting, she could see images of him. She could see him staring at her. On his face a half smile. Not part of his actual repertoire of expressions, but nevertheless a familiar expression in her current gallery. Her creations. How he would have looked. His eyes warm, but tinged with an understanding of what he had done.

The image was obscure in the crepuscular light. So now, in the darkness, with the open curtains throwing only a dull grey glow into the room, she watched him slowly. She spoke to him. Her voice in the silence bewitched the scene. The sorcery of the voice, unnatural with no audible reply. It made the silence all the more responsive. Answers seared through her ears. Like a prayer.

17

Mirrors and Matzos

They stopped the confessional process in order to clean up the breakfast things.

But even while she washed and he, without enthusiasm, dried, she was still mulling over the last hour. She took in a sharp breath and her hands were paralysed in the soapy bowl.

'I haven't told you that I ruined Sarah's life.'

He too paused. 'What the hell d'you mean?'

Maggie winced. 'She has nothing. I gave her nothing. I was never supportive of her.'

He tutted in frustration. 'Why do you deny yourself even the smallest break, Maggie?'

She shook her head and resumed scrubbing the plates with violence.

'You don't understand. I didn't want her.'

'She never went without.'

That wasn't the point and Maggie didn't answer. But her face fell. She looked instantly older. There was no sound but her angry sloshing of the water and his anxious setting down of the dried-up crockery. Then a few moments later she said, 'Anyway, what I'm saying is, it makes me feel like a confession from you is inappropriate. What you did was a single act. Running away from me in an understandable moment of panic. I have been doing this for years. Everything Sarah is, I've made her. I was cold, unemotional. I was closed up. I would never play with her.'

He was softly scoffing. 'You? Not playing? I don't believe that.'

She stared at the water as it turned grey. 'You don't know me either, Rudi. I changed, I had to and you wouldn't believe what I became. Sarah would never believe what I was once. What I was on that boat sometimes seems like a film, somebody else.'

'Nobody changes that much.'

'I did. Harry, my father, was a better parent than I've been. Better not to be there at all than to be cruel, like me.'

'You shouldn't blame yourself.'

She smiled, his choice of words pulling her out of a chasm. 'Why not? It *is* my fault, after all. You've been reading too many self-help books. Have you been in therapy? I hear all Americans go into therapy.'

He pulled a face. 'Only the sane ones. The lunatics, the politicians, people who think they've got all the answers, they don't do therapy.'

'So you've been in therapy?'

'Me? Are you kidding? Sure I have.'

Her eyes opened. Her reticence was quashed by interest in his life. Not a confession, just information. The washing-up done, she poured the dirty water down the sink and carefully rinsed the bowl. He watched her precision incredulously. Mimicking her, which was the only way to feel comfortable in the gleaming kitchen, he carefully folded the tea towel in half and handed it to her. She didn't notice his parody.

She turned to him and smiled, almost shyly.

'I don't want to read any more transcripts. I want to hear it from you.'

He nodded. He didn't mind now.

They were heading back to the lounge when he said, 'Hey, it's a beautiful day, why don't we go to a park or something? You got a park near here?'

'Well, Brockwell Park isn't far.'

'Can we walk?' He sniffed. 'It's easier to talk when walking, don't you think? That's the great thing about Chicago. It's a city where you can walk without being mugged. I love to walk.'

'Me too,' she said. 'That's something Sarah and I have in common. Although we never do it together.'

Once they were through the front gate and walking along the roaring open road he was able to speak and suddenly it felt like he was telling a story to a child.

'We arrived in Chicago in 1946. My father's cousin had gone over there in the 'twenties and he sent us money, plus we got some state aid. It was the only place to go. My mother wouldn't go to Israel. I told you she was an atheist. The war made everyone stronger in their beliefs. My mother wanted no more God.

'Her dream was to become American. She was learning English before we'd even gotten the plane tickets. We came alone as a family. There were so few survivors from Poland.

'We lived with my cousin for a few months. He had done well for himself and even after the crash he had kept afloat buying and selling cheap furniture in a shop on 53rd Street. By this time he had a better shop and had moved out of the poor Polish Jewish neighbourhood to the well-to-do Kenwood area. It was near the lake and a great place to live, close to the beaches and parks and not far from the university.

'My father worked all hours in a kitchen appliance factory fitting parts together. After the war was a good time to be in that line and his tailoring skills were way out of date for the West. My mother worked in the Sears Roebuck department store on Arthington Avenue.

'The school I went to, there were a lot of Jews. I still studied at the synagogue some evenings – at my father's insistence. He was sentimental about it.

'My other sister and my brother were born in the next few years. They are an all-American pair, Debbie and Michael, and they blended seamlessly into WASP Chicago. They helped my mother forget – she threw herself into raising her new children.'

Maggie looked appalled. He saw the look.

'No, but she wanted to. It was a new life, a new start. She wanted nothing from the world she left behind. I don't blame her for that.

'My father was musical. He had played the trumpet and he got an occasional evening job playing in the theatre. My parents loved American music – especially the blues. Of course the blues were songs of suffering. Maybe that's how my mother remembered my first sister.'

Maggie was so drawn into the story that, as they walked down Half Moon Lane towards Herne Hill and Brockwell Park, she began to feel that she was not walking on a bending South

216

London street with pedestrians in trainers and cars emitting white pop music. She was in this strange city he was talking about where the pedestrians wore dresses and suits – clothes that she remembered from her own childhood – and the noises were altogether different. She felt bad at having lost concentration.

'We never talked about Etta. My brother and sister only found out years later. But we couldn't hide everything. It was ironic that in trying to throw herself into white America my mother gave herself a harder time. When we had the money we moved even further away. We were so far removed from the old Jewish areas like Maxwell Street and Lawndale.'

Maggie interrupted. 'So you didn't feel Jewish at all?'

'I don't know what that means really. I felt like a kid. I had nightmares sometimes about the time before we came to America. I would wake up thinking I was still in the forest, dreaming that we had been discovered. I never could eat pork but that was after a year eating rotting meat, nothing to do with being Jewish.'

Maggie gulped.

'By the way, I meant to ask, what happened to your grandfather's jar of teeth? You don't have it now, surely?'

He looked down. 'No. I left it behind in a Polish farmer's barn. I was still a careless boy. My fugitive victim status failed to elevate me. Nothing dramatic. I just forgot it. Left it behind. Christ knows what the farmer thought. Can't have done much to enhance Polish–Jewish relations – they already half-suspected we used human blood to make matzos.'

Although he spoke with levity, Maggie could tell that he was angry at himself within. It was a trait she recognized. She moved on hastily.

'Look, you can see the wall of the park over there.' She pointed.

'Oh yeah.'

'S-so, what was your life like as an American boy?'

He carried on, more quietly than before.

'Typical, I guess. I loved the movies and especially the funnies. I loved laughing. And making people laugh. It meant I didn't have to explain anything. It didn't matter who I was.

'I loved *The Sid Caesar Hour*, Bob Hope, Lucille Ball, all those kind of shows. As I got older it was Lenny Bruce. Comedy that was dangerous. That made sense to me. Comedy should be dangerous.

'So all the while I was in high school I was practising in front of the mirror. It seemed the natural thing to do in front of the mirror. I didn't know that all the other guys were jerking off.'

Maggie was laughing as they walked into the park. It was refreshing for the eyes to hit the vivid green field after the dirty street.

'Seems like we all have our own uses for mirrors.'

He looked at her. 'Yeah, of course.'

But she didn't want to go there. She steered the conversation back, as she steered their course through the park. Her territory, taking her route. This was the way she liked to walk.

'So you started wanting to be a comedian? You know, I can't believe I wasn't demanding this information from you when I was young. It's as if I had no curiosity. I just took you as you were. It shows how selfish I was.'

He wasn't buying it. 'Or maybe just how we were living in the present. Not the past, and certainly not the future.'

'Oh, OK,' she conceded but then asked impatiently, 'so tell me now how you became a comedian.'

He stopped to admire a huge sweet chestnut tree towering over them. Its leaves had the slightest promise of autumnal gold.

'Even before my high school graduation I was sending my own material to the local radio station. None of it was ever used, of course. But I even loved the rejection slips. It made me feel a part of things.

'My mom was delighted. She saw that lots of Jews had made it big in Hollywood by changing their names. Particularly her favourite, Danny Kaye.'

'My favourite used to be Danny Kaye!' Maggie burst out, sounding about eleven years old.

He smiled at this flash of an earlier incarnation. 'My mother came out with some baloney about my grandfather being a great entertainer, that there were comics in the family, but I don't remember any of that.

'I graduated high school. Other guys seemed to be getting married to the girls they knocked up at the prom. I certainly didn't want any of that.

'I did a few amateur nights at some of the clubs. Mostly pretty seedy. I'd be on to warm up the crowd before a singer. I got regular gigs at a place called the Diamond Club.'

'But how did you make money?' It was her first thought.

'During the day I worked as a clerk at the Chicago City Council. It was easy to get a job as a Jew – it was good for their anti-discrimination rules.

'But really I wanted to go pro as a comedian. I had ambition. I knew I was as good as some of the guys who were doing really well. I got a bit of radio work. I couldn't understand why my earlier attempts had been rejected when I saw the pathetic material that they let through. I had a ball. I was writing material. I gave up my day job when I was working clubs four nights a week. It was a fantastic time. I was meeting women, I even began to get a few fan letters.'

'Fan letters?' said Maggie dubiously.

'I was never good looking of course, but in the era when Humphrey Bogart was considered a prime specimen of manhood I got my fair share of attention.'

You're not bad looking, she thought, noting with satisfaction that his carriage was upright and his pace quick.

He put his hands in his pockets and sighed. 'My folks kept pushing me to find a nice girl and settle down. Get one of those California bungalows that the Chicagoans were so fond of. I could see no reason to settle down when I saw the life that my high-school buddies had carved out for themselves. Anyhow, who would want to hitch up with a guy who was out every evening and had an unreliable income and no future?'

Maggie seemed surprised. 'But you had a future. You could have been really big.'

He smiled a small wry smile that seemed heavy. 'Maybe.' Then he shook his head.

'I got this fan letter from a woman in Chicago Heights, a southern suburb. She sounded pretty lonely. She was pouring her heart out to me. She lived in the middle of nowhere. She said the night she saw me in the club was the biggest night of her life.

'I felt sorry for her, don't know why, but it struck a nerve. Anyhow I wrote back. I encouraged her to get out more and said I was glad she enjoyed the show.

'She wrote back. She kept writing. It was no big deal. Even when the letters began to get pretty steamy, I could handle it.

Then she said she wanted to meet me. I didn't know what she looked like but I wasn't going to pass up an open invitation like that, so I suggested she come to another show.

'Anyway, a few days later, at the end of the set, I'm drinking at the bar when this woman comes up to me. She's young, quite attractive and quite pushy. So we start talking. Turns out she's the author of the steamy fan mail. I feel a bit uncomfortable, but she pushes it. She wants to go out drinking. I was planning something like that with a few other guys anyway, so I say, "Sure." She's not bad company.

'We are out for a long time. She smokes, she drinks – outdrinks all of us. She is clearly up for something. She keeps moving closer to me. Staring me down. But something tells me to back off. There is something about her that spooks me.

'We get home late. The other guys take a cab together. I don't want to leave her on her own so I get us a cab back to her place. She tries to get me to come in. I remember thinking it's a damn big place. I say this to her. She says her husband's wealthy – and out of town.

'That does it. I get the hell out. She doesn't want to let me go, she pulls at my coat and starts getting hysterical. I say as an excuse, "Not in front of the driver." I really didn't want anything to do with her but I didn't want her throwing a fit. As it is, she gets real short after that.'

'The next day she calls me up at the club. As sweet as cheesecake. Like nothing had happened. She says she wants to meet that night. I don't think it's such a good idea.

'She starts yelling at me. I'm glad to be out of it since she's obviously screwy.'

He paused.

Maggie, who was hanging on to every word like there was a ten-storey drop beneath her, almost snapped, 'So what happened?'

He lowered his head. 'A week later I get a letter from her folks. Turns out she's fourteen years old and claiming I molested her.'

Maggie felt her skin prick. 'My God.'

They both stopped. They were surrounded by a wide panorama of green. There was no one in sight.

'Yeah.' He couldn't look at her. He just said in a small voice,

'I swear, Maggie, the story I told you, it's the truth. I was completely innocent. I even asked her how old she was, and she said nineteen. I couldn't tell. She was all made up, the lipstick and everything. She carried it off. She fooled me and that's the truth.'

She stammered, 'Of course it is. I wouldn't doubt you.'

'Well,' he said, 'that wasn't how anyone else felt. They believed her. It suited the local papers to believe in the innocent young girl and not the seedy Jewish club man. It fit so many prejudices.' He hesitated. 'I often wonder what made her do it. Probably just boredom, a fantasy or frustration with all those mixed-up teenage feelings. I guess she didn't think too much about the consequences. They were nothing to her. By the time she realized, maybe it was too late – it was a big deal already and she was too afraid to own up.'

Maggie was shaking her head in disbelief and her eyes were aching with sympathy.

'My God, no wonder you were so worried about us!'

He looked pained. 'Yeah,' he said, 'there were times with you when I began to doubt my own memories. Thought maybe I was guilty.

'Anyway, the result of this fiasco was I had to get out of town. I couldn't expose my folks to any more trauma. Not my mother who'd devoted years in America to trying to fit in. No charges were ever brought against me. I got taken down the station and roughed up a bit by the cops but I think they knew it wasn't for real. They interviewed the girl and I never found out what she said. They dropped it. But mud sticks. Mom believed I was innocent but that didn't make it any easier to have the neighbours crossing the street to avoid her. It was anti-Semitic enough where we lived. Of course I had to quit the club.'

'So you ran away to sea,' she said in a flat voice.

'Mmm-hmm.'

He took a sideways look at her, while they were still standing motionless. He was wondering how many more surprises he could throw at her. But she wanted to know.

'So you must kinda see why I quit the boat in such a hurry. I was used to running away from trouble. So it was the obvious thing to do when Sally found out about us.'

Maggie looked at him sharply. 'I thought she was just

suspicious?' How clear her memories were again, now he was here in front of her and the time in between was driven away.

'She was, at first. But when she got her claws into something, she wouldn't let go. She wanted to pin something on me to get back at me for showing no interest in her. For a while she thought I was gay. Why else would I have turned down her generous offer? Then she stopped thinking and began watching. And when anyone really starts to look, I guess the truth is transparent.'

'But we were discreet.'

He raised his eyebrows. 'Physically, maybe. But we were always together. It didn't take a lot to guess what was going on. Remember the night your father died?'

Maggie thought she would never forget it – the yellow storm, her father's body, blue and bloated. But she *had* forgotten something. That when Sally came into her room to break the news, Rudi was sitting on the bed.

'Sally came and found you in my bedroom,' she said in a peculiarly still voice.

'Yeah,' he half-laughed. 'It was kinda ironic that we'd spent the night apart. But we were both barely dressed. That was enough to confirm what she already suspected.'

'And she blew the whistle?'

He shook his head. 'She was too desperate for that. She just threatened to. She told me she thought it was disgusting and criminal but that she'd say no more about it if I'd switch my allegiances to her – only' – he managed to smile at the recollection – 'you know Sally, she didn't put it as sweetly as that.

'So I had to go, don't you see? I couldn't hold her off much longer. She would have given me away at some point, out of sheer frustration. You were under age, remember. I know it seemed like a dream at the time, but I had committed a crime. And after what happened in Chicago, Christ . . .'

'God,' said Maggie, who slumped on to the grass in her shock. 'And to think she bored me rigid with her tales of how in love with my father she was. And how she knew the meaning of love . . . and' – Maggie was stuttering with the eagerness of her sudden flashback – 'she told me so patronizingly that "One day you too, little Maggie, might know love." So creepy, with the clear implication that she thought I was an innocent child. In fact I think she might even have called me that.' Maggie shuddered. 'I hated her for it. I really did. Having to cope with my father's death and feeling so sick, realizing I was pregnant and then her fawning all over me. It was the last thing I needed. I tried to be nice because I felt sorry for her in a strange way. But it was a complete lie.'

Rudi sat down beside her, after tentatively feeling the grass for dampness and checking it for dog shit. He stretched out his legs and knotted his fingers together and straightened them, palms outwards, as he often did when the joints felt awkward. Or perhaps it was his thoughts that troubled him. He asked, 'When did you know you were pregnant?'

She didn't need to think. 'When the storm passed and I still felt sick. At first I thought it couldn't be true, we'd been so careful, but I'd missed two periods. The evidence was irrefutable, even to me in my fantasy world.'

He looked worried. 'But you didn't know before I'd gone?'

'No,' she said firmly. 'I would have told you. I wanted to tell you. I was desperate enough to ask the Captain where you'd gone. I didn't have anyone else. I knew I'd have to leave the ship. I thought if I could get in touch with you . . .'

'And the Captain said what, that I'd left in Kingston?' She nodded. He shook his head. 'Goddamn tightwad, he charged me for breaking contract!' He remembered himself. 'Christ, you must have been desperate.'

'Yes,' she said blandly. 'That's when I persuaded myself you must have died. I couldn't face anything else. I handed in my notice, came up with some drivel about wanting to go back to England since I no longer had my father with me. The money I had just covered a passage back. I wrote to Great Edie but she claimed she never got the letter. She wasn't exactly pleased to see me. But there I was on the doorstep, carrying her only chance of a great-grandchild. Wasn't much she could do.'

Rudi stared across the grass.

'If I'd known I'd have taken you with. I wanted to. But I felt like I was becoming the monster that they all thought I was back home. I panicked. I didn't want to screw up your life by staying and having it all come out. I guess I kidded myself that I wouldn't screw up your life by cutting loose.'

The words came out in a storm. And afterwards she felt release. Rudi's head was bent.

Maggie took his hand, an old hand that was wrinkled and dotted with freckles that were spreading into age spots. It looked beautiful to her.

She said in a soft but intent voice, 'I think you underestimated the strength of my affection.'

He let out an anguished howl. Even now, with so many years gone, the emotion between them was real. Stoked as easily as embers. From between the rising sobs Maggie heard him say that he had ruined everything. She stroked his neck, feeling the black and white hair between her fingers.

18

The Last of the Lemon

Maggie had daily reminders. Sweet in memory but punishing in contrast.

She was washing her hair in the sink. Her hands hit the wet wooden side of the cabinet as she groped for the soap, a gritty oatmeal bar. Water sloshed over the edge of the basin, splashing her skirt. The wood felt so rough, she imagined it splintering. With her eyes gripped shut she saw shards following across the blackness. The simple ritual absorbed her completely; the monotonous rhythm, her youthful narcissism, the insight that she was female and her skin sensuous. Washing was a beautiful act.

She rinsed the thin suds from her hair, her fingers squeaking against the shiny scalp. The circles she drew. As she lifted her head, relieving her neck, putting her fingers over her closed eyes to rub away the water, she felt another pair of hands on her head. He had crept up silently behind her.

'Your skin', he whispered, 'is so fresh.'

She kissed Rudi and looked out across the ocean. Her mouth was resting on his cheek. Her left eye was consumed by the fleshly foreground of his skin. But her right looked through the porthole into the distance. The effect was dizzying. She did not know what she meant to him. She was untinctured, he thought, while he was weathered against the sky.

'Are you a child?' he asked earnestly, desperate for mental absolution.

She only smiled. The door blew open with the breeze from the sea. She felt the breeze on her face. It felt cooler as it dried her sweat.

'Let's stop,' he said, as he often did. 'Let's hold on to this. Hold my hands. Give me memories.'

She held on to his hand, not knowing what he wanted or why he wanted it. She was young enough then to believe that life would go on for ever.

The moment was broken by the screams. It had to be Sally. No one else had a scream that penetrating.

Maggie broke away. 'Sally, stop screaming. Stop screaming. Stop screaming. Stop screaming.'

It was the baby. The boat was gone. As she dragged herself from her bed Maggie still felt half enchanted. The bedroom carpet was still the wooden floor of the ship. The ground still swayed slightly in her head torn between sleep and consciousness. She walked across the floor. She turned the handle of the old door slowly. If she woke up Great Edie there would be trouble in the morning. The swollen door shuddered open. Sarah was screaming loudly, piercingly. Great Edie had a gift for waking only to the noises she took as a personal slight. The cries of the baby never stirred her. They struck Maggie like a stone.

Her milk had dried up. She had tried to breastfeed at first, half-heartedly, and the child had seemed reluctant – Maggie *believed* that Sarah would not want it. Sarah hung miserably on to the breast and refused to suck. Even when the midwife, amazed at Maggie's inability to master such a natural process, grabbed the baby's head and twisted it into the correct angle, Sarah would not cooperate. Maggie was grateful to the doctor who said that modern thought positively encouraged the use of the bottle. 'It makes them independent.'

She had not been pregnant, it seemed to her now, it was just misery swollen inside.

The birth had distracted her mind. Almost a relief, for eighteen hours she concentrated only on the pains and forgot the recrimination and the shame. The thoughts returned slowly and miserably over the five days that she languished in her hospital bed. It was no comfort to be visited by her cranky grandmother or the rest of the day to be surrounded by twenty-nine mothers who wanted their children. The white starched sheets. Being told when to sleep. Being helped to the lavatory. It was enough to drive anyone crazy.

She looked at her daughter who was held in a cot alongside the other infants, behind a glass screen at the end of the ward. She looked at the lines of babies, like a factory output. She looked at the sleeping face of the daughter. It didn't feel like hers. There was no sense of belonging. Only it didn't feel like nothing. There *was* a sense of pain.

As if to confirm her suspicion, her young body snapped back into shape and there was nothing to show that she had ever been pregnant – except the grisly infant. Maggie's skeleton was trimly covered by an even inch of flesh. She was glad. She had hated the invasion. The fear that something was inside her, listening to her thoughts.

But however much she hated being pregnant, resented being a mother, it was part of her. It was only possible to hate her child in the way that it was possible to hate herself. It was not as simple as a total hatred. She learned that it was possible to hate and love at the same time.

The screaming infant seemed full of hate. Sarah cried endlessly. Maggie felt impotent. And the angrier the baby became, the angrier Great Edie became. But the baby seemed to derive no comfort from her mother.

'Why Sarah?' Great Edie demanded by way of conversation, sitting in the visiting room sniffing censoriously. Princess Margaret had called her daughter Sarah and Maggie was short of inspiration. It was a nice enough name.

Rocking Sarah made her think only that she wanted to be rocked. Her mother and Rudi were gone. Maggie felt very lonely.

No one believed that her husband had died of typhoid. Particularly as Maggie had no information about the disease with which to be convincing.

'I had a husband. He died of typhoid.'

It couldn't have sounded less plausible if she had said her husband was gored by a mammoth. But she could think of nothing else. When Great Edie pronounced, Maggie found it very difficult to overcome her strength of mind. Sometimes it was simply easier not to; so typhoid it was. At least she did not have to feign grief.

She craved sleep because then she could return to the boat. She dreaded sleep because it meant waking up again. She could not sleep and when she did fall fitfully into dozing, Sarah would wake her screaming. She was miserable too. Of that there was no doubt. She look squashed. All babies looked squashed when they first leave the body of their mother. But over the days they unfurl. Not Sarah. She always looked cramped. As if she knew there was no room for her.

When Great Edie was in a better mood she let Maggie sit in the kitchen with her and listen while she talked. 'You might meet another man. Not now of course, not with a child hanging round your neck.' When her grandmother was advising Maggie on men, she always sat the same way. With her legs gradually opening and her skirting hitching inelegantly up her thigh.

Maggie said, 'But you didn't marry again.'

Edie looked sharply at her.

'Waddya mean, again?' she snapped. 'You ain't married once yet.'

The inevitability of the response, Edie couldn't let it go. Not once.

Maggie was feeling the roughness of the grater on her fingers.

Her grandmother snapped, 'Take your fingers off that thing, Maggie. I'll have to wash it up now.'

Maggie did the washing up, in fact all the cleaning. Her grandmother did not believe in washing pans. 'Lets all the flavour out.' (It was the only time she expressed an interest in flavours.) 'Nobody caught nothing off messy pans. Look at me, I've got a stomach of iron. Me, I never get ill.' She didn't. But that didn't explain why she never washed plates or knives or bowls or clothes or floors or her face.

It was eleven o'clock in the morning and Great Edie had recently emerged from her bedroom. It was a horrible vision. The years in which the most vigorous exercise she took was frowning were beginning to show. At sixty-three she was thick-set and shrinking. She was already beginning to smell old, the vaguely musty smell of someone whose clothing was all ten years old and more. And she didn't listen. She believed she had done her learning about life and now it was time to dispense wisdom.

The world was changing. Everybody said so. But the changing world, which was meant to be so liberating, only confirmed to Maggie how isolated she was. This changing world she experienced through the cinema screen or the monochrome television. Not only that but she was further distanced by the penetrating opinions of her grandmother. Somehow the derisive commentary that Edie threw on anything fashionable or 'swinging' tainted it all. 'Twiggy – she's the same age as you.' Edie came out of her *Daily Express* to look at Maggie's bored face. She eyed her up and down desultorily. 'Why can't you get one of them model jobs? You're skinny enough.'

Maggie put the kettle on, ignoring the remark. The handle felt sticky as she placed it on the hob. Her grandmother sniggered nastily from behind her paper, which was withering timorously in her hands. 'Mysticism?' spat Great Edie. 'The great fool! Meaning of life? What rubbish! What's George Harrison got to search for meaning for? I tell yer. These bloody Indians would give their eye-teeth to be in his position. He earns all that bloody money and then he wonders what the meaning of it all is.'

Maggie, seeing the feeble procession of clients who walked into the dim suburban light of her grandmother's Victorian house, looking for meaning in tea leaves and the crystal ball, couldn't help but agree. If George Harrison felt unfulfilled, there was no hope at all.

The day passed. Maggie dully changed her baby daughter six times. In between and after feeds. Folding the nappy into a rhombus and putting in the safety pin that seemed so big compared to the fragile legs it clamped. She boiled the nappies from the previous day. The bucket stank. Great Edie took refuge in the sitting room. The water was cold. Maggie boiled up kettles. Rinsed the cloth. Sluiced the muck down the sink. By the end of the day, when she was dragging the washed nappies through the mangle, her hands felt raw.

Her bedroom had a tatty Edwardian cupboard that she had picked up from a second-hand shop when she was expecting. There was a hanging space on the left-hand side behind a thin door. The right-hand side was split between five drawers at the bottom and above a half-length mirror set deep against the back. It was distinctly flat as a source of imagination. Seeking escape through its contours was not easy. Using it as she had long used mirrors, the way Grace had taught her, Maggie felt that she was squeezing the last drops from an overused lemon. The flavour grew fainter and fainter. But still there was a fragrant redolence to make it worth the effort.

And while there remained some taste it was better than nothing. Even though her old self was now fighting against her new common sense. The growing urge inside her to forget. To settle for this new life and not torment herself with thoughts of the past.

For now it still worked.

So this evening, as on many others, in the dusk she sat on the bed and stared into the mirror. Her hands felt the smooth veneer of the cupboard sides. As her fingers brushed the patina she felt herself falling into memory. Sarah's cries became the wail of the boat's engines.

She pushed through the mirror like thrashing through waves. And duck-dived into the water, the midnight depths. And as she swam to the surface, she felt a joyful weightlessness. When she pierced the surface, she was already dry.

The boat was still. And she and Rudi danced on the open deck. To the notes of a solitary piano, slightly off-pitch. This dissonance gave it a poignant fourth dimension as it reluctantly held the seconds. He held her as they danced a slow waltz, so slow it was walking in rhythm. Her backless dress had a full skirt of rich cream layers, which smelt of the mothballs in the costume boxroom. She wore white gloves but could still feel his warmth through the fingers.

The deck was dark. But though the boat was still, it was not empty. The people were statues. Rudi and Maggie waltzed round a white marble Sally Shezaar, frozen in an expression of surprise. And past Joe Moller, his fat rolling into marmoreal efflorescence.

They drank red wine from deep, heavy glasses. Rudi wore his normal shabby suit. She did not like to change him. And all the while they danced they were able to talk. They talked without breaking the flow. They talked about things with no strings. The shine on the water. The function of the earlobe – that it could only have been constructed for pleasure. His mouth brushed against it as he spoke into her ear. They waltzed down the steps to the alley below and, with the roar of the water behind him, he took off her clothes.

Yet slowly, inexorably, the world began to pull her back. One evening, her journey through the mirror was broken when a face flashed across her vision. It was a young man with eyes of gripping insouciance. He was not beautiful – the lips hung strangely and the eyelashes were too long and effeminate – but he had something. From her lips came the words that went with the face: 'Is every man an Alfie? Ask any woman.' Then with irritation, her eyes now fully focused again on her tatty room, she realized who her distraction was. The face belonged to an actor called Michael Caine. Last year, when the film came out, she had barely noticed the posters that were everywhere. Now this one tatty reminder seemed to jump from the hoarding. If the popularity of the film was anything to go by, roguish Alfie was the future of the male sex. Dancing on decks belonged to the past.

When Sarah grew older and Maggie herself was nearly twenty and when even Paul McCartney had got married, Great Edie thought that Maggie might attract one of her clients.

Several single solvent males came away from her readings convinced that they would shortly meet a woman, young, available and widowed from a husband who died of an unusual disease.

Maggie accepted it uncomplainingly. She had become more accustomed to her fate, more pliant. The boat represented unbearable freedom where she could walk without a pram and without the fear that people were looking at her. But she did ask why Edie was so determined to force a man on her, when she was so dismissive of their benefit.

'Well, how could you manage on yer own, eh?'

Maggie shuddered at the expression on her grandmother's face when her favourite syllable, 'Eh?' came out.

Whatever the strain in their relationship, Maggie certainly believed in Edie's strength. For all her sourness, her grandmother could conquer oceans. Maggie merely lived on them. Everyone was scared of Edie. And while Maggie suffered from the tongue that grew ever angrier, she felt safe. It was strange that she could be thoroughly miserable and yet fear the collapse of that same miserable world.

She missed her mother more than ever. As an adult, it was like losing her all over again.

As an adult she had to deal with her mother. Talk to the doctors, be aware of the situation. Great Edie abdicated responsibility with relief. Maggie wanted to be involved. She wanted to be closer to her mother. Even if that closeness was one-sided. Her renewed intimacy made no sense to her grandmother.

'You've got one baby on yer hands and you don't like 'er. What d'you want another one for, eh?'

Dr Spock reassured Maggie that it was quite all right that Sarah became independent quickly, that she did not crave affection, that she did not respond as some children do to physical closeness. Her physical relationship with Maggie was practical rather than emotional. Maggie held her when she needed to be held. She took her daughter's hand when crossing a road. She cuddled her when she wrapped her in a towel after a bath. She stroked her face when wiping food from her cheeks.

She had little physical closeness with her daughter but also her sense of physicality was slipping away. She had lost interest. She washed herself but did not beautify as once she did. There was a sense that such cleanliness was more than just washing away dirt. It was washing away her old self.

The care with which she had pinched her cheeks and applied the blob of rouge and smudge of lipstick in the make-up room on the boat – for him as well as herself – was long abandoned.

Sometimes she could not bear to look at herself. For it was the same face that used to live differently.

Later, when her own daughter was an adolescent, Maggie could not understand why she had not got over her early romance more quickly. Was it because of the circumstances? Was her situation a constant reminder that she was a victim with reason to be miserable? Was it the man she missed or her old freedom? After all, didn't every sixteen-year-old suffer heart-break? Wasn't love at that age only embryonic? Like chicken pox, if you got it young enough it was a minor fever. Only later in life did the disease leave disfiguring scars. Or was it more like German measles where everyone gets over it *except* the very young?

Maggie had hoped that she would get German measles. A deformed baby would have been taken off her hands. How could such thoughts *not* lead to a lifetime of self-loathing? She could never forget that she had thought such things. The hardest lesson she never learned was self-acceptance. She did not love herself. How could she possibly love someone who had ruined her daughter's life?

She sympathized with teenagers who killed children. She felt that she too had come close. That she had too often wished her daughter dead, or that she had never existed. She didn't know what the difference was between actual killers and herself. Her prison was metaphorical.

There seemed to be no way out of her living arrangements. That she would always have to live with her cantankerous grandmother because there was simply no affordable alternative. Her part-time cleaning jobs hardly paid for her cigarettes. She was hopelessly reliant on Edie for money.

But next door was a very wobbly, very grateful old lady. The kind of milky-cheeked, sweet-natured old lady that Great Edie would clearly never turn into. She had lived in the house for fifty years and was falling apart with the decorations.

Miss Reynolds was entirely alone. She had never married ('And that meant no children in those days,' sniped Great Edie) and had no family around. So Maggie watched out for her. Cleaned up ('One more won't make any difference to you, will it, Maggie,' said Edie), did bits of shopping and stopped to chat or at least smile through the old woman's stumblings that went in lieu of conversation. Maggie did not feel good about it. It was not, she reasoned, an act of charity, but because if she didn't look after her the woman would die.

And so it transpired. When Maggie, through tiredness or overwork or some other reason that she later could not remember, missed a week, on her next visit she found Miss Reynolds slumped in her chair. Dead. But still with a smile on her face.

'Not another one!' exclaimed Great Edie. 'Blimey, you do nothing except collect corpses.'

Maggie found out the old lady's first name only when she was called by the woman's solicitor and informed she was the sole beneficiary. Miss Florence Reynolds had no money after the funeral costs and urgent repairs to the house but she owned the property and she had left it to a rather surprised Maggie.

The funeral was attended by Maggie and, very begrudgingly, Edie who grumbled only half-jokingly as they sat in the crematorium, 'Why should I go to 'er funeral? I hardly knew 'er. It's not like the old girl's likely to return the favour, is it?' She jabbed her chin in Maggie's ear. 'What she leave you that house for? You killed the poor sod. Gawd save me from you when I'm old. That's all I can say.'

Maggie offered a pinched smile. 'That's not all you can say but let's hope it doesn't come to that.'

After the Gothic horror of Great Edie's and the superficial glamour of the boat, Maggie craved simplicity. She wanted no possessions. Great Edie's weakness for gloomy Victoriana gave her an almost permanent headache. Maggie yearned for light.

Almost for the first time she was thankful that times had changed. Now a single woman with a child could buy a property. She swiftly chose a semi-detached house in a cheaper area away from Herne Hill and nearer to Streatham. It was only ten years old. It had thin walls and low ceilings. But to her that was an asset. The moribund silence of the thick walls and vaulted ceilings of Great Edie's was oppressive by comparison. Maggie hated the shadows.

So in October 1976, after ten years with her grandmother, she took Sarah in the spluttering old Mini to the first real home she could call her own.

Her aspiring minimalism was abetted by the fact that she owned almost nothing. She went to Pratt's department store in Streatham and bought the cheapest, simplest essentials for kitchen and bathroom. Small ascetic towels and uncomplicated cutlery. What a release to leave Edie with her blackened silver dead-weight cutlery that was overlaid with curling patterns like ivy over a gravestone. What a pleasure this new independence, creating her own environment. After years in a dead house she was glad even to hear the noise of neighbours.

19

Different Colours

'It's a haven,' explained Diana. 'Somehow, in all the confusion, we have found ourselves.'

It was unclear whether by confusion she meant the world that they had left behind or the noise that they now made, the sound of clattering soup pans and full-volume Joan Baez.

Getting to know her new neighbours had proved easier than anticipated. Maggie went round one evening to ask that the sound be turned down so that her nine-year-old daughter could for once do her homework rather than learning protest songs. She found herself simply sucked in. She did not tell them that, in her opinion, bringing up a child alone (in her case without the father) was like running a bath without a tub – impossible – and so the women embraced the single mother and her scowling daughter as society's victims. Within a few weeks the wall between the two houses was, figuratively at least, knocked down.

'We all have dyke potential,' said Ann, sipping coffee and lighting a thin cigarette. She had removed the 'e' from her original name as part of her self-embraced de-floralization (her term).

'I haven't,' said Maggie. The women called her Mags.

Diana smiled in an indulgent fashion. 'Inside all of us is a fantasy to escape the aggressive sexuality of the masculine machine.'

Maggie valiantly fought the objections that initially rose in her mind when Sarah met the women. For if Edie had taught her anything it was the ugliness of blind discrimination. Great Edie was not prejudiced – she despised everyone.

The three women, Diana, Beth and Ann, had lived together for some time. It was unclear exactly how the three were attached. Maggie, although interested, couldn't bring herself to ask. The house had three bedrooms, but one was saved for guests.

Diana was the histrionic protagonist, given to loose flowing shades of purple. Ann an amiable yes-woman who lived in frayed denim. Beth, well spoken and elegant, Maggie found more convincing because of her reticence.

Beth had left her husband who was a brutal and violent man. She met Diana, who was then working in the women's refuge. Beth was, she admitted, a lesbian by default rather than design. 'I sought first a physical refuge but found myself better served in an emotional one.' She escaped from her husband only when a hospital doctor refused to believe she had fallen down the stairs again.

'It was ironic', she said ruefully, her eyes cast down, 'that I finally ran away with a smashed foot.'

Maggie could not believe what she was hearing.

'Yes,' sighed Beth, 'he crushed it with a paving slab. Before that he broke my wrist. I broke two ribs when he pushed me down the stairs and I've had more black eyes than a blighted potato.'

So that was why she walked with a limp.

When asked, Maggie explained, without reluctance, her own circumstances. The father of her child. Her mother's removal from normal society. Her father's ineffectual silence. She felt free to talk, realizing the women would be judgemental only in her favour.

Diana leaped on Grace's incarceration. 'Bloody typical,' she said. 'Who decided your mother was insane?'

'Well, it was obvious,' said the nonplussed Maggie.

'I mean, darling, by whose definition?' This question Maggie did not answer.

'You know who decides, Mags. Women have been accused of madness or evil or witchcraft ever since men realized women had something they didn't, that they have an understanding and intuition that goes way deeper' – she stopped for effect and lowered her voice – '*way* deeper than the infinitesimal piece of shit that men call their brains. With the physical superiority of brute force, they think they have overcome us. Well, no fucking way.'

Diana had worked herself up into such a frenzy, Maggie noticed, there were beads of perspiration on her forehead.

And then she remembered that it was not perspiration but sweat.

After a flurry of curiosity, Sarah accepted her new neighbours. 'Why do you all share beds?' she asked. Sarah was already blunt and she would remain so.

There was perceptible surprise on Diana's face. She looked at Maggie, who smiled encouragingly and made a gesture like a gate opening to show that she should proceed.

'Well,' said Diana, 'because sometimes women want to.'

Sarah looked at her, confused. Her small face curled in thought. 'Why?'

Ann, who had been relaxed into the kitchen seat, her naked toes hooked around the rung of the wooden stool next to her, a stance which displayed her flared jeans at their best, stiffened. 'Because some women fall in love with women, not men.'

'Why?'

Maggie knew Sarah wanted to know the unsaid. She said briskly, 'Because, Sarah, sometimes they just do and sometimes they do because they've had bad experiences with men.'

'Bad like how?'

Unless stopped, this would go on all night. Children have an insatiable attraction to the horrible. Sarah was never happier than when dripping in blood. And it would not be just a childhood trait.

'Bad like how?' she persisted.

'Aggressive, bad to live with.'

'Oh. So they're lesbians then?'

'That's right.' Maggie was mollified that she had not been introducing something entirely new to an innocent mind.

Maggie and Sarah referred to the women collectively as the Commune or the C. The women did not think of themselves as such but they did propound recognizably hippie values. They loved to be different from 'the hierarchical tradition of the nuclear family'. It was, they explained, the truly feminine

237

way. Nurturing, sustaining, growing. Equal respect and value accorded to all. That was the theory. What the women would not understand was that it didn't always work. That, for example, Maggie could not value and respect her daughter but now defined this relationship as a primitive love. She was protective of her daughter's physical needs. She was wearing decade-old clothes because she could not afford new for both of them. She loved her daughter on a profound level but this somehow did not translate into the more surface pleasures and affections that a mother might enjoy with a child.

Sometimes she reflected that, for the whole of Sarah's life, she had never yet felt comfortable. On occasions happiness, excitement (rarely) or amusement (less than most but she was not scandalously bereft). But she never felt content. There were holes in her life and she knew it. Even when the surface was calm, it was treacherous underneath.

She was not happy with her feelings for Sarah but she could not alter them. There was a dichotomy that she hated herself, but that didn't make things any different. She had even thought that if Sarah were to die she would be able to love her more. Alive, the feeling the daughter evoked in her mother vacillated between resentment and guilt.

If anything, Maggie overcompensated for her lack of feeling or negative feelings. Sarah had more pocket money than her contemporaries. A pound a week in 1977 was overgenerous and Maggie could scarcely afford it. Sarah had a record player in her bedroom. She went to the cinema. She had a Tiny Tears, a Sindy and a Barbie. But she didn't want them. She didn't like dolls. The plastic girls gathering dust on the floor could not have expressed the distance between mother and daughter more succinctly. It was surprising that Maggie could believe that Sarah would want to play with these dolls – she never had.

Sarah stayed up as late as she liked. And when finally the television closed down she would sit on the top of the stairs where they curved around and look down through the banisters as if in a cage.

It didn't make Sarah happy, this freedom. She was an intelligent child. Her brain was under-utilized like her mother's, but she was perceptive enough to know from very young that her mother's generosity was not love.

Sarah liked the Commune because it contrasted with the austerity at home. Maggie chose everything in shades of beige. The C had painted their white walls with symbols of feminine strength. Apples, colourful flowers, women holding hands. Sympathetic newspaper headlines pasted with Copydex, pages torn from women's press publications and stuck to the walls as bold statements of intent.

Her own home was sterile. Sarah longed for clutter. The C's kitchen was huge (the house was identical to Maggie's but the women had knocked down the wall dividing kitchen and living room). A huge oak table dominated the room. It was covered in leaflets, badges, books, tickets, loose change – all signs of activity and movement. Sarah nicked a badge with 'Cock-Free Zone' scrawled aggressively across it and pierced it into Tiny Tears's nippleless chest. Sarah smiled with satisfaction. Tiny looked a lot better that way.

In the C's kitchen there were always plates of leftover food. When Sarah first ate with the women and was offered a slice of solid quiche, she thought they said they were 'wedgetarians'. She couldn't understand why people would commit themselves to a cause that was so chewy.

Which was why Sarah and Maggie, despite frequent hostility between them, always went home for dinner together. The frozen food revolution was a bigger breakthrough than the women's movement as far as Sarah was concerned; she called the C's cooking 'turd food' and that made Maggie laugh. Maggie liked any jokes that went against right and proper thinking. Her approbation encouraged her daughter. Laughter eased the pressure.

Wholemeal food was not as unpopular with the more conservative residents of Trafalgar Road as the exotic aromas that emanated from the vents of Mrs Pillay's, two doors further down. This London street was typical of the time. The old and the new rubbed uncomfortably together. The Thomas and Glover families in numbers 32 and 34 were bastions of the old order, where women still had time to cook a proper roast on a Sunday and there were still men around to eat it. Mrs Thomas and Mrs Glover talked over the fence. There was plenty to talk about. They could not decide what brought the area into worse repute, lesbians, Asians or that shockingly young single mother.

'Come on,' Maggie prodded her daughter, who was slumped in front of the TV on a Saturday afternoon.

'Why do I have to come?'

Maggie gave no answer.

'I don't want to come,' said Sarah between her teeth.

'Well, what else are you going to do? You listened to the Sex Pistols three times this morning already.'

Sarah made a face. 'It's Siouxsie and the Banshees.'

'I don't care who it is, it gives me a headache.'

Sometimes Maggie could hardly bear to look at her daughter who seemed to be turning adolescent cruelly early. It made her feel old. She could hardly believe she was not yet twenty-eight.

Maggie said, 'I asked you to do the dishes this morning.'

Sarah stuck her bottom lip out.

'Why didn't you do them?'

Sarah looked bored and kept her eyes on the now silent television. 'I went to have coffee with the C.'

Maggie clicked her teeth. 'I told you not to go there so much. Why don't you ever do what I ask you?'

'You didn't ask me, you told me.'

Maggie was filling with rage. She was normally half full and it required little to top her up. 'Don't talk to me like that.'

'Why not?' Sarah was perfecting a magnificent petulance. 'You talk to me like that.'

Maggie made a noise of exasperation and angrily picked up the car keys.

'OK. Come on. Let's go. I'm not going to waste any more time having this conversation.'

Sarah clung to the sofa. 'Why don't you let me stay here? You're happier when I'm not here. You said so yourself.'

'I did not say that.'

'Yes, you did.'

Maggie had said it, many times, but she could not admit it. 'Don't be ridiculous.' Maggie might know how to placate Sarah, but she could never bring herself to. 'Get in the car,' she said, also through clenched teeth. She was particularly angry today because she had had a call from the hospital earlier. Grace was going through a periodic downturn. Until they could get a new drug regime going, the interim would be painful.

Maggie's Mini had such low suspension they felt they were scraping the ground.

Staff Nurse Brooks took Maggie aside when she arrived on Grace's ward. 'Doctor's put her in the acute ward just while she's bad,' she said in a lowered voice.

Under her breath Sarah asked Maggie, 'Is she in a padded cell?' Sarah had recently seen *The Return of the Pink Panther* on TV. Naturally the part that stuck in her mind was Herbert Lom, swaddled like a baby, scrawling 'Kill Clouseau' on his padded cell walls, with a crayon between his toes.

'No. Shut up,' muttered Maggie. To the nurse she said, 'How is she?'

The nurse's face looked pained and she consciously excluded Sarah. 'Perhaps you'd like to come into my room.'

Maggie nodded. Sarah was outraged. 'That's not fair!' she said. 'You drag me along here and then make me miss all the interesting stuff.'

The nurse smiled in a tired, kind way. 'We're just trying to protect you. Your grandmother is not a very well lady.'

'I know *that*,' snapped Sarah. 'I don't need protecting.'

'Yes, you do,' Maggie snapped back. 'Wait outside.'

Sarah flounced away, back to the waiting area of the hot ward. She saw and rejected a pile of dog-eared magazines on a low table and instead examined a huge wilting aspidistra in the corner.

The door closed. Maggie sat down. The nurse cleared her throat. She had been having these conversations with Maggie for years. Maggie clasped her handbag defensively.

'She was pretty bad on Monday night. So we sedated her quite heavily.'

'What kind of bad?'

'You'll notice the scars on her arms where she broke the skin. We cut her nails right back. She's been very distressed.'

'When did it start?'

The nurse thought back, playing with a biro between her lips. 'Over the weekend. She was at the art workshop with the others. The patients were trying to come up with ideas for the Jubilee party. Everybody was making Jubilee hats and paintings in red, white and blue. Grace became quite violent. Started screaming and hitting out at one of the helpers.'

'What got her upset?' asked Maggie pensively.

'I don't know, to be honest,' said the nurse, lighting up a cigarette and offering one to Maggie, who accepted gratefully. 'Since then she's been very depressed again, just like she was before. The fit was a bit unexpected. They're thinking of giving her more ECT.'

Maggie looked pale. 'Again? But it's only been a few months since the last time.'

'I know, I know.' The nurse drew deeply on her cigarette and tipped a satisfactorily large amount of ash into the overflowing tray. 'But it does no neural damage. Not long term anyway. Far less damage anyhow' – she took another drag – 'than she'd do to herself. We can't watch her every minute. And in her current state, she's a liability. To herself, and I'll admit it, to us.'

Maggie smoked silently. Then, with her eyes on the floor, she said, 'Sometimes I think she'd be better off dead.'

'Mmm,' said the nurse neutrally, 'that's a natural way to feel. It's not pleasant to watch someone you love torture themselves.'

'It's just . . .' Maggie's eyes clouded. The nurse touched her arm. 'After the ECT she's so dopey. She's worse than ever. I feel sometimes . . . we can have half a conversation . . . but other times, after the treatment . . .'

The nurse was slow and reassuring. 'The better times will come back. Don't worry. We're looking after her.' The cigarette, sucked soft, was finished. She stubbed it out and wiped a mark of ash off her fingers. 'Maybe you shouldn't see her today. Certainly I don't think your daughter . . . Grace really won't notice if you don't come.'

Maggie looked up, resolute. 'I must go. I told her I would. I can't let—'

The nurse interrupted, saying gently, 'I just wonder if sometimes you let your devotion to your mother obscure your daughter's needs.'

Maggie's face turned stony. 'I'm sorry, that's none of your business.'

The nurse was subdued. 'I know. I'm sorry, I shouldn't have

said anything.' She removed her hand and stood up. 'Come on then.'

She opened the door and the two women walked out. Sarah, who was behind the ancient aspidistra, her nose inserted into its dark layers, looked round expectantly.

Maggie shook her head slightly and said, more kindly than before, 'No, love, you stay there. The nurse thinks I should go alone.'

Sarah thrust her face back into the plant.

The nurse was fretful. She smoothed the front of her uniform pointlessly.

'Well, since you won't know the way I'll get Nurse Donaldson to come along with you.'

The acute ward had its own music, stereo wailing and moaning. An elderly woman held the metal sides of her bed as they walked past. Maggie was drawn towards her. Then she saw that the woman was not looking at her, as she had first thought, but was stretching a piece of saliva from her mouth like bubble gum.

The nurse, a well-covered blonde with dark roots and a nose like a miniature garlic bulb, walked on. Her soft-heeled, un-fashionable shoes made a squelching noise against the highly polished floor. Maggie noticed details when the rest of her mind went blank.

Nurse Donaldson stopped and lifted the black partition side-ways in a slightly awkward movement.

Maggie squeezed her body round. 'Hello, Mother,' she said, so softly the nurse didn't hear and felt obliged to fill in the silence.

'Grace.' She raised the volume. She had a Cockney accent. 'It's your daughter to see you.'

'Don't worry,' said Maggie monotonously, 'she knows. And if she doesn't, it doesn't matter.' She turned to the nurse. 'You don't have to stay. I'll be fine, honestly, I'm used to it.'

Seemingly affronted, the nurse left. Maggie was glad. A young girl, probably hadn't been here more than a couple of months. It was obvious. There were none of the give-away changes she noticed took place in the nurses who had been working here for a while. They began to assume the mannerisms of their patients. It was like any foreign country; after a while the language rubbed off on even the most recalcitrant. The experienced nurses stopped looking so crisp and turned a little wilder round the eye. They all smoked heavily.

Maggie took a cheap grey plastic chair with an unsupporting back from the corner of the ward and pulled it into the cubicle. Her life was full of uncomfortable seating arrangements.

She sat down. 'Hello, Mother,' she said again.

Grace, who had been sitting bolt upright in her bed, heard something. She turned slowly to the side.

'Hello, Mother,' Maggie repeated.

'Hello, Mother,' echoed Grace. Then she said in a high pitch, 'I'm ill.'

'What you been doing to yourself, eh?'

'I'm ill,' snarled Grace, baring her teeth. Animation was unusual and alarming in her.

'Why are you ill?' This was the pattern of their more cogent conversations. Repetition from Grace and efforts by Maggie always to move the words slowly along.

'I'm ill.'

Maggie moved her hands very slowly towards her mother's face. Even so, it was too sudden. Grace flinched and raised her own hand as if to strike.

'I'm ill.'

'Mmm. What do you feel?'

'I'm ill.'

'How are you ill, where does it hurt?'

Grace's eyes raced suddenly. Maggie could see the flashing whites of an animal in pain. 'I can feel her, she's angry.'

'Ruth?' said Maggie softly.

'She wants me. And with this—' Grace threw her head against the bar at the back of the bed. Maggie rushed take her mother's head in her hands.

'No, no, she doesn't want you to hurt yourself. Ruth doesn't want that. Ruth was happy. She wants you to be happy.' It was best to speak in a gentle rhythm.

'I killed her, I killed Ruth, I killed her, I killed—'

Maggie held the head very tight, cradling it in her arms, soothing the anguish.

'Ssh, Mother, you didn't. You loved Ruth. You never would have killed her.'

'I killed Ruth. I killed her. Mother said I killed her. I kill—'

'Ssh.' The rocking was calming her slowly. 'Mother doesn't know anything. I reckon she's ill too.'

'I'm ill. I'm ill.'

Maggie regretted repeating the word. 'Don't worry, Grace, don't worry. I'll look after you, Mummy, don't worry.' She held her mother in her arms until the tension relaxed a little and her heart stopped racing.

'Don't let Ruth come!'

Maggie could feel her mother's breath on her arm. 'No,' she said, 'I won't let Ruth come. Don't worry.'

'I'm ill. I'm ill. I'm ill.'

'I know, I know, I know.'

And Maggie sang in a familiar tune:

'Uncle Will, he fell ill
He can't afford the doctor's bill.'

She sang again, taming her mother's white hair with her strokes. And Grace, bent inside her daughter's arms, sang broken words with her.

Sarah was waiting in the hospital garden, aiming pebbles at a little pile of stones some three yards away. She didn't look up when her mother's shadow fell over her hands.

'Don't do that,' said Maggie wearily, her voice perceptibly changed from the soft, loving tones of reassurance that were directed towards Grace. 'Who do you think is going to pay if you break a window?'

'You've been ages,' Sarah retorted. 'I was bored stiff.'

Even now she had a place of her own, Maggie still cleaned Great Edie's house every week. She had developed the habit. If she didn't do it, it wouldn't get done and she could no longer bear the thought of her grandmother living in squalor. Edie would sit in the corner of the kitchen with her legs spread comfortably round the old boiler, which Maggie had paid to be repaired.

The old woman never expressed gratitude. In fact she was quite unpleasant about it. 'What you want to keep cleaning for? Isn't it enough that that's how you earn your money?'

Maggie scrubbed grimly on. There were stains that would never come out of Edie's kitchen floor. Still, once a week, Maggie cleaned to a stream of invective. Sometimes aimed at her, but more often at some irrelevant victim.

'The only good thing about this bleedin' Jubilee', said Edie, 'is that the TV gets better. Not all that pomp and ceremony mind you. Lighting damn bonfires? Whoever heard of it? The Queen ought to be careful she doesn't set fire to that bleedin' great castle of hers, lighting bloody bonfires all over the place.' Edie was scanning the *Radio Times*. 'Now *My Fair Lady*, I like that one. It gives a girl reason to hope.' Maggie was unable to switch off from her grandmother's monologues and in fact found herself sweeping in time to them. 'Audrey Hepburn is nothing but a lowly cockney and she gets to marry a rich man who looks after her. That's what you need, and if not you then that poor wretched Sarah.'

This was not the message that Maggie had picked up from the film, but she generally knew better than to contradict.

Edie was casting her narrowed eyes through the films of the bank holiday weekend. '*Secret Life of Walter Mitty*, Hmm. *Love Among the Ruins*, Katharine Hepburn and Laurence O-livier. Gawd, maybe you should watch that. *Henry the Fifth*. Gawd, bleedin' Laurence O-livier again. What they want to keep putting him on for? He gets on my nerves he does. Mincing around. Bleedin' poofter. Ooh, I've got no time for 'im, poncey git. Different rules for the likes of him.'

And so it went on.

' "On Monday John Noakes cleans Nelson's Column" – 'ere,' Edie cackled and leaned forward to give Maggie a poke in the ribs, 'you'll enjoy that one, eh? It's about cleaning.'

Edie had bought a new television. She thought it would be nice for Sarah when she came to visit. At least that was the excuse. Maggie had only black and white. 'How else will she learn the different colours of the Union Jack then, eh?' Edie's was a very timely patriotism. It came out occasionally to serve a purpose.

Once Edie believed in an institution she took its word as the Bible. This did not happen very often but she had made an icon of the consumer magazine *Which?* 'The champion of decency and common sense,' she said self-righteously as if the words might apply equally to herself. She read it religiously, quoting pertinent comments to Maggie and Sarah for moral uplift.

Naturally her colour TV was the most highly recommended of a test reported in *Which?* January 1977. 'A Sony KV – 181OUB MK II,' said Great Edie with the pride of a mother who has watched a child say three words in the school play. 'That's the best there is.'

The television had come out best in terms of value for money and reliability. The price was down to £260. The viewer could reckon on only two days of unwatchability a year according to the test ('When it's snowing,' said Edie, who was showing off her new vocabulary after reading the instruction pamphlet in detail).

Sarah was as fascinated by the set itself as by what was on it. The twenty-two-inch screen, the controls on the left-hand side, the switch at the wall, the flickering dots that brought life into the living room. This colourful television was much more real than black and white. When her great-grandmother went on her long trips to the lavatory, Sarah held her cheek to the static screen and felt the warmth of the cathode ray world. When she felt shaky the TV was staunch and sturdy, quelling her fears. If Sarah was ill (which she was, as often as possible) she now liked nothing better than to be 'looked after' by her great-grandmother.

Maggie couldn't understand it. 'But, Edie, she's perfectly capable of staying on her own. There's always someone next door if she needs anything.'

The grandmother was indignant.

'You let that poor wretch of a child into that house of depravity? No. No, no, no. She's better off with me.'

And so round went Sarah. She was met by Edie at the door, who came armed with a copy of the *Radio Times*.

Sarah noted early on that her great-grandmother had a fondness for bits of the body. There was a surprising amount of flesh on the morning programmes for schools. *Good Health*, a programme aimed at eight- to ten-year-olds and dealing with hygiene, showed a group of schoolboys washing in a communal shower.

'Ooh, yes, they're getting lovely and clean. All lovely and clean,' commented Edie. Sarah, who had never seen a naked boy before, was equally fascinated but she was still struck by Edie, whose eyes were welded to the set. Sarah wasn't sure if the comments were just an outpouring of genuine enthusiasm or covering up her embarrassment. They ogled together through the filming of a birth. A sweat-covered woman, straining on her back, whose hand was held by a rather feeble-looking bearded man. 'Fat lot of good he's doing,' grumbled Edie. 'Hairy bugger.'

The Commune decided to organize an anti-monarchist party in the garden. Hoping to drown out the official Jubilee street party.

Maggie was torn. She didn't want her daughter to be alienated from the other children but the sight of the bunting-festooned lamp-posts depressed her. It signified the smiles she would have to give those neighbours who normally patronized, ignored and carped at her as an example of the social disgrace that was destroying the country. Yet here they were knocking on her door asking if she wouldn't mind baking a Union Jack cake.

'Maybe you could write "Anarchy in the UK" on it,' Sarah suggested. Maggie laughed and Sarah looked pleased.

'I don't want to cause a fight and anyway there wouldn't be enough room and anyway again, how do you spell anarchy?'

'A – n – a – r – c – h – y,' said Sarah, who had picked up some useful spellings from the Sex Pistols.

Maggie escaped by volunteering to make a salad, protesting, 'You wouldn't want a cake of mine, really.' Mrs Thomas and Mrs Glover glanced at each other. Of course a wanton single mother would know nothing of the genteel art of cake making.

Maggie decided that she and Sarah would attend the beginning of the street party and sneak off to the alternative event once the food was finished. Thus they could both avoid too much street conversation *and* the politically motivated turd food.

It turned out to be one of the first times she felt a true affinity with her daughter.

The street was, it might be said, swinging. Which meant that under grey skies and on top of the grey street lay ten trestle tables covered in Union Jack paper tablecloths. On top of which was a rather bedraggled picnic tea and plates of sunken cake oozing in tricolour. Parts of conversation brushed against Maggie's ears as she toyed with a soggy rice salad.

'Why do we do it?' shrieked the tinkling voice of Mrs Glover.

'Oh, I'm exactly the same,' responded Mrs Thomas sympathetically.

'I know you're right. I know. But isn't it difficult?'

'It's very strange.'

'Sometimes I swear I'm going senile.'

'You don't do it for the same reason as me.'

Mrs Saville was saying, 'It's been touched up . . . you don't think it's too short?'

'No, no.' Mrs Pillay shook her head emphatically, hoping to ingratiate herself with these icy women. Her mild chicken curry lay untouched in the middle of the table.

When silence fell there was always someone to say, 'Well, aren't we lucky with the weather?' And someone to reply, 'Oh yes, ever so lucky with the weather.'

'Chanson d'amour' blared from a couple of transistor radios playing Radio 1. Old Mrs Pillay beamed generously round at her neighbours. 'Yes, yes, a lovely song,' she nodded.

Sarah pulled a face. Maggie, sitting opposite, chewed distractedly now on an egg sandwich triangle that seemed to harden as she ate. She abandoned it and said to Sarah, 'Go on, go and play with the others.'

Sarah hated her mother. She was being sent from comfortable boredom, watching the cake crumbs on Mrs Pillay's face, into the morass.

The faces turned to her.

'Yes, dear,' said Mrs Saville, whose daughter was in Sarah's class. 'Lucy's over there, I'm sure she'd love to play with you.' Lucy had stood and watched the previous week while Sarah's head had been held under a running tap.

Adults believe that children will get on together merely because they are all children. They forget that wild animals destroy their weak ones by instinct. Maybe it was because Maggie was so isolated as a child that she did not understand. She saw isolation as a purely physical thing, created by the absence of people. She did not understand that isolation could, in fact, be exaggerated by other people.

Sarah slunk off scowling. She murmured, 'I hate you,' in her mother's ear.

'I hate you too,' Maggie mouthed back.

She was preoccupied with her own self-consciousness. The truth was that while most of her neighbours may have disapproved of her, they did not think about it most of the time. They were distracted by the broken latch on their outside toilet, by the chance of promotion, the ailing aunt, the state of the cricket, the country, their impotence – the blinding preoccupations of the everyday. Maggie clung to the world's disapproval. It avoided the need to address her own role in her disappointed life. That she had allowed herself to be blinded.

Half an hour later she began to see again.

She was walking back from the toilet. Thrust into a sudden scented silence, a person had to re-evaluate physically and mentally. Am I drunk? Am I bored? Do I have blue, red and white icing on my teeth?

So she was looking again. As she walked back to her seat she spotted the street's children. Or at least six of them huddled together around a small brightly coloured object. Looking closer, she recognized it as a Miss Piggy pencil top. A pink and blond rubbery trinket. The children gathered round, enjoying its tawdry appearance. Gripped in a magic circle. Maggie smiled. And then she saw her daughter.

Sarah stood three feet away. But that three feet could have been the ocean. She was standing with her hands in her pockets, displaying an excruciating awkwardness, her body apparently fighting between pushing forward to feel part of the group and pulling back because she knew she was not welcome. The others completely ignored her. Sarah looked desperate. Her eyes seemed bigger, her jaw dropped and her hair was pathetically limp. She leaned on one foot. Her elbow stuck out in frail embarrassment.

Maggie was suddenly torn by an unbearable pang. An ache inside herself. It lasted only a few seconds. But in those seconds she was so knocked she had to struggle to stay on two feet. She was hit with the weight of nothing other than the loneliness of the human condition, encapsulated in her vulnerable, unfortunate daughter. If people didn't notice it was because they didn't want to. *She* hadn't wanted to. The polite chatter of the party that before had been merely annoying now seemed to shout out that the world fails to meet our emotional needs. The strain of conversation, the tinny sound of the radio. So thin and ineffectual in this vast great space.

Years of self-control promptly pulled her together.

She marched up to Sarah, apparently oblivious. 'Come on, I think we should go. The C will be wondering where we are.'

Sarah was relieved that her mother never noticed that she talked to no one, but did wonder why Maggie was so good-humoured with her that afternoon. She was quite cheerful the next day too. Maybe, thought Sarah, it was the Jubilee party at the hospital. It was a refreshing experience after the seriousness with which both the street and the C took the Jubilee, albeit from different angles.

The confusion of the patients was a highly rational response, mother and daughter agreed, to a nationwide celebration of twenty-five years of a powerless German monarch. Most of the patients didn't have a clue. They didn't know who the Queen was. That's why they were incarcerated, after all. They didn't know why they were being led to the hall to make merry. What had happened to the art therapy workshop? That's what was meant to happen on Tuesday afternoons.

They weren't hungry or they didn't like the blue in the icing. They spat it out. They didn't want to dance. Or they wanted to dance at the wrong time. They objected to being allowed only three colours of hat, and when the nurses' backs were turned, hats became orange or brown or vomit colour.

The singing of the national anthem was the best, Sarah decided. Of those who knew the words, some refused to sing them and sang something else of their own choosing (there was a particularly drowning rendition of 'Over the Sea to Skye' in one corner of the hall). Some merely screamed with excitement or anger, or both. The rest, who attempted to accompany the reedy singing of staff and guests, sang the words with a wild and tuneless gusto that sounded closer to the Sex Pistols' version. Sarah thought it was a huge improvement on the original.

Grace was still on the acute ward and so not at the party. And while Maggie laughed along with Sarah at the extraordinary scenes in the hall that afternoon, she became thoughtful towards the end.

Sarah noticed. 'What's the matter?' she said, not unkindly.

'I've just realized why Grace has got so bad now.' Sarah merely looked at her. Maggie could have been talking to herself; she was not looking at her daughter. 'It must have been the Jubilee celebrations. All the talk of the Queen and flags and nonsense and reminiscing and everything must have jolted her memory. Because Ruth died in 1953, on the day of the coronation.'

20

Cantonese Girl

'Did you know David Sylvian was born in Catford?'

Maggie looked up from a sandwich to the magazine snap of the blond singer. She wondered why pop singers had stopped smiling. They stopped, as she recalled, in 1967. Probably, she mused, when they discovered drugs they lost control of their facial muscles.

'No,' she said, 'I didn't realize. Catford, huh, that's not far from here.'

'I *know*,' said Sarah, rolling her eyes. 'Why the fuck d'you think I said it?'

Maggie no longer cared that Sarah swore. It was the lashing attacks that upset her. Revenge, she accepted, without asking. Too late, she now realized the impact of her cold nurturing, the permanent damage.

Maggie thought often of the moment when she first realized what she had done. It was the Jubilee (funny, she thought, how her family's moments seemed to coincide with the royal family's). On that warm June day four years ago she saw that Sarah was a person, an autonomous entity, not just a cramp in her own body, pulling at her, at her womb.

Sarah could simultaneously crave attention and be angry when it came. So now that the ham and cheese sandwich was drifting from Maggie's fingers and her gaze with it, Sarah was desolate. But she had learned how to get attention.

'You never listen to me. I'm not surprised my father left you.'

Instantly Maggie came back from her reverie. 'You don't

253

know anything about that,' she muttered between clenched teeth, her forehead pulsing.

'Well, why don't you try telling me?'

Maggie didn't answer. She turned her head away. At fourteen, Sarah was disappearing for nights on end. Maggie knew she would not like what Sarah was doing. She knew that asking her not to would push her further into it, but that not asking meant that she didn't care. Conversation was reduced to imploring questions and Japan.

Late morning, Sarah stumbled downstairs in an old and dirty towelling dressing gown. Great rings underlined her eyes.

Maggie looked at her daughter and burst out, 'I wasted *my* life, why do you have to as well?' This was not the harmless opening gambit she had planned.

Sarah said, 'What have I got to waste?'

Maggie tried to smile. 'You should think about the future. You don't want to be stuck here, you might want to go to university.'

Sarah shouted like a harridan, 'Why would I want to go to university? To meet boring fuckers with beards?' She slumped further in her chair, then sat up to emphasize her point. 'When David Sylvian formed Japan he couldn't even play a guitar, nor could Mick Karn – they just handed him the bass and said, "Play this." David knows more than all the stupid people decomposing in fucking university.'

Maggie clamped her lips together and said nothing, ruefully.

Sarah screwed her face up unpleasantly. 'Anyway, you don't know anything about university.'

'Unlike you, of course.'

Sarah spat, 'At least I don't pretend I'm some fucking expert. Oh Go-od.' She gave a long exhausted sigh and raised and dropped her hands in frustration. 'I can't even come downstairs without you bloody going on at me.'

Maggie saw friends, worried and cleaned houses. Sarah went out. She went to the ice rink. She couldn't see much from behind her dyed black fringe, but she managed to trip up a decent enough David lookalike all the same. He had a layered blond-and-black wedge cut. Afterwards, he took her to the fish bar opposite. By this time she had realized that he was not a Japan fan, but a casual. He had put two gold chains round his neck and changed into Farahs. Still, one couldn't be choosy, not in South London, in 1981, aged fourteen.

He had expected resistance. Girls normally had rules – strictly no groping under the T-shirt. Not this one. They had barely got round the back of the shop before she was egging him on. Encouraged by her silent yielding as he pawed her tits, he started fumbling at the zip of her Falmers. She pulled at him violently.

'Hey,' he cried, winded, 'what if people see?'

'Who gives a fuck?' she said.

Her sexual confidence was at its aggressive peak because at this age her mind operated in black and white. She did not worry about consequences, she only knew that the act of sex, loveless, brutal sex, controlled by and for herself, took away a physical ache inside her – temporarily, until the next time. It was an extreme enough action at this point in her life to overwhelm anything else. Only later, when her body and mind grew numb with experience, when casual sex was no longer enough to shock her, only then did she know she needed something more. At thirty-two, when sex with a stranger was a nothing, as memorable, she had decided, as a visit to an all-night garage, she realized that it did not protect her from fear.

At fourteen, self-loathing convinced her that she was doing the right thing. She developed a taste for the immoral minority. Because the moral majority didn't want misfits, people like her grandmother, like herself (and, though she did not realize it, like her mother). They thought she was bad, and so she would be bad. She also knew she was more intelligent than her life.

The Commune next door were all for rejecting the moral majority but they couldn't understand why Sarah wore so much make-up. 'Sisters shouldn't pander to stereotypes of beauty,' said Diana.

'I don't have a sister,' retorted Sarah, sick of their preaching.

Sarah had reached a stage in her life when she needed to know everything about Grace. She said provocatively (since this was the most effective form of communication she had yet discovered), 'She doesn't seem that ill to me.'

Maggie was patient. 'That's because the illness goes through different stages, manic and depressive.'

'And what is she now?'

'Depressive, that's why she's very withdrawn and quiet.'

'I feel like that,' said Sarah immediately.

'No, it's not the same.'

'How do you know?' she demanded. 'How do you know what I feel?'

Maggie worried that Sarah was identifying too much with Grace. She realized that Grace's abstract existence could appeal to a vulnerable adolescent. Sarah had always been protected from her grandmother's more alarming sides. All she saw was her grandmother left alone to think her thoughts, while she had to go through the daily torture of education among hostile classmates. Maybe it was time to stop hiding it. She said, 'What Grace has is different from how you feel.'

'What exactly do *they* say she has?' Recently, Sarah had developed a deep distrust of 'they' – by which she meant any figure or body of authority, particularly doctors, politicians, the legal profession, teachers and those selfish individuals pompous enough to call themselves parents.

'It's called schizo-affective psychosis,' said Maggie, as if reciting a poem off by heart. 'This means her illness follows a course of remission and relapse, or depressed and manic episodes. She can believe that her thoughts are hijacked by a third party. She jumps from topic to topic. When depressed she often thinks and says nothing at all. Her speech is affected by constant repetition, neologisms (which means she makes up words) and rubbish which is known in the trade as "word salad". She can't feel emotions properly, which means either that she shows nothing (although you can never be sure how much her emotional deadening is a reaction to her drugs) or, less frequently, that she is hypersensitive, and her deadpan behaviour gives way to hysterical anger and fear. These fits can, in my experience of her, often be provoked by hallucinations; she hears voices and sometimes she sees things that upset her. She can get violent, suicidal and physically destructive. Her violence is not normally aimed at other people. Her brain is deteriorating as she gets older because of her institutionalization and being on drugs for so long. She has made little or no progress since she was diagnosed in her late twenties. All attempts to wean her off antipsychotics have resulted in severe relapses. She is best off with a combination of an antipsychotic and an antidepressive but that too has failed on several occasions, at which point they normally wheel her off for another dose of ECT. ECT is electroconvulsive therapy where they administer a controlled electric shock to her head to liven her up. It sounds horrible, but really it can be quite effecti—'

'All right, all right!' shouted Sarah, covering her ears to the onslaught. 'I accept I'm not like that.' Maggie closed her mouth. Sarah continued, 'But I might be one day, mightn't I? Schizophrenia runs in families, doesn't it?'

'Yes,' Maggie admitted. If her daughter wanted the truth, she could have it. 'But a lot of people who develop schizophrenia as adults are withdrawn and eccentric as children.'

'Fuck! That really is me,' said Sarah.

'No, it isn't,' Maggie cut in swiftly, 'nothing like it.' She moved on. 'If you want to see your grandmother as she really is, I've no objection, if you feel you're ready.'

'Yes,' said Sarah, her face airy, her voice wavering only slightly. 'I am ready. I'm not a child any more.' Saying it was easy.

Make-up gave her confidence. Putting it on took Sarah two hours every morning. She smudged her cheeks with white creamy foundation. She elongated her eyes with heavy kohl. She cut her eyelashes to remove their western curl. The result was androgyny. David Sylvian looked like a girl-boy and she looked like a boy-girl. They were a perfect whole. Sarah wore simple black peasant clothes (a pair of her Japanese slippers would later crawl into Maggie's wardrobe).

She listened to his silver voice. She looked at pictures of his beautiful blond face and hair. She imagined bumping into him on a London street where he, immediately recognizing some-thing indefinably special about her, would ask her to join the band. They would plan their revolution and the cooperative rice paddy they would run afterwards (she never saw herself as a rice picker).

Many unprofitable afternoons Sarah spent in the second-hand record shops of Brixton. What joy, after fruitless hours scouring dusty piles of magazines, to pull up, like the one good plant in a blighted crop, a Japan fanzine from 1978, the forgotten early days. Her feet were scarcely out of the door before her hands were feeling into the brown paper bag and pulling out the floppy treasure.

'Why do you dress differently?'

'We're just individualists,' said Dave (as he was known before he became too deep for such a prosaic diminutive). 'We are making a point of looking individual.'

Sarah renamed herself Go – the pseudonym of an ancient Japanese artist. She was pleased that now her hair was longer, dark and straight, it could almost be oriental. She told boys that her father was Chinese and murdered in an anti-Communist plot. (This seemed no more stupid than the typhoid that killed him first time round.) 'He was a spy,' she said breezily. 'It was the brink of a huge scandal when he was fucking my mother. He had to be assassinated by MI5 in the toilets at Heathrow.' It all drew her further away. The make-up covered her skin, the name concealed her identity, the clothes hid her body and the fringe masked her eyes. She was untouchable.

Her bedroom seemed very small, hemmed in by brooding posters, but not many boys objected to the eyes on the walls which followed their every furtive move. Nor did they mind that Sarah did not want to talk. Maggie noticed that Sarah never had girls round to play. But boys were better than nothing. There have always been strange men wandering through my house, reasoned Maggie. First it was Edie's clients and now it was Sarah's boys.

'Doesn't your mum mind?' said Tony, the catch of the evening, who she had met against a wall.

Sarah Go recoiled. Her heavily lacquered hair did not move. 'My mum doesn't give a fuck. Why should she?' She nodded impatiently at the spinning record. 'Listen to the words, they're the best about fucking. David sees sex as an expression of alienation and release of pain. Don't you think that's great?'

'Do men wear make-up in China?' said the bewildered Tony as Sarah Go smeared his face with white face paint – a ritual she habitually performed; it was a kind of initiation rite, a small price.

'Sure.' He squirmed as she drew on kohl eyeliner. 'Do you want sex or not?' she demanded. He capitulated and held still. She finished with lipstick, a cherry blob more vertical than horizontal. 'There,' she said, with a flourish, 'the lips of a beautiful Cantonese girl.' He stretched his neck towards her, unable to wait any longer. She twisted her face away, her neck struggling free from the body lock. 'Don't kiss me. It'll spoil my make-up. I hate kissing.'

'Well,' he said, 'you're the first girl to say that.'

She made a face. 'Mother birds regurgitating their food for their young – that's all kissing is. Don't you think that's disgusting?'

'Huh?' He raised one confused nostril. 'But my mum used a Kenwood mixer.'

She was getting bored. She changed LPs and turned up the volume. 'Their first album,' she said. '*Adolescent sex*.' His penis bulged at these welcome words. She fiddled with the needle on the record player and added, 'This is my favourite . . . "Despair".'

He looked around shiftily. 'Don't you think it's a bit loud? Isn't your mother asleep in the other room?'

'My mother wouldn't hear me whatever I did. She's only got ears for herself.'

But she was wrong. Halfway through the song the door opened and Maggie's weary form appeared. She didn't see Tony because in terror he had moved, faster than a lizard, under the bed. Sarah was not scared but angry. 'Haven't you heard of knocking?'

Enraged, Maggie retorted, 'Haven't you heard of sleep?' She stormed to the record player and pulled the needle, cutting dead the droning French lyrics.

'Don't,' screamed Sarah, 'you'll scratch the record!'

Maggie sniffed the air that smelt strongly of the greasepaint Sarah smothered herself in.

'And why have you put even more damn make-up on?'

'Because there's a guy under the bed and we're about to have sex.'

Maggie didn't believe her. She took it as teenage fantasy and so played along. 'Well, how's he going to get near you with three feet of make-up in the way?'

Sarah said calmly, 'I don't care what you think about how I look.'

'All right, OK, do what you like, but do it quieter. It's three in the morning and I have to see Great Edie tomorrow. You know what she's like.'

'No,' Sarah said belligerently, 'I don't know what she's like. I know you treat her like a pain in the arse, but she's not as irritating as you fucking are.'

Maggie closed the door, shaking her head. She had been a bad mother, but did she deserve this?

Sarah finished the job with Tony. It was four in the morning when she pushed him to the front door. 'Aw, man,' he protested, 'aren't you going to let me have some kip?'

'You can't sleep in my bed,' she said, shocked at the question. 'That's for David. How can I talk to David with you there farting? Piss off.'

Tony walked from the door in the growing light, wiping the make-up off his face with the back of his hand. In her bedroom, Sarah lay naked under her duvet. She held David next to her and they talked quietly.

'Oh, David, I know,' she murmured, stroking his cheek, which was rippled with a soft stubble after the long night. 'It's so hard when no one listens to what you're really saying.'

1982: the Falklands' war, death of President Brezhnev and, most importantly, Japan broke up. Of course it was typical of David's artistic integrity. He was sickened by fame, where his looks meant more than his message. Sarah understood, she suffered the same misunderstanding. Her own artistic integrity – which compelled her to take large breaks from school – had seen her hauled before an educational psychologist.

Maggie and Sarah sat at opposite ends of the plastic table. 'My mother doesn't care, she would be glad if I left home and never came back.'

'I'm sure that's not true,' said the educational psychologist.

Sarah turned to Maggie with a petulant look on her face. 'Why don't you admit it, Mother?'

Maggie sighed. 'Because it's not true.'

Sarah looked sick. 'You're a liar.'

Maggie's lip trembled because she could not entirely deny it. 'You can be so unkind, Sarah.'

Sarah whistled. 'Well, I wonder where I learned that?'

Maggie looked at the professional who averted her gaze. The

woman glanced for confirmation at a thick wad of handwritten notes. 'It's a shame, Sarah, because your teachers all tell me that you're an intelligent girl. And from what I can see, you could do very well.'

'I don't want to do well. I want to leave school and leave home.'

The woman spoke with certainty. 'You think that now, but you will come to regret it. A few years of freedom will mean a much tougher time afterwards. You will find it harder to do well in a career. It will be frustrating for you. You will have to get a job that will not fulfil your potential.'

'David Sylvian didn't,' said Sarah, looking pointlessly at the bin in the corner of the room.

'I did,' said Maggie quietly.

The psychologist and Maggie exchanged looks of stalemate. This was her chance. The school had done its duty. That was that.

The educational psychologist probably overheard, as the pair walked away, because Sarah was deliberately loud when she said, 'Mum, I wish you'd had an abortion.'

But she probably didn't catch the wobble in the girl's voice because Sarah had learned to steady that, even from herself.

Grace

'She looked at me. She looked at me. She could see. He knew. I killed my sister. I killed my sister. Was a slut and a bitch.'

She pulled at her hair. It was twisted in clumps. She pulled again, with more force. As her fingers slipped to her lap, stray hairs stuck in her loosening grip. 'Gev me zuster. Me stront. Me vermoordene. Gev me zuster. Gev me zuster.'

She refused to sleep in her clean sheets. She would not put on her clean clothes. She said her sister had washed them in poison. She would wear the same clothes or none at all. If they tried to persuade her, she screamed. A piercing scream of terror.

'Zuster vermoordene. Deadshadegiftig.' *She smelt flowers and thought it was the poison. She gagged and held her throat. There were no flowers.*

She did not sleep. She sat in her chair in her dirty dress with her eyes open until the day came again. Murmuring like a spell, 'Gev me zuster. Gev me zuster. Gev me zuster. Gev me zuster.'

Sarah was a year older. Since their discussion Maggie had stopped regulating Sarah's visits to her grandmother. She could see her when she liked and even alone, while Grace was on the normal ward. Only in the manic phase did Maggie insist that she go with her daughter (Maggie could not visit herself without the staff nurse's knowledge). Grace had not been this disturbed for a long time and Sarah wanted to see.

It was a bad morning. Sarah and Maggie had yelled viciously at each other. They started speaking again only en route to the hospital. Maggie led the way on to the acute ward. Sarah would

*not walk in step with her. 'You can leave whenever you like,'
Maggie called back. 'Don't feel ashamed to say if you want to
go.'*

'I can manage,' said Sarah tightly. 'I'm not a child.'

*The nurse warned them not to sit on the poisoned bedcover.
Grace was likely to think they were infected. Instead, they sat on
two stools.*

*Grace's bent head lay between her hands. But her hands were
never still. They moved in and out against her head, hitting the
sides, blocking her ears. The rest of her body was paralysed.
While she often looked out of the window, today she had her
back against the wall and faced the ward. She did not look up at
her visitors.*

*Maggie smiled at Sarah in what she hoped was a comforting
way. Sarah's mouth acknowledged this with a swift nervous
upturn.*

*'How are you, Grace?' Maggie spoke in a low steady tone.
'How are you?' Grace did not respond directly but murmured
and banged her ears. She spoke words they could not understand. 'She might be like this the whole time,' muttered Maggie.*

*A quarter of an hour passed. Sarah stared at her distant
grandmother. Then unconsciously, straining for connection, she
placed her hand on Grace's wrist. To this, the reaction was
immediate. Grace jumped in horror. Her face came up, her hair
a mad rage. Her fingers in her mouth seemed to stifle an
outburst. Boiling water might have splashed on Sarah's hand, it
moved away so fast.*

*'It's all right,' said Maggie soothingly but neither Sarah nor
Grace was listening. Sarah stared in shock into the eyes of the
woman who seemed to be changing before her.*

*Grace screwed up her face to summon strength. She opened
her mouth, pulled her fingers out and screeched. 'Slut! Bitch!
Slut! Bitch! Slut! Bitch!' She repeated these two words until they
melded into meaninglessness. Her eyes were wild. Grace's face
was bright red. She was sweating. She was banging her ears in
distress. 'No! No! Vermoordene, vermoordene!'*

*Sarah was pale with shock. She did not know what she had
done. 'What is it, Grandmother? What's the matter?' she said
desperately.*

Grace spat like a terrified cat, ssssteeeeeeeetz ssssteeeeeetz!

Sarah choked. 'What's the matter?'

Maggie turned to her. 'She can't hear you. She's not talking to you. Don't worry.'

Ssssteeeeeeeeetz ssssteeeeeeetz! It didn't matter that these sounds meant nothing, they sounded so full of hate.

Sarah gasped and ran from the bed in tears. Maggie followed her, but her daughter pushed her away. She ran off. Maggie walked back to Grace, who was still staring angrily at the space where Sarah had sat, cursing as venomously as ever.

Sarah had left her jacket behind. Maggie picked it up for her and wondered what upset her daughter most. The shock of the sickness, the suffering of her grandmother or the fear (perfectly realistic to a suggestible young woman of active imagination) that a similar fate was lined up for herself?

21

Down the Plughole

Sarah lay on Alex's sofa. She was dressed in a wrinkled T-shirt. Her hair was dishevelled. A crumpled duvet covered her feet. She was writing. Writing feverishly on plain paper. Single sheets that when she had covered them were tossed on to the floor. They settled like snow.

Sarah Lockyer's Diary

Chapter One: How I learned to swear.
   (And how I met Alex.)
   (And how we became friends until I ruined it by fucking his fat mate.)
   In the summer of 1989 when the sun blazed and everyone was raving, I did not rave.

She liked that line. She felt it was modern and yet expressed a universal and timeless loneliness.

I did not want to wear a stupid smiley-faced T-shirt and shout, 'Mental!' I thought that was crap. It was crap. But I also did not want to be like my mother and not have a fucking clue where my generation went. So I went out.
   Alex and I met on a hot night. Unlike now, when I can hear the rain banging on the window like it wants something from me.
   I went to a party. I don't know whose. That was part of the

vibe. Free party spirit bollocks. Of course it was all bollocks. There was no great new movement. No new spirit of peace and hedonism. Least not at the places I went to. It was just another excuse to go out and get high. I went with a girl from work, which, by the way, was in the admin department of a large London insurance company. It sounds glamorous and it was. Let me tell you. Every day a different insurance claim. Oh yes.

It was not cool because it was a fancy dress party. Everything cool that year was fluorescent. Anyhow, the theme was numbers. The girl I went with, Claire, who was overweight as well as stupid, was wearing a bikini and too much perfume. She said, 'I'm Marilyn Monroe. It's really clever, actually. When somebody asked her what she wore in bed she said—'

'Chanel No. 5, yeah, yeah, I know.'

I had to interrupt her. You'll think it was mean of me, but she was so fucking irritating. The most stupid people are always the ones who think they know everything.

So with this girl I went into this sad suburban house. We walked out through the sliding French windows, on to a patio, with paving like Battenberg cake. Ugly shrubs round the edge; beyond, all shiny in the evening, was water.

I said, 'I didn't know there was a swimming pool.'

Claire, who bloody knew everything, said, 'Oh yeah. That's why I wore my cossie.'

Thank fuck I didn't know. There's no way I would be swimming. And it was too suburban for anybody to be swimming without costumes.

Luckily she sees someone she knows. I stand in the corner. The room is very square. I feel kind of hemmed in. Particularly as I am getting barged by these sweaty bodies grinding revoltingly. People that ugly should not be allowed to dance. I never dance. At least not in public. Or at least not unless I am pissed. And often not even then.

I laughed when I saw a guy wearing a pair of trunks and smelling of Chanel No. 19. Claire couldn't believe someone else had had the same idea. I can't believe that I still feel pleased about how miserable she was, even though I haven't seen the girl for ten years. But that's me, celebrating small moments of victory.

Like at most parties, I was bored. And at twenty-two I had yet to come up with a better solution to boredom than having inappropriate sex (I still haven't actually – I just don't go to parties so often).

I got talking to a bloke wearing a T-shirt with 'Wine me, Dine me, 69 me' written on it in purple.

The bloke, who, even in the dark, I could see was ginger, said that it wasn't his, it was his flatmate's. The mate bought it on holiday as a laugh and now he wore it only to fix his bike. There were oil marks on it.

This bloke I recall as very skinny. Very pale. See-through like a salamander. I could see whole rivers of veins. But that might be poetic licence. What would I expect of a ginger guy? I wasn't a ginger virgin, you know. He didn't think much of me but he was pissed as a fucking salamander. He said, 'Waddya come as a nun for?'

'I don't know,' I said. (I pride myself on a good comeback.)

It didn't matter because like a lot of people, I find, he didn't seem to have a fucking clue what I was talking about anyway. I was not on his vibe, as they say. Do they? They should.

Anyway, something didn't work. We didn't connect on a higher level. Maybe I was the only person there not on e. I would have, happily, but I couldn't get any. I said, most politely, to two girls in the queue for the loo, 'Do you know where I can buy any pills?' But they completely fucking ignored me. Not even like I wasn't there or didn't exist but as if I'd never fucking existed. Maybe I hadn't, I thought. How do you tell?

Someone wrapped in Spar bags had come as seven-eleven. A man with disgusting stomach muscles said he was a six-pack. The house was quite big but it was too full and too dark and too loud.

Everyone else was drinking water and Lucozade (not because they needed it but because it was cool and told everybody that they were 'e'd out of their brains' which was the de rigueur way to be) so I drank most of the litre bottle of vodka myself.

I couldn't feel anything.

Over and over again that orgasm song by Lil Louis – 'French Kiss' – was playing. It was huge that summer. You heard it everywhere. The beat that got faster and faster with a woman moaning herself to a climax. 'Uh, er, er, er, er' (OK, it doesn't look so very realistic written down). It wasn't exactly good music, but it was kind of appropriate. I don't mean for me. I mean it was appropriate for the kind of time people wanted to go home thinking that they had had.

I remember getting off the bed after I'd done it with the ginger guy and looking out the window. Down into the garden. People without costumes were using the swimming pool after all. Ginger guy was putting his trousers back on. He was away quicker than I was.

I put my knickers back on (somehow we'd done it in my smock and wimple) and walked out across the landing to another bedroom at the front of the house.

I think maybe the ginger guy put something in my drink because I've been very drunk plenty of times before and it's always gone one of two ways. Either I spend the night with my head down the toilet or I collapse semi-conscious and spend the following morning with my head down the toilet (which is worse). This time I did neither.

I just opened the window and jumped.

I had often contemplated suicide in theory. As a spectator sport. I liked the idea – surely anyone who's worked in life insurance does. Oh, the temptation to fuck up statistics. Like a lot of people I enjoyed tipping over the edges of cliffs or bending over motorway flyovers, just for the thrill. Or reading Samaritans' ads and thinking how nice it would be to have someone persuade me out of it. But I never really tried it. I'd be sure to fuck it up. I spend too long picturing all the things that could go wrong. Like I throw up all the pills before they do any damage. And I can't remember if you're meant to use hot or cold water when you slash your wrists. So I'd never really do it. Which was why I'm saying that I must have been doped. It was like falling in a dream.

I used to dream I was falling or flying or both. One time I shrieked, 'I'm flying! I'm flying!' Everybody was gathered around admiring until my mother pointed out that actually I was lying on top of a red car with my arms stretched out. I was so embarrassed, I woke up blushing.

So I thought I was flying. But because I'd been humiliated before I wasn't going to shout about it. And I looked down and I realized I'd landed in a tree. This huge tree that took up nearly all the small space between the house and the road. My outfit helped. The billowing smock must have hooked over a branch. I was hanging upside down. I don't know how long for. But it can't have been long. My arm was feeling very heavy, swinging. I hadn't thought of anything to do about it. I hadn't thought anything much. Then this male voice shouted up to me, 'What are you doing?'

My eyes were bulging.

'What are you doing?' he asked again.

'I'm lizzening to the muzic.'

Have you ever tried saying 's' upside down? When your head is swimming in blood? It's difficult.

There was music falling out of the open window. Sounded awful. You could still hear the stereo from further back in the house. But there was also this racket.

'What is it?' he asked. He really seemed like he wanted to know.

I said, 'Iz a zagzaphone.'

It was a saxophone. Might even have been a great saxophone but it was a fucking useless saxophone player. He was playing notes that didn't seem to hold together. Like a string of pearls – with the string missing.

Alex asked me if it was a fancy dress party.

I said, 'Ez.'

He said, 'Tarts and vicars?'

I said, 'No, numberz.'

'Numbers?'

'Ez. You had to come az a number.'

'You had to come as a number?'

'I came aza none.'

'Oh, a nun . . . oh, you mean a none!'

I didn't know why he was so interested. But he was the first person in the entire evening who'd got the point of my costume.

And he laughed. He's never laughed like it since. He said afterwards that it was my ears. That the laugh was perfectly normal and that since I had been listening to that saxophone torment quite happily while hanging upside down in a tree, my memory was not to be trusted.

But I swear it was huge. I've never heard anything like it. Rising higher in pitch, 'Eh-heh-heh, eh-heh-heh-heh-heh.' A stutter and then a roar, over the top. Falling down to the bottom of his lungs like a roller coaster.

He started to help me out of the tree. I don't know what happened exactly but at some point, when I was half rescued, I got impatient. I pushed too far and fell to the ground, socking him one in the mouth with my foot in the process.

I was all right. Since I was drunk my muscles were relaxed. I was bruised but nothing worse. Later I pointed to this as irrevocable proof that drinking is good for you. But Alex (trust him) said that it was the drink that got me there in the first place.

I woke up in Alex's house wondering if he'd fucked me or not.

I didn't know Alex then.

I stayed a couple of days. He wouldn't have let me if he hadn't liked me. He's like that. He doesn't do anything he doesn't want to do. That was probably what I liked about him in the first instance.

But we got on as well. Once my tongue was back to its normal size and the helicopter in my head had turned its engine off. It was a new experience for me.

I can quite honestly say that I made no friends at school. You will think this is just nostalgic self-indulgence. That everybody had a bad time. I wouldn't say it wasn't a bad time exactly, it was just that the girls despised me and the boys didn't notice me at all. And the trouble with kids is, once you start being unpopular, it just snowballs. Because even the kids who might otherwise have liked you have to hate you too, to be safe themselves.

Being safe is the most important thing. Children don't judge one another the way adults judge one another. Not on intelligence, beauty or (then at least) money. It's like poker. All that matters is how cool you are. And since this mysterious alchemy doesn't exist, since there is nothing solid about 'cool', you can't get it, you just are. Or not. And being cool compounds your coolness. Being cool, you actually become a definition of cool. So you can't not be cool any more, you see? And it works the same in the other direction. Not being cool is a dead end. Any efforts you might make make you look twice as uncool. But it's completely important. And you have to try because you are a child and desperate to please.

Others gained strength from my weakness. It suited them to have, in me, an agreed definition of uncool. The cruellest behaviour often came, paradoxically, from the kids closest to me, who needed to work harder to distance themselves.

From the age of about nine to eighteen my sole aim in life was to become cool. Eventually I did become cool, by that criterion, but by then it didn't seem to matter any more. Now I do all the things I was desperate to do as a child but couldn't. But now it's too late. They don't impress anyone any more. Not even me.

When I was young I couldn't swear. I don't know why, I just couldn't.

There was this thick as shit girl who expended huge amounts of energy on making my life as unpleasant as possible. I think now, why did she bother, what did she gain? But at the time there didn't need to be a reason. She just did.

I was walking out of the school grounds at the end of the day when I saw a fellow loser about to be attacked by this girl for carrying books home. This was worthy of contempt because it could mean only one thing: she was planning to do her homework.

Thick Shit is waiting propped up against the tree by the gate. She is eyeing Fellow Loser. You can feel the tension. Fellow Loser knows she is under surveillance. She starts to walk funny. Suddenly she can't remember how. She stops, reddens, sets her eyes non-confrontationally to the middle distance and moves on again. But Thick Shit has picked up Fellow Loser's anxiety and is now determined to cause trouble. She feeds on weakness.

Thick Shit moves towards Fellow Loser just an inch or two. It's all that is needed. The threat is enough to pin Fellow Loser to the ground. She is taut with fear.

Thick Shit says, 'What you taking fucking books home for?'

Fellow Loser is petrified.

Thick Shit carries on, 'Running home to do your fucking homework, are you, Loser?'

This rather weak insult is bolstered by the accompanying titter of Thick Shit's mates who suddenly appear from behind the tree, holding their mouths in a disingenuous display of hilarity. Of course they were there all along. Thick Shit is never alone. I thought then that it was because she was so popular. Now I realize that this was weakness too, that she couldn't cut it solo.

It looks to be all over for Fellow Loser. She is about to be utterly humiliated. Possibly robbed, possibly thrown in the mud. It depends how Thick Shit is feeling.

But then Fellow Loser sees me. Watching. From behind her, trying not to be noticed but unable to turn away. Watching is weird. Fellow Loser draws strength from me. She can console herself that at least she is not the complete loser that I am.

There is an altered tension in her. From fear to renewed strength. She pulls herself up. She looks Thick Shit full in the eye, lifts her third finger into an aggressive gesture and shouts, 'Up yours, you thick shit,' and storms past.

Thick Shit is stung. The invisible power is broken. It suddenly seems so easy to overcome her. All you have to do is swear. Wounded Thick Shit is now flailing. She needs to restore her image in the eyes of the tittering chorus who, she instinctively knows, will support her only while hers is the winning side. Thick Shit does not have bright ideas. But she has tried and tested strategies that will always come through in the end. She looks at me. I look at her. But of course I look away first. She has found her victim.

'What you fucking looking at?'

Later, at home, I shout into my pillow, 'I'm looking at you, you fucking stupid twat, what do you think I'm fucking looking at, you thick cunt?'

It might have been a tad overstated but it would have worked better than what I did say, which was, 'Nothing.'

Particularly as I said it so quietly I don't think she could even hear me.

She looked at her friends. And there was a hush. A light wind rippled through my hair and I could feel the goose pimples rising on my arms and neck – the evidence of my cowardice.

She sauntered up to me and said, 'You're so fucking weird. They should put you in a fucking loony bin like the rest of your fucking family.'

And they laughed and laughed and laughed.

We all get what we want in the end. Only not always when we want it. I did become cool. And cool when I was eleven meant swearing a lot and getting attention from boys. Now I can't fucking stop myself.

And long after Thick Shit had stopped swearing and started producing children and bringing them up in a model of the middle-class family, there I was swearing my arse off. She was being procreative, fulfilling God's purpose, while I was having sex for no purpose at all.

Consequently, thanks to unresolved issues in early life, I am lumped with a screwy philosophy that serves only to fuck my life up:

1 You must never be seen to try.
2 Being caught reading books is a sign of insanity.
3 There's nothing worse than being insane.
4 Your coolness can be measured by how often you say the word 'fuck'.

And I can say it now, as easy as anything.

Sarah sighed and paused and looked around the empty room, without Alex, seeking inspiration. Chewed her pen and resumed.

Well, Alex was the first person I really liked. Obviously I had known people who were friendly enough. But I never felt much.

Alex introduced me to people he knew. They all seemed to want to be weird. I couldn't understand that. I had spent so long trying to be the same and here they were trying to be different.

With Alex, for the first time I began to discover what it was to be myself. I stopped caring. Which was good, in a way. But the trouble is it hasn't been replaced by anything else. With Alex's support, I felt able to walk away. Then I walked out of so many jobs that it stopped having any effect on me. I stopped feeling like it mattered. The trouble is that Alex had a nice little set-up that allowed him to opt out. I had no back-up plan. I wanted to leave the world I was in but I felt I had no alternative.

Alex offered me one. He let me sort out his house. It's a bizarre job but not unfitting. For a while I was happy. But it turned out I couldn't join his world. I wanted too much. I wanted a final escape. Having been given a visitor's visa, I then wanted citizenship. Full rights. I pushed things too far. And when I didn't get what I wanted, I did the only fucking thing I knew. I fucked around. That was not a good idea. I should have trusted Alex, I suppose, to have my interests at heart. But I couldn't. Because I've never had anyone like that.

She stopped writing. Her hand ached. She had pushed the pen harder and harder. Her fingers were hot. The lines had begun to slant wildly across the page. She looked up blinking. Then she wrote again on the pad.

The end. Bored of writing fucking diary. No one would publish my life anyway. Shut up.

And she lay on her back and sighed. It was a week since Alex had walked out of his own house. She had no idea where he was.

Alex was gone. Sarah had pushed him away. Through her childishness, her innate need to spoil everything. To spoil life before it spoilt itself. Squashing flowers. Leaving an inky smear and not even enjoying the pleasure of destruction.

She winced now at how she had taunted Alex with the thought of Matthew. And the taste of Matthew. The giant slug in her mouth. He left a trail from her mouth, over her chin and all the way down her body.

She didn't really know Alex. What had bound them together for this long was a mutual respect for each other's privacy. They both lived mainly on the inside. Alex knew himself well enough to know that. Sarah lived so much on the inside that even *she* didn't know it.

Alex had looked after her from the beginning. He had no idea what had made him stop to talk to a drunk nun hanging from a tree. It was totally unlike him to initiate conversation with a stranger. Something about the expression on her upside-down face, something he recognized. He would not have had words for it but it was the look of the unloved.

And then Alex had slammed the door on her. An unthinkable thing for him to have done. A physical action. Alex was not demonstrative. Alex was not supposed to care about her actions either. That was how it had always been. Until now.

At first she had absurdly got on with her job. As if at any moment he might return. Working in silence. Well, of course, it had been silent before. But she noticed the silence now. It was reproachful. At other times she did nothing. She did not think. Her head echoed with emptiness. The work seemed pointless, *was* pointless.

Until Alex came back, she had no money. She would soon run out of food. She would be found on the floor. This had a pleasing ring of drama. It faded with the discovery in a small kitchen cupboard of a kilogram of rice and almost the same in lentils, evidently bought in a drive for economy and forgotten ever since. She would not starve though she might die of boredom.

After pretence of normality she gave in to self-pity. She no longer pulled on the sweatshirt and leggings but stayed in her night T-shirt. She made herself tea but she did not climb down the staircase to the rooms below.

Instead she sat in the kitchen and thought. The phone rang sometimes. She ran towards it and waited for the message, hoping that it would be Alex, but it was always people Alex knew. Names, mainly unfamiliar. It was clear they did not know where he was either. How many people he knew.

Her mind was spiralling downwards.

She had pushed away the one person who was interested enough to put up with her. From the beginning Alex had ignored the defensiveness that other people found so hard to take. Maybe because he was defensive too. What better hope is there than that one could find another whose faults one can tolerate because they are one's own? Alex did not mind her drunkenness because he was inclined to it himself. He did not balk at her sexual encounters because they were a different response to a similar feeling, his own hostility to intimacy. She shunned intimacy by fucking anybody. He by fucking nobody.

Alex was as unripe as Sarah. She told him about sexual exploits that meant nothing to him as they meant nothing to her. Alex *had* never laughed like it before. Because he had never before met someone like himself.

While the food was unappetizing, at least there was a good supply of beer. Soon Sarah initiated a new routine. Unable to sleep at night, she slept until three or sometimes four in the afternoon. She rose. She turned on the video. At the beginning she would feel secure. Knowing that there was at least an hour and a half before she had to emerge and think for herself. For that period she could live in someone else's reality. She stuck to familiar films. She watched not for interest but for consolation. As such she could watch the same films over and over again. Each film had an atmosphere she loved. Always happy endings.

And at the end of the film she climbed out of the cocoon, walking out into the light, shedding the protective atmosphere like a skin. At first the music would still be playing in her head.

Her life would have accompaniment and be sweeter for it. Slowly the music would fade away. So slowly she would not notice the moment when it first ceased to be audible. But later she would be aware that it was not there any more, that her world was silent again.

There was still no sign of Alex. She made a decision to return to her flat. It was the first decision for she couldn't remember how long. She didn't normally make decisions. Things happened. Things just happened.

Strange how soon the verisimilitude of normality falls away.

She left Alex's, closing the door behind her. A heavy sound. Slamming, she hoped, all those memories behind her. The letters, the boxes of hair, the games, the pervading presence of Alex that hung in the lifeless air. And the older, dimmer presence of the people she had never known but now, after these last weeks, almost felt she knew. His parents, their friends, their thoughts, the shadows that filled the rooms.

She walked back to her flat. A journey that took at most seven minutes seemed interminable. She almost couldn't face it and went back. Only the knowledge that she couldn't go back since she had left the key on Alex's kitchen table propelled her legs forward. She had left the key on purpose. She wanted to forget her debt.

She walked in, pushing the door awkwardly past a pile of post. The flat was stale. A few flies buzzed weakly round the scabrous plates. Sarah opened a window. But the air outside seemed just as fetid and she was disturbed by the sound of drilling. She closed it again.

On the answerphone were five messages. Four were from Maggie. One was from a cold-call guy leaving a request to speak to the person responsible for purchasing the stationery. Sarah scrawled the cold-call number on the back of unopened junk mail with blunt eyeliner – well, she needed pens.

She kicked the crap off the sofa and lay on it staring at the blind. Straight lines. It was a small room that looked smaller because of the mess of dirty laundry, videos, old magazines and plates. She had not spoken for over a week. She was beginning to fear it. But she had to talk to her mother some time. Oh God.

She shook her head at herself and in one swift movement picked up the receiver. How hard could it be?

The phone had been cut off. However, the thought that she had taken the first step to a rational existence by attempting to make a social phone call eased the strain a little. She had earned a rest.

She lay on the sofa and picked up the book that lay face down on the floor. *Through the Looking-glass.* She knew it almost off by heart because Maggie loved it. It was the one book that her mother had agreed to read to her. Maggie normally hated reading out loud.

Sarah liked the White Knight best. His entirely self-sustained good humour. That he was so pointlessly wandering through the wood. Sarah too was good at the pointless wandering, but there was no place for it now.

And she loved his phlegmatic nature. He sang his nonsense song and told Alice happily,

'Everybody that hears me sing it – either it brings the *tears* to the eyes or else—'

'Or else what?' said Alice, for the Knight had made a sudden pause.

'Or else it doesn't, you know.'

How wonderfully simple things could be. And then she slept.

She awoke hours later. It was morning although she didn't know what time. Still wearing the same clothes, unwashed and unfed (there was no food here at all), she went out for a walk. The fresh air might help, she thought, but help what exactly? She wasn't sure. She just knew she didn't want to think about it.

She wound around South London. She was convinced people were looking at her and consequently became hopelessly lost through crossing the street whenever she caught someone's eye. And she made sure to avoid the lines of the pavement squares. Didn't want to get eaten by bears on top of it all. And she was watching how people dress alike. Two girls with straight long ponytails both wearing tight navy pedal-pushers, pushing the pedals of their cycles in rhythm. Two men in black apart from lime-green jackets. A couple. Both slightly overweight. She had dyed black hair and a bright yellow Fila shirt. He had dyed blond hair and a black Fila shirt. Her nose-ring matched the ring through his eyebrow. Two black guys with rolling muscles that must fit together like fingers, their mirror sunglasses reflecting distortedly her own walking figure.

Who was she meant to walk with? Was that why she stood out? Did people always come in pairs? She saw *her* other half only when she looked in the mirror. No one spoke her language. Sometimes she did not speak it herself. When the same incomprehensible thoughts ran around her head like water down the plughole. Which way did the water spin in the northern hemisphere? Clockwise or anti-clockwise? She must experiment when she got home, must look more closely.

Maybe, she thought, after seeing a woman of dubious character standing in a neglected doorway of what had once been a Caribbean café, the green letters still falling off the façade, maybe she could become a prostitute. Isn't that what the self-help books recommended? Finding a way of making money from what you liked to do? Except she didn't much.

The fear that was rising unchecked in her was not for the immediate future. Even though this was actually where the danger lay. Since closing the door of her home of two months she had left behind all food and drink and she had no money. Her bank account would long since have been drained by the rent that went out on standing order. But these risible, mundane fears were not what consumed her. It was a fear of the void that seized her stomach and pulled it downwards, unrelentingly, until her legs felt bloated. That left her head pricking and reeling and isolated. Strange pains at the back and the front that seared through her like a cheese-cutter. The terror, or was it gratitude, that she would slip into total delusion and never come back. Let someone else take care of her. It had worked for Grace.

As the thoughts travelled through her, more real than the blood in her veins, she passed many streets without noticing her surroundings. But she was now arrested by a cooler wind. She turned to her left where the breeze led her and saw a dark alleyway. Without thinking, she walked down it.

The messy streets of South London with their welter of people, shabbily dressed, overdressed and hardly dressed, were vibrant and secure. But here, moments from the noise and light, she felt instant alarm, encouraged by the smell of piss and the ubiquitous beer cans, a couple of used condoms and a dirty syringe, rotting cabbage leaves and cigarette butts trodden in the wet.

The alley became darker and thinner and was heading to the door of an old building and a corner, so tight, like part of a maze. She felt anxiety. A refreshing, tangible anxiety. Not the more terrifying anxiety of the unspecific, of fear for fear's sake. She heard a noise and her breath caught. It sounded like someone flicking a knife.

As her eyes grew accustomed to the darkness and sought out more details, she felt the damp side of the wall. There was no person there but there was something moving. A flick of a disappearing tail. The shine of oily rat fur. It scuttled away. She smiled. And then she noticed that the noise that she thought was the knife was the sound of a bottle falling and rolling on the ground. Knocked by the rodent and still swinging. She picked it up. It was a bottle of vodka. Full and, more importantly, sealed.

She almost didn't take it, thinking that the rat might have been planning a party. But reason told her it had most likely been left by a down and out.

She had once left a bottle of whisky behind a bin on New Year's Eve – the police were frisking people at barriers round Trafalgar Square. When she returned at one in the morning naturally it was no longer there. So now she felt – as right-minded people think about umbrellas – that it was part of life's checks and balances to claim this vodka as her own.

While she walked outside she felt better, with the motion, the tread of her feet against the solid concrete. But inside the flat, she deteriorated.

She looked at herself in the mirror with the first glass of vodka. She had definitely lost weight. Her face was developing a fetching cadaverous look. She had dark circles around her eyes. Her pale skin was turning liverish. She smiled and her smile looked ghoulish in the dusty air. She smiled and felt miserably, utterly alone.

22

James Joyce Makes an Unexpected Appearance in Weston-super-Mare

Alex walked out of his house slamming his own front door behind him. He was angry. It was an entirely new feeling. He decided this rash inside him was an allergy, a sickness responding to Sarah's behaviour. He had never stormed from anything in his life.

This did not make any sense. Until now he had been profoundly unconcerned by any (and there were too many to remember) of Sarah's lascivious exploits. Uncensored details had wafted past him, like a familiar and unremarkable scent that registers only subconsciously.

He never felt anger but inexplicably he was now shaking. Energetic rage had pulled him as far as Paddington station. Often he arrived at a random terminus and took the first train out. Something about the destinations, lined up before his eyes, signified possibility. Train travel meant escape. There was, then, no reason why this morning he found himself at Paddington, other than that he had to be somewhere and he wanted to go somewhere else. He scanned the blue computer screens. There was a train to Weston-super-Mare at ten o'clock. He bought a ticket. Why not.

He did not think about Sarah. That is, he actively did *not* think about her. Which was not easy, for it meant not thinking about a lot of other things too; the rambling house he had left behind, his work, his feelings. It was a struggle to find something else, when there were many areas of his life he already avoided.

For the first time ever he had left the house with nothing to read. He left with nothing but a wallet and keys. That's how angry he was.

The bookseller on the station glittered with shelves of titles, fat and fluorescent. He felt, though, inexplicably, too unsettled to read a book. Instead, he bought four broadsheet newspapers and a pen. Then a sloppy coffee in a polystyrene cup that he would later chew to nothing in his distress and an almond croissant that he would not finish. The coffee spilled over his fingers as he struggled to carry all these awkward new possessions.

'Oh bloody hell,' he cursed aloud, but his words were swallowed in the noise of the irate trains and the adenoidal announcer.

His Intercity train stood parallel to another and, as the other moved off, he experienced the illusion that it was his train that moved. As he adjusted his vision, he caught his own face in the reflection of the two windows, a stronger image in the darkness created by the pieces of glass sucking light from each other. His expression was thunderous and painful but he didn't see that.

'The aspects of things that are most important to us are hidden because of their familiarity (one is unable to notice something because it is always before one's eyes).'

Wittgenstein's words had been stuck by his mother Hilary, in her own hand, to the inside of the toilet door. Alex had read them with every bowel evacuation, every day in the 1970s. On the outside of the toilet door was a sticker popular at the time, an attempt at wit: 'This is it'. Some guest added 'sh' to the 'it' in a stoned hand. The two comments, outside and in, complemented one another. Not that Alex disagreed with Wittgenstein, what he disagreed with was having thoughts force-fed in the toilet – an uncomfortable idea no matter what the message. Alex had long ago removed both stickers but the outlines stayed on the door, and the words remained in his mind.

In his reflection, he recognized the face, the features, the movement, and the slight lean to the left (his face followed his politics). The straight nose, the eyes with lids that lowered slightly, creating the impression (quite accurately) of scrutinizing disbelief. But he couldn't see his feelings. He couldn't understand himself because his obscurity was so familiar, so present.

These thoughts and the crosswords carried him to Bristol. The journey to Weston-super-Mare was called three-legged – he envisioned a long, articulated monster, limping along in tripodal misfortune. He changed trains at Parkway and caught another to Temple Meads. Less angry now and more dazed, he swung from thought to thought like they were lianas. From the platform a violently green piece of plastic – shiny, moulded, the size of his thumb – caught his eye and urged him to pick it up.

The train from Temple Meads to Weston-super-Mare was called the Sprinter. Named by a marketing man with a sense of humour, the creaking exoskeleton swayed and clanked across the countryside, through Long Ashton and Yatton.

He sat with an overweight group of addle-pated middle-aged women and four raucous young girls clad in a rustle of cotton dresses.

The eldest not more than ten, the girls were arguing in a language that Alex didn't quite understand. It sounded like English until he tried to catch on to a meaning. And then it wasn't right.

'Great bolshy yarblocks to you,' said one.

The other, her face spitting hate, replied, 'You shouldn't give me that uncalled-for tolchock.'

Then the youngest, her front teeth missing, with a perfect bowl of a haircut with a high fringe and freckled dots all over her nose and the poise of unlikely ancient wisdom, turned her head slowly to join the fighting. 'I'll meet you with chain or nozh or britva any time.'

Alex stared, eyes wide open for once. Surely they were speaking Nadsat, the fictitious teenage language of *A Clockwork Orange*? He could scarcely forget, his mother had made him read it over and over. Nadsat was the language created by the main character Alex, his namesake and his mother's dream son. A boy who flaunted convention and lived by instinct alone. *A Clockwork Orange*, a broiled broth of delinquency, of torture perpetrated by and against Alex, anti-hero. Of illegal sex, violence, murder and state brainwashing. His mother loved it.

It could not be so, they could not be talking so. He shook his head and tried to listen harder, even prodding his ears with a finger to make sense of the world.

The fat middle-aged women, entirely undisturbed by the hysteria around them, were in fact in charge. Only when the cacophony paused did they look round in concern. The children were never still. There was a constant shifting and palpable aggression. Though they were children, Alex found himself bristling with unease.

He heard one of the women say, 'Don't fight against it please, there's no point in your fighting, you can't get the better of us.'

At least he was not thinking about Sarah. Then a high-pitched squeal demanded, 'Give me back my grahzny sodding leg, Alexander the large!'

A sweet-smelling waft of air preceded the arrival of a comical button nose and the palest peach features of an angry child.

'What?' he said, flummoxed, holding back his head in panic.

She wrinkled up her face and opened her mouth wide to create maximum volume. Inside was rosy pink and moist, lined with tiny teeth. So white they looked blue, those at the front were bigger and there were several gaps.

She repeated in an educated tone, 'My grahzny sodding leg, you've got it.'

And he realized what it was. The green piece of plastic, which his fingers fiddled with, was the lower limb of a toy android of some kind.

Everything belongs to something else, he thought. He handed it back to her and closed his eyes to avoid further interaction. But whenever he allowed his eyes to open slightly he could see her staring.

And when he closed his eyes and slouched, with his long legs stretching easily underneath the opposite seat, he found the thing he was trying not to think about coming ever more starkly to the forefront of his mind.

The sallow features, the dark lustrous hair. The malicious voice that wanted him hurt.

'Fat sex, have you, Alex?' The words reverberated. The pictures she had painted in his head. Matthew, rolls of flesh, his tongue so fat she'd almost gagged. He opened his eyes again, his hand protecting his face, his mouth tight.

'How could she?'

The little girl still stared. He was convinced now that she was not a little girl at all. How else could she quote a shockingly adult book? He was hearing things. He was disturbing himself with a trick of the ears. He hated *A Clockwork Orange*, he hated children dressed as adults and adults dressed as children.

It was his first visit to Weston-super-Mare and yet it was entirely what he expected. He walked out of the station building to be hit by a roundabout and an enormous supermarket. Not a seagull in sight.

He followed signs to the beachfront. An athlete compared to the rest of this population, both the transient and the permanent; late holidaymakers swallowing sausages, sauntering truants, pensioners steadied on shopping trolleys and mothers chained to prams. At last, the twisted pavement, which wound past chain stores, old-style chip shops and the sweets and cancers shops (newsagents in Nadsat), opened on to the broad vista of the front.

Pronged by the pier and steps that led down to the brown sand was a huge grey sky. A little pale sun came through the cloud. It fell, behind him, on to the long, jumbled front of incongruous buildings, not the peeling pastel terrace he had assumed all British beachfronts to be. One in particular seemed to be shining at him. Summer View was not an old building, just a neglected one. Alex walked towards it, drawn to its total defiance of beauty, decaying without charm.

He sat on the badly sprung double bed, his palms irritated by the synthetic cover. He looked at the old television in one corner, the apricot towels that had been washed too often, the net curtains, the view across the sands to the twinkling sludge-green sea. A tiny pink sink with the scrape of soap that would make a person smell worse, not better, brought a patch of damp in the corner of the room to his attention.

Alex did not dwell on feelings. He avoided. He got on with his life by getting on with his life. He had developed, like everyone, unconscious comfort strategies. For reasons that he shunned, he was uncomfortable with intimacy: emotional intimacy, sexual intimacy, physical intimacy. But he had never articulated this.

Alex's language protected him. Non-emotive, non-confrontational, obscured. He spoke in games and on the surface; he was an intelligent foil. People liked that, it kept them both amused and at a distance. When intimacy threatened he ran away. Now, for instance, he kept moving. He had no sooner sat down and looked around the room than he shifted up again and went back outside, to go nowhere.

Oh but he did like to be beside the seaside – in the erosion. He stopped at a second-hand bookshop and bought five anonymous 1950s paperbacks. Forgotten authors, styles outmoded, plots pulpish, covers sub-Hitchcock hysteria, dusty black with yellow torchlight and screaming female faces, hands holding their mouths with perfectly manicured bright red nails.

Each morning he read in the same café where the bad coffee was masked by the cigarette smoke and smell of burnt cheese. Every afternoon he wandered along the front, round the town and stopped at amusement arcades. In the evening he retired to his small room in the guesthouse of one Mrs Brand-Pullen and spread his tired feet on the rough nylon carpet. He took a bath in the communal bathroom, only mildly distracted by the smell of the long-wet carpet and by the grains of sand on the bottom of the tub that grazed his back. Later he swigged from the bottle he kept in a plastic bag under the bed. He drank when the clouds in his mind began to clear. Thus he ensured that not once in seven days did he have to think.

At the beginning of the second week, Mrs Brand-Pullen demanded interim payment, fearing Alex to be not a legitimate guest but a thieving squatter. Why else would a single male with so few clothes and keeping such strange hours be staying so long in Weston-super-Mare? She asked him as much, straight, and he had no answer. He was as suspicious as she was. Why am I staying here?

But the question shook him. Stagnation had overrun him like mould in the shower and Mrs Brand-Pullen was the spray-on mildew remover. She was not a scent he would have chosen.

That afternoon he wandered as usual into the beachfront arcade. Yet it felt different. On this new week only a few people were gripped to machines. The room buzzed and flashed as brightly as ever but the holiday season was ebbing away. 'The universe is overridden by a blinding green smog,' cried out an electronic American voice. 'Save the earth from a deathly emission from planet Carthon.' The voice of doom was drowned in the sudden revving of a virtual car rally. A small boy squandered his lunch money vying for a pink rabbit he did not want.

Alex walked slowly. A long flat table created a visual space in the dark room where everything else stood vertical. It was a dormant game of air hockey. A woman stood by the sleeping machine. He felt a shock. Suddenly Alex was arrested, by *her* paralysis. For the first time he could remember, he had a feeling so rare he could hardly identify it; he felt longing.

Everything about her was delicate. Her face was so chiselled as to be almost pointed. Her skin was scratched with fine lines, not ageing, but the slight imprint of expression on a translucent wrapper. A thin white dress hung so lightly to her, it chilled him.

She noticed him staring at her. He never stared at anybody and she could somehow tell. His stare was fresh. This intrigued her and was probably why she did not wave off the ogle as she normally would.

'Do you want a game?' There was a lick of a west-country accent.

He started and coloured. He had not spoken to anyone but Mrs Brand-Pullen, Helen in the coffee shop and the man in the off-licence for more than a week.

His money lit up the metal surface of the table, the air blew the disc puck into life.

Despite her frailty, she was an aggressive player. The fingers that tapered delicately were now white with pressure as she gripped her bat, as she bit her lip and her eyes gleamed with competition. She laughed jubilantly and, as her mouth opened wide with delight, her pearly teeth caught the flashing lights of the room.

She cheated. He liked a woman who played games with the same passion that he did. Too often they were half-hearted. They thought games were only for fun. That there was no point. They didn't realize that that *was* the point. Pointlessness was the very best motive for almost anything. That was what he liked about Sa—

But he wasn't thinking about her.

They played in silence for half an hour. Then, because his

hands were too sore to continue and she had thrashed him so completely, he said, 'Do you want to go and get a beer?'

She smiled. 'All right then.'

They bought beer outside and walked with the bottles on to the beach. There were a few people but it wasn't crowded since the sky had grown leaden and the wind now felt uncomfortable.

'You like air hockey then?' he said.

'Mmm,' she said, her mouth enclosing the bottle, curved lips feeling the open neck.

How beautiful, he thought, stunning himself with this sudden desire.

'What's so good about it?' His conversation had become blunt, childlike.

'Ooh, well now,' she said, considering, wiping drizzle from her face, her so pale face!

They sat on the sand. He gave her his newspaper to park on. She sat on the back cover, the sport. The headline: 'It's all over now'.

He watched her with a smile on his face as she thought aloud.

'Air hockey seems sexually symbolic to me – I guess most sports are, if you're playing them properly. The opponent has to be just right. Playing with someone for the first time is finding out whether they're a worthy opponent or not. When they're not it's completely pointless and a boring waste of time. Playing against women is not nearly as satisfying for some reason. Even though, of course, men have an unfair advantage because of their physical strength – my arm muscles don't have much stamina despite my fierce determination.'

'Your fierce determination takes you a long way,' smiled Alex.

'Yes. Only when I'm being well and truly thrashed do I find it hard to muster the strength to go on.' She looked at him coyly and giggled, not like a girl, artless, but as if she knew exactly what she had said and simply found it amusing academically. He was silent.

Her paper face crumpled in fervour. 'I'm prepared to risk physical injury. My right thigh suffers serious bruising where it gets forced violently against the table – you have to get side-on to get the force behind your wham – but I don't feel it at the time. My wrist gets sore, bruised, because I'm blocking the goal' – she paused and looked up – 'which is cheating, of course, but justified when the opposition is male.'

She gasped for breath. Every link in her neck was separate as she stretched upwards.

'Winning the game is not as important as scoring a goal. Scoring, especially really impressive goals, is the best and the addictive part of air hockey. It's like "Wow, did you see that – look what I can do." '

He was entranced by her energy. She drained her bottle and her clear eyes came back from the sea.

'I have to go,' she said, without reluctance. 'I have to pick my kids up from school.'

'You have children?' he said incredulously. People Alex knew did not have children. How could a body so thin have gone through the process of birth without snapping? He had no experience of birth but he knew it was mysteriously painful.

'Yes,' she said, laughing at his amazement. 'Why not?'

He looked nonplussed.

'I don't know.'

She laughed and stood up. 'It's been nice talking to you . . .'

'Alex,' he said, extending his hand.

She looked at him, knowingly. 'Yes, it's been nice talking to you, Alex.'

And she got up and, waving her fingers, walked away, her thin white dress blowing in the wind.

Framed by artificial lights twinkling round her like stars, she reminded him of a mirror in a dressing room, lit by bright bulbs. Illuminating everything. For the first time he saw clearly.

A picture of Sarah, her image flashing across his eyes. The sea, crushing water against sand, enunciated the name with a stress on the first syllable as it hit and slung back. Sarah. He was dazzled yet the sky was so grey. He believed that James Joyce had been born on a cloudy day, but he had never before believed in epiphanies. His soul swooned slowly.

He spent many hours that evening thinking about her. Their friendship, who the hell she was, who he was and what they made together. He wanted more than anything to be with her, and once his mind was unlocked he could think of nothing else. Enlightenment in Weston-super-Mare: from nowhere it had come to him, in a wave of sea air, in the whiff of sewage and seaweed and fried fish.

Later, past eleven, when he had unsuccessfully sat in his squalid bedroom and found the walls closing in, cramping his burgeoning thoughts, he escaped again to the front. He bought a bag of chips and thrilled at the greasy smell of proper potato chips, dripping in oil, that promised a fat-coated mouth and demon indigestion. He shook the salt pot dully, feeling the crystal spray hit his fingers. It is important to apply the salt first, or the vinegar makes the chips soggy. They tasted astonishing.

He had spent many years believing feelings were unsophisticated, that intelligent people didn't besmirch themselves with anything so grubby as emotion. It was Weston-super-Mare and a game of air hockey that taught him otherwise.

Early the next morning he told Mrs Brand-Pullen that he was leaving. She eyed him with fear, imagining he would take the furniture with him. But her mouth opened; she was never short of words. 'Well, well, and it's about time too, isn't it?'

For once, she was right.

23

Sarah's Bath

She shuffled several times in her seat, conducting a conversation inside herself before speaking. When she spoke, the words seemed to tear through the quiet, like she had pushed through a membrane she did not know existed.

'I'm worried about Sarah.'

Rudi looked up. 'Well, she's gone quiet but you say she's done that before.'

Maggie's voice was beseeching. 'I must have rung her a dozen times.'

He was calm. 'Ring her now – it's been a couple of days.'

Maggie paused. 'I just did. The phone's been cut off.'

'Ah.'

Maggie started to tidy the breakfast things. Rudi was staying over for a few days, just staying over. He looked at Sarah's old bedroom, he didn't know why. How could it tell him anything about a woman he didn't know? Inside the cupboard 'Japan is beautiful' was etched in a thin line with a compass. He pulled a curious face. He couldn't imagine a daughter interested in the Orient.

Maggie wondered whether he wanted to meet his first child or if it was too much trouble. She hadn't made Sarah sound easy. Maybe it was enough to deal with the past, enough to enjoy the equilibrium they had achieved. Digesting change was exhausting and her appetite had faded.

She thought. Then she said, 'I'm going round to the flat.'

He looked startled. 'How will you get in if she's not there?'

She smiled wryly. 'I have the spare key. Sarah is inclined to get herself locked out.' Her levity concealed her nerves. She knew something was wrong. Even in their worst moments now she still knew and felt her daughter's suffering. It had not always been so, but such, now, was the hold that Sarah had on her life. It overcame even the grip of Great Edie. Twice in the last week Great Edie had voiced explicit concern for Sarah. The charm of Edie's delivery had made Maggie consciously put off doing anything, but she couldn't keep ignoring the problem since she felt it too.

The 1930s block that Sarah lived in was on a busy street, not far from a small grocery store called Mr Naik's.

'I'll get some milk,' said Maggie solidly. 'She's always out of milk.'

Rudi's eyes registered surprise. 'But she might not even be there.'

'She's there,' said Maggie, her mouth betraying her grim expectation, turning white with the pressure she was putting on her lips.

'How do you know that for sure?'

'I just do.'

'OK,' said Rudi, unconvinced.

Armed with milk and a bag of cleaning fluids that she had brought from her own house, Maggie marched towards the block. Rudi found himself running along behind. There was a fatalistic propulsion about her that reminded him of when she marched to her dead father on the ship. That was the day she grew up. She had been grown up ever since, he thought. She had spent her whole life looking after other people. Only with him perhaps could she be anything else. He wanted her to be looked after. An overwhelming urge to make her comfortable filled him. Comfort more than anything – comfort is an under-rated pleasure.

His thoughts were interrupted by the sound of Maggie talking to a young man standing outside the communal door to the block.

'I've been ringing and ringing,' said the young man rather desperately.

Rudi took him in in a discreet glance. An unkempt gangly guy, over six foot, dressed casually in a sweatshirt with something incomprehensible written on it, worn over a pair of rather grubby loose pale trousers. His hair, black, straight, came down only to his collar, but still seemed longer than he was able to control.

'You're not Alex, are you?' Maggie was asking.

The young man looked surprised. 'That's right. How did you know?'

'I guessed,' said Maggie, sticking out her hand. 'How do you do. I'm Sarah's mother.' She rarely said her own name if she could avoid it.

'Maggie?' Alex almost whispered.

'Mmm,' said Maggie, scanning up the wall to what would be Sarah's window. It betrayed no clue, she noted, except that it needed a clean.

Rudi looked at Alex and raised his eyebrows with curiosity.

'I'm Sarah's friend.' Alex looked lamely at the pair, though he had not been asked to justify himself.

Rudi stretched out his hand. 'How's it going? I'm Sarah's father.'

The expression of surprise on Alex's face deepened. It made him look young and vulnerable. Defences were crumbling but there was nothing to replace them; he was left with a void, like a facelift.

He blustered, 'But Sarah doesn't know her father.'

'No,' said Rudi. 'Unfortunately not, things have been difficult.'

'I see,' said Alex, which meant he wasn't going to ask.

Maggie had not been listening. She was carrying out a reconnaissance. She spoke like a general. 'Let's go in.'

'Should we?' said Alex, who felt it an invasion of privacy.

'Well, I'm not going to serenade her in the street,' said Maggie firmly.

Alex looked to see if she was being deliberately facetious. It was hard to tell from her immobile expression. He decided she was.

He knew very little about the family. He knew that Sarah had never met her father. That her mother and she didn't get on that well but that was hardly unusual. Sarah was more revealing about her cantankerous great-grandmother and the

292

mad grandmother locked away. He suspected she talked about them not because she wished to confide but because they made good stories.

Maggie put the key in the lock. The three walked in and called the small lift.

As they waited and it shunted slowly downwards, long cables and steel latticework, it looked to Alex like a torture piece. He should bring a lift into his next game. No one spoke.

The lift was so small that Maggie found herself pressed up against the two men. Both made her feel uncomfortable for different reasons. Alex, tall, good looking in a rather intense way, not someone easily ignored, the effect multiplied because he was towering over her head. She wondered if her grey was showing through. And then Rudi, here, now, squeezed against her, still an extraordinary thing, when his significance for so many years had been his absence. She could feel the warmth of his body. She was ashamed that it made her knees wobble rather. She dismissed such folly from her mind.

There was no discussion of what had brought them all here but there was a shared feeling of anxiety. At least Maggie thought so. Perhaps there wasn't. Perhaps it was just her, magnifying her fears in their presence. Perhaps they felt nothing. You could never tell with men. Thirty seconds' ascension seemed much longer.

There *was* an exaggerated sense of drama surely when Maggie put the key in the lock of Sarah's front door. It opened slowly and they all peered round.

'God,' said Maggie, 'it smells *awful.*'

Even Alex had to agree.

'God knows what the landlord would have to say.' Maggie waded across the hall to the sitting room, over unopened post and through the heavy, sickly air. The two men lingered impotently by the door – until Maggie let out a muffled shriek, whereupon Rudi and Alex both ran for different women.

In the war-torn sitting room Sarah was apparently asleep under a quilt on the sofa. Her face was a deathly white.

Maggie sat beside her, perched on an inch of cushion, shaking her daughter gently.

'Sarah. It's Mum. Sarah.'

Alex felt cold panic crawling over him. A pricking sensation at

293

the base of his skull. His fingers and toes shrank, his stomach turned.

Rudi said nothing and thought nothing. Except that, having thought she looked like her mother, now, in the face on the sofa, he saw himself.

'Christ, she's barely conscious,' said Maggie.

Alex felt relieved. He had assumed she was dead.

Rudi walked across the room, inadvertently splintering a CD case that lay underneath a crumpled mess of magazines. He crouched down beside Maggie and picked up Sarah's wrist. 'Her pulse is quite weak,' he said.

The shaking was having an effect. Sarah was moaning softly and moved a little under her duvet. Her eyeballs rolled.

Her mother rubbed her lifeless hand. 'Come on, you stink to high heaven, the first thing for you is a bath.' It was no leap for her to talk to people who couldn't answer. She moved briskly across the flat and the squeaking of taps was soon followed by the sound of running water.

The two men looked at each other.

Rudi fetched a glass of water for Sarah and Alex held up her chin.

Maggie returned. 'It's ready.'

'I'll carry her,' said Alex, jumping up from his kneeling position.

'Thanks,' said Maggie.

He scooped her from the sofa. She felt so light. He was carrying a phantasm. She felt cold. She clearly did not notice who was carrying her, or else in this state she had forgotten that Alex had disappeared and so was not surprised that he should be carrying her. Her head lolled backwards and her arms swung feebly from her torso.

Water frothed from the taps. The bathroom was full of steam. Alex stood Sarah up. Her body contorted and would have fallen, but he held on to her.

'You hold her while I take her pyjamas off,' said Maggie.

Alex obeyed the command. Despite the overwhelming need for practicality he felt weak at the thought that he was standing by Sarah's stripped body. He looked away, although this made the job harder. Maggie gave him a strange look.

Rudi was standing in the hallway; he was always a presence.

'What shall we do?' he asked Alex anxiously.

Alex, not sure where the words came from, said, 'Well, I think I'll change her bed and tidy up a bit.'

'Oh, yeah, sure, good idea.'

Sarah, in the bath, was babbling incoherently. 'The sky . . . the sky . . . the sky above my head.'

'How lovely,' said Maggie, and, feeling that her daughter needed to play, added cautiously, 'I can see it too.'

And she could really. The moisture bubble that formed on the cracking paintwork of the ceiling bulging with stains of steam looked like a cloud on a white sky.

Sarah said with precocious interest, 'Where am I?'

'In the bath.'

'Is it going to rain?'

'Well, if it does, we'll find an umbrella.'

'You be an umbrella.'

Maggie sighed. 'OK, I'll be an umbrella.'

She thought momentarily of spreading her arms as spokes but was inhibited and so she tried to think in an umbrella-like way: protective, waterproof, spiky. She saw herself quite clearly as a black umbrella of medium size. Certainly not an automatic, she wanted more dignity than that.

There was little time for daydreams.

'I think I'm going to be sick again.'

Maggie wordlessly picked up the red bucket by the side of the bath and held it while her daughter retched and spewed. The product was unimpressive. Maggie, examining the contents, shook her head and tutted, 'Your stomach must be completely empty. What have you been doing to yourself?'

'I don't know,' said Sarah weakly, burping but more coherent after the emission. 'I drank a lot.'

'I gathered that,' sniffed Maggie, grimacing. She wet her daughter's hair with the shower hose and gently applied a shampoo through the wilted locks. She wiped her daughter's mouth with a damp flannel.

'That's my freshwater flannel,' said Sarah with mild indignation. 'Won't he mind my sick?'

'Oh I shouldn't think so.' Maggie was talking only to keep her daughter's mind peaceful while she restored order to the body.

'Am I turning into Grace?'

'No.'

'How do you know?'

'Because I saw what happened to Grace and she wasn't like you at all.'

'How's that?'

'Well,' said Maggie, searching for evidence of sanity, 'Grace didn't know what was happening to her. If you are worried about going mad you won't do.'

'Are you sure?' Her daughter was able to look at her for the first time.

'Well,' smiled Maggie sharply, 'it's always worked for me.'

'Oh.'

Maggie rinsed the hair and rubbed the soft skin of Sarah's back. She held up her arm and cleaned the armpit. It had a tangy fragrance.

'Ugh,' said Sarah, 'that smells revolting. Sorry, Mother, and sorry that my stubble's coming through.'

Maggie snorted. 'Why did you let yourself get like this, eh?' She looked swiftly at her daughter who was pondering this question with difficulty. 'And I'm not talking about your armpits.'

Sarah looked almost relieved. 'Oh, right, I don't know. It seemed the right state to be in. What else was I supposed to do?'

Maggie raised her eyebrows and rubbed Sarah's other armpit, the right one, more firmly.

'Well, you could try asking for help.'

'Instead of?'

'Instead of letting yourself drift into misery.'

'But it feels so pathetic,' whimpered Sarah.

'Come on, don't want you staying in there too long, it'll make you more wobbly.' Maggie went to get a clean towel from the cupboard but found to her pleased surprise that there was one waiting outside the door. She held the towel between outstretched arms and, though shaking, for the first time Sarah walked in willingly.

The men waited on the balcony.

'Will she be all right?' asked Alex. By asking he was deferring responsibility.

296

'Oh, sure.' Rudi dragged nonchalantly on his cigarette. 'Not that I know anything about it, of course. You know her better than I do.'

There was a silence.

'Where are you from?' asked Alex.

'Chicago.'

Alex nodded. 'I thought your voice sounded Midwest.'

'Oh, do you know America well?'

'I know quite a few Americans,' said Alex.

'Oh, good.' It was all Rudi could do to stop himself from mentioning a few to see if they had any in common. Instead he said nothing. They both looked over the balcony to the dustbins below.

'How long have you been over in London?' asked Alex, thinking this was safe territory.

'Oh, just a few months.'

'Like it?'

'Yes,' said Rudi darkly. 'Though I must say this isn't my favourite part.' The view was a tangle of drainpipes and bits of buildings, the grey air infused with the chemical smell of the dry cleaners somewhere nearby. It was all accompanied by a permanent buzzing noise of roadworks and traffic.

'No,' agreed Alex circumspectly. 'No.'

'I'm staying in a bed and breakfast in Pimlico,' Rudi volunteered.

'Well, yes,' said Alex, still looking away, 'that would be nicer. But there are good things about South London when you get to know it.'

'Oh, sure, sure.' Rudi knotted his brows.

Alex was beginning to sound like a tour operator, but when he said, 'And are you staying long?' he regretted it instantly, for it was, in the circumstances, such a leading question. He put his hands in his pockets and moved his body, without thinking, into a more open stance. He was strangely intimidated by this elderly man who seemed somehow so comfortable in himself. Alex was thrown by how appealing this made him.

But Rudi was used to tougher interrogation and in response to the question merely smiled and murmured, 'Maybe.'

Then, uncomfortably shifting, Alex said, 'Have you met Great Edie yet, the family tyrant?'

'Not yet,' smiled Rudi again. 'I've been putting it off.'

'Well, with any luck,' pushed Alex, who didn't think it would go down badly, 'with any luck she'll die before you have to.'

Rudi laughed. 'I'm not going to disagree with you. I don't think she'll like me.'

'My family always do the decent thing and push off at the proper time,' said Alex. 'None of this dragging out.' He paused. 'I met her once.'

Rudi took one last drag and stubbed out the dog-end. He looked up at Alex. 'And?' He picked up the stub and buried it in the earth of a plant pot. The plant inside was dead. It seemed, to Alex, unnecessarily scrupulous with the flat in the mess that it was.

'She didn't take to me much.'

Rudi laughed again. A billow of smoke wafted in front of him. Alex found his laugh comforting. Rudi gave the impression that whatever life threw at him it couldn't touch him any more. Alex wondered if this was an inevitable process of age and decided it wasn't.

Rudi said, 'I didn't realize she "took to" anyone.' Lowering his voice though there was no one to hear, he added, 'She's a spooky old bat though – that weird psychic thing.'

Alex's eyes widened. He had heard this information previously only from Sarah whom he had taken to be a little over-credulous. Now here was a perfectly rational man with his feet firmly on the balcony concurring.

'Well, Sarah did mention—'

Rudi whistled. 'Crazy old broad! Maggie can't keep anything from her. She knew I was back. Been gone thirty-three years and she knows the minute I'm here.' He pointed an emphasizing finger into the air. 'She told Maggie before I'd even gotten to see her.'

Alex could think of nothing more intelligent to say than 'Wow'.

Rudi sighed and lit another cigarette. He smoked Marlboros. 'Yeah, it's a real problem. With the old lady sticking her evil nose in, the rest of them will never be let off.'

Alex squinted. 'I don't believe in that kind of thing though. It's not logical.'

Rudi looked with screwed-up old eyes into Alex's drained but young ones.

'Logic, huh? What is it you do again?'

Alex hadn't said. 'I write computer games mainly.'

'Oh, OK, I see.' He nodded sagely. 'And that's logical, is it?'

'What, the fact that I make them or the games in themselves?'

Rudi drew back his head to reappraise the tall youth in front of him. The movement showed Alex that the elderly neck was crêpey and he noticed for the first time the white beard stubble that was coming through.

'Well, that's certainly a logical deconstruction of my question.'

Alex bit his lip.

'You went to college, right?'

Alex nodded.

'Waddya study?'

Alex mumbled, 'Maths, stats and computing.'

Rudi smiled. 'There's no logic in math.'

Alex looked perplexed and said in a polite tone, 'There is, actually.'

'Well, yeah, I guess,' said Rudi provocatively, 'if you believe in a self-imposed logic. Which as it happens I don't.'

'Oh,' Alex said, floored rather. He propped himself up on the stone ledge round the balcony as his feet were now aching. He was not used to standing up.

Rudi, who was, took this shuffling for mental discomfort and spoke quickly. 'I didn't upset you, did I?'

'No, not at all.' Alex was sincere and settled again. 'Are you interested in maths?'

'Not really,' replied Rudi. 'I'd like to be, but I'm not the quickest at that kind of thing, though I love the idea of it. The limitlessness, infinity in both directions – if you know what I mean.'

'Not really,' said Alex who was nevertheless gripped by the old man's voice that was bathing in these thoughts that excited him. He sounded suddenly delicate and fresh, where before he had sound tired and smoke-croaky.

Rudi explained. 'I know that logically infinity can't go in any direction. It can't move because it's infinite, right? And yet you get something that, in the mind at least, is infinitely small or infinitely big and yet because they're both infinite they're the same size. It's the same thing and yet entirely different. How is that logical? Infinity is just a concept and yet apparently it exists. They say the universe is infinite. Well, I find that hard to believe. I figure somewhere there's a door or maybe a turnstile where you have to show your ticket. There's no such thing as a free universe, right?'

'Well,' said Alex, thinking that the conversation was not following the course he might have predicted and that Rudi was so like Sarah it was uncanny. The same aura; that he might look shabby and a little run down but something was shining within – that intensity. Rudi seemed to have lived many times. Would Sarah be that way some day? These thoughts interested him more than the answer he gave suggested.

'But of course logic doesn't preclude paradoxes.'

'Oh no – no, you don't,' laughed Rudi derisively. 'You can't shift the rules. That's like the Pope suddenly saying it's OK to masturbate.'

'No, it isn't,' said Alex, laughing himself now. Rudi was displaying a habit he had witnessed in Sarah too; she would create a stupid argument when she was ignorant about the issue and didn't care much. It was one of her more charming sides and one she displayed only when she felt confident. When she didn't, she would climb down or get nasty.

The conversation ended with Maggie walking out through the kitchen door. Rudi clapped Alex cheerfully on the back. 'You must tell me some mathematical paradoxes some time. I'd love to know . . . really,' he added to Alex's unconvinced smile.

Maggie looked tired but calm. 'I've given her some more water and a cup of tea. She threw up three times in the bathroom.' She shuddered and addressed no one in particular. 'God, you'd have thought I'd be past the sicky stage with a child of thirty-two, wouldn't you.'

Rudi turned to look at her and smiled vaguely. 'Hmm?'

'So is she all right?' Alex was anxious.

Maggie nodded. 'Yes, she'll be fine. She was lucid for a while in the bath but then she sank back into mumbling. I think she's just depleted of all her strength. She's in bed now. Thanks for changing it, Alex.'

'No problem . . .' His voice trailed off. She sounded so down to earth. He was surprised. After all the bad he'd picked up from

Sarah he found himself liking Maggie just as he had warmed to Rudi. He rarely liked people at once. Maggie seemed so different from Sarah's creation that had developed over the years in his head. She never explicitly talked about her mother, but things had slipped out. Maybe Maggie had changed.

People could change, he was beginning to realize. Certainly he seemed to be changing. Maybe Sarah hadn't noticed or couldn't notice change in her mother. Sarah dismissed the possibility of kindness in her mother as a belated assuaging of guilt, but at this moment she seemed to show nothing but sensible, genuine concern. It struck him particularly forcefully because genuine parental concern was something new. Maggie and Rudi were overwhelmingly genuine in a way that his parents had never been.

They walked back into the flat. Maggie sighed with the heat. 'It's so stuffy in here.'

'I think we should take Sarah back to my house,' said Alex. 'There's plenty of space there.'

'Your house?' said Maggie.

Alex shifted in his seat. 'She was staying there before.'

Maggie looked at him curiously.

Flustered, Alex said, 'She was working for me . . . sorting out, for her board and lodging . . . after she left her job.'

'She left her job?'

'Yes,' said Alex uncomfortably.

'I don't know very much about my daughter,' said Maggie.

Rudi winced.

For the first two days at Alex's, Sarah was almost feverish. She lay in bed, rarely opening her eyes, drinking and eating only when forced to do so and without recognition.

Then on the third day she sat up in bed when Alex walked into the room and said, 'Why are you here? You left.' She sounded grumpy. She looked so cross, Alex knew she was recovering. Her hair was once again a mess, her face was still pale but at least her expression was moving.

'Welcome back,' smiled Alex in warm relief.

'Where have I been?'

'You've been out of it,' he said, 'for days.'

She registered this.

Maggie, hearing life stirring, came running in.

'Oh God, it's my mother,' groaned Sarah. 'What's she doing here?'

Alex looked up at Maggie, a little embarrassed.

Maggie shrugged her shoulders amiably. 'Don't fret yourself, Alex. She's been like this for a long time.'

24

There Is a Fault

'Am I ill then?' said Sarah weakly in a half-attempt at humour.

Maggie was taking her daughter to the doctor's.

Travelling with her mother made Sarah feel not just feeble but also angry. 'What am I meant to tell him?'

'Just tell him what happened.'

The time allocated for a GP visit is eight minutes. This seemed like an ocean of time to Sarah. She had nothing to say. Eight minutes is too long to say nothing.

The doctor smiled, registering only minor surprise that a woman of Sarah's age had her mother with her. They sat down at the doctor's indication. Her smile was unwavering. 'So what's the problem.' It didn't sound like a question.

Sarah stared into space. Maggie nudged her and it was she who broke the silence. 'She's been losing control of her life. She doesn't sleep.'

The doctor stared at her pad for no apparent reason.

Sarah spoke. 'I have become non-functional.'

'And how long for?' asked the doctor in a gentle voice, without looking up.

'Oh, about the last thirty years.'

Maggie let out an exasperated sigh. 'Sarah, try and be helpful, there isn't much time.'

Sarah tried these days to fight against the contumely inside her. It bit at her throat like bile. She said in a strangled voice, 'Old habits die hard, Mother. I find it hard to be helpful.'

'Maybe' – the doctor coughed – 'maybe your daughter would find it easier to talk with you out of the room.'

Maggie held her breath and turned her eyes to her daughter questioningly. They said, would you, in an expression not of hurt but of caution and long-held unease. Probably, the eyes of her daughter replied, always with mistrust. Maggie stood up and walked slowly out.

'Do you have a close relationship with your mother?' asked the doctor.

'Ye-es,' answered Sarah, 'but sometimes we have trouble understanding each other. We're too similar probably.'

'So,' the doctor nodded at this unexpected clarity, 'what's the matter?'

'Oh God,' sighed Sarah, 'nothing, absolutely nothing.' She paused and then continued in a contemptuous voice, 'I'm unhappy. I've been unhappy. I have trouble sleeping. I am inclined to solitary and anti-social behaviour. I have headaches, stomach aches. I have unidentified terrors. I can't relate to other people – but that's nothing new. I mistrust genuine motives. I lack motivation. My life has no point or purpose and although I know that's true for everybody I find the truth hard to deal with. I get very angry.' She tapered off.

'At yourself or other people?' the doctor enquired dispassionately.

'Both. Myself mainly. I have the misfortune of being in my own presence more than anyone else after all. I have suicidal thoughts but despise myself for never having the balls to carry it out. Is that enough?'

'Yes.' The doctor smiled at the self-consciousness. She rested her fingertips together with the thumbs against her mouth as doctors do. 'Well,' she said, 'you're depressed.'

Congratulations, doctor.

'The question is,' she continued hastily, seeing the look of unmitigated scorn that flashed across Sarah's unhappy face, 'the question is what we can do about it.'

Sarah spoke wearily. 'I guess if there's anything to be done, I have to do it myself, right?'

'Well, that's true to a certain extent but there is plenty we can do to help.' She ploughed straight on, leaving Sarah to mull. 'There is the chemical or the psychotherapeutic approach, in other words, drugs or counselling or' – she paused, trying to win over her audience – 'both. I can put you on the waiting list to see a counsellor attached to the practice. You'd have a wait of a couple of months. You are entitled to six sessions.'

Six sessions, Sarah mouthed silently, how unutterably depressing.

The doctor was positive. 'I would recommend you go. It can be surprisingly helpful if you normally find it difficult sharing your problems with other people. Talking to a stranger can be . . . easier. However I'm going to prescribe you some anti-depressants too. What these will do,' she said, scurrying around her keyboard to bring the options up on screen, 'is calm down your anxiety. They'll help you sleep. These seem to have fewer unwanted side effects than other anti-depressants. But as with the others, even Prozac no matter what you may have heard, you won't notice any difference for two to four weeks.'

Two to four weeks? Sarah walked blackly from the surgery holding her prescription in front of her like a dirty rag. Two to four weeks – what good was that? How did anyone ever survive? Maggie followed.

It seemed very unsatisfactory that the side effects kicked in immediately while the relief took time. And the side effects storm-trooped her body. Her mouth was like a desert. She couldn't eat. She was lifted above the ground. Her head and neck detached from her body, her legs kicking futilely in the air. She couldn't hold on to anything. Conversation, thought, even solid objects seemed insubstantial, flimsy, untrustworthy. As if the slightest wind could carry her away from the world around her, the chair, the sofa, the bath, into the blankness of her mind. When she swallowed the blood seemed to bounce around her head. She saw through a camera lens. She blinked and blinked in hope of finding a focus. She slept fitfully. Panic consumed her and the world was magnified in the darkness.

She was so afraid. She screamed one night with a nightmare and ran sobbing to Alex's room. He was woken by the naked figure swaying in the doorway, framed by the light behind.

'What goes on in your head?' he said tenderly as he held her. She clung to him.

'I'm frightened of the darkness,' she said, letting out dry gasps.

'The dark's fine,' he said in a full, strong voice. 'I like the dark.'

'But it might always be darkness. I might always be in the dark.' And a sudden weight on her stomach squeezed the tears again.

'I am the dark. I have nothing inside me.' She gasped.

'You do,' he soothed, finding the words from somewhere. 'You have everything inside you. That's why nothing comes out.'

She wept some more, in short shudders. For ever, she thought.

He shook her. 'Come on, get up, let's go. Put some clothes on.'

'I don't want to wear any clothes, I can't face it.'

He was wearing a T-shirt and leggings. He got out of bed, pushed her upwards, though her body was evasive like water, spilling and spewing through his arms. He yanked the sheet off the bed in almost one movement, such was his sudden energy. 'Then wear this sheet.'

Though it was three in the morning, Alex made a phone call. Twenty minutes later a car slipped to a gentle brake outside the front door. There was always someone Alex knew, for every situation. When the car arrived they were sitting on the front steps.

'Hello, Vic.' The short-haired, cheeky-faced, swarthy, stubbled character grinned as Alex climbed into the car pushing Sarah before him. He drove at 120 m.p.h. all the way.

'Why wasn't he asleep?' murmured Sarah.

Alex enveloped her. Despite everything, he found space to enjoy the soft tactility, just a thin layer of cotton separating them. Vic didn't speak but he shuffled in his seat, gripping the steering wheel. The miles licked past. The road broadened into a motorway and, almost as quickly, narrowed again.

Sarah felt wrapped in a shroud. The darkness punctuated with only occasional flashes of artificial light, blurred with speed, confused her but still it was better to be moving. She grazed her face against Alex's hand gratefully. He stroked her fingers and the form of her body against him prickled like a bur. Unconsciously he was allowing himself now to feel more.

Wind sliced through an inch of opened window. Sarah smelt the car; the ageing upholstery, the ingrained smell of cigarettes and melted fruit sweets that reminded her of Magic Orange air freshener that hung from rear-view mirrors that in turn made her feel slightly sick. She was more sensitive since going on the drugs.

She lay moving with the motion of the car, staring at the back of the driver's seat. Little holes were scattered across the plastic and a rip had pushed out a handful of yellow foam padding.

She felt comforted because she did not feel alone. This was the first time she thought that with certainty. Her mother had always been somewhere else. Sarah had grown accustomed to it; she had come to expect solitude but now she craved good company, more than anything.

'Beachy Head is a funny place to take a depressed person,' said Sarah. She saw a sign as they finally wheeled into the deserted car park. Sarah immediately released herself from the cocoon of the car and started stumbling towards the edge of the cliff, over the dark land, pocked with rabbit burrows and wind-stunted gorse, to the chalky edge, the South East's favourite suicide spot. Alex slammed his door and ran after her.

Not just because she was wrapped in a billowing sheet did Sarah look like a ghost. Her face was luminous. The wraithlike hollows round her eyes gave her head a skeletal third dimension. The vision imbued her with the aura of a consumptive heroine, Alex thought. She felt none of this, but wafted onwards because she had been set in that direction. Somnambulant.

Vic saw nothing but his rather odd acquaintance, Alex, drooling after a bird in a sheet and for some reason wanting to chase his fancy to a spot of self-extinction. 'You go ahead, man,' shouted Vic to Alex's disappearing form, pointlessly waving his hand in the direction of the edge. 'I'll mosey around here for a while. I need a dump anyway.'

Alex bounded after the wandering waif. Like a dog, thought Vic, snatching his Lucozade Sport drink, slamming the car door and retiring to the bushes.

When Alex finally caught up with her, Sarah was sitting down, looking down at the sea, huddled, with the unmastered sheet flapping around her.

'I feel so light,' she said. 'I'm not sure if I did jump off that I would fall. I'd just float on the breeze. It's strong enough.'

Alex smiled, although she didn't see. If he was concerned by what she said, it didn't show. 'You'd break,' he said. 'You'd break all right,' and he took her arm. He held the white limb between finger and thumb. 'Your arm is so fragile, I could easily snap it.'

'Would you like to?' she said.

He didn't understand why she asked but he stroked her arm.

She looked down hundreds of metres below to the foot of the cliff with the beach, the tiny pier and the toy town.

'I'm already broken,' she said flatly.

'You're not,' said Alex softly.

The water churned in black ruffles. She said, 'I got an answer-phone message from this girl I was at school with. Last time we met, five years ago, she was overweight and depressed about being single. This time she sounded totally transformed. She was married, pregnant, bursting with life in every direction. It was obvious to me that she was making contact to confirm for herself how much she'd changed. I was her benchmark.'

'And did you call her back?'

'No,' said Sarah. 'The phone was broken. I told you every-thing's broken.'

Alex smirked. 'The phone was not broken, it was cut off because you didn't pay the bill. That's not the curse of fate, that's economics. You chose to get into a situation where the phone would be cut off.' He paused for recovery and took a deep breath. 'Christ, I'm not used to having to play Pollyanna.'

She almost laughed. But she refused to drop the lugubrious behaviour so easily.

'It doesn't mean', he continued, 'that it has to stay that way. You pay them the money and the phone'll be mended again. They just want your cash, they don't care about the customer's fractured soul. It's sick, but it's functional.'

She smothered a laugh this time in the fold of the sheet.

'And as for your condescending so-called friend – as if you'd want to be Mrs knocked-up swollen-ankled domestic wifey in the suburbs.'

'I know. I know, Alex, don't worry. I told myself that I didn't envy her. But I couldn't help but think that however much I didn't want that, I have no alternative. I have only ever known what I don't want. I know what makes me miserable but not what makes me . . .' She stopped and bit her lip; it felt chilled.

'You see, I can't even say the word. I find the whole concept alienating.'

The grass felt wet to the touch. A smudge of grey light was appearing on the horizon at the very lowest point where it touched the sea. 'My mother', she said, 'has been miserable her whole life. Nothing makes her happy. I sometimes think that it is only her misery that she feels is authentic.'

He clicked with exasperation. 'You don't have to be like that.'

'No? Isn't happiness genetic?' She turned to him. His face was tinged with the blue-grey of the approaching dawn. 'My mother's unhappy. My grandmother's mad *because* of her unhappiness. My great-grandmother is as miserable as hell. Everybody's unhappy. Why should I be any different?'

He said without thinking, 'Your father seems happy enough, considering.'

She turned round with such a jolt that it looked to him as if she could tip off the edge of the cliff.

He realized what he had said. 'Ah.'

She said quietly, 'You've seen my father?'

He nodded.

'Oh.'

He looked at her for signs of reaction. She seemed calm. 'What's he like?'

Alex wondered what to say. 'He seems nice.'

'Nice?' There was an edge of irony at this wholly inadequate answer.

He thought harder. 'He seems nice. Yeah . . . nice.' He trailed off hopelessly.

'Oh.'

'Are you interested?' He was unsure.

'I don't know,' she said. 'It seems peculiar. I don't think I can face thinking about it.'

Light was swelling over the littoral line. They both sat and stared. Sarah realized that she was not blinking and her eyes had stuck to the shore for so long she could see only a radiant blur.

'Why did you bring me here?'

'I think it's beautiful.'

His entirely uncharacteristic words made her shiver. 'In a rather morbid way.'

'I know,' he said, 'that's *why* it's beautiful. I wanted you to see that things weren't so bad.'

She continued to stare, her eyes glazed with a film of unspecific emotion – loss, regret, fear or equanimity? 'They feel bad.'

'But getting better.'

'Are they?'

'You know they are,' he said patiently. 'You just can't feel it because you're numbed up with drugs. That's part of the process.'

'How come you're so knowledgeable?'

'Weston-super-Mare,' he said enigmatically. At this she gave him a genuine look of curiosity.

There came, as always, a sense of renewal with the dawn. That nothing could be the same. Every day had to be different. Alex stood up and pulled her up with him. They walked slowly towards the telephone box. She smiled. 'I love this.' She was looking at the small notice next to a public call box. It said, 'The Samaritans: always there, day and night.' It gave phone numbers too.

'Hmm, even if you hadn't thought about it before, that'll put suicide into your head.'

'Well, I guess it helps,' said Alex generously, 'or they wouldn't put it there.'

It was a very desolate spot, in the grey dawn. They walked on, to the concrete plinth that shone in the darkness. Sarah read aloud the inscription. 'Mightier than the thunders of many waters. Mightier than the waves of the sea, the Lord on high is mighty. Psalm 93:4. God is always greater than all of our troubles.'

There was nothing to say.

Now they were moving, the air felt humid. 'It's going to rain,' said Sarah.

'Mmm,' said Alex, 'I expect so.'

A man was walking his dog. They were approaching from the road. Beetle blobs that grew, with propinquity, in size and animation. Signs of life, the cycle continuing.

'Let's go,' he said.

They had a lot of incomplete conversations. It didn't matter. Who needs endings, she thought, when you can just shut the fuck up.

He dragged her away. Her eyes were glued to the message on the plinth, her vision almost fully lit. Grey air chased away lingering shadows. And for the first time in a week she felt her body weight. It almost bowled her over. She buckled with the sudden impact of feeling the ground again.

'I do feel better,' she said, turning her head round at last.

'It's the fresh air.'

She was recovered enough to pick. 'What, are you PR manager for the great friggin' outdoors now? Since when? You've resisted going outdoors since the day I met you.'

'I've changed,' he said.

Maggie's face crumpled. 'You told her about Rudi?'

Alex shuffled uncomfortably. 'It kind of came out.'

'How did she take it?'

'I don't think it really sank in.'

'Did you tell her the history, why he left?'

'On the way home in the car, I told her what you told me.'

Maggie looked down. Odd, that she now saw Alex as some-one to confide in. She knew nothing of him, but there was an acceptance about him. He didn't ask questions, which made her more inclined to answer.

'Rudi's probably going to be in London for a while.'

Alex nodded as if this were not news.

'I'm very glad you're here,' Maggie confided, touching Alex on the arm. 'It makes everything easier. I find Sarah is . . . still resistant to me. I probably provoke her, I feel uncomfortable sometimes with intimacy. It sometimes seems that it's too late for us to get over everything.'

'I don't see that,' said Alex seriously. He surprised himself. He didn't usually have opinions about other people's lives. He enjoyed this sudden responsibility. He felt useful for once, although he had never noticed a lack of usefulness before.

She interrupted his thoughts. 'Did you have a good relation-ship with your parents?'

'No,' he said.

Since her illness – but perhaps that was too strong a word. Then exactly what had afflicted her? Sarah could reflect now in the vacant days of recovery. She lay on the leather sofa in Alex's parents' library, surrounded by characters. She fingered the dictionaries. She played with words, throwing them up into the air and letting them fall to the floor.

It was not a definable illness, she mused. I merely fell into the morass of my mind. She flicked through pages. I choked on reflective quagmire. Introspection is nearly always fatal. We walk on quicksand, the trick is to keep moving. If you stop, look back or take notes you will inevitably slip through the slime of self-consciousness. If you search for a point, of course you get a puncture. It's obvious. Start swimming through mud, unavoidably you will no longer be able to see. I fell through a crack in concentration.

Her gaze, that had danced through the dictionary, backwards and forwards like the dip in a tango, fell suddenly on the letters 'BBC'. She looked up from the page, assuming a blank face. She spoke aloud in an official announcement. 'There is a fault. Please be patient. Normal service will be resumed as soon as possible. The BBC apologizes for any interruption to your viewing pleasure.'

Then Maggie walked in carrying a laden tray. Sarah stopped speaking to herself. 'Hello, Mother.'

Maggie smiled, glad to see her daughter dressed and engaged in conscious thought. 'I wondered if it was time for a cup of tea?'

Sarah closed the dictionary. She sat up and moved along the sofa to give her mother space to sit down. 'Yeah, OK.'

Maggie sat down and smiled while she poured out the tea. Sarah could never be bothered to brew tea in a pot herself but she was appreciative of the superiority of the drink thus prepared by others. Her appetite was still far from normal, but craving tea was a sign that she was no longer at the bottom but beginning to climb the slope to health. Maggie was pleased. They both drank their Yorkshire tea black. It was a reassuring ritual.

Maggie's smile was not so reassuring and Sarah was no longer blinded by fever. After silence as the water gurgled from spout to cup, Sarah said, 'What is it?'

'I've been talking to Alex,' Maggie answered, her face white.

Sarah paused for a moment to calculate the sum of these

words. The total registered on her face. She said quietly, 'I'm glad that Rudi has come to see you.'

Maggie felt shock pulse through her body at hearing his name on her daughter's lips. She didn't say anything, she couldn't, she was floundering. She had no idea of a response, of a thought, of anything at all.

So it was Sarah who continued, as if, with Maggie's silence, pre-empting a question. 'I don't really want to be interested. If it happens that we meet, and I suppose it will at some point, then fine. But I'm not going to put my best frock on.'

'Oh, OK.' Maggie hid her disappointment in her stupor.

'But don't get me wrong, whatever you want, you do.'

'What do you mean?' said Maggie stupidly.

'I mean, I'm sure it might be very good for you. You deserve a break. If you can forgive him, then I don't have a problem. It's you he let down, really it's nothing to do with me.'

Maggie could hardly see that this was true but she didn't say so. She didn't want to provoke determined resistance in her daughter and she knew how easily that could happen. 'What are your feelings towards him?' she ventured.

Sarah screwed her face a little in consideration. What a relief to see it moving again. 'I don't know,' she said. 'Not much really. You've said so little about him ever. Great Edie always slagged him off but of course she never met him. I don't feel angry with him. I don't feel anything much. Well,' she said more expansively, 'I'm sure deep down I'm a raging torrent of fucked-upness about him, but it doesn't show on the surface because I'm too busy being fucked up about other things.'

'Sarah . . .' Maggie's voice was tired.

'What?'

While Sarah had been ill (she called it dispossessed because it was exactly as if her daughter's spirit was missing) Maggie herself had been tortured by self-hatred. Clearly she had been wrong her entire adult life. How could she have meant right and done so wrong? She had stifled her own life for the sake of someone else's but it left her so resentful.

Here was Rudi and she felt drawn to him as ever. Was this right now? She could no longer trust herself. Maggie was confused. Had she done wrong in clinging to order and security and closing the shutters on her old brightness? At the time it felt like the only option but, in fact, she had made a choice.

Maggie closed her eyes for a moment in dread. She was no longer sitting in the dark, airless library, but in a vacuum of herself. As she opened her eyes again and began to speak she was not aware that Sarah was still talking. Her louder, more urgent voice silenced her daughter mid-breath. 'Sarah, I just don't want you to be unhappy. I know I caused most of your unhappiness but it was never because of you. You were an innocent victim.' Sarah looked bleak and said nothing. 'I know, I know,' Maggie said desperately, 'you hate therapy talk. I just want you to know that I'm sorry.'

'For what?'

'Don't make this harder for me, Sarah.'

'Why should I make it easier?'

Sarah was trembling in weakness and dilemma.

'Please,' begged Maggie, 'you're my daughter. I need you.'

'What do you want from me?' Sarah's dark brown eyes were violent, enlarged, betraying the emotion her words and tone denied.

'I need to be forgiven. I need you. I need you as a daughter.' Maggie's eyes were full of tears.

This shook Sarah who had never seen her mother cry. Her voice was still brittle. 'I forgive you, Mother, if you want to be forgiven. There's nothing to forgive. I have no resentment towards you. I know you did your best. You don't have to worry anyway, I'm not your responsibility any more. And it was never your fault.'

'It *was* my fault,' said Maggie through her tears.

Sarah was now desperate too. She had no idea how to react to her mother. Her overriding urge was to run away, but she could not. She could not leave her mother like this.

'It's not a question of fault, Mum, there is no fault. If there is a fault, then where does it stop? Was it Rudi's fault? No, he had every reason for doing what he did. So maybe it was that stupid girl in Chicago. Or maybe it was Grace's fault for giving you up? Or Ruth for dying and sending *her* mad? And, since we're calling up all the suspects, what about old Edie? She's as guilty as any of us. She set the whole fucked-up ball rolling.' Sarah said this all in a rush, in an excited breathless stream. She shook her mother whose head was hung in shame. 'And who are we to blame Edie? We don't know what kind of cruel and vicious depravity she had to endure. There is a fault? I'm sick of fault. Maybe fault is to blame.' Maggie sniffed loudly and wiped her eyes. 'I'll pour you some more tea, OK?'

'Thanks,' said Maggie, looking at the bookshelves to hide her face from her daughter.

Sarah found her mother's tears unendurable. She couldn't even bear to think of her crying. It made her feel too uncomfortable. She spoke sharply. 'Just stop hitting at yourself, OK?'

'That's what Rudi says too.'

'Well, he's right,' said Sarah decidedly. 'There's nothing wrong with you. You meant well.'

Maggie, her head still turned, fighting to control herself, said, 'You think so?'

'Of course. For fuck's sake, Mum, I forgive you. I don't want you to be unhappy either.'

I don't want you to be unhappy. Theirs was the language of the unsaid. It had to be. The wish that her mother should not be *un*happy was, for Sarah, a considerable leap. It was too much for Maggie. She knew it was wrong but she fell at her daughter in an awkward grasp. Sarah felt too but she could not entirely submit. She sat stiffly and managed to reciprocate with a pat on her mother's back.

Maggie pulled away, calmer again. She said in a wobbly voice, 'I'll leave you to your reading.'

'OK.' Sarah forced a smile. 'Don't worry about me, Mum. I'll be OK.'

'OK,' said Maggie, getting up and moving towards the door. Sarah looked pointedly at the dictionary on the first page she came to.

obs. **homely** adv. ME. (f. home *n* + -ly².) 1. Familiarly, intimately. ME-M17. 2. In a kindly manner. LME-L16. 3. Plainly, simply, unpretentiously. LME-L18. 4. Directly, without circumlocution. LME-L17.

Homelyn *n.* M17 [origin unkn.] A coastal fish of the skate family, *Raja montagui.* Also called *spotted ray*.

She looked up, aware that her mother was still lingering by the door. She looked at her questioningly, her eyebrows raised.

'Will you meet your father?' said Maggie tentatively.

Sarah closed the book. She sighed. She rubbed her forehead with her palm wearily.

'Yeah, I expect so. If you want me to.' Maggie's face lightened as Sarah spoke. 'Just don't make a big deal of it, OK?'

25

Deconstruction

Alex smiled. Sarah sat in his parents' dusty sitting room looking out over the garden, or the knotted puzzle of brambles and snails and the broken slabs reclaimed by nature that it was now. It was definitely still his parents' sitting room. Before she arrived these lower floors had been uninhabited for twelve years. Alex lived above a mausoleum, an elaborate burial chamber full of photos and trinkets of the dead.

She remembered the day, weeks ago, when she had heard voices here. The sound of a party, music and polysyllabic words, with the tang of dope, which, in a moment, was gone. Now she questioned her senses; was this experience Edie or Grace? In other words, was all this the house or her head? It could be either, she reasoned, since they were both largely undiscovered. She was glad to be here. For probably the first time in her adult life she felt at home, which was odd since she wasn't.

'Are you going to take the food or not?'

Sarah jumped. She had forgotten Alex had even entered the room. He stood in front of her holding a tray. The curtains cast a shadow on the floor. French windows, heavily leaded and warped, were pushed open. The sun shone through the thick film of dust. Floating particles streamed with golden autumn sun around her head.

'I like this room,' said Sarah. 'Even though it's so heavy.'

'Heavy?' said Alex.

'Yeah, you know, full of the past. Hanging heavy. It makes it hard to breathe.'

'Can you hear something then?' said Alex who, after his encounter with Rudi, was beginning to take such comments as perfectly rational.

She looked surprised that he should ask. Last time, when she mentioned the voices to him, he had been dismissive. 'No, I can't hear anything. Not like that time when I was looking at the garden. I was thinking about that just now. But I can feel something. It's eerie, but kind of exciting. I'm not afraid any more.'

'Really?' Alex looked pleased.

They were alone. Maggie was working. Sarah was stable enough now that Maggie felt able to leave her alone in Alex's hands. She sensed too that Alex did not mind. Perhaps that he even wanted it.

He had made a plate of salmon and asparagus. Light slices of brown bread and butter decorated the circumference.

'This is delicious,' she said, licking her fingers, 'but odd. What has come over you?'

Alex coughed. The cough sounded strictly unnecessary. Sarah looked at him penetratingly, with a lack of self that before would have been beyond her. She was broken. She was waiting for the fracture to heal. In the meantime she was plastered in a numb calm. This gave her space. Space to look outside and see others not purely as an influence, good or bad, on herself but as separate entities. So she was looking at Alex as an individual, no longer as her osteologist. She said, 'What's up?' He looked awkward. His self shifted, though his body stayed in the same place. He was blurred, like a bad exposure, a thin green ghost. He was never comfortable in this room, surrounded by memories of his parents.

He said, 'We haven't talked about when I slammed the door on you.'

'No.'

He looked at his plate. 'I'm sorry I did that.'

His first apology. The intimacy embarrassed her. She said glibly, 'Well, that's OK, I'm sorry I shagged your mate.'

Alex smiled briefly. 'Well, that's fine. Why should I mind?'

'Oh.' She pursed her lips and raised her eyebrows. 'Everyone seems to be apologizing to me at the moment, I must go mad more often.'

'That wasn't why I apologized.'

'No? Why was it then?'

'Weston-super-Mare made me see more clearly.'

'You said,' she replied, feeling for some reason anxious. 'Well, that's all right then.'

'Except . . .' His face quivered, green again.

He was looking at her, staring now it was his turn to speak. Now he knew where her face came from. The dark, haunted eyes and the pale skin of her father. 'Except . . . you dared me to kiss you. Why did you do that?'

'I don't . . . know.' She turned her head away from his gaze. Her eyes were closed when she felt his hand on her shoulder. Her skin moved in empathy. She shuddered. He took this for revulsion and shrank back. She smiled. 'No,' she said. 'It's not . . .' She smiled feebly as if it confused her too. 'It's all right, really.'

She took his hand and felt the fingers, slender but long and square. She had never looked at them before.

It was a paradox, this tension now. When it was actually their long friendship of shallow ease that had revealed their worst sides. Still he looked at her warily.

'You don't have to worry,' she said, though he had voiced no fears.

After eating, they went up to Alex's TV room and sat on the sofa. She had chosen *To Have and Have Not*, the movie where Humphrey Bogart and Lauren Bacall, champions of the understatement, met. The frisson between them was such that, with hindsight, the film seemed an irrelevance, a front obscuring their real agenda, which sang out with every lowering of her eyelashes, every widening of his eyes, every quiver of her nostrils and every knowing glimmer of his pained smile.

Sarah liked being ill, now she was well enough to sit in front of a film, in Alex's spacious rooms. Suddenly from being permanently busy he seemed to have nothing better to do than to keep her company.

'Shouldn't you be working?' she said pettishly. She would never stop wanting to spoil things.

'Stop being grumpy.' Now when he smiled there were warm lines by the side of his eyes. 'Anyway it's Sunday.'

'Is it?' She was genuinely surprised.

Sarah had read that Humph's smile wasn't so pained actually, but that some form of facial paralysis meant he was unable to smile properly. Though she could now not avoid thinking this every time she watched him, it was too distressing, particularly in her weakened state, to tolerate. So she pushed the thought away and let herself fall into the picture, drunk with delight. All she had ever felt or could ever feel for another human being expressed in the flick of a cigarette lighter.

She shuffled and leaned against Alex, against his seated body. (It was the only way to get comfortable on such a spartan piece of furniture.) She rested her hand under her head as a cushion because she could feel his ribcage through his T-shirt. It curved away from her.

This was time and peace. Her eyes wandered from the film. He too turned away to look at her.

'What are you thinking about?' Never would he have asked before, never.

'The order of your books.'

He raised his eyebrows, questioning.

'I'm glad', she said, 'you don't put them in any order. I much prefer them thrown together.'

'They're not thrown together!' he said indignantly. 'I put them very carefully in the way that feels right. A way that gives me pleasure when I look at them.'

She was silent but felt inexplicably pleased with the answer.

'*Oliver Twist*,' she said, having looked at it earlier in the day. She enjoyed the sound of the words, the elegance of the phrase, the way it fell around the mouth. 'Is it a good book?'

'Yes,' said Alex, 'but the Jewish character is not very sympathetic.'

He stood up and sauntered from the room. She watched his long feet roll against the floor. She heard him going down and then back up one storey. He came in with the dark copy of *Oliver Twist* between thin fingers.

'Every great book has a wisdom beyond the story,' he said on his way back to the sofa. 'That's what I believe; pick a paragraph randomly and it will always have something to tell you.'

From where she was lying with her arm over her face she could see only the lower half of his body.

He sat down again beside her. She lifted her body to accommodate him and flopped down again.

'Let's see what *Oliver Twist* has to say. Give us your finger.'

He fanned the book, took her finger and let it fall.

'OK,' Alex said, holding the book closer so he could read.

' "We have a consciousness of all that is going on about us, and, if we dream at such a time, words which are really spoken, or sounds which really exist at the moment, accommodate themselves with a surprising readiness to our visions, until reality and imagination become so strangely blended that it is afterwards almost a matter of impossibility to separate the two." '

Alex looked at her. 'Good choice.'

'How does that work?' she said, astonished at the perspicacity of the paragraph.

'I don't know,' he said. 'My mother taught me the trick. Chomsky said that literature would give us a far deeper insight into the human person than anything science could do.'

There was a sudden sound of voices. It flashed past their ears like traffic on a motorway.

She stopped. 'What's that?'

He strained for a moment. She could feel a quickened pulse in his neck and the muscles of his chest were taut.

'I didn't hear anything.'

'Liar,' she said.

'Come on,' he said when the film had finished and Lauren Bacall had walked off the picture, snaring her prey with a sway of hunter hips.

'What?' She was disturbed to be dragged from her comfortable reclining position. It was eight in the evening.

He smiled. 'I thought it was time to show you that game I've been working on with the others.'

Her mouth dropped open. 'But I thought that was tied by a privacy agreement?'

He nodded. 'It is . . .' He swallowed as she put her hands on her hips. Her strength was returning. 'But I thought' – he let out a curt breath – 'I thought to myself, well, who is she going to tell?'

She looked quizzical. 'My, I've never been to Weston-super-Mare but it certainly seems like a life-changing place.'

'Oh yes, it is.'

She followed Alex to the dark room that led off his bedroom. It had the thrill of the forbidden. He had raced ahead, newly enthused, but she hesitated at the doorway. He looked at her. 'What?'

She smiled. 'All I ever wanted was to be *allowed* to know.'

He raised his eyebrows. 'You mean you don't actually *want* to know?'

'No, of course not,' she said smiling. 'It's much more interesting as a mystery, as an unknown. I'm sure the details would be a real let-down. It's the *idea* of it I like.'

He laughed. 'You should study deconstruction, you'd like it.'

'Eh?'

Miracles happen every day. We take them for granted. Nobody celebrated then, when the phone rang and Sarah answered it not just without reluctance but actually without thinking. Two months ago she would have fallen into an agony of indecision.

It was Leona, the girl Alex knew, on a mobile. Leona, the mixed media concept artist, funded by dope-smoking parents who wanted their child to scandalize the artistic establishment and open a fashionable bar on the proceeds. 'Oh,' said the languid voice when Sarah answered the phone, 'this is Leona, who are you?'

Still she stayed cool. 'This is Sarah, I'm someone Alex knows. I came to your "End of Art" concrete-bashing performance.'

'Oh.' Leona did not sound impressed. 'Right. Well, I was ringing to invite Alex to my new private view . . . but I suppose you can come if you like.'

'Thanks.' Sarah laughed. 'I'd be grateful if I didn't know you had to drag people off the street.'

There was a sound on the end of the line like someone unblocking a nostril with a menthol inhaler.

'Well,' said Leona snuffily, 'bring whoever you like. I'll put the details in the post.'

'OK,' said Sarah breezily, 'I'll try and make it. Are you all right? You sound like you have a cold.'

'No,' said Leona pointedly, 'I don't,' and put the phone down.

Only afterwards did Sarah realize that of course Leona was snorting a line. It had been so long, Sarah realized with pride, it hadn't even occurred to her. Imagine needing it to get through the afternoon. That must be why Leona was so thin, the insecure cow.

The renewed ability to despise others is a medically proven sign of recovery. The heat of the fever had cooled.

Alex had invited Maggie to the private view (he had appointed himself as unofficial peace broker) but at the last minute there was trouble with Grace. She was having one of her fits, tearing her skin with her fingers. The doctors were concerned and wanted to talk through options with Maggie.

Alex told Sarah.

'Oh God,' she drawled, 'not again. She's only just got over the last turn.'

'Maggie sounded quite worried.'

'She always does,' said Sarah flatly. So Alex and Sarah went to Leona's big night alone. Sarah was prepared after last time. Waltzing through the hubbub of indolent artist voices without the protection of chain mail, she said to Alex so loudly, so impudently imitative, that the band of tractor-heeled, black-coated, skinny people all turned and stared. 'You know,' she shouted, 'it's the iconoclasticism of her work that I find so enthralling.'

Alex laughed appreciatively but poked her in the spine, saying quietly in her ear, 'Iconoclasm is the word for which you grapple, I think, my dear.'

She looked at him imperiously. 'Pompety-pom.'

And she strolled confidently to the drinks table and whisked up a glass of champagne, thinking, I can play anything for an hour and a half.

'London is Rubbish' would allow Leona to bask on critical barbed wire as her parents had always dreamed. One huge floor of the warehouse was taken up by the piece, a giant map of London with each area illustrated by rubbish found on the actual streets and in the bins.

There were two ways to view it. The whole was best seen from a narrow iron walkway that followed the rectangular parameters, high above the 'space', accessed by steel staircases at the two far ends. But to look at the detritus up close, street by street, one could walk along clear single-file paths which approximated the pattern of the tube lines. Underground stations and major thoroughfares were marked with standing signs, written in broken glass stuck to abandoned cardboard.

'London is Rubbish' stank. Oozing beer bottles, mouldering fruit, thick shake dribble and chip grease soaked into the matting base of the installation. Fast-food packaging was the mainstay of every district. (In the commentary notes Leona had written, 'In *our* kingdom of the blind, the Burger is King.')

Rubbish distinguishes us. Sarah started in the north-west. Golders Green was mapped out with bagel bags and VW parts. Park Lane had two twenty-pound notes. Bank had computer paper strips and a letter from Goldman Sachs inviting 'Tim Young' to an introductory tour of the trading floor before lunch in a local bar.

Heading east along the Central line, the fag packets got cheaper. Cans replaced the beer bottles of Notting Hill and the polystyrene cappuccino cups around the City. As living conditions changed, so did the nature of what people would chuck on to the street. Portobello Road had a microwave oven, Bethnal Green a caffeine-stained denture plate, an empty 'economy snack' noodle pot and a coconut-oil hair conditioner tub.

What really gripped Sarah was a letter ripped into tiny pieces and meticulously taped together by Leona. It was almost illegible with many scratchings out and rewritings.

Dear Music of Chance

I too like drinking red wine with friends. I am an economics student in London but I come from Munich. I am one metre 95 with dark blond hair. I would very much like to meet you and get to know you better.

'I wonder,' said Sarah sadly, 'whether this was the rough version or if he was too shy to send it. So sad a thing to leave in a public bin.'

26

Sludge and Skeletons

'I could be a nun,' she said. After years of squandering her intelligence in going-nowhere jobs for zero profit, Sarah had made a decision. She was going to squander her intelligence on a going-nowhere degree course for zero profit.

After some time in the library, she had returned set upon reading Medieval Studies at a former polytechnic in South London.

Alex, out of interest not objection, had asked her why.

'I'm going to become a silent nun helping the poor.'

Alex looked up. 'Silently?'

Sarah smiled. 'Yes, then they won't laugh at what I say. It's a mad plan but that's why it's perfect. I think the last thing I should do is something sensible.'

'Absolutely,' agreed Alex. 'You certainly don't want to do something practical that's going to send you off the rails again. Some people just aren't made to take Business Studies even in the real world.'

Hitherto Enid Blyton was the only novelist Sarah had read voraciously of her own volition. Since her illness, or whatever it was, something had changed. She wanted to be different. Encouraged by Alex, and inspired by the house of ten thousand spines, she began to read other books with enthusiasm as well. Whatever it was that had held her back before – suspicion of success, fear of failure, maybe a long-held need to spoil her own chances – there was now a door open to her. She could read and explore without pain. She had been drawn to medieval writers.

The distance appealed to her and the simplicity of belief, the lack of ambiguity, the sense that all that mattered was the pursuance of good and avoidance of evil.

St Augustine wrote, 'I will describe the twenty-ninth year of my age. A Manichean bishop named Faustus had recently arrived at Carthage. He was a great decoy of the devil and many people were trapped by his charming manner of speech. This I certainly admired, but I was beginning to distinguish between mere eloquence and the real truth, which I was so eager to learn.'

Well, she told herself, without flinching, I'm only four years behind. Sincerity was progress, but progress was going to be slow; she had no education worth mentioning. To get into university Sarah needed to take an access course. And to build the confidence to take the access course, she had determined to read her way out of her perceived ignorance. Alex said he would support her through any course she wanted to do, but she was reluctant to be totally reliant. Instead she got an evening job in a bar to refresh her after a day of dry thinking.

The Falcon felt like one of the few London pubs to escape modernization. There was no non-smoking section, no bleached beech floor, no coffee machine or Thai food selection in the evening. It remained a warren of corners, with a dull-red, ash-pocked carpet and yellowed walls, knobbly like rice pudding. A dartboard attached to one wall and in a tiny corner a pool table with blunt cues permanently guarded by menacing regulars who had earned their entry to the late night lock-ins. Toilets dark enough for the clientele to carry out their drug deals in privacy.

The landlord, Gerry, was spherical, his legs bending under the weight of his stomach. His wife, Leigh, was thin with sun-dried skin. Her dark hair was dyed mucky yellow-green. Even when she wasn't smoking, her lips stayed clasped to some fictional fag.

He stole from the till and she stole from the customers. Her unctuous conversation, combined with deeply exposed scrawny cleavage, was thrust demandingly in front of men's wallets and kept her in vodka all night.

Ironically, Sarah's nose was too clean. Gerry chastised her for checking the watermarks on £20 notes.

'Watcha fink yer doin?' he shouted, emitting a spray of spit and missing consonants. 'You wanna drive me outta business? 'Arf the dough we get in 'ere is fake, the uvva-rarf is nicked. You leave it alone, yer stchewpid caa.'

Sarah enjoyed it immensely. Almost as much as she liked St Augustine's piety and self-flagellation. By day she learned from the heavy pen of ancient scholars. By night from the barmaid, Brenna, a lumbering sloppy-lipped bovine creature whose frazzled perm and white bleach were competing to destroy her hair. Brenna, culled from the miry flats of the Shannon, was, unlike St Augustine, not blessed with spiritual wisdom, but she did know how to handle drunk perverts, which in the twenty-first century may be a more useful skill.

John, recently out of Wandsworth, with fingers like spiders, told Sarah, as she was stretching up to change the Glenfiddich, that her breasts were 'not too small and not too big, just how I like 'em'.

She said, 'Uh, thank you.'

This was a mistake. For the very next day he beckoned her over to where he sat at the bar in pretence of ordering a drink. Instead he said with a sneer, 'I'd like to stick my tongue up your arse.'

Sarah curled her upper lip in disgust and walked away. The truth was she was a little intimidated by the sheer obscenity. She could bite back in her own environment but here she was outclassed. Brenna propounded a more robust approach. When John threw a compliment her way she would say, 'Fack orff, yew great piece o'shoit.' And it worked.

'They say,' smiled John with his mouth sucking at his 'pint of shit' – he nicknamed his Guinness as well as his penis, 'they say this place was built on a plague ground. That's why it's so full of bad people.'

Sarah found it oddly comfortable to be with a different kind of misfit. It preserved her stability, maintained a balance. To throw herself completely into a self-improving world would be to guarantee that she would rebel from her own decision. She still liked rats.

At the same time, as a kind of transitional occupation, she spent a couple of days a week cataloguing Alex's house. There was still much to do. Alex didn't ask but she wanted to continue. In truth, she was increasingly desperate to know what it was he was really looking for. This mystery should be resolved, for she knew that it held the answer to Alex's story. In November she found it.

The job became more and more pleasurable as the year darkened and chilled. It was a form of hibernation. She had moved into the cellar, the very bottom of the house. It seemed for a moment as if her task would never end. She quavered at yet another room stacked with boxes.

But, as ever, once she started, the fascination gripped her. Only now she did not allow the fever to consume her. She no longer feared the house. She felt initiated. She knew this house better now than anyone and that gave her strength. She felt protective of it almost. She had felt a pattern in its secrets, in the way it yielded up the seemingly random information. Boxes and shelves and piles of material. Drawers so full she could hardly open them. Something in almost every book. A postcard, a letter, a photo or occasionally another lock of hair with a number attached by a silk thread. Random or significant? It no longer seemed important. To find the part was to get a glimpse of the whole. She put all the hair together with the rest in the box she had discovered months ago.

It was early one chilly morning and she had just opened a box of holiday souvenirs, a trip to the seaside. Shells of different shapes and sizes, coloured pebbles and lumps of wood. A once-white cotton hat with the red words 'Brighton Belle' fading from its brim. Old-fashioned sticks of rock in two shades of brown. One plain red flip-flop with the imprint of the owner's foot still clearly visible on the sole. The innocence was sinister.

But it was the next box that answered the question. For behind the holiday snapshot was a black tin box the size of a shoebox, with metal clasps at the two shorter ends. The other containers had been ordinary packing cases, orange boxes, or cupboards and drawers. Some of the stuff was simply stacked in columns against a wall. This was different. This box was specifically chosen. Almost at once she was convinced it was what she was looking for.

Her fingers tingled as she opened the lid. She was trembling and the clasps were awkward. The lid was slightly bent and came off haltingly. It was only a little way up when she heard noises; a tiny laugh, wheedling from the box. As she raised the lid further it grew louder, slowly releasing a long blast of sound, easing the pressure of a cacophony within. It hissed in relief. Quiet at first then reaching a crescendo, building discordant, indecipherable speaking voices mixed with screams, moans and always in the background the dull thud of electric rock music.

With misgiving she wrenched the lid off and looked inside. The noise vanished, dispersed. At first she thought it was just another box of hair and she felt disappointed. For the first thing she saw was rows of locks, the same length but different thicknesses, some straight, some curly. Asian hair, black hair, grey hair. She picked up one lock of hair after another and rubbed them between her fingers, with her mouth open in puzzlement. They had been undisturbed for so long that the shock was as much theirs as hers and some fell apart with the first touch. They were held together delicately with a numbered label.

But there was something underneath. Her heart beating faster, she scrabbled to pick it out. Locks of hair overflowed in her haste and fell to the floor in hirsute chaos.

Photos (more photos!) but these were different from any of the others because all of them were of people having sex. Many people, in different combinations. Such variety, thrust before her, that it was like a butcher's shop, a display of flesh. A woman, whom Sarah just recognized as Alex's mother Hilary, lying naked, half on her side, on the kitchen table with a man (not Alex's father) behind her kneeling, holding her buttocks with his hands, impaling her. Her attention was focused not on him but on the camera. She stared into the picture with her eyes widening and self-conscious. One arm stretched out, as if she were trying to communicate with me, thought Sarah shuddering.

There were literally hundreds. Hilary with three women, all naked, imbibing one another; Hilary bent over backwards, her hair hanging down, her upside-down eyes staring, always staring into the camera. Another saw Alex's father standing naked, seemingly supporting a drinks tray with only his bare erection – the caption on the back read 'Look, no hands!' Closer inspection revealed that the trick was achieved with the hands of another, dark and scarcely visible, holding the tray from behind, his naked body almost hidden in Ted's shadow.

Her taste soon soured and she poured out the entire contents of the box on the floor. With the scattered photos fell an unsealed envelope and in it some folded sheets of paper. A list of numbers and dates and next to them a person's name, a number and, in one of two hands, a comment.

7 April 1974, for example, had twenty names attached.

75 Alan McReady 4/10 Too sweaty and small. Whined. Do not reinvite.

76 & 77 Estelle and Mark Planter 6/10 She was too keen, he not enough. Such an undignified pair – and she's a lousy writer.

78 Cyril Matthews 8.5/10 Quelle surprise! Old Cyril surpassed us all. As he exploded he puffed out Mahler. Will never be able to watch him lecture again.

And so it went on.

She looked back to the photos. What held her were not the preposterous positions, where, just like the newsagent's top shelf, the sheer glut lessened the individual impact. No, what she was drawn to was the expression on the face of Hilary. Ted looked into the camera slightly sheepishly but Hilary was different. Her true object of lust was the camera.

Sarah stared, hypnotized by this woman. Hilary, large eyes and pale skin, thin long face, all like Alex, her head tilted provocatively sideways, her straight hair in a ponytail, stared back, penetrating her gaze. Sarah felt defiled, as if somehow this woman had looked into her. She tried to turn the picture face down on the floor when she was frozen by a woman's voice. In her head or outside, she didn't know.

'Alex, come out, darling, come and take the photos.' The eyes in the photo seemed to mock and yet cajole. 'Come on, honey, you'll enjoy it.'

And Sarah felt a child within herself cower in horror. She was sickened by the smell of trapped bodies, of sweat and the unmistakable female scent. And the woman's voice that taunted, 'Alex, don't hide from me . . . that's not my leader of men . . . that's not my little rebel . . . I want to make an artist of you.'

Sarah gagged and clutched her mouth and the photo dropped from her hands and whistled to the floor. The noise and the smells evaporated into the still air as she frantically threw everything back into the box and slammed down the lid. She sat on it to keep the demons inside but ran from the room when she became convinced that she could feel it throbbing.

She was still breathing erratically when she ran to Alex at his desk. He made no mention of her interruption.

'I think I've found what I was looking for.'

His lips thinned. 'Good,' he said boldly, 'you'll understand why I wanted them located before the house was cleared.'

She looked grim. 'You had to take those photos.'

'Yes,' he said calmly, 'my mother liked me to explore what she saw as the limits.'

'And the hair . . .' She trailed off.

'The trophies of their exploration. The virgin territories they colonized. It was like Vasco da Gama only it was scarcely scurvy they were risking.'

He spoke curtly as if he could have found it funny, except it was clear from his dazed expression that he didn't at all. That this was just the way he dealt with it. Sarah noted and matched him. She said laconically, 'No, they must have got plenty of vitamin C with all that forbidden fruit.'

Alex smiled and said, casually, rather as if she had found a missing sock, 'Well, that's a relief.'

Sarah's face was filled with desperate compassion but she spoke like a man delivering furniture. 'OK then, where do you want them?'

'In the garden. I want to make a fire,' said Alex, standing up.

The act of clearing and burning an overgrown garden in November was cathartic. Alex was a man inspired. He found a collection of outdated but serviceable garden tools from the shed that they would later destroy, since it was eaten by fungus.

Hacking through the snarling brambles, Alex was filled with energy. His body looked powerful. He was clearly enjoying the destruction. He had waited a long time for it. Sarah swept up the litter Alex produced and built the bonfire. She shovelled dead plants, aggressive branches and the long tentacles of winding creepers that, for years, had strung the garden from end to end. They worked in silent pleasure for much of the early afternoon. It was work of dark joy. They both understood; it did not need to be voiced.

'Look,' said Sarah finally, when they were almost done, when the dark afternoon was beginning to fade. She held up a bleeding finger, torn by a rusty nail in the undergrowth. 'I've pricked myself. Does that mean I'm going to fall asleep and be woken up by a handsome prince?'

'I hope not,' said Alex bitterly, 'if it means I'm going to be cutting this forest down for the next hundred years.' She laughed. 'Anyway,' he continued, cheerfully prosaic, 'you're more likely to get tetanus.'

But then he looked at her again. He seemed to consider for a moment. Then he put down his shears and walked over to where she stood holding the bleeding finger, stemming the flow. He took her finger, drawing the wound close to his eyes, and then, without warning, moved the finger to his lips and kissed it. He put her finger in his mouth to clean the wound and sucked away the blood.

Her mouth fell open and she looked at him, with her eyes screwed in self-conscious curiosity. There had been an undeniable increase in their physical affection since Sarah had been ill and Alex had come back from wherever he had gone. Maybe it could be dismissed by either of them as comfort in the horror. This now, though, was a direct challenge, an aggressive move. She stared at him and said nothing. He stared at her as if waiting for a reaction. He slouched a little and, after returning the finger to its owner, pulled his own fingers through his hair that was matted and had fallen forwards with the dirty work. He sighed heavily and rolled his aching shoulders, moving his neck from side to side. He looked at Sarah.

'Let's do this bonfire.'

It was built like a pyramid, a shrine to the past, only built to be burnt, to destroy the dead, not preserve them. Dead wood, peeling furniture that had swollen and shrunk in hot and cold, the decaying deckchairs on top. Above the bigger, dryer layers, strange objects of lost summers were piled: clothes, garden gloves, chipped plastic cutlery, plant roots and broken pots.

At the side of the pyramid, Sarah raked a rank heap of decomposed leaves, a mass of sludge and skeletons. She moved rhythmically, watching her work and thinking about Alex and herself.

The towering shrine to putrefaction was set ablaze. Alex lit the pile of dry wood, unused pieces they had found, long neglected, in the garden shed. Together they inserted the flaming torches into the heart. With some hesitation, as it garnered its powers, it crackled and sparked and, with a deep breath, the conflagration leaped into the sky.

'Fuck,' mouthed Sarah noiselessly though no sound could be heard over the roar of the fire.

The flames obscured the pile in minutes as the two watched in awe and the rubbish hissed and spat. It singed their faces. They were soon forced back from the intense heat.

'Come on,' shouted Alex, 'let's get some stuff from the house.'

They went inside, admiring the easy path they could now tread because of their own labour that afternoon. Sarah picked up the tin box. There was a barely perceptible shiver from Alex as he saw it. She carried it out into the garden. He stayed inside to look through the piles she had isolated as rubbish weeks earlier. At least that was the ostensible reason. It also meant that she was to burn the photos alone.

She carried the box into the garden, trying not to think about the contents, and left it by the side of the pyre to go back for the rest of the hair.

She walked to the fire and, without ceremony, opened the lid of the tin box and emptied its contents into the flames. In a last attempt at infamy, the photos flipped and tossed as they struggled in the heat. There were flashes of vulgar positions, of limbs and breasts impossibly contorted as the photos curled. It was a matter of seconds but in that time Sarah saw once more Hilary's provocative gaze before the oily destruction was complete and the smoke bulged with the noxious smell of burning chemicals. Next the hair was thrown on the pile. It fizzled lamely to nothing, gone in an instant.

Some time later Alex arrived, behind boxes filled with trivia to throw on the fire. He seemed happier already, knowing that she had performed the cremation. There was a new agility in his step. He set down the boxes and tipped their contents one by one on to the mound. That done, they stood again, staring into the orange and black, seeing patterns and faces and spirals of thought.

*

They sat later in the kitchen, reflecting on the day's work. Sarah was amazed at the change in Alex. She could not define it exactly. Maybe his body was looser. He sat more easily, his legs stretched out and open on the floor. Yet she had never noticed that his mien was tense before.

She sat opposite. They ate a simple meal of cheese, bread, olives and salad. They drank water. They had both showered. As they ate in companionable silence and she glanced at him, she realized what the difference was. The afternoon's exertion had left Alex with a rosy glow. He looked healthy. He looked alive.

At last she spoke. 'It seems like a relief,' she said.

'It certainly is,' he said.

She smiled. 'You sound like Oliver Hardy.'

He sniffed. 'I'd rather sound like Stan Laurel.'

'Well, yes,' she said, 'who wouldn't?'

Further silence and then, for no reason, unplanned, she abandoned her plate and came round the table to sit next to him. She turned the chair so it now stood at right angles to his. And she rested her feet on the rung of his chair.

He turned and looked at her, down his nose. 'Hi,' he said.

And she smiled again and stroked his cheek with the back of her hand.

'You have colour in your cheeks, I've never seen that before.'

'Does it make me look devastating?'

'It does rather.'

He paused. Turned away from her. Picked at an olive. Seemed to compare his two thumbs for length and then said, with a sigh, 'Come on then, we'd better get this over with, hadn't we?'

'Yes,' she said, 'I suppose we better had.'

And they walked sombrely to his bedroom.

'Thank God your mother changed the sheets,' he said lying back afterwards.

Sarah outwardly agreed but also mused that no matter what, good or bad, caring or indifferent, her mother was never very far away. 'She probably did it on purpose, hoping this might happen,' she said. 'She approves of you.'

'Your mother', he said pointedly, 'approves of anything that she thinks might make you happy.'

'You reckon?' There was genuine doubt in her voice.

'Yes. Maybe she didn't used to, but right now that's what she wants more than anything.'

'How funny.'

They lay silent. She was pleased that they were having a normal conversation, despite the activity of the last hour. She did not want that to change.

It was the first time that she had spent the night in bed with a man and wanted to stay. Not among all the men she had had sex with – the few who had lasted months, or weeks, and the great majority who were with her only a matter of days or just one night – not one among them had she wanted near her at night. If she found sleep in their presence at all (and often she would leave the room, for another bed, the floor, the sofa, anywhere alone) it was hard won, against her creeping dislike.

When, rarely, she could sleep, she woke early, disturbed by some movement or noise from the alien beside her. It was not their fault. It was hers. For choosing to go to bed with people she did not like. It was not always an active aversion, just displeasure, perhaps with the particular individual but more likely with herself. Sometimes it was as mild as ambivalence, but such lack of feeling was still too much to allow her a restful night.

This was different. She did wake early – it was still dark and the clock showed it was not yet six – but there was no discomfort. In fact, when she thought back to the experience, she felt warm inside. There had been no wild thrashing, no screams of ecstasy, no engorged faces sweating with lust or alcohol. None of the usual nonsense, she thought. None of her histrionics, where her volume increased, she sensed, as her enthusiasm waned, her external voice drowning out the objecting voices inside.

She ran through it in her mind. Last night she was gripped with a need to nurture Alex. To cleanse his palate of the foul taste his parents left behind. She had held him for a long time. She had stroked his pale skin and they had embraced each other. His skin felt so cool. His eyes looked so vulnerable. When she kissed him it was to kiss him better. So it had to be slow and restorative. She had to draw him in, to wash him, to protect him and to heal. And in offering healing, it seemed she was healing herself.

She had given and received, she was shocked to admit, an expression of love. How strange, how exposing, how incredibly embarrassing.

She sat up and turned to his sleeping form. She moved to ease a pain that was growing in her chest. She inhaled deeply, wondering if she had slept awkwardly. The pain grew worse and her heart beat painfully.

She tapped Alex on the shoulder and said in an alarmed whisper, 'There's something the matter with me, I'm in pain.'

He had not been asleep, for in a smooth roll he turned and looked at her with open eyes. He drew his finger across her brow, down her cheek, her neck and out across her collarbone.

'I think I have a temperature,' she moaned, 'I'm so ho—'

'Ssh,' he murmured, putting his finger to her lips. 'I feel the same. I think it's normal,' and he pulled her towards him again.

27

Butterflies

Maggie had fallen silent. Her voice had been slow since the beginning of the phone call. She had asked after Sarah's health. She had reiterated her support of the university plan. She expressed concern that her daughter was overdoing it by taking on a job at a bar. That it was all too soon. But there was something else. Sarah knew it. She burst out, 'Something's going on, isn't it? Don't do this to me, Mother. What's wrong?'

There was a long pause. Then the words came out with a curious flatness. 'Grace has cancer.'

'Cancer?' Sarah stumbled as if the word were foreign. 'What do you mean?'

Expressionless, 'I mean she has cancer.'

'Is it bad?'

'Yes.' A halting sentence, 'It's apparently in the final stages. The lump in her breast was enormous . . . it was almost breaking through the skin.'

'Didn't she notice?' Part of the conversation and yet separate, Sarah felt the words leave her lips but outside her control. She could hear a mental shrug.

'I don't know . . . they don't know.'

'Didn't *they* notice?'

'Apparently not. Well, you know how she hates to be touched most of the time.'

Sarah could feel the blood at the side of her forehead pulsing. 'Where is she?'

Maggie sighed. 'She's been transferred to the normal hospital.'
Sarah sounded weary. 'When are you going?'

The ward was noisy. A middle-aged woman sitting beside the next bed was crying inconsolably at a hoarse whale incumbent next to her. The whale wheezed, every breath a miracle of survival. The chin pointing upwards, gasping for fresh air but in the hot ward there was none.

Maggie was glad that her feelings were not pouring out like that. Although inhibition was hardly required while senile geriatrics wandered hopelessly to the toilet with the door wide open.

The heat made Sarah feel rather sick and she went frequently to breathe in the yard directly outside the ward. An unmaintained area with gravel and a few weeds and a dead creeper climbing up a cracking wall. Two plastic seats stood unevenly on the loose gravel in lieu of a bench.

Sarah could not remember ever having seen Grace's bare arms before. She was always serenely covered, long sleeves and long, grey dresses. So now she seemed violently naked. She pulled at her nightgown, struggling to free herself. She ripped the material up the front to her stomach and found the strength to wrench the sheet from her bed. She pulled at the bloody bandages where the lump had been removed.

Grace had now been put in a sleeveless NHS nightdress.

'Why did they do that?' asked Maggie bleakly.

'Does it matter what she dies in?' said Sarah gently.

'My mother is not going to die in uniform.'

Next day Maggie bought her mother a pair of beautiful sea-green nightdresses. Grace no longer objected to colour. Even properly covered, the bright ward lights shone through her, sunshine through a colourless butterfly.

The flesh had already withered. Grace was thin before but she was now half her former self, her skin transparent. Maggie stared at the other breast, exposed and shrivelled. 'I find myself looking through it to see cancer there too.' Sarah and Maggie sat around the bed for several hours at a time. The nurses told Maggie there was no need, that Grace would be unlikely to notice if they were there or not, and if she did notice she would not remember.

'But they don't understand,' said Maggie. 'I've always been sitting pointlessly around her bed.'

Medical wisdom thought that this quick end was really a good thing, better than years of distressing infirmity. What if Grace had lived to Edie's age? That was the oncologist's unspoken consolation.

Rudi offered Maggie support but was secretly relieved (rather than glad) that he would no longer have to look into Grace's mirror eyes. They reflected his guilt. At least that's what he saw; to him the mother in Grace was always apparent.

Great Edie was angry. Her daughter's weakness was fatally confirmed. 'Seventy? That's no age. I was still working at seventy. What 'as she *ever* done except cause other people trouble?'

Maggie silently thought otherwise. If nothing else, her mother had burnt a flame of hope inside her that kept her daughter warm.

Edie refused to visit. 'I wash my hands of her, I don't want to think about her ever again.' And she locked up her face with a key. It would have been difficult anyway.

It seemed that disagreement was for once to bind Sarah and Maggie together. Agreeing with each other and disagreeing with the rest of the world. Sarah could not see how this had happened while she wasn't looking, before she was ready.

'But I don't know her yet!' she said as if that must make Grace's death impossible.

'*Why* do they say this is for the best?' Maggie demanded.

Nothing happens to schedule.

Terminally ill, crabby old women can cling to life indefinitely. Others, younger, slip so fast it is easy to miss. A matter of weeks ago, Grace was a certainty. Her condition varied but the problems were always the same. She was a permanence in Maggie's life but now, soon, she would be gone.

The consultant sat with Maggie and Sarah in the staff nurse's room. The heat burned against Sarah's cheeks and she had to rest against the wall.

'We've removed the lump and made her more comfortable but at this late stage there is little point in trying anything else. It will only cause her needless suffering and confuse her all the more.'

Maggie said, 'You make her sound like a dog.'

The consultant smiled. 'I don't mean to. All I mean is that your mother is not going to live very long whatever we do, and we don't believe she has the mental resilience to deal with any of the more radical treatments – and anything else would be entirely pointless. The best we can do is to keep her out of pain.'

By this time Sarah was doing most of the talking since Maggie's usual competence seemed to have abandoned her. 'How long is she likely to live?'

The man smiled cautiously. 'I'm afraid that's impossible to judge. It's such an individual thing. It could be a few weeks or even months but more likely less. It depends how the cancer spreads. We can't really say how aggressive the tumour is because we don't know how long it's been there and the patient is not in a position to answer the question.'

'She's not the patient,' said Maggie in a low bitter tone, 'she's my mother.'

Sarah was shocked at seeing her mother out of control. Her mother was so restrained, so sensible, too sensible if anything. Now here she was losing it; it was almost heartening. She had to indicate to Maggie that it was time to leave the room.

Nothing happens to schedule. When they got back to Grace's bedside, Rudi had arrived.

Maggie could not see her daughter's reaction because Sarah was a few steps ahead. Her gait remained steady but Maggie found her own legs dragging. She had dreaded this. She wanted Sarah to meet him, but she had wanted to do it carefully. She wanted to organize it so that it caused her daughter minimum trauma. Now, with Grace, that plan had gone. There were no plans currently, just reactions to circumstances. It was all so immediate.

Sarah had spotted the seated figure and knew it could only be one person. She walked confidently though she did not feel it. She knew that she had nothing to fear, that all responsibility was his. That she owed him nothing and could walk away if she chose. Still, her palms were sweating.

She was glad actually that the meeting turned out to be

chance. The thought of a meeting organized by her mother, no doubt with tea, warmed pot and milk in the fiddly jug, which in her opinion was less attractive than a plastic carton . . . Her thoughts were wandering.

Rudi was initially terrified. He had to face it. He had seen Sarah barely conscious, helpless. He had seen her when she couldn't see him, but now she was returned to the conscious world, to her living difficult self. He had heard much about Maggie's guilt and Sarah's anger. He felt culpable and not a little anxious at the reaction of this volatile Frankenstein's monster that they had created and rejected.

Fear combined with fascination, fascination at this embodiment of his feelings for her mother. As interested as he was in her, as he *wanted* to be in her, he had known three daughters before her. What interested and terrified him more were the feelings that her presence provoked in him. She was a ghost of a happier time. A ghost walking translucent across the shining floor towards him. Pale still, and risen almost from death, if he surrendered to hyperbole. A reawakening of long ago. She was the years between them. How long it had been. He automatically stuck out his hand.

'Hi.'

She stuck out her hand but did not smile. She did not smile as a formality. Rare smiles were evinced when provoked. When there were no other options.

'You must be my father.'

'Yes,' he said, responding to her detached tone. 'I guess so.' Fear never showed in his face.

She turned to look at the huddled form under the sheet and sighed. 'No change then.'

'No,' he said, 'she hasn't stirred.'

Maggie was now at the bedside. The sight of Rudi and Sarah together, before her, temporarily obscured thoughts of Grace.

She faltered, 'I didn't mean it to be like this, so sudden. I meant to let it happen more easily. You don't feel sprung upon?'

She didn't address this to anyone in particular. Rudi said, 'No, no,' and Sarah shook her head.

'No, it's probably better this way,' said Rudi. 'Am I right, Sarah?'

'Whatever,' said Sarah, looking at Grace. She did not wish to be pandered to. She was not used to her wishes being taken into consideration and her response indicated an urgent need for distance.

But Rudi was unaware of this modern term of non-commitment and did not want to say the wrong thing. He did not want this living consequence of the most important thing of his life to turn sour.

He said, 'I'm pleased to meet you.' She said, 'Yeah,' which he took as positive but it was hard to tell, since her face was turned away and fixed on Grace. 'But this isn't the time,' he persevered. He walked round the bed to where Maggie stood rigid. He didn't touch her though he wanted to. He said, 'I don't want to interrupt. I'll go.'

'Don't go on my behalf,' said Sarah languidly. 'It really doesn't bother me. Stay, I'm sure Mother would appreciate it.'

He smiled tentatively but she wasn't looking. 'That's thoughtful.'

'I'll go.' Sarah was brusque, decisive.

'No, don't.'

'No, really.' Sarah turned round, somehow avoiding his face as she picked up her jumper from the end of the bed. 'I was going anyway. I've been here ages and Alex will be wondering where I am.'

He asked, 'Are you feeling better though?'

'Sure, much better. Alex is doing a great job of looking after his feeble invalid.'

Seeing that she was really going, Maggie said, 'I'll call you later, OK?'

'OK,' said Sarah in a monotone and left without another word.

Maggie and Rudi looked at each other. They said nothing. They didn't know what to say; it was too extraordinary.

Then Maggie sighed at her mother and said to Rudi, 'She's in a real mess. They can't do anything for her. She has a few weeks at the most apparently.'

'Oh lord.' His voice was heavy. 'I'd get you something to eat but you'll want me to leave you here, won't you?'

'Yes,' she said unresponsively. She didn't think it then, but it nevertheless left a favourable impression with her that he understood.

'They can't expect me just to swallow everything and start playing Happy Families.'

'I don't suppose they do.'

Sarah banged Alex's denimed leg in vigorous frustration. 'Fuck you. You're always so damn reasonable. Why can't you be hysterical just once in a while?'

'I'm hysterical inside,' he said darkly. 'Which is much more unhealthy. I'll be ulcered up on a diet of milk and Zantac in a few years.'

'And I'll be in an institution.'

'Oh, stop it,' said Alex laconically, 'you say that too often.' He stretched and yawned and focused on her curled form on the chair opposite him. 'So come on, tell me how you're getting on.' Sarah's study motivation had slumped since the double blow of Grace and Rudi. Alex had persuaded her to do some reading this afternoon only with the bribe of a game of Monopoly afterwards.

'Not bad. I'm one hundred and fifty pages into Bede now.'

'Very good,' he said, bringing back a couple of chilled Cokes from the next room. 'You have earned your Monopoly for being a good girl.' This produced one of the rare smiles.

'I don't think I've ever been called a "good girl" before.'

'I hope it doesn't put you off,' he said with mock concern. 'I know what a polarity responder you are.'

He thought how beautiful she was when she smiled. Her dark features lit up. Her otherwise hostile expression gave way to a humorous one. Even her hair looked lighter. Her smile was to be valued for its rarity. He knew that no one else would look at her as he did. To most she looked mistrusting and sullen. And it remained thrillingly hard to obtain. Her body might be available but her smile was precious. He touched her creased cheek with his hand. Then he kissed it and she didn't even flinch. Before she would have run at even the suggestion of such sensibility. He kissed her again and said, 'Oh, by the way, I invited Rudi round to play Monopoly too.'

She drew her face away from his lips and said, 'What?' not in outrage but sheer incomprehension.

'Well,' he said, 'you know how much better Monopoly is with more than two people.'

'Oh yes,' said Sarah, 'that's right.'

Alex had gambled wisely. He ventured that if it was organized by him, Sarah would be much more amenable to a meeting with her father. And this way there was something comfortable to do.

He had put it to Rudi, who was both keen and nervous after the first encounter at Grace's bedside.

'But what if she refuses and I'm already on my way?'

'I'll tell her before you leave. If her head starts spinning, I'll give you a call.'

'I guess I'll take the ship, huh?' Rudi found this funny, even if nobody else did.

Hilary had left Alex with a theory about Monopoly pieces. The iron was too submissive. The flash car was too material. The ship was too big and masculine an organ. The hat was a little whimsical and the dog a revolting symbol of unquestioning loyalty.

'I wish there were a cat,' she once said. Whereupon his father, Ted, made her a tiny model cat out of plaster and painted it black. 'It's lucky too,' he said.

'I'll be the boot,' said Sarah.

Alex aimed the cat at the bin and missed. 'I'll be the car. It seems appropriate for a money-making game.'

Sarah did not need to speak to her father about anything other than the game.

Once she said, 'Nuts?' proffering a bowl of roasted almonds that Alex had bought in especially from Mr Naik's. Rudi looked at her to see if she was being funny. She still would not look at him directly but there was a half-smile curled around her lips.

She felt freer without her mother there. It allowed her to ignore the fact that he was her father and merely treat him as someone to get along with. She remained aware that everything she said and did would subsequently be analysed, so she set out to be as perplexing as possible and as inconsequential and as disrespectful of the occasion, all at the same time.

She felt free to shout, 'You bastard!' when Rudi landed on Vine Street, depriving her of her favourite orange set. He sprang back at the insult, but she wasn't looking. He looked at Alex, who smiled encouragingly. 'You total and utter wanker,' she shrieked when he later missed her yellows with three houses and then sailed round to Go. 'I can't believe it! Arse face!'

It was quite a battering. When Sarah left the room to relieve herself, Rudi looked a little wild-eyed. Alex consoled him.

'It's going very well.'

'Is it?'

'Oh yes.' Suddenly Alex sounded old and Rudi young. 'She's appallingly rude when she feels comfortable. Only yesterday she called me "turd paper" when I wouldn't get her a beer.'

'Is she still off the sauce?'

'Not if she doesn't want to be, but I said if she was well enough to drink then she was well enough to fetch it and to get me one while she was at it.'

Rudi managed to laugh a little. 'Guess this is stressful for her, though. I'm sweating.'

'Mmm, I know,' said Alex guilelessly. 'Monopoly's a tense game. It all becomes so real, doesn't it?'

It was gone midnight when Rudi finally called a cab. While still technically solvent he had donated his remaining assets to Sarah's pile. He could still play. 'Here,' he said caustically, handing over a heap of paper money and a cluster of weakened properties, 'it's about time I gave you something.' She twisted her lips in appreciation. A subtle reaction that he knew from Maggie. Meaning, yeah, yeah, OK, it was a good thing. Alex saw him to the door.

'See you,' they said almost together.

Sarah's head had dropped on the table, she too was exhausted.

'He's not bad, is he?' said Alex, beginning to put things away. He had taken to tidying up since Sarah had come back. He equated the old confusion that *he* lived in with *her* mentally scattered thoughts. It seemed advisable then to keep everything in order. In his new role as carer this was surprisingly easy.

'No, not bad,' said Sarah. 'He should have sold me Vine Street though. That was very unkind.'

The gauze between Grace and the world grew daily more opaque. Her eyes seemed milky.

Morphine meant that she slept a lot of the time. She would pick at the uncomfortable wound on her breast, pulling at the bandages where the blood had soaked through with fingers like talons from the weight she had lost.

One afternoon, Maggie was by her side and Rudi was reading her notes at the foot of the bed. Grace had her eyes shut, and had done for some hours. The eyeballs moved erratically under the lids. She lay perilously close to the edge of the bed. Maggie herself was drifting off in the sickly heat of the ward; she fell on her elbow that rested on the bed trolley. She was woken by a nightmarish vision of Grace's frail skeleton smashing to the floor. But somehow it never happened.

Grace's head was propped upright again by the nurse and rested on a wall of plump pillows. She had been asleep or unconscious since Maggie had arrived. Then without warning she raised her arm, opened her mouth and a strange childish wail came out.

'Aa . . . ah!'

Maggie started and looked up to see her mother's mouth, tiny but producing a great volume of sound. Then words coming out. Strange words. '*Vlinder, vlinder,*' in the very real voice of a little girl. '*Vliegen zuster. Vliegen in de garten.*'

Rudi dropped the notes on the floor. 'What the hell's she saying?'

Maggie was undisturbed. 'She comes out with this stuff sometimes. It's a language she used to share with her sister.'

'What is it?'

'Kind of bad Dutch. Edie is Dutch, of course, well, Dutch Jewish, so when she married an Englishman and came over here, she talked a bit of Dutch to her babies. Then she was widowed and had to fend for herself in England. The girls grew up English, went to English school but a lot of words stuck.'

He took this in. 'Why didn't Edie go back to the Netherlands, to her family, when her husband died?'

Maggie sniffed. 'Who knows? She was too bloody-minded probably. They'd all been strongly disapproving in the first place of her marriage to a foreigner – and to a non-kosher husband. She never had much to say for them. I don't think she got on with her parents.'

'Not another one,' said Rudi, massaging his brow.

Maggie laughed a little. 'But maybe they wouldn't take her back . . . would you?'

Since the day Grace went into hospital, Maggie had asked Rudi to move into a hotel. She needed to be alone. Her flat was reassuringly empty and cool after the furnace of the ward. She didn't take her coat off but went straight to a drawer in the kitchen. She pulled out a thin, leathery A5 pad and sat down with it at the kitchen table.

The pages were divided into two columns. Maggie's neat handwriting had headed the left-hand column 'Idioglossia' and the right 'English'. Then followed pages and pages of words.

Vlinder	–	butterfly
Zus/Zuster	–	sister
Ermoordene	–	murderer
Vliegen	–	to fly

Maggie stroked the worn cover absentmindedly. Remembering the time she had written all this down, years ago, when her mother was first lost to her. When Maggie had thought that learning Idioglossia would be a way to reach her again. But she learned that to Grace, Idioglossia *was* Ruth, and thus, when speaking it, she could hear only her sister. Later Maggie realized that each relationship between two people had its own private language, even if that language was unspoken or the relationship was no longer real, existing only in thought or memory.

Grace

Grace felt pain in the side of her chest. When she looked at her fingers there was blood on them. She closed her eyes and the hospital faded from her mind.

The world looked muddy. The man said, 'You'll get used to it.' The large group of children chattered loudly with intrigue and alarm. Ruth looked at Grace. Grace looked wide-eyed with anxiety. Ruth put up her hand.

'My sister's scared.'

The man clucked impatiently. He strode towards where Grace had taken her gas mask off and turned white. 'Don't worry, love,' he said, picking it up. 'You'll be grateful when the poison gas comes, won't you . . . cheer up, be a brave girl.' He nudged her in the ribs and lowered his voice. 'You should be setting an example for the younger ones.'

I couldn't see through the mask. I couldn't breathe. The man walked away; he had many more children to deal with. But he shook his head. I heard him say, 'They're never satisfied, never satisfied.' I heard it.

I was never scared, Grace.

I know, Ruth, I know. When that plane came down, you marched up bold as brass.

Yes, I ran ahead, even though they shouted after me.

I couldn't understand. The pilot might still be alive. I saw your silhouette, Ruth, by the smashed plane. I looked at a cornflower. Brilliant blue petals.

Sometimes we had only each other and then you loved me.

We were butterflies, Grace, vlinderer *fluttery.*

You were a light, Ruth, and I was a moth.

You were stupid.

I found Idioglossia, Ruth. In the dictionary. I found Idioglossia, our secret language. Idioglossia, impossia.

When we were evacuated, when Mother wasn't there, we were closer. Mother was divisive. Mother didn't like Grace because she was a dreamer. Mother liked Ruth because she was beautiful.

You're stupid, Grace, you always were. You should have gone through the spiegel, *not me.*

I go through the mirror, Ruth, but you're not there. Stop laughing, Ruth, stop laughing. Stop.

She saw her sister behind her eyes. She was young and beautiful. She saw her expression, bewitching. She saw herself, young and cold. Her silent face, her silent eyes. She saw her husband, hypnotized by her sister the bewitcher. The beautiful bitch. And she saw her mother laughing.

'Get the nurse,' said Maggie, rubbing her eyes. 'She's in a state again. She needs something.'

Grace was living in the past where thoughts seemed to make more sense.

28

Water

Watching Grace die was like watching a swiftly shrinking sea. Her illness progressed tidally; she was stronger in the morning than at night, but each morning she was weaker than the day before, though some days she partially rallied. The regular rhythm of Grace seemed to affect the people watching her. Her visitors arrived and left separately, meeting in different combinations, sometimes at random, sometimes planned. Thoughts, speech and silence flowed in waves.

* * *

It occurred to Rudi for the first time that he was much the same age as Grace. That he and she had lived through times that Maggie was too young to remember. That was weird. Grace seemed timeless yet there had been a war for her too. He looked at her sleeping face. It didn't feel real. And even Harry could have been only ten years older; on the boat he had always thought of Harry as a different generation.

* * *

Sarah visited every day, as much to show solidarity as anything else. Maggie was there most of the time. Rudi could not match her stamina, nor would she want him to. He kept in the background. He feared that Maggie was holding on to the impossible hope that Grace would show some lucidity before the end. He watched Maggie drawing into her mother's twilight.

*   *   *

Sarah wondered if Great Edie would ever die. Losing Grace was one thing but life without Edie would be unrecognizable. Who could she moan with then?

*   *   *

Sometimes they talked about his life in America. 'Have you spoken to your children since you've been here?' Sarah demanded.

'Of course.'

'I didn't mean it offensively.'

'No problem.' He did not react to her. She was not sure if that was a good thing.

'How can you afford to stay here?'

'What are you, Immigration?' He smiled. She half-sniggered, and slouched on her stool. He said, 'I'm retired, I have a pension. I worked thirty years in the City Council when I went back to Chicago.'

'Why did you go back there, after all that trouble?'

'I had nowhere else to go and I wanted to see my family. Time had passed and people have short memories. I felt I oughta go back, I hadn't done anything wrong. Besides, I'm not a quitter.'

'Oh,' Sarah said fervently, 'I am.' She felt good with the smile he gave her.

*   *   *

Rudi wondered, was it Victor Frankl, Auschwitz survivor and psychiatrist, who said that whatever happens, no one can take away a person's right to think? Some guy said it. Maybe Grace was worse off because her right to think was taken away. Or did she choose to leave it behind? Was it a family thing? Sarah, after all, was dragged under so easily.

*   *   *

'I had therapy once,' said Maggie, when she and Rudi were alone. 'It was the hospital's idea and their therapist. They had this idea that families work like a system. That anything one person does will always have a knock-on effect on someone else.

351

Sarah wouldn't come, of course.' She paused. 'Do you think I kept Grace ill by treating her like an invalid?'

'No,' said Rudi, who had no idea.

*   *   *

What the hell was Rudi doing here? Maggie had not asked him to come back. She wanted to suffer alone, she had always suffered alone. She stared angrily at him – even when he wasn't there – and inconsolably at her mother.

*   *   *

'It's nice of you to come, Alex.'

'Oh, no problem, I wanted to come.'

The chair looked comically too small for him. He couldn't sit comfortably for long. He stood up and paced around. Why can't men sit still? Maggie wondered. But I'm not going to complain about any man who can put up with Sarah. Just hope it lasts.

*   *   *

Sometimes Maggie let go. One wintry afternoon they were in the hospital coffee bar while Grace had her bed bath. 'Were your parents happily married?' Maggie asked Rudi, unprompted.

'I guess so, why?'

'What did they like about each other?'

'I dunno really. Mom liked Dad to play the piano. She had great legs.'

'It's all very haphazard, isn't it? It can be the tiniest of things.'

He nodded unblinkingly. He was restraining his real thoughts because he knew that anything he said would be taken amiss. He said, 'Why did Grace marry Harry?'

Maggie thought about it. 'Because he was the first man to ask. Edie didn't do a lot for her confidence. Ruth was the one who was supposed to be the great catch. Ruth was the complete opposite of Grace. She was more like Edie. Loud, wild and always right. She was a troublemaker and Edie loved that. Ruth was engaged three times, never married but hardly a virgin. Can you imagine, in the early 'fifties?'

He looked puzzled. 'But if Edie gave you such a bad time for

352

being a single mother, why did she approve of Ruth playing around?'

She looked at him as if he was stupid. 'Edie doesn't mind people causing trouble. What she despises is getting caught.'

*   *   *

In the late November darkness, Sarah and Maggie sat together.

'Her skin looks like dead leaves,' said Maggie suddenly.

'I was just thinking about them,' said Sarah.

'Dead leaves?' Maggie turned to her, perplexed. 'Why?'

'Alex and I were having a bonfire, getting rid of some of his rubbish. There was a mush at the bottom of sludge and leaf skeletons which were too wet to burn.'

'Make good compost,' said Maggie, seeking relief in her practical side.

'Mmm. His garden is one big rotting pile.'

'Maybe you could plant something.'

'Maybe.' Sarah was doubtful.

Tentatively Maggie squeezed her daughter's arm. 'I could help you.'

Sarah turned a weary eye but she said, quite positively, 'Yeah, maybe.'

*   *   *

Maggie was happiest on her own. She would have stayed all night if the hospital had allowed it. But until Grace was truly on the edge, she had to go home. Alone Maggie could think as she liked without fear of being questioned.

Great Edie was a bitch, she really was. She could have visited, just once. She was such a witch. Edie said it was amazing Grace's marriage had even been consummated. What kind of thing was that to say to her?

*   *   *

'Did I tell you Ruth had an affair with my grandfather?' said Sarah, rubbing her eyes.

'No,' said Alex. 'What, Harry, Grace's husband?'

'That's the one.'

Alex whistled. 'Do you think she can hear us?'

'Who, Ruth?'

353

He raised his eyes in consternation. 'No!' He gesticulated at the unmoving form in the bed.

'Oh, Grace. No, I shouldn't think so.'

*　　*　　*

Maggie rested her elbows on the tray attached to the bed. It was dark already. Seemed like she was the only one here today. Grace had not opened her eyes for two days. She breathed irregularly and picked at her wound. Maggie closed her eyes.

When she is seven years old, Maggie's mother tells her that she had killed her sister, Aunt Ruth. Maggie does not know what to believe. But she doesn't like her mother to be sad. She likes to look in the mirror with her, and she likes the magic that her mother works, that makes them see 'happy Mummy' and 'happy Maggie' waving back. But she is scared of her mother too, now; when she holds her daughter desperately and won't let go. Maggie can't really remember when her mother was normal.

She doesn't remember Aunt Ruth, just the sound of her. She laughed very loudly. When she was little, Maggie thought it was because Aunt Ruth was so happy but, now she is older, Granny Edie has told her it was because she was a drunk. But Granny Edie seemed to like Aunt Ruth more than she likes Mummy. Maggie doesn't like that because it makes her mother funny and ill. She doesn't think Granny Edie should say horrible things if they aren't true.

Her father doesn't say anything about it. He is very shy. He doesn't talk to Maggie much. Granny Edie says that he liked Aunt Ruth better than Mummy too, because Mummy is a bit stupid. Maggie doesn't think that is right, but Granny Edie knows most things. Maggie asked Granny Edie why her father never plays with her and Granny Edie said that he doesn't like playing any more. He used to play with Aunt Ruth and she died. Maggie doesn't realize that parents are meant to speak to each other. She used to think that they weren't allowed to. Father would say, 'Maggie, can you ask your mother to pass the salt?' and Maggie would ask Mummy and Mummy would pass it without looking up. Mummy never says anything to Father. Granny Edie says that it's because Mummy is cross that Father went to sleep with Aunt Ruth when he shouldn't have. Father is a 'dirty bugger'. But Granny Edie says that if Mummy didn't want them to, she should have given them a jolly good talking to, not let herself be trodden on 'like a bleedin' doormat'. She says that Maggie must never let this happen to her.

Maggie remembers the day that Aunt Ruth died and she doesn't understand why it is Mummy's fault. The Queen was getting crowned and Granny Edie had bought a television specially so everybody could watch it. But when it started Aunt Ruth and Father weren't there. Mummy was strange. Maggie sat on her lap. When Father came into the house he was strange too. He fell over. He sat down and watched the Queen for ages without saying anything. Granny Edie said some rude words and asked him where Aunt Ruth was but he didn't say anything. Then Father needed to be sick. He ran up the stairs. Then he came back again and he fell asleep in the armchair.

After the television programme ended Mummy went upstairs to the toilet. But she came back really quickly. She was scream-ing, 'Ruth's gone through the mirror!' Nobody knew what Mummy meant. Maggie thought that Ruth must have been waving at Mummy. Granny Edie ran upstairs. Maggie didn't know what was happening. There was a lot of noise and an ambulance came. Maggie had never seen an ambulance man before. Then Mummy told Maggie that Aunt Ruth was dead. Mummy went into the bathroom to wash her hands and when she looked in the mirror she saw Aunt Ruth's face. A dead face. Aunt Ruth was drowned in the bath. That was because she was drunk. It was an accident. Maggie must always be careful not to fall asleep in the bath.

At first Granny Edie said it was Father's fault. She said if he weren't such a dirty bugger, he would have washed his hands after he was sick and he would have seen Aunt Ruth in time. Maggie doesn't understand. Father always makes her wash her hands. But now Granny Edie says that really it was Mummy's fault, that if Mummy had any sense she wouldn't have let Father go out with Aunt Ruth and Aunt Ruth wouldn't have got drunk and so she wouldn't have drowned.

Mummy isn't here at the moment. Granny Edie says she has been taken away to a castle, because she is very ill. Granny Edie hopes that Mummy doesn't come back. Maggie hopes she does *because if she doesn't, she is going to have to live on a boat with Father and she doesn't want to do that.*

*   *   *

Maggie sighed and dragged her fingers through her hair. She looked at her watch. Five o'clock. She looked around her. To her surprise she saw Rudi walking towards her. He saw her looking at him. 'Hi,' he said cautiously. 'I wasn't going to disturb you, but then, I dunno, I thought you might be able to use a little company.'

She smiled gratefully. 'That was nice of you.'

'How is she?'

Maggie turned to her mother. 'Pretty ghastly, she's been making that tortuous noise all afternoon.'

He pulled up a chair beside her. Maggie was rubbing her eyes. 'I know I've got to let her go. It's just that being with Grace was such a magical place to be. The world was different through her. Grace wanted to climb into the mirror with Ruth. She would brush her fingertips against the glass and it would melt to her touch. The mirror became soft and thin like a net curtain, and it parted so easily.' Maggie's eyes looked red.

Rudi was thinking, for some reason, of the year he spent hiding in the forest with his parents. It *was* possible to disappear in impossible spaces. He still had the piece of paper on which Maggie had written him a riddle, when they were on the boat together.

> Walk into my parlour, said the spider to the fly, water hides inside a glass and look straight through my eye.

She was hiding right in front of him but somehow he couldn't see her. He looked at her now, exhausted, beside him. 'I'll take you home,' he said. 'We'll have some drinks and some cigarettes and you can tell me what the hell you're talking about.' Maggie stood up without resistance.

At two in the morning Rudi was woken by the phone in his hotel room. He was alert instantly.

'Hello, Maggie.'

She was breathless. 'Grace is dead. They just called me. I'm going round there now. I can't believe I wasn't there when she went.'

'No, Maggie, don't be dumb. Wait till the morning. You can't go now, you'll just be in the way.'

'In the way?' she echoed in a voice that made him crack inside. 'She's my mother, what are you talking about?'

Rudi held her firm. 'There's nothing you can do until the morning. You can't go to the hospital now, nothing's open and you know how lousy the coffee machine is.'

'I could take a thermos flask,' she wailed in a tragic voice that broke into sobs.

'Just stay there, don't move. I'll get a cab.'

His new hotel was much closer to Maggie's house. He was in her kitchen in less than half an hour.

'I can't get the water to boil,' she said. 'You won't be able to do anything, you don't even have a kettle.'

He had a look. 'You haven't plugged it in,' he said softly. He made tea. She would not sit down. 'Don't you want to be comfortable?' he said. 'Try and relax.' She shrugged. In the end they stood together at the top of the tiny back garden, just outside the back door. He looked into the darkness to where the pear tree was swaying in the breeze. The branches were completely bare now and the only sign that it was ever different was the corollary mulch of rotten fruit around the base of the trunk. This pear tree was the garden. It was a small space and the tree had grown to fill it.

Rudi was cold and tired but he bore it uncomplainingly. He looked at her staring ahead. 'You're not going to sleep tonight, are you?' She didn't answer. 'C'mon, let's have a game of poker.'

They played as they had not played for over thirty years. She was reluctant at first, as if this were disrespectful. But she grew distanced from her melancholy. She seemed calmer, her eyes less staring. But then she said, with apparently no stimulus, 'Don't think this . . . your being here, playing like this, makes everything all right.'

'No,' he said seriously, 'I wouldn't.'

But it did calm her. She was falling asleep in the chair. He pulled the big cushion off the sofa and rummaged in the airing cupboard for two blankets. He did not want to leave her alone. He watched her sleeping, legs tucked under in an awkward ball.

The dim light smoothed her middle-aged lines and she looked very young. He was filled with a surge of love for her, from his stomach to the back of his mouth. An ending was always a beginning. His eyes stung and he had to move away.

He thought about all she had told him that night. He didn't know why she had agreed to tell him now. Maybe he had caught her at a weak moment. He thought about the impact on a person of a mother like Grace. Because her love was incomplete it was more gripping. Maggie would always want more. Her mother was never reliable; as often as she was an escape, for Maggie, from the world, she would not know her daughter, staring straight through her with those almond eyes. It was not surprising that Maggie was so attached. Grace's world was more attractive than Harry's silence or the grim words of her angry grandmother. No, that all made sense. What bothered him more was Edie. She hated one daughter enough to blame her for the other's death. It was crazy. He couldn't figure it out. What possible motive could she have?

He sighed. The death of Grace was indeed the death of a butterfly. For years she lived in a mirror-house, staring out. Maggie's relationship with Grace was profoundly unfinished. Now the mirror was broken and Grace had flown away.

29

Sisters

When Maggie left the next morning Rudi tried to go with her but she wouldn't allow it. She was sullen.

It was eleven when she walked into the vast hospital building. It seemed suddenly bigger and she felt lost. She was lost. She went up the far staircase rather than the near one through distraction and came out at a different place, by a window. The ward was peaceful. She was confused. She had expected the bed to be empty or for it to be a mistake and for Grace to be propped up still. But there was another woman in her place.

The nurse greeted her. Maggie signed to take away the possessions. Grace's one gold ring and the nightdresses were accounted for on an inventory. They were handed to her in a see-through plastic bag. Maggie felt the arm of the nurse on her back. 'You can go and see her if you want to, in our chapel of rest.' She handed her a booklet. 'Here, this tells you what to do about the funeral and everything.'

Maggie looked at the body of her mother. She kept thinking she saw movement in her unlined face. The air was charged. She did not know what to do. What was she supposed to do? She flicked through the booklet but it did not cover this. She looked at the body again. In some ways her mother seemed no different. And it did take just a moment. No time was needed to commit the vision to memory. Now what was she supposed to do?

She floundered for a few seconds then she turned away, opened her bag and took out a spiral-bound reporter's notebook. She sat down on one of the wooden seats, took a pen. 'To do,' she wrote in a careful hand at the top of the first sheet. She wrinkled her forehead into a concentrated frown.

1 Ring undertakers to compare prices.
2 Go to Registrar of Deaths in Brixton.
3 Don't forget piece of paper from hospital that confirms she died of breast carcinoma.
4 Need death certificate *before* going to undertaker.
5 Set date for funeral (undertaker will arrange with crematorium).
6 Invite mourners. Edie, Sarah, Alex, me . . . Rudi? Maybe some of the people at Westfield?
7 Food for afterwards. Quiche, salad, etc . . . M&S.
8 Get dress dry-cleaned – what's Sarah going to wear?
9 How to get Edie there?
10 ?

To-do lists always had ten points. But she couldn't think of another one.

Maggie was more distant with Rudi. It was more than grief. It was rejection. She mourned privately. To express it was to let it go. She liked to hang on to things although they were gone. He suspected she believed that her mourning was all she had left. He feared she regretted having confided in him. She made no mention of it.

She became closed up, cruelly efficient. She insisted on making the funeral arrangements on her own. When Rudi got round early to her house on the second morning, she had already risen, cleaned the lounge and rung the undertakers.

'Thanks for your help but I feel better doing it this way,' she insisted. 'It's all very straightforward. There's no estate, no money, no will. Hardly anything that it's even worth giving to charity. I'll just dump it all.' She spoke through closed lips. Her face was drawn. He felt for her, but he knew that in this state she would not respond to kindness, not positively at least. He simply smiled at her.

'To be honest I'd rather be left alone for a few days, while I'm sorting stuff out. You'll only get in the way.'

*

The day of the funeral was normal. The rain did not drive down in angry streaks. No poignant mist shrouded the trees. No piercing sun suggested better times ahead. The weather itself was normal, neither cold nor warm, neither wet nor absurdly dry. The wind was light but not suggestive of anything. It blew no gentle reminder to all who gathered round the fountain at the entrance to the crematorium.

Rudi arrived first, on his own. He put his hands in his pockets and thought such thoughts as one thinks. The slight discomfort with seeing the cars already in the car park, knowing that it was continual, that while they were lining up, the previous incumbent was still sliding into the incinerator. After Grace would come another corpse pulling at her shroud tails.

Maggie had organized that Alex and Sarah should pick up Edie, in a cab. In fact, subsequent to the Beachy Head trip, Alex had thought that calling friends up at three in the morning was a little impractical. So he had pulled himself out of his constructed world and bought a car. And not even a second-hand car but a spanking grown-up new one. He was paying for it in mature monthly instalments. It was all very unnerving.

Sarah was stronger with Alex. Sitting next to him in the front seat, she felt more able to cope. She berated herself for this, that it took a man . . . but then interrupted herself. Surely seeking comfort in other people was no more than what the vast majority of the population did? Give yourself a break, for fuck's sake, this is a funeral.

She and Alex had come to a sensible decision. They were happier together so they might as well stick with it. In a casual, non-committal, no-pressure kind of a way of course.

'What do we do if I get a sudden urge for life-denying, self-negating, ugly sex?' she asked him as he tried to turn the wrong way down a one-way street. It was an important question.

'Well,' he said dubiously, keeping his eyes on the road, only minor panic fanning in his eyes as he realized his error, 'I'll try my best.'

'No,' she said scornfully (she had not noticed the traffic problem), 'I meant with someone else. I might need an outlet from all this good behaviour.'

This did drag his eyes from the oncoming traffic. He turned and looked at her sternly. Strangely, this thrilled her. 'No,' he said with force, 'we'll have none of that nonsense any more.' He paused and thought for a moment while cars hooted at him to get out of the way. 'If you do get an urge, you must cross your legs until it goes away.'

Maybe she would and maybe she wouldn't. A lifetime of spoiling is a hard habit to kick. But they would be happy for now. And Alex was prepared to understand her. And she was sympathetic to him. But we are weak.

Great Edie did not answer.

'Oh God,' said Sarah, 'here we go.'

Alex rang the bell again and Sarah banged the door, shouting through the letter flap, 'Come on, open up, you're not fooling anybody.'

There was a reluctant shuffling sound. A light switched on in the hallway. The sound of slippered feet dragging across the ground grew louder. ' 'Oo is it?'

'Great Edie, you know perfectly well who it is, it's me and Alex.'

'I don't know any Alex. Go away and leave an old lady in peace or I'll call the law!'

Alex snorted.

'Open the bloody door!' hollered Sarah.

Great Edie opened it with a look of rage consuming her face. 'What a way is that to talk to your great-grandmother?'

Sarah smirked. 'Nice outfit, Edie, very suitable.'

Edie was wearing a polyester dressing gown, white and skagged on the inside, pink and orange fantastic flowers on the out. It might have been easy-clean, but hadn't been.

'What you talkin' about? Suitable for what?'

'You know, stop causing trouble.'

'I ain't going.'

'Yes, you are.'

'I ain't,' screeched the old lungs, with such violence that it shook the rest of her body.

Alex and Sarah forced their way in. It was Alex's first time in the house. It smelt of dust and piss and the strange potions of the old witch.

362

The party gathered in the concrete square outside the crematorium. Sarah and Alex had finally pulled Edie into a grubby outfit of navy blue. Maggie had a sober black skirt and jacket and a grey shirt. Sarah had found a black suit, but it could have done with a press. Alex had pointed this out. Sarah said, 'Oh, it's all right, the creases'll come out when I'm sitting on them.' Rudi wore a dark suit, it was all he had with him. Alex had a suit. Still in its dry-cleaning polythene bag. Sarah had been amazed.

'I didn't know you had a suit.'

'Of course, do you think I'm such a troglodyte?'

'Well, it's not the kind of thing—'

'Does it look all right?'

Sarah narrowed her eyes to get a better look. 'Kind of, it makes you look like a criminal.'

That morning the crematorium was running late. There was nothing to do but wait. Death was like that, sighed Rudi, nothing but waiting. There were only so many cigarettes that Rudi and Maggie could smoke while they were waiting. There had to be some conversation. There was a lot of shuffling.

Sarah thought of something to say to Rudi, who was altogether an easier conversational prospect than her mother at the moment. 'Who are my other grandparents?' she said.

'I'm afraid they're both dead,' Rudi replied. 'My mother died twenty years ago. My father died last year. It was a real fight, he was a tough old guy.'

She nodded sagely. 'I hear he got you out of Poland.'

'Something like that.'

'Oh,' she said, 'it must have been quite an ordeal.'

'Yes,' he said, amused, 'I guess it was.' He put his hands into his pockets and bounced up and down on his heels. Sarah looked at Alex. It was his job to keep Edie on her feet and she, clutching his arm, had steered him to the central fountain and pond and the surrounding rose bushes, with their dead heads still clinging.

Rudi spoke again, drawing her attention back.

'So, Alex has told me about the university course you're going to do.'

Sarah bristled. 'That's right.'

'Well,' interjected Maggie, instinctively knowing that the best encouragement would be few questions. 'It's very good news.' Sarah smiled a little.

But Rudi did not know Sarah so well. 'Medieval Studies, isn't it? What, bodkins and jousting and bloody battles, huh? Sounds fun, I guess . . . but what are you going to do with it afterwards?'

Maggie looked anxious but Sarah was calm. 'I don't know. I'm sure it's totally useless for any worthwhile future occupation. But by the time I'm finished I'll be too old to start anything sensible anyway. I can't even apply until next spring.'

'Well,' said Maggie rather too cheerfully, 'I'm sure it'll sort itself out one way or another. As long as it makes you happy.' Since everyone could hear the strain in her voice, this was scant consolation. Alex wondered if Maggie knew that her attempts at cheer fooled no one, or if she, in fact, wanted no one to be fooled.

'If you really want to know,' creaked Great Edie, 'I can tell you what Sarah's going to do.'

But she was murmuring into the rose bush so no one heard her and anyway the conversation was broken because finally the door opened and the previous mourning party trooped sedately out of the crematorium; it was time for Grace's meagre ceremony.

A pair of nurses from Westfield, Grace's hospital for so many years, who had attended the ceremony expressed their regrets and went back to work.

The funeral party – Edie, Rudi, Maggie, Sarah and Alex – went back to Edie's house. Not the ideal venue for a wake but it was an easier option than coaxing Edie into somewhere else. Rudi's nose wrinkled in distaste as he brushed past the heavy curtains hanging at the front window. The grime that held them together stuck to his fingers.

Maggie had bought in some quiche and dips from Marks and Spencer. Sarah had made some vol-au-vents, saying mysteriously, 'You have to eat vol-au-vents at funerals.'

'But you never cook!' said Maggie indignantly, as if behaviour change at a time like this was in bad taste.

'Well, obviously sometimes I do.'

Rudi raised his eyebrows and opened a bottle of wine.

At funerals, even more than weddings, visions of past ceremonies crowd into the head.

'I remember my parents' funerals,' said Alex, wiping vol-au-vent crumbs from his lips. 'They were ill at the same time, but my father died first. I always thought my mother hung on because she wanted to get an idea who was going to show up for her.' Rudi balked but said nothing. Alex sipped some wine. 'My mother should have gone first. She was diagnosed first and was given less time. But she beat him. And she turned up at his funeral and was the centre of attention for that day. There was a huge turnout, people they hadn't seen for years. Everyone was very nice to her, of course, even though she was so appallingly rude about them behind their backs. But it seemed to satisfy her because she died less than three weeks later.'

Rudi smiled gingerly. 'Oh well. That was good, I guess.'

'Not really.' Alex returned the smile. 'The last laugh was on her. Because who was going to make the effort twice in a month? A lot of people begged my forgiveness but told me they'd said goodbye to Hilary when they said goodbye to Ted. I told them that I understood completely and so would my mother. Complete bollocks, of course. She would have scratched their eyes out.'

Rudi nodded. 'I take it you weren't close to your mother.'

Alex laughed.

Edie was taken to the parlour, to give her – or possibly everyone else – a rest. 'Prop her on the chair and she'll be asleep in a few minutes,' Maggie told Alex, in an exaggerated whisper. He escorted the old woman to the room, marvelling at the frailty of her limbs. Edie was reassuringly ungracious. She dismissed him with a wave of her hand. 'All right, that's enough, I can sit down on me own. No need to treat me like bone bleedin' china.' Alex returned to the living room without saying a word but nodding rather formally. Then Great Edie was alone. Or she thought she was.

She did not sit down but stayed shakily upright. She was

standing by the mantelpiece in front of which Maggie had once bathed in the fecundity of George Crouch. On the mantelpiece stood the same row of photographs that were there when Maggie was growing up; there had been few additions in the intervening years.

The old woman gripped the wood of the shelf to steady herself. Her arm trembled with the effort. Her watery eyes strained to look at the photos through her cloudy cataracts. She stopped at the photo of Ruth, the gold-framed, grinning snapshot that looked so large compared to the others because it was taken from the neck up. She held out a wobbling finger to the dusty glass and traced a line down Ruth's cheek. The words that came from her were barely audible. 'Yer shouldna left me, left me all alone.'

She had heard no sound but, at that moment, instinct made her turn her head. Rudi was standing right by her, smiling charmingly, like she could have softened his hard edges. In her shock, she upturned the corners of her mouth stiffly and slowly. It was more unpleasant than anything, but he appreciated the effort.

'Well,' she snapped, 'what do you want?'

He was still smiling. 'Thought I'd come and have a little talk, check you were OK, seeing as you hadn't sat down yet.'

She squinted at him. 'What yer want ter talk ter me for?'

Suddenly, she was distracted. Out of the corner of her eye, she saw a flash of red at the window to her right. She turned her head with such unusual speed that Rudi turned too – and saw net curtains, grey with dirt. Edie was transfixed by the brightness, the vivid red. She felt the heat of breath against her cheek. She raised her hand to her face as her mouth fell open. She felt her cheek with the back of her hand as though she did not recognize it.

'What is it?' cried Rudi, his avuncular smile vanishing in his alarm at seeing her petrified in this way.

She pointed a finger at the window. 'Can't you see it?'

'What?' He craned his neck but saw nothing.

'Red, that red skirt, I can feel 'er, it's Ruth. I ain't never seen 'er, not in thirty years.' Stunned, she fell heavily towards the chair, catching her knee on the arm. She tumbled on to the cushioned seat, and was forced to grip the edges of the chair till her feeble veins bulged, to save herself from crashing to the ground.

Rudi's concern for her safety was obscured by his anxiety to seize the opportunity he saw before him. He almost stuffed her into a more balanced position before squatting down beside her.

She was staring again at the window, pathetically crying, 'Where are yer, Ruthie? Where are yer, gel? Speak to me! Why have I had the bloody rubbish of the dead of half of London ringing in me friggin' ears all these years and never a word from you? And why now, back for yer sister's funeral? How could yer do that to me? Why did yer never come to me?'

She had clearly forgotten Rudi was there. He didn't want to break this trance but he had to say something. His best idea was to utter in a sonorous tone, fitting, he hoped, for such occasions.

'Edie,' he said tentatively. Then he spoke a little louder. 'Edie, why did you hate Grace so much?'

He was afraid he had broken the spell because she turned violently towards him. But her eyes were vacant and wide open. There was movement on her face. He saw images, like film frames, running backwards across her eyes. He stared, trying to make it out. He saw the figures of two people.

And then she spoke in a voice that he didn't recognize. But its depth, clarity and resonance made him think it must be the voice Maggie had spoken of.

The old woman said, 'I see two girls, Edie and Elli, growing up in a small village on the reclaimed land. They live on the outskirts in a big house made of wood. They look out of the window and see the dyke. From another window they can see the houses where their mother teaches the piano. The girls play in the fields by a lake where their father takes them on his way to work. He is a signalman on the railways. Even in winter, when they are not in school, he takes them and they skate on the thick ice.

'Edie is the eldest and the leader. She is stronger and more vigorous. She has mousy hair. Elli, the younger, is dark and frail. She is insubstantial, like a spirit. Sometimes in the tall fields she disappears. She is so quiet and thin, she can hide in the reeds. She sings, but the sound she makes is the noise of the wind.

'Elli began to sing when she was three years old. She has a voice like the breeze. Edie is six years old and she already has big feet. She is loud, like thunder. Edie is a clumsy child but Elli, their father believes, is a gift from God. Edie loved her sister and did not mind that Elli had a gift. How could she when her sister is such a soft soul?

'The parents cherish Elli. She has a rare talent, she will be a huge success. A tutor comes to the house three times a week. There is no time to play any more. Their mother must work more to pay for Elli's lessons, but she knows that one day Elli will bring fortune to the family. Elli falls behind at school. Edie goes out alone. She is quick-witted and thrives with other children. Her skin is dark from the sun. Elli stays pale and thin. Her fingers are so delicate, she says it aches to play the piano. Edie's hair is cut short because it is always knotted. Elli's hair is long and black. Their mother loves to brush Elli's hair.

'Edie is practical. Her parents need not worry, she will always look after herself. She becomes independent and they do not notice. Elli lives in a world of her own. She can do nothing on her own. Her parents do everything for her. Elli never grows up.

'When she is a young woman, Edie meets an Englishman. He is not interested in singing. He does not understand the dark world Elli lives in, he lives in the light. Edie is drawn to this foreign brightness, she sees it as an escape. Her parents do not like him but they don't prevent the match. They marry in the village church and for once the wooden house is full of the sound of talking, not music. Half the village comes to celebrate. Elli hides under her bed. She can face strangers only when she sings.

'Edie and Jack move into a home in the village. Edie is pregnant with their first child. There is a long winter that year. The lake is frozen solid, so thick somebody rides a horse on to it. Soon many people are on the ice. Edie is skating for hours despite her condition. She skates till she feels dizzy, her face glowing with the cold. Elli stays inside the wooden house. Her throat is sore and she has wrapped it in a scarf. That night Edie visits her sister to cheer her up. In the morning Edie realizes that it was not with cold that her face glowed, nor the skating that made her dizzy. She has influenza. She is ill for three weeks. She loses her baby, a boy. But Edie herself is strong, a survivor. Soon she is well enough to see the blame in her parents' eyes. The night of her visit she infected her sister. Elli is not strong enough to fight. The influenza kills her. The parents are broken. The frail beautiful spirit is gone and the daughter who is left can only torment them. Seeing the life force in their other daughter reminds them always of Elli. Edie leaves with her husband for England. She never returns.'

Great Edie trembled slightly. Rudi saw the tension in her change. He said nothing but stood up and walked to the mantelpiece and looked along the row of pictures. Different eras, different settings and sizes thrown together in discord. Half the people he couldn't put a name to. A childish Maggie, under a pine tree in a wood, with sad black eyes. Rudi's heart wept. Edie as a young woman with her husband. A picture of young Sarah scowling or squinting against the sun. At the end was the picture of Edie as a child, a wide smile engulfing her face. Next to her a smaller, darker girl holding her hand, standing in shadow.

'You looked after this picture better than the others,' he said, dragging a finger across the glass and finding it still clean afterwards.

His words shook her back to life. She twisted impotently towards his voice, trying vainly to stop him picking up the photo. He walked round to face her, holding it in his hands. She gulped as if trying to swallow the enormity of what she had just revealed. He looked into her old face, the lines of fear, hatred, pain and power.

She whispered, 'You won't tell anyone, will yer?'

He hesitated. 'Why don't you want them to know?'

'I want to be left in peace.'

Edie? Peace? He drank this unlikely brew. It tasted strange. He said, 'It might help them understand you better. It might make everything easier.'

She snarled. Her face curled up. 'I don't care about any of them no more! They're nothing but trouble. Leave it alone, can't yer?' Something in this peevish outburst touched him. He nodded.

'Sure, I can keep a secret.'

He was almost out of the door when she called weakly after him, 'I did love Grace once, yer know. But her darkness just finished me.'

'Forget it,' he said, walking out and back to the others.

'What have you got there?' said Maggie on his return, seeing that Rudi was holding something in his pocket. Rudi pulled out a snow-shaker that had lain behind the photo of Edie and Elli. Maggie sighed. 'Oh God, Edie hasn't been boring you with that old thing, has she?'

Rudi smiled. He shook the ornament and watched the snow-flakes swirling round the pair of polka-dot girls holding hands. The flakes floated slowly through the water to the ground.

30

The Golden Segment

She did not want to go but Sarah encouraged her.

'Go on, Mother, you really need a break, you're so tired.'

Rudi wanted Maggie to come away on holiday with him, just a short trip. Maggie came up with many reasons why she couldn't possibly.

'Mother, I'll be fine.'

'She'll be fine,' agreed Alex helpfully.

Maggie looked down. And then up again. 'And what about Edie, what's going to happen to her?'

'Mother, you're not indispensable. We can manage her perfectly well. For God's sake, stop making such a fuss.'

'Well, all right then,' she said, seeing she was beaten. 'But it doesn't mean anything, you know. Don't start getting any ideas.'

'Oh no,' said Sarah with a serious face. 'I wouldn't.'

'What are you going to do while I'm away?'

'Mother, you're going away for four days, I'll be fine. Alex and I are very busy sorting the house out and I've got lots of reading to do. I'm sure I'll manage.'

Since Grace's death, Maggie had lost her purpose. At least that's how Rudi explained it to Sarah.

'She feels empty. She put so much of herself into her mother. It's going to take her a while, I think, to feel complete again.'

Maggie seemed very raw, very open and yet at the same time, to Rudi, she was cold.

Sarah tried to be understanding, though it was difficult. It was a little late for her mother to start worrying about her.

Maggie said, 'I'll ring you on Saturday. If Great Edie dies, there's a leaflet about what to do by the phone. I've left a list.'

'Mother, stop worrying.'

Rudi had hired a four-man barge from Potter Heigham, a small harbour on the Norfolk Broads. They could take this boat and explore the region, the expanse of canals and lakes, which would be desolate at this time of year. Maggie was unsure about the wisdom of the choice. It was December after all. But she didn't say so.

Rudi smiled. 'Of course I wanted to hire a cruise ship – that would have been more appropriate – but I couldn't afford it, not just for you and me and I don't have three thousand pals.'

Maggie climbed aboard and walked round the boat with a disapproving nose. 'The toilets are disgusting,' she called back to Rudi.

His joviality was undimmed. 'It can sleep four, or you can put half of yourself on the upper bunk, half on the lower, if you really want to spread out.'

She came back out and looked at him. 'Now you're just being silly.'

'Yes, my darling,' he said, 'you can't deny me that. The older you get, the sillier you are allowed to be.'

'Or the sillier *you* allow yourself to be,' she said.

'Exactly.'

They bought provisions in the grocery store by the harbour. The barge had a tiny battered kitchen at the far end. Maggie cheered up a little when Rudi boiled her a very serviceable cup of tea.

'Not bad for an American,' she admitted begrudgingly.

'And look,' he said, pulling a curtain at the side of the kitchen, 'central heating.' It was a small, smelly oil heater.

'What's central about it?' she demanded.

'Well, it's in the middle of the boat.' He gave her a quirky look. 'I used to be a comedian, you know.'

It was impossible not to forget the mundane, the routine, on this boat. The isolation, the serenity, calmed her pulsing head, despite everything. Though she did not want serenity. Calm, she thought, meant forgetting.

And it was breathtakingly beautiful. Waking in the morning, sticking her head out of the hatch on the roof of the kitchen. Staring out across the water with the hoary mist rising, enveloping the horizon. There was no edge to the world.

'I want the rest of your life to be your golden segment,' said Rudi softly in her ear. 'You've had the two-thirds in poverty, I want the rest to be precious.'

She turned and frowned. He knew he had spoken too soon.

'You're so sentimental,' she sighed, 'so impractical. You want me to be a child again, but things have changed. I have so much else to think about.'

'I don't want you to *be* a child. I want you to be happy. I want to be happy too. And I will be happy by making you happy.'

'And what about your life?' she shouted. 'What about your kids in America, what about the rest of your family? What would they think of such nonsense as you going back to your lost love, like *they* had never happened?'

Rudi turned to fill the kettle. How sad that she had to do this now. That she could no longer dream. He said soberly, 'My kids are grown up, they have their own lives. I think they can handle it. They know my relationship with their mother – she walked out on me, remember.'

He changed the subject, knowing that she was not going to let go. She had her reality. If he did not test it, she would allow them a pleasant time.

The following evening though, he had to try again. They had eaten a gristly tin of stew with rice. A bottle of red wine had washed the flavour away.

They played cards amiably by the tiny lights pinned to the walls.

Maggie said, 'Stop looking at me.'

'I'm not looking at you.'

'Yes, you are.'

'OK, I am, waddya want, I like looking at you.'

'Why do you like looking at me?' She looked up at him angrily.

'Because I love you,' he said.

She threw her cards down on the table.

'You have to understand,' she said with violence in her voice, 'we do not and we will not have a relationship again. I accept your apologies. I know that you had a lot of terrible things happen in your life, and I'm sorry for that. I consider you an old and valued friend. But that is it. I have been on my own for too long. I am happy with things as they are.'

'Liar,' he said. 'You're not happy.'

She blinked heavily, thinking for objections. 'Anyhow, this is madness. It was mad enough that we were together in the first place. What did we ever have in common? What did we really have together?'

He shrugged. 'You got me!'

She looked puzzled.

'I don't know, Maggie!' He waved his arms in an attempt to get his point over. 'How the hell should I know? Of course it's crazy. But it was even more crazy that we both spent thirty years miserable, thinking about each other. How stupid was that?'

'Well, it wasn't my decision,' she said sulkily.

'You're so damn difficult! Ha!' He slammed his hand on the table and let out a wild laugh. 'Well, I guess I ought to expect it, that's what I always liked about you. That you were an awkward pain in the ass.'

Serious again, he leaned across the table. 'Maggie, I'll tell you what we got together. I know what you might have been. I'm the only one that does. I'm the only one that knows you, Maggie.'

'I know myself,' she said stiffly. 'I thought you liked me to be independent?'

'OK,' he said, holding his hands in the air in a conciliatory pose. 'I guess I have to respect that.'

She nodded and gave a polite smile. 'Not that I don't enjoy your company,' she said formally, as if declining an invitation. 'I do, it's been a lot of fun and you've been very supportive.'

'Even when you haven't wanted it,' he said tersely.

'Well, yes. I'd like to see you as a friend.'

'You like me around?' he asked dangerously.

'Well, yes,' she said, 'I can't deny that. We've always got on very well.'

He nodded knowingly. 'Well, that sure is a shame since I have to go away,' he said. 'I'm not staying in England.'

She looked shaken. 'What? Why not?'

He shrugged. 'Waddyou mind? You want me to go.'

She bowed her head at the sting. 'I know but . . . I thought you wanted to stay?'

'I can't, Maggie, don't you realize, my visa will run out in a couple of months.'

There was silence. Winter silence, even nature stilled.

'I can write maybe . . .'

'No,' she said.

'No?'

'I've had your notes before.'

'Ah, yes.'

She looked out of the window, into the darkness, the glistening water and the waving bulrushes lit by the lights from the boat. He heard his watch tick.

'You cunning bastard,' she said, shaking her head, avoiding his gaze. She turned around and said with a sob, 'OK, I give up. I suppose I'll have to marry you then.'

He sighed in silent relief. 'I think that would be the best thing.'

She laughed an unnatural laugh. 'Well! Don't things turn out strange?' She shook her head in confusion and all the while he watched her. When she was still he saw there were tears in her eyes.

'One good thing,' she said.

'What's that?' he said simply.

'It'll kill Edie . . . figuratively speaking of course.'

'Oh, sure, I doubt she'll see the spring out.'

He stopped holding her to say that they should go for a dip.

She was aghast. 'Rudi, it's gone midnight, it's raining, it's freezing, the sewage from the whole of Norfolk, I should think, is pumped into the water. I'm not being difficult, really I'm not. It's just not sensible.'

'And that is exactly why we're going to do it.' At the last word he sprang up, nearly banging his head on the roof of the cabin in his enthusiasm. He grabbed her with both arms, under her shoulders and her knees. She screamed and kicked but he was too strong, too determined for her.

'What?' she spluttered. 'You're going to throw me in the water, I've only got one pair of pyjamas!'

'Well, you'd better take them off then, hadn't you?'

With her still in his arms, like an escapologist, he removed his own gown. She gawped. 'My God,' she said in shock.

'Yeah,' he drawled. 'It's all still here.'

The shock seemed to fuel a new energy in her, a difference. For in silence she took off her pyjamas. If he could do it, so could she. She stripped in his full view, uncowering, unashamed.

'My God,' he said. 'Your body,' he faltered, 'it's been so long.' His old voice cracked.

'Yes,' she said airily, 'it's all headed southwards I'm afr—'

'You're so beautiful.'

She allowed him to touch her, a voyage of rediscovery.

He took her hand and they ran, without hesitation now, and slipped from the far edge of the boat into the water.

The chill knocked the scream from her. Her heart was beating wildly. She saw Rudi bravely thrashing. 'It's deep!' she gasped. 'I can't touch the bottom.'

He tried to laugh but he couldn't.

'Gogga geg ow!' he panted.

She had floated on to her back and was looking at the sky. Clouds were rushing past the moon. He pulled at her hand and brought her vertical again.

'It's time to go in,' he muttered, 'otherwise I think I may die.'

'I'm so cold,' she said between chattering teeth. 'What a stupid idea.' She was wrapped up in a towel and two blankets. 'I can't feel my feet,' she moaned.

'Yes,' he laughed, 'it was a crazy idea, and I want to be crazy. And I want you to be crazy. And you might have to be even crazier for a while until you get used to it again.'

He handed her the hot chocolate and then he poured a little brandy in it. He sat down on the bed and said, 'Here, I brought something to read to you.'

From his bag he pulled a worn copy of *Through the Looking-glass*.

'That looks like my book,' she said in surprise.

'It is your book, dummy.' He pushed her wet hair away from her face.

'I've read it before,' she said, pouting.

He laughed. 'I wanted to read you the poem at the end. I guess you didn't read that very often.'

She thought, holding the mug between her frozen fingers, the steam feeling warm against her nose. 'Oh, what, not the sentimental nonsense where Lewis Carroll is waxing nauseatingly lyrical after the story proper?'

'That's the one.' He opened the book.

'No, I never read that bit much. Who did? All I remember is the editor's note that said the poem was an acrostic. If you took the first letters of every line, from top to bottom, it read the name of Alice Pleasance Liddell. That was fun, but apart from that it was Victorian slush, wasn't it?'

'Dreadful!' he agreed 'Here, catch a load of this bit:

'Long has paled that sunny sky;
Echoes fade and memories die;
Autumn frosts have slain July.

'Just awful, huh?'

Maggie raised her eyes. Rudi read some more.

'Still she haunts me, phantomwise,
Alice moving under skies
Never seeing by waking eyes.'

'And wait there,' Maggie shouted, wrestling the book from him, into the spirit now. 'Listen, the end is totally sickening:

'In a Wonderland they lie
Dreaming as the days go by,
Dreaming as the summers die.

'Ever drifting down the stream –
Lingering in the golden gleam –
Life, what is it but a dream?

'Yes,' sighed Maggie, warm at last, 'revoltingly trite but I suppose it's very sad, when our summer ends.'

Rudi put his hand to her face. 'Depends on the summer,' he said. 'Personally I prefer autumn.'

Maggie pulled a face. 'Surely you mean "fall"?' She tutted reprovingly. 'I speak strange languages, you know, you don't have to pander to me.'

'Oh, I wouldn't dream of it.'

Bibliography

Mental Illness

Jennifer Barraclough and David Gill, *Hughes' Outline of Modern Psychiatry*, John Wylie, 4th edn, 1996.

German Berrios and Roy Porter (eds), *A History of Clinical Psychiatry*, Athlone Press, 1995.

Kathleen Jones, *Asylums and After*, Athlone Press, 1993.

Harold Kaplan and Benjamin J. Sadock, *Pocket Handbook of Psychiatric Drug Treatment*, Williams and Wilkins, 2nd edn, 1996.

Chicago and Poland

Saul Bellow, *The Adventures of Augie March*, first published 1949, Penguin, 1981.

Irving Cutler, *The Jews of Chicago*, University of Illinois Press, 1996.

Lucy S. Davidowicz, *The War against the Jews*, first published 1975, Pelican, 1987.

Martin Gilbert, *Holocaust Journey: Travelling in search of the past*, Phoenix, 1997.

Eva Hoffman, *Stetl: The history of a small town and an extinguished world*, Vintage, 1999.

June Skinner Sawyers, *Chicago Sketches*, Wild Onion Books, Loyola Press, 1995.

Simon Wiesenthal, *Krystyna: The Tragedy of the Polish Resistance*, Ariadne Press, 1987.

The Ship

Laurence Dunn, *Passenger Liners*, Adlard Coles, 1965.
Commander Geoffrey Marr, *The Queens and I*, Adlard Coles, 1973.
Byron S. Miller, *Sail, Steam and Splendour*, Angus and Robertson, 1979.

General

Chris Freddi, *The Complete Book of the World Cup*, Collins Willow, 1998.
A. Robert Lee (ed.), *The Beat Generation Writers*, Pluto Press, 1996.
John Maher and Judy Groves, *Chomsky for Beginners*, Icon Books, 1996.
Arthur Marwick, *The 1960s*, Oxford University Press, 1998.
Radio Times, June 1977.
Which?, 1977.
Virginia Woolf, *Diaries: Volume 5, 1936–41*, first published 1984, Penguin, 1985.

Acknowledgements

I would particularly like to thank my agent Jo Frank, my family and Sara Conkey.

There a number of other people for whose information, advice and memories I am extremely grateful: Kat Barrett; Roger Bennett; Anne Collins; Michael J. Lawson; Anna Moore; Christine Nerurker; Claudia Peach; Margaret Purdy; Kate Robinson; Ruby Runner; Bill Scott-Kerr; Georgie Spear; Sharon Walker; Geinor Warr.